P9-DHF-821

# MR. CHURCHILL'S
# SECRETARY

BY SUSAN ELIA MacNEAL

*Mr. Churchill's Secretary*
*Princess Elizabeth's Spy*
*His Majesty's Hope*
*The Prime Minister's Secret Agent*
*Mrs. Roosevelt's Confidante*

# MR. CHURCHILL'S SECRETARY

## A NOVEL

*Susan Elia MacNeal*

BANTAM BOOKS TRADE PAPERBACKS

NEW YORK

*Mr. Churchill's Secretary* is a work of fiction. All incidents and dialogue, and all characters with the exception of some well-known historical figures, are products of the author's imagination and are not to be construed as real. Where real-life historical figures appear, the situations, incidents, and dialogues concerning those persons are entirely fictional and are not intended to depict actual events or to change the entirely fictional nature of the work. In all other respects, any resemblance to actual persons, living or dead, events, or locales is entirely coincidental.

A Bantam Books Trade Paperback Original

Copyright © 2012 by Susan Elia MacNeal

Excerpt from *Princess Elizabeth's Spy* by Susan Elia MacNeal copyright © 2012 by Susan Elia MacNeal.

All rights reserved.

Published in the United States by Bantam Books, an imprint of The Random House Publishing Group, a division of Random House, Inc., New York.

BANTAM BOOKS and the rooster colophon are registered trademarks of Random House, Inc.

This book contains an excerpt from the forthcoming book *Princess Elizabeth's Spy* by Susan Elia MacNeal. This excerpt has been set for this edition only and may not reflect the final content of the forthcoming edition.

Library of Congress Cataloging-in-Publication Data
MacNeal, Susan Elia.
Mr. Churchill's secretary : a Maggie Hope novel / Susan Elia MacNeal.
p. cm.
ISBN 978-0-553-59361-7
ebook ISBN 978-0-553-90756-8 1. Americans—England—London—Fiction. 2. Private secretaries—Fiction. 3. Churchill, Winston, 1874–1965—Fiction. 4. World War, 1939–1945—Great Britain—Fiction. 5. Nazis—Fiction. I. Title. II. Title: Maggie Hope novel.
PS3613.A2774M7 2011
813'.6—dc22        2011027603

Printed in the United States of America

randomhousebooks.com

20  19  18

Book design by Caron Harris

To Noel, who always believed

In wartime, truth is so precious
that she should always be accompanied
by a bodyguard of lies.

—WINSTON CHURCHILL


I read about the guts of the pioneer woman
and the woman of the dustbowl and
the gingham goddess of the covered wagon.
What about the woman of the covered typewriter?

What has she got, poor kid,
when she leaves the office?

—CHRISTOPHER MORLEY, *Kitty Foyle*

# MR. CHURCHILL'S
# SECRETARY

# PROLOGUE

HALF AN HOUR before Diana Snyder died, she tidied up her desk in the typists' office of the Cabinet War Rooms.

She looked up at the heavy black hands of the clock on the wall and sighed. There were no windows in the War Rooms, the underground lair used by the Prime Minister's staff, reinforced by concrete slabs and considered to be bombproof. The ceilings were low; signs warned *Mind Your Head*. The once-white walls had faded to a dull yellow, and the floors were covered in worn brown linoleum. Overhead were lines of drainage pipes from the Treasury. While the air was filtered by a special ventilation system, there were still lingering odors of floor wax, chemical toilets, and cigarette smoke.

The windowless typists' office was lit by four green-glass pendant lamps and adorned with several gas masks, along with steel helmets and whistles for air-raid drills. It was quiet in the small room, but outside, in the hall, the subterranean air was punctuated with the clatter of typewriters, conversations in low voices, and the piercing ring of telephones.

The only evidence it was spring was the calendar on the wall. *May 1940.*

May 12, 1940, to be exact. Winston Churchill had just been made Prime Minister. Armies of Nazis were marching across Holland, Belgium, and Luxembourg—and it looked as though the entirety of Belgium was about to fall. If and when Belgium fell, France would be next. And after France, well, what then? Attacks on England from the air, invasion from the sea? St. Paul's Cathedral a smoking ruin from bombs dropped from Messerschmitts and Heinkels? Red, white, and black flags with swastikas flying from the Houses of Parliament with Nazi troops goose-stepping down the Mall, through Admiralty Arch, to knock over Nelson's Column? Would they set up military headquarters at Buckingham Palace, execute high-ranking officials at the Tower of London?

The people to whom Prime Minister Neville Chamberlain had promised "peace in our time" were now trembling on the edge of a terrifying abyss. It was a strange moment in time, a limbo-like state when the horror was fast approaching but barbarity hadn't yet quite descended.

Diana sighed again and pushed back a limp wave of pale hair that had held a curl when she'd begun her day, nearly sixteen hours before.

Pulling the last sheets out of the typewriter—the special noiseless kind Mr. Churchill insisted upon when he'd taken office so that the secretaries could type directly while he dictated—Diana separated the original from the carbon and added each to its respective stack. Then she said her goodbyes to the other typists, pinning on her navy-blue straw hat, the one with the daisies and cherries.

It was late and the sunlight was fading as Diana made her way to the bus stop. Silver barrage balloons floated high in the sky, turning pink in the slanting sun's rays, negligible protection against threatened Nazi air raids.

No lights glowed against the encroaching darkness—blackout regulations had been in effect since Neville Chamberlain had declared war almost eight months before.

Like most Londoners, St. James's Park was looking unkempt around the edges. The metal gates had been dug up and taken away to be melted down for munitions. Most of the grassy lawn had been turned into victory gardens. Men with pale faces and black bowler hats, carrying gas masks over their shoulders, walked with tense and hurried steps. They were leaving Whitehall or Parliament, or whatever government building covered in thick barbed wire and sandbags they reported to. There were women, too, in their gray-and-brown uniforms, carrying on with their work as secretaries and nurses and drivers.

Diana groaned inwardly as she saw the queue for the bus that she usually took to her flat, a third-floor walk-up in Pimlico.

"Damn," she muttered as she eyed the long line. Her mother, back in Kent, would have been aghast. No umbrella, hat pinned at a rakish angle, heels just a fraction of an inch too high. Her mother always complained about the way Diana dressed. Sweaters too tight, lipstick too bright, curfew too late—and this was before Diana had moved to London. That was the last straw. No respectable young woman went to London to work, even for the P.M. Especially for *this* P.M. Better to stay in Kent, playing tennis and bridge, rolling bandages and knitting socks for soldiers, until the right young man from a proper family came along. Of course, these days, any so-called "proper young man" was going to be in the army, navy, or air force.

Diana stood still for a moment, contemplating her options, her delicate features momentarily creased with worry. She had her mother's face, she'd have to admit—

the sparkling eyes, the high cheekbones, and the tiny, pointed chin. Normally, despite the war and threat of invasion, she wasn't one to worry. She was well-off financially. She had a large circle of what her mother would call "the right sort" of friends. She had a number of "the wrong sort" of beaux—which were just right for the present moment.

"Damn," she repeated. She looked up at the darkening sky, then back toward the bus stop. She'd never get on the next bus; she'd be lucky to get the one after that. So she decided to walk, a good half-hour to forty-five minutes, in the dark.

Her mother would be appalled, of course.

Diana took off at a brisk clip, heels tapping smartly on the pavement. The sun gave its final golden explosion and then sank past the horizon, leaving a few clouds of rosy gray. The winds picked up, and she shivered, ducking her head down and keeping a firm grip on her pocketbook.

After the sunset, blackout swallowed her. Her mother, terrified of the city, was always ringing to warn her about rapists and muggers. Diana had laughed and told her not to worry. London was her city; she'd be fine. More than fine, in fact. Still, she shivered again in the damp darkness. She thought of the small flat she shared with two other girls. With work and parties and dates, they all kept irregular hours. No one expected her home at any particular time.

Her killers knew this.

She heard the heavy footsteps behind her and walked just that much faster in the inky darkness, her heels making a delicate staccato rhythm on the pavement. Instinctively, she pulled her twill coat around her and gripped her handbag even tighter.

She heard the heavy pounding of the man's boots as

they hit the pavement, faster now. Diana sensed it—the primal smell of danger. He was the hunter, and she was the prey. She tried to search the gloom for a policeman or an air-raid warden. But there was nothing and no one. She began to run, her breath burning in her lungs, feet squeezed by her pumps.

Diana turned around, her heart drumming, ready to scream—when she heard a car's engine rattle behind her. The Humber coupe's large, round headlights were covered by blackout slats. As it passed, she nearly choked on the noxious exhaust fumes.

The car pulled up to the curb in front of her, liberally covered with thick, white paint visible in the blackout, and stopped.

"Are you all right?" came a breathy voice through the car's window.

In the faint gleam of the rising moon, Diana could see that the driver was female, a young girl like herself. She breathed a sigh of relief.

She looked behind her for whoever had been following her—and saw nothing in the shadows. *You silly ninny,* she thought, *imagining ghosts and goblins at your age. Probably just some poor man trying to get home to his wife and children. Serves you right for not waiting for the bus.*

"Fine, thanks," she said, approaching the car. "Just a bit spooked there for a moment." In the murky darkness she could now see that the girl was in her early twenties, with a blue Hermès silk scarf tied smartly around her neck.

The girl assessed the skies. "Need a lift? I'm heading to Pimlico—you're welcome to ride along if you'd like."

Without hesitation, Diana ran to the passenger's side and got in. "Oh, thanks *so* much. There was such a long queue at the bus stop, and then there's the blackout—"

The driver smiled as Diana settled herself in the leather seat. "Not to mention high heels."

"Well, you know, a girl's got to make *some* sacrifices for beauty during this damn war."

"And don't we all know it." They laughed together as the car wound its way through the shadowed streets.

"My name's Diana, by the way."

"And mine's Claire," the other girl replied. "Pleased to meet you."

At last, they reached Diana's flat, a brick terrace house. She looked up at the building—one of her flatmates had a light on—and had forgotten to close the blackout curtain. *There'll be a fine for that,* Diana thought absently. "By the way," she asked Claire, "how did you know I lived here?"

Those were her last words.

There was the sound of heavy boots on the pavement, and the car's door opened with a sudden jerk.

Diana turned and looked up at a tall man wearing a black woolen mask. The only part of his face she could see were his eyes, cold and unblinking. He was muscular but lean and wore leather gloves on his hands. "Get out," he said.

Diana did as she was told, in a fog of shock. "Turn around," he barked. "Hands on the roof of the car."

Diana looked to Claire and saw that her face was set; she was part of what was happening. Heart in her throat, breathing shallow and labored, her armpits damp with fear, she turned and placed her hands on the roof of the car.

Without preamble, she felt the hot shock of the metal blade as it pierced through her flesh and could hear the tearing as it went through cloth and skin and muscle.

There was pain, more pain than she'd ever thought possible, and she fell to the street, her cheek lying against the hard pavement. She gave a few gasps.

And then a cloud of benevolent black velvet closed around her.

# ONE

"I WOULD SAY *to the House, as I've said to those who have joined this Government, I have nothing to offer but blood, toil, tears and sweat. We have before us an ordeal of the most grievous kind. We have before us many, many long months of struggle and suffering,"* intoned Winston Leonard Spencer Churchill to the House of Commons and the British nation in his first speech as the new Prime Minister.

There must have been complete silence in the House, although there was a burst of static over the airwaves as Maggie leaned forward to listen to the BBC on the wireless. She and Paige sat at the kitchen table and clasped hands, listening to the address. Charlotte, better known as Chuck, entered the kitchen quietly and leaned against the door frame.

*"You ask, what is our policy? I can say: It is to wage war, by sea, land and air, with all our might and with all the strength that God can give us; to wage war against a monstrous tyranny, never surpassed in the dark, lamentable catalogue of human crime. That is our policy. You ask, what is our aim?*

*"I can answer in one word: It is victory, victory at all costs, victory in spite of all terror, victory, however long and hard the road may be; for without victory,*

*there is no survival.* Let that be realised; no survival for
the British Empire, no survival for all that the British
Empire has stood for, no survival for the urge and im-
pulse of the ages, that mankind will move forward
towards its goal."

Chuck nodded her acknowledgment of both girls. Together they all listened to the speech's conclusion in
tense silence.

*"But I take up my task with buoyancy and hope. I feel
sure that our cause will not be suffered to fail among
men. At this time I feel entitled to claim the aid of all,
and I say, 'Come then, let us go forward together with
our united strength.'"*

The three girls were perfectly still and silent for a moment, as the words' gravity washed over them.

"Well, at least it's the truth," Maggie said, pushing
back a stray lock of red hair. "He didn't try to pretend
everything's all right and fob us off with easy comfort
and lies."

"I just don't know," Chuck said to both girls as a
tinny version of "God Save the King" played, and she
walked over to click off the wireless.

"Look what happened in Poland. Look what's happening in Belgium and Holland and France," Paige said.
"Maybe Ambassador Kennedy was right. He said Hitler
doesn't want England. And if we'd just—"

Chuck gave a snort. "Oh, right. And then they'll stop?
You really believe that?"

"This is a different kind of war," Maggie said. "A
people's war. It's not just soldiers on the front line, it's
civilians. *We* are the new front line." As she said the
words, her chest constricted a bit. It was true. England
might still be in the "Bore War," where nothing dangerous was really happening, but things were about to
change. Nazis had invaded most of Europe and were undoubtedly moving toward England. Would troops try to

invade by sea or parachute down from the sky? Either way, the scenario was grim.

"Yeah," said Chuck. "We're as likely to be bombed here in our own home as the soldiers over in France."

"Stop it!" Paige said, covering her ears. "Just stop!"

Chuck frowned and pulled her bottle-green cardigan sweater around her, rather like a general settling his uniform before going once more unto the breach. "Tea," she stated in her deep, booming voice, deliberately changing the subject. "We all need tea. There'll be no blood, toil, tears, or sweat until I have some goddamned tea."

That was Chuck, practical and pragmatic. More handsome than beautiful, with rich chestnut-brown hair, strong features, and thick black eyelashes, Chuck McCaffrey had worked for U.S. Ambassador Joseph Kennedy, along with Paige Kelly, before the war had started.

Maggie Hope had come to London for another reason altogether—to sell her late grandmother's great leaking, creaking pile of a Victorian house. But when Britain declared war, and Joseph Kennedy began being quoted in the papers spouting pro-Nazi sentiments, both Paige and Chuck both quit their jobs with the Ambassador—and lost their Embassy housing. Maggie, admiring their resolve, invited them to move in, and they gratefully acquiesced.

Paige and Maggie had met years before either had come to London, at Wellesley College, an all-women's school in Massachusetts. Paige was a rich debutante from Virginia with perfect waves of glistening golden hair and a heart-shaped face, and Maggie a red-haired and pale faculty brat far more interested in fractions than fashions, but they'd become fast friends nonetheless. Finding each other in London had been pure serendipity; becoming housemates made a pleasure of a financial necessity. The flatmates' rent, along with Maggie's work privately tutoring students in math, allowed her to stay in London.

Chuck made her way toward the copper kettle on the stove but stopped short at the state of the sink, piled high with dirty dishes. "Jesus H. Christ!"

Maggie shrugged. "The twins." The twins in question were Annabelle and Clarabelle Wiggett, two pixielike young blondes who also lived in the house, known as much for their thick Norwich accents and incessant giggling as for the catastrophic messes they left. Chuck referred to them, not necessarily unkindly, as "the Ding-belles," "the Dumb-belles," and "the Hell's Belles."

Chuck made a low growl in her throat. "Off with their heads," she muttered, rolling up her sleeves and taking up a dishrag.

The telephone rang, and Paige jumped to get it. "Hello?" she cooed, as if expecting to hear from one of her numerous boyfriends. Then, "Oh, yes, David—she's here." David was David Greene, one of Maggie's good friends, who worked as a private secretary to Winston Churchill.

Maggie took the heavy black Bakelite receiver and sat down at the kitchen table, running her fingers over the nicks and scars in the wood. "It's just that the girl's gone missing," David said, his voice solemn. "Actually, it's a bit more serious than that. But the thing is, we need a re-placement. Yesterday."

"Wasn't she murdered a few days ago?" Maggie asked. "Mugged for a few pounds? I saw something in *The Times* about it. And in Pimlico, too—"

Paige and Chuck both turned, listening.

"Look, it's a terrible situation, Magster, but there's still a war on and work to be done. Now more than ever. We need to fill the position."

"Paige and I have already decided—we're going to be drivers. The call of the open road and all."

"Maggie, my dear, I know you can take dictation and type well. And that's what's needed right now. And please, let me emphasize the *right now* bit."

Maggie leaned back in the chair. She could see where this was going. "Well, then, why don't *you* do it?"

"I'm already a private secretary, research and that sort of thing. Besides, I don't, well—"

Maggie raised an eyebrow. "You mean you don't . . . type?"

"Not very fast, I'm afraid," he said. "But *you* can, and quickly, too. And that's what's needed." Then, "We need you."

Maggie was silent. Dishes done, Chuck had turned back to her tea, the mug dwarfed by her large, capable hands. Paige busied herself with the newspaper.

"Merciful Zeus, woman!" David exclaimed over the crackling line. "It's a chance to work on the front lines. You'd be doing something important. Making a difference."

The knowledge that he was right stung. She could make a difference. But not in the way she wanted, with her mathematic capabilities. As a typist.

"Working for Mr. Churchill would be one of the hardest and most challenging jobs you can do. And vital as well. But it's up to you, of course. I can't say it's going to be anything but difficult. But if you're interested, I can make it happen. We've already started the paperwork, proving you're a British citizen in good standing—despite your dreadful accent."

Maggie smiled in spite of herself; David loved to mock her American accent. "Would there be *any* chance of my being involved with the research and writing end of things? After all, with my degree, I could be of more help, especially with things like queue theory, allocating resources, information theory, code and cipher breaking—"

He sighed. "I'm sorry, Maggie, but they're only hiring men for those jobs. I understand your frustration. . . ." Maggie had already tried for a private secretary job, a position traditionally held by young Oxbridge men from upper-class families. Despite being more than qualified, she'd been turned down.

"No, David. You don't." It wasn't his fault, but still, the truth hurt. She could type and file, while young men her age, like David, could do more—research, reports, writing. It just wasn't fair, and the knowledge made her want to throw and break things. Immature, she knew, but honest. "I'd rather drive or work in a factory, making tanks."

"Maggie—why?"

"Look, you of all people should know why." David, after all, wouldn't be there, either, if they knew *everything* about him. "*You* don't get to judge *me*."

"I'm sorry. . . ."

"You're sorry? *Sorry?*" she said, her voice rising in pitch. In the kitchen, the girls all pretended to be very, very busy with what they were doing. "Perfect. You're sorry. But it doesn't change anything." Her pronunciation became more distinct. "It doesn't *change* that when I interviewed for the private secretary job, I was *more* than qualified. It doesn't *change* that Dicky Snodgrass was a condescending *ass* to me. It doesn't *change* that John sees me as a mere girl incapable of anything besides typing and getting married and having babies. And it doesn't *change* that they hired that cross-eyed *lug* Conrad Simpson—a mouth breather who probably still has to sound words out and count on his fingers—all because his daddy has a fancy title and he has a . . . a . . . a *penis!*"

There was silence on the other end, and then the line crackled. In the kitchen, the girls looked at each other in shock.

"And the fact that you're absolutely right, I know, doesn't make it any better," David said.

"All right, then," Maggie said, slightly calmer now that she'd gotten that off her chest. Then she added, "What about Paige?"

Paige looked up from the paper; "Fifth Column Treachery" was the headline. "What *about* Paige?" she asked. Maggie waved her hands and shushed her.

"Paige is American—only Commonwealth citizens allowed," he said.

"Chuck?"

Chuck was still bent over the tea, but her back tensed.

"Chuck's training to be a nurse, and she'll be more than needed soon," David said. "Besides, Ireland's not the Commonwealth, you know. Things are still a little . . . iffy between England and Ireland, if you know what I mean."

"Ah," Maggie said. "Of course." Chuck was Irish. And with all of the violent history between England and Ireland, as well as the recent IRA bombings in London, Maggie could see why an Irish citizen at No. 10 wouldn't be considered, let alone approved.

Maggie took a deep breath. Despite her frustration at the system in place, she knew it was time for her to give up her pride and do what needed to be done. *Here's something I can do for the war effort,* she thought, *something I can do, and do well. There's a need, and I can fill it.* It was as simple as that. And in wartime, it was all that mattered.

"All right, then," she said with a dramatic sigh. "Yes, I'll do it. Fine. You've got yourself a secretary."

"Good girl! I had a feeling you'd come through. We'll see you at Number Ten tomorrow then, eight sharp. There's a lot of work to be done."

"I know. I'll be there." And then she added, "Thank you, David. You can count on me."

*          *          *

Michael Murphy left his flat in Soho early, forgoing an umbrella even though the skies promised worse weather.

He paused at the curb while he buttoned his old mackintosh against the morning chill, tucking a small worn-leather suitcase tightly between his feet. Around him was a regular Tuesday morning in London—traffic getting heavier, a siren wailing, shops and cafés opening, people walking quickly on the sidewalks or waiting patiently in queues for red double-decker buses. A few drab sparrows picked at crumbs, and the damp air was cut by car exhaust.

Satisfied he'd never seen any of the faces in the crowd before, he set off for Piccadilly Circus. The statue of Eros with his bow had been removed for safekeeping, and the Shaftsbury fountain was boarded up with wide wooden planks. The area, edged by the London Pavilion and the Criterion, was already mobbed with RAF pilots on leave, Wrens in brown uniforms and bright lipstick, and young boys shouting and selling newspapers.

They were overlooked by huge billboards: *Guinness Is Good for You. Bovril Schweppes Tonic Water. For Your Throat's Sake, Smoke Craven A.* And just in case one could ever forget the war: *It Might Be YOU— Caring for Evacuees Is a National Service.*

Murphy walked down the steep flight of steps to the Piccadilly Circus Underground station, bought his ticket, and then descended further into the bowels of the Tube. As he sank lower and lower into the earth, the cool air smelled of exhaust, rotting rubbish, and stale sweat.

The train arrived with a loud rumble, and he pushed his way in with the others—businessmen in rumpled suits and felt hats with newspapers in hand, a few soldiers, a nurse with a white winged hat. He transferred from the Piccadilly line to the Northern, noticing a particularly beautiful young woman with a dove-gray pill-

box hat and red lipstick, somehow disconcerting so
early in the morning. He gave the woman a grin and
tipped his hat. She blushed and dropped her eyes.

He remained standing on the train, then got off with a
crowd of passengers as the doors slid open at Euston
station. Instinctively, he reached into his coat and felt
for the butt of his pistol.

It was there, hard and reassuring.

He walked along with the rest of the crowd, hanging
back just slightly, until most had proceeded up the staircase, leaving a momentary lull before the next train arrived.

In one smooth, practiced move, he reached into the
case and released a catch activating the bomb inside.
Then, in another quick motion, he dropped it in one of
the gaping rubbish bins.

Walking briskly now, he headed up the stairs. There
was a man with a fleshy, florid face playing "The Sailor's
Hornpipe" on a slightly out-of-tune violin. Murphy
threw a few coins into the open case, pausing to wink at
the woman in the gray hat, who'd stopped to listen. She
blushed again.

Continuing through a turnstile, he jogged up another
steeper set of stairs and then into the open air. He
walked a few blocks and spotted a café across the street.

He went in and took a seat by the large plate-glass
windows, the dark wood chair scraping over the black-
and-red tile floor.

Then he looked up at the waitress and ordered a pot
of tea.

Murphy was enjoying his first sip when the ground
shook slightly and the battered wooden tables and
chipped flowered china dishes trembled for just an instant.

There was an uneasy silence as the other patrons stiffened, wondering what had happened, waiting.

The crowd began murmuring, some rising to see what the outside commotion was about. A baby began to cry, and his mother held him tightly against her.

Then people, some battered and bloody, faces contorted with shock, began to walk past the café's window. *And they're the lucky ones,* he thought.

The man caught sight of the young woman in the gray hat, the one he'd favored with a wink. It was askew, and her lipstick had smeared. A gash on her face wept blood, dripping dark and red onto the light gray of her suit. She walked past the window of the café, unseeing.

From a distance, the wail of sirens could be heard, growing louder as they approached.

Murphy left a few coins on the table for his tea and then went out into the throng, savoring the confusion and chaos he had caused.

# TWO

No. 10 Downing Street, the historic black-brick office and home of the British Prime Minister, appeared austere and unassuming, especially compared to Parliament, Big Ben, and all the other grand Gothic government buildings in Westminster. It was almost ascetic in its simplicity—as if to say that while the other buildings might be there for display, this was where government actually met, where work was really done.

Downing Street had been closed to the general public since the previous September. The building itself was sandbagged and surrounded by coils of thick barbed wire, braced for imminent attacks.

Maggie Hope walked up the steps, past the guards, and knocked. The door opened, and she was led by one of the tall, uniformed guards past the infamous glossy black door with its brass lion-head knocker, and through the main entrance hall. She passed through, barely noticing the Benson of Whitehaven grandfather clock, the chest from the Duke of Wellington, and the portrait of Sir George Downing. They continued up the grand cantilever staircase. From there, they took a few turns down a warren of corridors and narrow winding passageways to the typists' office, ripe with the scent of floor polish and cigarette smoke. The guard left her there.

She took off her brown straw hat with the violet faille bow and removed her gloves. The silence was cut only by the loud ticking of a wall clock and the low murmur of conversation a few rooms away.

Then, a voice: "How do you do, Miss Hope."

Standing in the doorway was a tall, slim woman in her early fifties. Her glossy black hair was threaded with silver and pulled back into a sleek chignon. The inherent beauty of her face was obscured by heavy black-rimmed glasses perched at the end of her nose. "I am Mrs. Catherine Tinsley," she said, her mouth pursed.

"How do you do, ma'am? My name is Margaret Hope—but please call me Maggie."

Mrs. Tinsley looked down her nose and took the girl's measure. *Pretty little thing,* she sniffed, *but too young, too thin, and far too pale. And that ghastly red hair pulled up into a bun. At least she had the common sense to dress in a plain suit and flat shoes. Not like that other young chit, Diana. Poor girl. Nasty bit of work, that.*

"Well, Miss Hope," she said, taking a seat behind the larger of the wooden desks, which had a brass lamp, "please call me *Mrs.* Tinsley. I am Mr. Churchill's senior secretary. Even though Mr. Churchill has been Prime Minister for only a short while, you should know that I have been with the family for more than twenty years."

She looked at Maggie over her glasses to make sure she was suitably impressed.

Maggie tried to arrange her face in such a way as to show that she was.

"I *do* hope you'll work out better than the other girls we've had."

"Yes, ma'am." *Especially the last one,* Maggie thought grimly as she took the small, hard seat opposite Mrs. Tinsley's desk. "I'll do my best, ma'am."

"That's why you're here. And don't think Mr. Churchill will be too pleased about it. He doesn't like new staff."

*This is going well,* Maggie thought with a sinking heart. *Is it too late to go melt scrap metal?* Her office skills were good—but would they be good enough?

After all, she wasn't really a secretary but a Wellesley graduate, summa cum laude, Phi Beta Kappa, fluent in German and French, about to start working toward a doctoral degree in mathematics from M.I.T. Or she had been. *Not that Mrs. Tinsley—or anyone else at No. 10—cares.*

"In any case." Mrs. Tinsley sighed, shaking her head. "It's bound to be difficult at first."

Maggie drew herself up in her straight-backed wooden chair and lifted her chin. *I'll show you,* she thought. *I'll show all of you.* "I'm ready for anything. Ma'am."

"Very well, then," Mrs. Tinsley said. "But remember—if you leave now, no one will hold it against you."

It was a long day.

Maggie met Miss Stewart, a petite and plump older woman with watery blue eyes and snow-white hair with a wide pink part, another of Mr. Churchill's secretaries. She spoke in a soft, melodious voice. She whispered that because "He" was spending the week at Chequers, the Prime Minister's official country house, the office was quieter. The atmosphere was much more intense, she said, when "He" was in.

*Fantastic,* Maggie thought. *I can only imagine Mrs. Tinsley under pressure.*

Maggie was also introduced to Richard Snodgrass, head private secretary. *The bastard who kept me from getting the private secretary job,* she thought.

"Thank you, Mrs. Tinsley. But Mr. Snodgrass and I have already met."

Several months ago, Maggie had been up for a job as one of the illustrious private secretaries but didn't get it. No women allowed. *No girls in the precious private secretary sandbox,* Maggie thought. In the caste system of No. 10, women were the secretaries—the typists. Men, usually Oxford or Cambridge graduates of the upper class, were the private secretaries, who did the research, drafted reports, and ventured opinions, while the women took dictation.

Richard Snodgrass was short, made to look even shorter by his striped double-breasted suit. His greasy black hair was combed over his bald spot. His hands were small and soft, and he blinked rapidly, as though coming into the light after a long stretch of darkness. *Like a little mole,* Maggie thought. She caught a whiff of vetiver cologne.

"Mr. Snodgrass, Miss Hope is our new typist," Mrs. Tinsley said.

"Of course," he said stiffly, the name ringing a bell.

"I obviously made quite an impression with my sparkling personality," Maggie said drily.

"So glad to see you've found your proper place here at Number Ten, Miss Hope. I'm sure you'll do well—with the rest of the ladies."

Maggie forced her lips into a tight smile. "Thank you."

"Miss Hope. About the private secretary job . . ."

*Oh, this should be good,* she thought.

"You may be very smart. For a woman." He coughed. "But you see, women—even smart women, university-educated women—have the bad habit of going off and getting married. You just can't count on them to stick around and get the job done. Especially in wartime."

Maggie was silent, inwardly fuming.

"After all, if we made an exception for you, pretty soon there would be all kinds of women insisting on doing work on higher levels. And then where would we be? Who'd do all the typing?"

Snodgrass laughed.

The two women didn't.

Maggie had the feeling Mrs. Tinsley was just as angry as she was.

"Mr. Snodgrass," Maggie began, before she could stop herself, "how is Mr. Simpson working out?"

Snodgrass looked confused. "Mr. Simpson?"

"Yes, Mr. Conrad Simpson. Who was hired as a private secretary. Instead of me. How's he doing in his new position?" Maggie knew very well from David that Conrad had been let go—he'd been terrible at his job.

"He, ah, moved on."

"Really?" Maggie said. "So, you just couldn't count on him to stick around and get the job done, then?"

"Miss Hope, that's not—"

"And so—I'm here, and he's not."

"Miss Hope!" Mrs. Tinsley sounded shocked.

"I merely wondered what happened with Mr. Simpson," Maggie said. "Thank you for enlightening me."

Snodgrass spluttered, "That's not—" before collecting himself. "Carry on!" he barked as he waved one hand, turned on his heel, and walked away.

"Back to work, Miss Hope," Mrs. Tinsley said sternly.

Later, that evening, two young men in dark suits passed by the office door.

Mrs. Tinsley saw Maggie glance up and frowned. "You should know, Miss Hope, that the private secretaries, while young, are men of considerable standing. Under the guidance of Mr. Snodgrass, they act as a buffer between Mr. Churchill and the rest of the world, making sure he has everything he needs—conducting research, writing drafts, producing reports. They will go on to their own illustrious careers."

"Yes, I—" *I know all too well,* Maggie thought.

"The private secretaries have the very best education, and their work calls for the highest degree of intelligence, care, and sensitivity. You must realize, Miss Hope, that this is a serious business. We are at war, and that doesn't leave much time for beaux and the like. The private secretaries don't have time for mooning schoolgirls. We expect all staff to act with the dignity accorded to Number Ten. Is that clear?"

"Of course, Mrs. Tinsley." *Me? Moon over the private secretaries? Oh, just drop a bomb on me now and get it over with.*

"Well, then," Mrs. Tinsley said, looking up at the black hands of the clock. "You've put in a full day's work. You may go."

At that, a black-and-white cat jumped onto Mrs. Tinsley's desk. "Ohhh!" she exclaimed, trying to shoo him with her hands. "Dreadful creature!"

Maggie picked him up and gently deposited him on the floor.

Mrs. Tinsley sniffed. "That is Nelson, one of the Churchills' cats. Named after Lord Nelson, of course. You'll find their animals are allowed to roam about quite . . . freely."

A sprightly young man burst into the room, Anthony Eden hat in hand, trench coat over his arm. David Greene—who'd telephoned Maggie about the job—was short and slight, with sandy hair and bright eyes framed by wire-rimmed glasses. There was an impish look to him, as though he could play the role of Puck at a moment's notice.

John Sterling followed, a few paces behind, head down. He was taller than David, with serious eyes and a fiercely angular face. He looked as though he'd cut his thick, curly brown hair himself, without a mirror. Lines between his brows hinted at worries beyond his years.

"Good evening, ladies," David said, performing a courtly bow. "And how are you, Mrs. Tinsley?"

"Why, Mr. Greene, Mr. Sterling," she said, her hands toying with her creamy pearls, "is there anything you need?"

John's face was drawn. "Did you hear about the bombing?"

"What? No," Mrs. Tinsley said, startled. "What bombing? Germans? The Luftwaffe?"

John shook his head. "Euston station. IRA, most likely."

Momentarily subdued, David stated, "Five dead, more than fifty wounded."

"That's *horrible*," Maggie said, blood draining from her face. *Those poor people, just going about their business,* she thought. *One minute getting on or off a train, the next . . . Isn't it bad enough anticipating air attacks from the Nazis, without the IRA mixing it up as well? Not to mention that young girl who was stabbed.*

"Control yourself, Miss Hope," Mrs. Tinsley snapped. "You'll most likely witness much worse by the time this war is over. By the way, these young men are Mr. David Greene and Mr. John Sterling, two of Mr. Churchill's private secretaries."

*Of course they are.* Maggie had known them both for more than a year, introduced by Paige and Chuck. David was one of her closest friends. John was . . . well, John was an enigma. Serious, patronizing, and generally infuriating was how Maggie would characterize him.

"So, how was your first day, Magster?" David asked, leaning against Maggie's desk as she straightened up.

"Fine, *Mr.* Greene," she said in measured tones, catching his eye and trying to give him the hint to keep things formal, at least in the office. She rose to get her coat and hat from the hook near the door. "Thank you."

"Did you know, Mrs. Tinsley," David continued, "not only does Miss Hope hail from the good old U.S. of A.—as is apparent from her atrocious accent—but in fact she was a cowgirl on a ranch in Texas."

There was a sharp intake of air from Mrs. Tinsley.

"I assure you, Mrs. Tinsley," Maggie said, with all the dignity she could muster, "I'm a citizen of the United Kingdom. I was born here in London; my father and mother were both British citizens. However, I was raised near Boston."

"I wasn't aware Boston had ranches," Mrs. Tinsley said, knitting her brows.

"Certainly not." Maggie glared at David, who affected an innocent pose. "Mr. Greene thinks he's very clever."

"It's all right, Magster," David said. "The Boss is half American, after all, on his mother's side. He even claims some Iroquois Indian blood. So you'll fit right in."

Mrs. Tinsley pursed her lips and folded her hands. It didn't bode well. "Miss Hope, you may be excused. I still have work to do—there's a war on, you know. Good night, Mr. Greene, Mr. Sterling."

And the three left.


"You mean I'm *not* very clever? Maggie, you cut me to the quick," David said as they made their way from No. 10 to the path flanking St. James's Park in the mild May air. The rain had stopped. Slanting lemony sunlight pierced the clouds, although a few birds—sparrows, crows, ravens—chirped warnings of more rain to come. "So, really—how did your first day go?"

"I didn't realize it was going to be so much like Miss Minchin's Select Seminary for Girls."

John looked over; his eyes, Maggie noticed, were rimmed with shadows. "Sorry?"

"Never mind. You had to be there."

"Oh, the Tinzer is all right once you get used to her," David said, "and it's Number Ten Downing Street— what did you expect?"

"It's fine, really," Maggie said with bravado she didn't necessarily feel. "I know I can keep up with the work, it's just a matter of learning the ropes."

"Let's take you to the Rose and Crown to celebrate your first day," David said as they strolled down Birdcage Walk bordering St. James's Park, the Gothic arches and towers of Westminster Abbey visible in the distance. The area, with the Foreign Office, the Treasury, the Houses of Parliament, and the Horse Guards Parade, was one of arched importance, exuding both pomposity and grace.

Maggie always loved Monet's paintings of the Houses of Parliament, which she'd seen at the Museum of Fine Arts in Boston—the Gothic arches in the different lights of morning, late afternoon, and sunset. As they made their way along the park, she caught a glimpse of the Houses' peaks, towers, and pinnacles. She thought they looked more like a fairy-tale castle than Buckingham Palace ever could. And it was easy to imagine Peter Pan and Wendy flying past the clock tower on their way to Neverland.

In the thick green grass of the park, set precariously near the sidewalk, a nest of seven newly hatched ducklings lay on the ground, brown and soft and breathing in unison. A protective mother duck waddled nearby, gazing balefully in warning at those passing. From its dark pagoda on high, Big Ben gave seven low mournful chimes through the fading saffron sunset.

"Merciful Minerva, *I* could use a drink," David said.

"And Paige has us under strict orders to bring you along so we can celebrate."

Maggie smiled and linked her arm through his. "Well, we can't disappoint Paige, now, can we?"

They walked the cobblestoned side streets of Westminster, past sandbagged Victorian government buildings, black-painted corner pubs, bone-colored Georgian homes turning violet in the dying twilight. Maggie loved the sense of collapsed time that permeated the twisted streets, where the clip-clop of horses' hooves could still be heard. The air smelled of the salty Thames, car exhaust, and horse dung. In the growing darkness of the blackout it was easy for time to wash away and to imagine London several millennia ago, when it was just a cluster of huts along the banks of the river Thames, faces of ancient Britons painted blue.

The last rays of sunset illuminated the exterior of the Rose and Crown. Although the pub's blackout curtains obscured the lamps within and the windows were taped in large crosses, when David opened the door, golden light spilled out, along with the sounds of laughter, music, and the clatter of glasses. Inside, the smell of spilled stout mingled with cigarette smoke. Men in uniform on leave and women in spring dresses like colorful blossoms shouted over the dull roar.

"Cometh the crisis, cometh the crowd," John muttered.

Scanning the throng, Maggie saw Paige at a worn wooden booth in the back, waving frantically.

"Hello! Hello!" Paige exclaimed over the din as they all sat down at the wooden booth with her. Her voice was childlike and breathless. "David, John," she said, angling her cheek to be kissed by each man. "Do you like my new hat? And, Maggie—love the outfit. How was your first day?"

Maggie hugged Paige, who was wearing Joy—jasmine and roses. Her nails were long, perfect ovals impeccably painted with one of the increasingly rare Elizabeth Arden reds Maggie knew Paige kept on her dresser.

Behind them, Chuck and her beau, Nigel Ludlow, threaded their way through the crowd. Paige waved them both over.

"Well, they didn't fire me, that's a good sign," Maggie said, sliding over to give Chuck and Nigel some room, then reaching over and taking a sip of Paige's shandy.

Chuck was coming from a shift at Great Ormond Street Hospital, wearing her usual serge trousers, battered shoes, and bottle-green cardigan pulled tight across her impressive breasts. Her brown bobbed hair was flattened by the exertions of the workday. She wore no lipstick, but a single string of pearls around her neck was a nod to femininity.

Nigel was a barrel-chested young man with ruddy cheeks and thick dark hair that flopped over one eye. He'd gone to Magdalen College at Oxford with John and David. He'd worked as a private secretary, as the others had, but for then Prime Minister Neville Chamberlain. When Chamberlain had stepped down, Nigel had revised his pacifist ideology, and was now in the process of joining the RAF. He was spending his last days in London with Chuck.

As David went to the bar for more drinks, Paige offered, "I still have nightmares about typing for Mr. Kennedy."

"Did everyone hear about the Euston station bombing?" Maggie asked the table.

"Dreadful, just dreadful," Paige said, shaking her head.

"Terrible," Chuck said. "I love Ireland and her green, white, and orange flag with all my heart, but the IRA makes me ashamed to be Irish. That's the point of the goddamned flag, you know. Green for the Gaels, orange for the Protestants—and white for the peace between them."

Nigel leaned in and put his arm around her, giving her a loud smacking kiss on the cheek. Chuck smiled, and when she did, her stern face blossomed into something approaching beauty.

"Ireland's still neutral, though," Maggie said. When England declared war on Germany, Ireland chose neutrality. It was a bitter pill for many English.

"Most people in Ireland really do support England and the war effort," Chuck said. "My family does." Chuck's parents were originally from Dublin but had immigrated to England when she was four. Her father had a medical practice in Leeds.

"But what about those who don't—who support the IRA? Who's setting off the mailbox bombs in London?" Maggie asked. "Who's bombing the Tube?"

"I told you—terrorists, extremists, nutters," Chuck said. "Like your, what do you call them in the United States? The Ku Klux Klan."

"Well, we'll see what happens if 'neutral' Ireland's used as a base to launch an attack against England," John said.

"I'm personally just bloody sick of having people think that just because I'm Irish, I'm some sort of terrorist," Chuck said. "Even today, I was pulled off a case because some paranoid mummy didn't want her 'precious darling' contaminated by the horrible Irish nurse." She shook her head. "Stupid bint."

John reached down and pulled the *Evening Standard* from his briefcase. *"PREPARE FOR THE WORST!"* screamed the headline. "Well, regardless of Ireland's neutrality, it's starting in earnest now," he said, taking off his jacket to reveal red suspenders. He sat down and rolled up his shirtsleeves. "Norway was neutral, and it didn't stop the Nazis from invading. And now Belgium's officially surrendered."

Maggie set her lips in a grim line. "France is next."

"Thanks for the reminder," David said, returning with glasses of beer.

Chuck turned to Maggie, trying to change the subject. "So, your first day—how was it? Tell us everything!"

"It was fine, really," Maggie said, smiling once again, trying not to look as tired and frazzled as she felt. "I'm sure it'll get better. Oh, and I stood up to the odious Mr. Snodgrass. That was a plus."

"Dicky Snot-ass," David said. "That's how he's known around the office. Don't take it personally, Magster."

John took a sip from his sweating pint glass. "I still don't understand why you and Paige stayed. You're Americans, after all. You could have left months ago. Probably should have."

*How to explain?* Maggie thought. Yes, she'd originally come to London to sell her late grandmother's house. Yes, at first she'd felt angry because she'd had to give up a doctoral program in mathematics at M.I.T. to do so—no small achievement for a woman, even a Wellesley woman.

When she'd first come to England, she'd been full of resentment—of the narrow-minded people, of bad food and weak coffee, of the dilapidated houses and antiquated plumbing. But when the house didn't sell, Maggie was forced to settle into Grandmother Hope's battered old Victorian. And she found the house was repairable, the tea was lovely, and the English people were of a much kinder character than she'd first given them credit for.

Those people, whom she now thought of as *her* people, were being killed at Calais and Dunkirk. England herself might any day be attacked—by sea, by air, by marching armies of ruthless brown-clad soldiers. The cheerful, ruddy-faced youth; the children playing jacks under Mummy's watchful eye; the old grizzled men in the parks, walking their even older and more grizzled dogs—all mowed down by Hitler's goose-stepping troops.

Maggie had come to see the Nazis not as a people, as selfish and misguided and ultimately defensible as any other, but as robots blindly following the orders of a madman. One article she'd read in *The Times* was the catalyst for her hatred: about Nazi soldiers who'd invaded a town and lined up all the older Jewish women. They'd made the women, most of them grandmothers, climb up into trees and then chirp like birds. They must have been terrified, Maggie thought. And there was something about the new technology of waging war that made her realize this was an entirely unprecedented conflict.

In spite of her own ego and inherent selfishness and petty concerns, she'd grown to love England. London was not just the place where her parents had lived before their tragic car crash but where she would have grown up if that hadn't happened.

She found she'd given her heart to England and wanted her to be safe. She couldn't leave now. Running back to America would have meant turning her back on her heritage, on her home—ultimately, on herself. It didn't matter whether John understood that, or whether Aunt Edith did, either, for that matter. Maggie had made her decision to stay, and she was going to stand by it.

"True," she said finally, "but if we left, then where would you lot be?"

"If only we could get the United States—and not just

you two—to join in the fray," David said wistfully. "The Old Man's trying everything, you know. Practically getting down on his knees and begging Roosevelt for some old warships."

"I can see Roosevelt's point, though," Paige said. "Another war? After the last one? And the Depression?"

"Americans," John said, snorting. "Late to every war."

"The Americans *will* join!" Maggie said, annoyed, for John took every opportunity to snipe at what he saw as a lack of American involvement. "And not just to supply boats and bullets but troops, too."

John was nonplussed. "I fear your President has the moral compass of a windsock."

Maggie glared. "And Britain didn't sit by and watch while Hitler annexed Austria and invaded Sudetenland? What about Czechoslovakia? And Poland?"

John was taken aback. "Not if it had been up to Churchill—"

"And up until the last few months, Churchill's been painted by the papers as old, insignificant, a warmonger—spilling English blood thoughtlessly, and trying desperately to preserve a way of life that's been over since the death of Queen Victoria," Maggie concluded.

"All right, all right, you two!" Paige exclaimed. "Do we need to separate you?"

"*And* I'm not so certain it's such a good idea to let foreigners have such sensitive positions in wartime," John added.

*Annoying, annoying man.* "John, not only am I British by birth, but I'm doing my part for the war effort." Maggie put her hands on Chuck's and Paige's. "We *all* are. So maybe you should be grateful for a little help."

David grinned. "Ah, that charming Yankee modesty."

"Look, I don't mean to insult you," John said, tracing an ancient pint ring stain on the wooden table. "It's just that . . . these are uncertain times—as Diana Snyder learned too late."

"The girl who worked at Number Ten?" Nigel said.

"The papers said she was mugged," Chuck said. "Her wallet was missing. Open-and-shut case."

"Of *course* that's what the papers say," John said. "It's wartime. Things happen. Unpleasant things. And sometimes they aren't as straightforward as they seem. Certainly you don't believe everything you read in the papers, do you?"

"So *you* think she was . . . murdered?" Maggie asked. "Why?"

"Let's just say it's an ongoing investigation."

"Mercy, John," Paige said, conjuring her best southern-belle accent and wrapping her arm around Maggie. "Just because *you're* paranoid doesn't mean everyone's out to get you. Besides," she said, sniffing, "no one's even noticed my new hat—spent nearly all my clothing rations on it."

Chuck rolled her eyes; Maggie gave her a gentle kick under the table.

John didn't rise to the bait. "Wouldn't be a problem if the U.S. was actually in this war."

"I truly believe that America will join the fight," Maggie said.

"Yes, one can always count on the United States to do the right thing—after all other options have been exhausted," John said.

Maggie was about to retort when David rose gracefully to his feet. "Right-o, then, let's not tear each other apart when there are plenty of Germans just waiting to do that very thing. Let's go dancing, shall we?"

"Fine," grumbled Maggie and John simultaneously.

David turned to Paige. "And may I say, my dear, I love your hat. You look absolutely adorable in it."

Paige glowed beneath her confection of bluebells and ribbons. "Why, thank you, David. *You're* a true gentleman."

# THREE

At the Blue Moon Club, the light was dim. Trumpets and clarinets blared through clouds of smoke and Shalimar as the group crammed into a small velvet banquette lit by a low-shaded lamp. As the Moonbeam Orchestra played a cover of Jelly Roll Morton's "King Porter Stomp," a group of dancers on the floor twisted and shimmied through intricate turns and lifts. There was a narrow marble bar and a small sign next to the bald, nervous-looking barman, proclaiming *NO GIN.*

"Well, we'll just have to drink champagne, then, won't we?" David said. "Might as well, while our money's still worth something."

Chuck and Nigel hit the dance floor, moving with more enthusiasm than grace, while the rest of the group settled into their seats.

David elbowed John. "Look—over there. Is that . . ."

John squinted. "Simon Paul? I think it is. Heard he's been working for Halifax."

At a table across the dance floor was a young man, tie askew, a distantly amused expression on his pale, fleshy face. He reminded Maggie of a painting of a young Henry VIII at the National Portrait Gallery, a big fellow, good-looking in a slightly paunchy way. His ginger hair was wavy, and his skin, especially around the nose, was reddish. David waved him over.

A jovial expression transformed his features as he walked across the dance floor to the table. David rose to his feet. "Si, it *is* you, you old sod! How long has it been? Five years now?"

Simon gave a tilted smile. " 'Thirty-six, old boy. Graduation—spring of 'thirty-six."

"Ah, the infamous Simon," Paige whispered to Maggie as the young men talked.

" 'Infamous'?"

"He was up at Oxford with John and David. NSIT."

"NSIT? What's that mean?"

" 'Not Safe in Taxis.' A real taxi tiger. As opposed to 'Very, Very Safe in Taxis, Probably Queer.' Now, hush . . ."

" . . . lifetimes since Magdalen," Simon was saying. "I've heard what you two have been up to, working for old Winnie. Is he really as drunk as people say?"

John's eyes narrowed. "Hardly."

David remembered his manners. "Maggie, Paige, may I present Simon Paul. Oxford man—friend, scholar . . ."

Simon laughed. "You forgot drunkard."

Paige held out her hand for Simon to shake, but instead he leaned across the table to kiss it.

"Delighted to meet you," he declared, keeping Paige's hand in his. Then, to Maggie, "And you—you look just like one of those glorious Rossetti redheads."

"Why don't you sit down, Mr. Paul?" Paige cooed. Under her breath, "Maggie, move over." Maggie slid in farther, and Simon sat down next to Paige.

"Please, call me Simon."

"So you all know each other from school?" Maggie asked.

"Oxford, Magdalen College," David said. "Parties, punting, picnics, Pimm's . . ."

Simon took out a pouch of tobacco and a paper and proceeded to roll a cigarette. "Those were the days, eh, boys?" He finished rolling his cigarette and put it in his mouth, removing it only to pull a few stray tobacco leaves off his tongue with his broad fingers before lighting up.

"And now he's working as a private secretary to Lord Halifax," John concluded.

"Halifax?" Maggie said. "Britain's Foreign Secretary, right? He was with Chamberlain for appeasement, right?"

"Now, now," said Simon. "Just because he's a Tory and hunts the occasional fox . . ."

"He was tight with Ambassador Kennedy," Paige ventured. "Saw him around the offices quite a bit. Quite the hatchet-face—not at all attractive."

"Halifax believes in realpolitik," Simon said. "Without commitment from Russia and America, this war . . ." He shrugged.

"Thank God he didn't become Prime Minister, and Churchill got the job instead," Chuck rejoined.

"Had a bit of a falling-out there, didn't we, boys?" Simon said, taking a long drag on his cigarette.

"Nice to see you've come around to our viewpoint," John said.

"Wouldn't say that, really—wouldn't say that. What are we fighting for, anyway? Hitler doesn't want England. If we leave him alone in Europe, we'll all be having dinner together by Christmas."

"How about for the duration of the war," John said, "there's *one* national government—*one* England. Come, now—even Halifax is part of the coalition."

"I still don't see why British blood needs to be spilled in this mess," Simon said, rubbing out his cigarette. "Goddamned waste, if you ask me. If we keep going along Churchill's path, this entire island could look like

Calais. Western Europe has fallen. France is falling, even as we sit here with our pints. There's only going to be about twenty miles of English Channel between us and the Germans once they take France. Perhaps a poor peace *is* better than a miserable war."

"A 'poor peace'? Are you mad?" John said, his voice tight.

"If we don't survive, there's no hope," Simon rejoined. "As Lord Halifax was quick to point out."

David colored. "I doubt a 'poor peace,' as you say, would ever come to pass," he said. "As the Boss once said about Hitler annexing Austria, 'After a boa constrictor has devoured its prey, it often has a considerable digestive spell'—that is, before attacking again. What do you think a 'poor peace' would ultimately bring?"

"That's why we need to act now," Simon said. "Play the Italian card."

"The 'Italian card'?" Paige asked.

"Some people," John said, giving Simon a pointed look, "believe that Hitler listens to Mussolini. And if we give him some of our Mediterranean territories, he'll have a little chat with Herr Hitler. Convince him not to invade."

"Otherwise," Simon said, "we're going to end up fighting them both."

The table was momentarily silent, a chill falling over them.

Maggie looked at Simon. "Do you actually think that Hitler and the King could really someday sit down to tea and crumpets together? Really? Because I don't. Maybe it's because I'm an outsider, but surely you know this war is about more than that."

"Really, darling?" Simon said with a smirk.

Maggie caught his sarcastic tone but was undeterred. "It's, it's—" She flung her arms wide, encompassing the dance floor, the park, the city, the country itself.

"It's . . . this. Your island. Your England. What makes you different. And if you can't see that, well, then maybe you don't deserve the"—she fought for the word—"*privilege* of being English."

She took a breath. "Yes, things need to change in England. It's not an empire anymore, and the days of colonialism are over. It's time for there to be more opportunities for the poor and working class—and women, of course," she said, giving a hard look to John and David. "But the point's moot if England's invaded by Nazis."

It had been a long day and Maggie grabbed Paige's wrist. "We're going to freshen up," she snapped, leading a surprised Paige away to the ladies' room.

As the girls left, David gave a soft whistle. "Not bad—for a Yankee. If we could get a few more like her, we might actually win this thing."

The lounge area of the ladies' toilet was papered with a silver art deco print that glowed pink in the soft rosy lights that circled the mirrors. Paige took a look at her reflection, smiled, and pulled out a tube of lipstick. "So," she cooed, painting a crimson bow on her lips. "Feel better now that you've got that out of your system?"

A blowsy woman in a low-cut dress left, and Maggie leaned against the marble counter. The ornate gold-framed mirror showed both girls, the same middle height and slight build, one redheaded and one blond.

"It's just . . . the waiting, the stress, the talk of invasion. That bastard Dicky Snot-ass. And then that man, that Simon . . ."

"He's not that bad, really," Paige said. "I think he's just trying to play devil's advocate. Personally, I think he's rather handsome."

"I noticed," Maggie said. "Simon was acting very . . . friendly with you."

"Simon's *such* a flirt!" Paige blotted her lips with a tissue. "Want to borrow? Go on, just a little bit. It'll look so nice with your hair." Even at Wellesley, Paige had always been generous with her things, lending out lipsticks and Worth satin ball gowns indiscriminately. Maggie smoothed some on.

"Ta-da!" Paige said, spinning around, her shining blond hair floating around her like a halo. "And David's not an option, of course," she said, considering, "being Very Very Safe in Taxis, Probably Queer, but—have you ever considered John? You'll be working together in"— she gave Maggie a significant look—"*close proximity* now."

Maggie had a sudden image of John, trim in his dark suit and tie, his expression wry, a stray curl straggling across his forehead.

"He's a dish, isn't he?" Paige said, reaching down behind her and straightening the seams in her stockings. "Even with that dreadful hair."

"No, no, thank you, Emma Woodhouse. I don't need a matchmaker. And John and I got off on the wrong foot ages ago." *I have enough to worry about,* Maggie thought, *without—how did Mrs. Tinsley put it?—"mooning" over one of the private secretaries. And an annoying one, at that.* "I've had enough of bad dates and taxi tigers," Maggie said. "Besides, *you're* the one who seems interested."

"I'm interested in everyone, darling. But in a purely hypothetical way. I'm too much of a gadabout to settle down anytime soon." Paige reached into Maggie's bun and took out the tortoiseshell clip securing it. Maggie's red hair tumbled free over her shoulders. "Much, much better. Oh, let's just forget it for tonight and dance. David's a terrific dancer, you know," she said, linking her arm through Maggie's as they made their way back to the table.

A tall and elegant brunette had joined the group and was seated at the velvet banquette. "Sarah!" Paige squealed, leaning down and kissing her on both cheeks. "Where have you been? We've missed you *desperately*."

"Hello, Sarah," Maggie said.

"Hello, kittens." Sarah slouched back and stretched out her long, slender legs as she took a drag on her clove cigarette. "And I've been in the studio, of course. If we're going to have a season this year—and in my opinion, the show *must* go on—there's a lot of work to be done. But I tell you, if I have to do *Giselle* one more time, just take me out into an alley and shoot me." She was as beautiful as any fairy-tale princess, but her voice was disconcertingly low and raspy, almost froggy.

"Sarah," Paige said as she and Maggie took their seats, "did the boys do a proper introduction? This is Simon Paul, an old school chum of David and John's. Simon," Paige continued, "meet Sarah Sanderson. Sarah's a ballerina with the Sadler's Wells Ballet."

Sarah and Simon looked at each other, locked eyes, then looked away. "We've met," Sarah said curtly.

"The Sadler's Wells Ballet?" Maggie asked, sensing Sarah's discomfort and trying to change the subject.

"The Vic-Wells Ballet until just recently. We perform at the Old Vic and the Sadler's Wells," Sarah said, taking another long drag. "Lots of scurrying back and forth with our dance bags."

Nigel and Chuck returned from the dance floor to the banquette, flushed and breathing heavily. "Oh, it's *wonderful*," Chuck said. "What are you all doing sitting here, just waiting for bombs to drop? Dance, damn you!"

"*Speaking* of dancing," Simon interjected, looking to Paige. "Maybe you'd do me the honor?" The band switched into a rousing version of Glenn Miller's "Stairway to the Stars."

Paige graced him with her most radiant smile. "Why, I'd *love* to!"

"David?" Maggie asked. "Take a spin?"

David looked surprised but pleased to be asked nonetheless. "Of course, m'lady," he said, standing and offering a hand. "After you."

On the scuffed wooden dance floor, David held Maggie lightly, guiding her gracefully through intricate maneuvers. "So why didn't you ask John?" he asked finally.

"He's a bit of an ass," Maggie said over the trumpets.

"What?" David said above the din.

*"Ass!"* Maggie practically shouted.

David seemed amused. "Ha!" he said, spinning her farther into the crowd. His hands were a bit sweaty, but he was a fantastic dancer.

As the orchestra beat out four, the lead singer segued into "Blue Orchids." The clarinet player licked his lips and launched into his part as the drummer switched to wire brushes.

"May I cut in?" Maggie looked up, startled, at John.

*Good Lord,* Maggie thought. *What's he doing here? Did he overhear?*

"Good luck, you two." David smiled as he turned and left.

As they moved around the floor, the color rose in her cheeks and at her throat. She noticed, under his chin, a tiny sliver of unshaven hair that his razor must have missed. She found herself worrying about the possibility that her nose was getting shiny and that John might notice. *Oh, stop it,* she thought. *You've had too much champagne.*

Maggie closed her eyes and relaxed into John's arms as they moved around the floor. It was a mistake—the room started to spin.

"Do you mind if we take a break now?" she asked.

"Of course," John replied. He had a strange look on his face that Maggie couldn't quite place.

They broke apart and headed back to the table. As John and Maggie sat down, Sarah looked up expectantly. Men were in short supply, after all. "My turn?" she said to John.

John sighed. "What is it with women and dancing?"

"Oh, Johnny, don't be such a prat and come on," Sarah insisted, offering her hand. She rose to her feet, the sharp points of her hip bones jutting out through the silk of her dress. "Mind the toes."

The music had changed into a waltz, and John and Sarah glided together. She was amazing, Maggie thought, all long legs and sinuous arms, her dark hair floating behind her.

"Take a look at Fred and Ginger," David said at her elbow, as if reading her mind. "Don't they look fabulous?" Maggie had to admit that they did—whirling, spinning, and twirling. When the song ended, they wandered back to the table.

"Why can't we do something like that at the Wells?" Sarah said breathlessly as she sat down. "Instead of bloomin' *Giselle* all the time."

"But you'd make a beautiful Giselle!" Paige exclaimed.

"Yes, I would," Sarah replied. "And I wouldn't complain so much if I actually *were* Giselle and not 'second peasant girl to the left.' "

They laughed, and Sarah slipped her red high heels from her feet and began to massage them. Maggie gasped at seeing her toes—bunions distended their shape, and they were covered with calluses and barely healed blisters.

"Yeah, gorgeous, aren't they? That's what you get for

wearing those pretty pink satin slippers." Maggie considered Sarah with newfound respect.

She glanced at Paige, who was flirting shamelessly with Simon, her hand ruffling his hair; David and John, engrossed in political debate; and Sarah, who was talking intently with Chuck and Nigel. As the light glimmered on the golden trumpets, she realized the day—and evening—had gone rather well, all things considered.

Suddenly, unbidden, her thoughts flashed to the late Diana Snyder. *The poor girl,* Maggie thought. *And she'll never know any of this.*

# FOUR

THE MAY MORNING threatened rain. A cool wind blew from the east, and a few birds chirped in alarm.

People walked with a hurried step along Herrick Street in Pimlico, and a few plump, gray pigeons flapped down and took shelter under the roof of a café. The sky opened abruptly and cold rain poured down, drenching a group of rowdy soldiers as they made their way down oil-stained streets, passing reddish-brown brick buildings in the growing darkness of the storm. Under the heaviness of the water droplets, flowering trees wept pale pink petals down into the gutters.

A young woman, caught without an umbrella, dashed under the eaves of a building, desperate for cover. Grimacing, she looked up at the sky. The rain drummed loudly on the overhang and flooded down the verdigris gutter pipes.

"Are you coming in, miss?"

She looked up to see a gentleman in a well-tailored gray suit. He had thick, white hair, rosy cheeks, and dimples that made him look younger than his years. "Are you coming in?" he repeated.

"Oh, no."

"It's not going to let up, I'm afraid," he said, shaking his head.

She sighed.

"You know," the man said, "I'm going to be speaking here in a few minutes. Why don't you come in and have a listen? It'll get you out of the rain, at least."

The young woman looked from his face up to the sign above his left shoulder. *The Saturday Club,* it read. *Today's Discussion: Whose War Is It, Anyway?*

" 'Whose war'?" she asked. "The Saturday Club—what is it?"

"We're, well, we like to think of ourselves as . . . pacifists. After all, no one wants this war. Do you?"

"No, of course not."

Their eyes met, and she gave him a smile in return.

He opened the door for her. With another look up at the leaden sky, she turned and allowed herself to be escorted inside.

"Neil, how many?" the white-haired man asked.

"Almost thirty, Mr. Pierce," replied a younger man at a battered wooden table, hastily scribbling the last names. A few angry red spots of acne dotted his chin.

"Let's get on with it, then," he said, giving the woman another smile. "Please stay?"

"Yes," she said, unpinning her hat and smoothing her hair. "I think I will."

The young woman took a seat at the back of the room and looked around. The yellow paint on the walls was chipped and scuffed. Worn black linoleum covered the floor, and the ceiling was water-stained. The audience was made up of mostly middle-aged, middle-class women and a few older men. The humid air was rank with strong Oriental perfume and liniment. The woman looked up as the man walked through the room and up to the podium.

"Thank you all for coming today," he said, turning and smiling reassuringly. "My name is Malcolm Pierce, and I'm the president of the Saturday Club. I'm happy to see familiar faces in the audience—and a few new ones as well." He winked at the young woman, who smiled in return.

He leaned back on his heels. "We at the Saturday Club are united in our belief that this is a waste of war, that Britain has no call to fight against Germany. Hitler is not our enemy. Who is our real enemy? The Jew. The Jew is our enemy—our common enemy, Germany's and ours. The Jew is our absolute enemy who will shrink at nothing. He knows but a single goal: our complete destruction. And most important to us here in England, let me ask you, *Cui bono?* Meaning, who benefits from this war?"

A few in the audience started nodding. "Hear, hear," said an older man with a cane in the front row.

Pierce looked around at his rapt audience. "The Jews, of course! Some here may say, 'But there are decent Jews, after all!' However," Pierce raised a cautionary finger, "the very phrase 'after all' proves that these exceptions—mythical exceptions, based on rumor and gossip—are meaningless in our battle against the Jews. Even Martin Luther saw this 'decency' for what it was: 'Know, dear Christian, and have no doubts about it, that next to the Devil you have no more bitter, poisonous, and determined enemy than a genuine Jew. . . . If they do something good for you, it is not because they love you, but because they need room to live with us, so they have to do something. But their heart remains as I have said!'"

Pierce looked at the upturned faces gazing at him in rapt attention. "I think of myself as a patriot, one who speaks out against this war in hopes of saving the lives of Englishmen and women. Germany is not our enemy. Hitler is not our enemy. Who is? The Jews! The Jews are our real enemy—and how they must be rubbing their hands together and laughing as they think about how much British blood will be shed.

"And this is the truth—the real truth—that the current British government, especially the warmonger Churchill, is determined to keep from you. But now you know the truth. And you—we—will not be fooled into going along with Churchill's propaganda. We will do everything possible to keep Britain out of this war—this unnecessary, unnatural war." He smiled, dimples flashing. "Thank you for your time."

When the speech was over and the applause subsided, weak tea and stale biscuits were offered in the back room.

Pierce made his way around the room, shaking hands and offering words of welcome. When he reached the young woman, who'd helped herself to a cup of the steaming tea, he stopped. "And what did you think? Are you glad you came in out of the rain?"

"Interesting," she replied slowly, taking a sip of tea and looking up at him. "Most interesting."

"Come back and see us next week?"

She smiled coyly. "I might."

"And may I ask your name?"

The young woman's smile grew, and she showed tiny, pearly white teeth. "Claire."

It was inconceivable to Maggie that they were in the garden on such a beautiful Saturday afternoon not to prune the roses but to build a bomb shelter. As in a shelter from bombs. Bombs raining down from the sky. Exploding. That sort of thing.

And yet here they were.

Maggie, Paige, Chuck, and the twins—Annabelle and Clarabelle—had each chipped in a few pounds for an Anderson, a shell-like hut made out of corrugated steel. Two curved pieces of steel acted as the roof and two were the walls, while two other flat pieces of steel, one with a door, made up the other walls. When finished, the shelter was supposed to be six feet high, four feet wide, and six and a half feet long, and in a pit four feet deep with at least fifteen inches of earth heaped on top of the whole contraption.

Under the hot cerulean sky, the girls surveyed the garden, tied pinafores around their waists, and picked up their shovels. They'd marked off the area to dig; now they just had to do it.

Chuck groaned. "Of course it *had* to rain this morning. Makes the dirt even heavier."

"All right, ladies," Paige declared, scanning the directions with the same take-charge attitude she'd used for party planning. "We've marked off the proper dimensions. Let's start digging!"

Clarabelle and Annabelle exchanged a look and then started giggling. Although they weren't that much younger than Maggie, Paige, and Chuck, with their pixielike physiques and tendency to laugh, they seemed like children sometimes.

Paige was not amused. *"What?"*

Annabelle, the slightly taller, firstborn twin, often spoke for the two of them. "It's just that . . . you sound just like one of our schoolmistresses."

Clarabelle began. "Miss—"

"—Poulter!" Annabelle finished. "Isn't she just a dead ringer for Miss Poulter?"

Paige narrowed her eyes.

"Oh, Miss Poulter was really quite nice—" said Annabelle, sensing Paige's annoyance.

"—and *very* pretty. And smart. Like Jo March in *Jo's Boys*—" Clarabelle chimed in.

"—or Anne Shirley in *Anne of Avonlea*—"

"—and not at *all* like Miss Minchin in *A Little Princess*—"

Chuck glared. "The fucking Nazis are going to drop fucking bombs on us, and all you two twits can talk about is fucking *books*?" She grabbed hold of a shovel, stalked off, and began digging with a vengeance.

"She's still annoyed about the dish situation," Maggie explained. "Maybe . . . if you two could wash up a little more often?"

The twins exchanged exasperated glances. Then Annabelle whispered, "She's just so—"

"—bossy," Clarabelle said.

"And *loud*!" both twins said simultaneously, setting off a fresh explosion of giggles.

"And her *language* sometimes," Annabelle said.

Maggie's lip twitched; Chuck was indeed bossy, loud, and prone to using profanity. Still, she had her reasons. "Just do your dishes," she said gently. "And I'm sure everything will be fine."

They turned back to digging. After months of the "bore war," the threat of bombs wasn't just hypothetical anymore. Overhead, Hurricanes and Spitfires roared by in V-shaped formations of three, on their way to France, most likely. German Messerschmitts and Heinkels could be on their way to London any day. Some of the port cities had already been bombed. It was just a matter of time for London.

Shovels in hand, they all ripped up the sod, rolled it back, and then began digging in earnest. The earth smelled damp, rich, and loamy, warmed in the sun. A hundred years and a gallon of sweat later, the five had barely scratched the surface. The back of Maggie's blouse was soaking wet, and beads of sweat stung her eyes.

They rested on the back steps leading up to the kitchen, gulping glasses of cool water as the sun's rays slanted and deepened. As Chuck lit a cigarette and pushed back a brown curl, Paige ventured, "You know, I'm sure if we called the boys, they would—"

"*No!*" Maggie exclaimed. Then, in a more reasonable tone of voice, "We can do it ourselves," she said, rubbing her sore forearms. A blood blister on her forefinger was starting to ooze. "Eventually."

The twins sighed. "We don't really need an Anderson, do we? We could always just go down to the basement. . . ."

"And be crushed if the house collapses?" Maggie asked. "Or burned to a crisp if a bomb sets it on fire?"

The twins looked at the house and shared a chagrined expression, realizing Maggie's logic.

"I don't know how you can stand it, Chuck," Annabelle said, leaning back and swatting at a buzzing fly. "With Nigel enlisted in the RAF now." She looked at Chuck sideways. "Any idea where he's going to be sent? And when?"

Chuck took a long drag on her cigarette; her hands were shaking. "No, no idea," she said. "Could be anywhere . . ." Her voice broke. "He's training now. Probably up north, in Scotland maybe. I know he can't say anything, but—"

Clarabelle patted Chuck on the shoulder. "It'll be fine, Chuck. You'll see. Everything will be all right."

Maggie, Paige, and Chuck, and then even Annabelle, looked at Clarabelle, then at the pieces of the Anderson shelter, then back to Clarabelle. "I mean, *Nigel* will be fine. More than fine. A hero, in fact."

Chuck blinked hard. "Bloody hell," she said finally, wiping her eyes with her sleeve.

"Right, then. Back to work, ladies." Maggie stood up, brushing dirt and leaves off the seat of her trousers. "And do you know what I think our shelter needs? A nice big bottle of gin."

Across the Atlantic Ocean, in one of Wellesley College's faculty apartments, Edith Hope couldn't sleep. It was her age, she told herself; it was hot flashes and night sweats and needing to use the toilet every few hours.

She looked up at the bedroom ceiling, shadows from the maple tree branches outside the window dancing in the silvery light from a waning moon.

Not to mention the fact that her niece was in a country about to be invaded by Germany.

She turned over and flipped the down pillow to the cool side but still couldn't get comfortable. She threw off the gray-silk duvet, the one her hair was beginning to match. *Guilty conscience, Edith?* she thought. *Maybe. Probably.*

Edith's last argument with Margaret still rang in her ears and haunted her dreams. She hadn't wanted to send her to London. But when her mother, Margaret's grandmother, died, there wasn't any other option. Edith wouldn't—couldn't—go back to London, to that place where time compressed and old hurts would feel just as raw as they had twenty-some-odd years ago. And she was still, after all this time, determined to keep her word.

And yet.

And yet it had been hard on Margaret. Edith sighed. Margaret hadn't understood. And why should she? She was young and had her life in front of her.

"I'm a college graduate now," Margaret had snapped any number of times before she'd left. "Don't you think it's time to start treating me as an adult?"

*An adult?* When Edith looked at her she still saw a newborn, small and mewing like a kitten. She saw an inquisitive toddler, a precocious child, and a determined teenage girl. But a grown woman? Edith tried not to let her lips twitch into a smile. "I'm well aware of your age, Margaret. And if you want me to treat you like a grown-up, you will need to behave like one. . . . I'm sorry, but there it is."

And that was the end of the discussion.

Until, of course, Margaret started to make noise about staying in London—poppycock and nonsense about truly living in London, not merely getting a job long enough to sell the house and then returning to Boston, where she belonged. *What's that girl thinking?* In response, Edith had sent off the letter, revised and rewritten so many times, she knew it by heart.

*Wellesley, Massachusetts*

*Margaret,*

*I feel it is my duty to write to tell you how disappointed I am by your decision to stay in England. When I asked you to go, it was simply to oversee the details of the house sale, so that the money would offset the cost of M.I.T. It seemed a perfect opportunity for you to see something of the world before going back to your studies.*

*However, now that war is beginning in earnest, I feel that it was the wrong decision; I should never have allowed you to go. Perhaps you've been too sheltered all your life, and this first taste of freedom was too intoxicating. But I will warn you that ultimately it will come to naught. Why do you think women such as myself have fought so hard to be educated, to work in academia? Do you realize the sacrifices we made for your generation?*

*And for you to throw it all away, to stay in a country hunkering down for war, to waste your talents . . . It's a slap in the face. Why do you think I left London for the States? One reason was the Great War; believe me, you don't want to go through something like that. Leave it to the British.*

*Come home, Margaret. I insist. You can't do anything more in London.*

    *Edith*

There was the war, there was the threat of imminent invasion.

There was also the chance, however slight, that Margaret would find out the truth about her father.

And that was what worried Edith the most.

## FIVE

A̲t No. 10, Maggie had seen Mr. Churchill only in passing, always in a hurry, his endless Romeo y Julieta cigars leaving a pungent trail of smoke behind him wherever he went, faithfully shadowed by his private detective, Mr. Walter Thompson. But it was obvious when he was in—the office crackled with electricity and there was a sense of urgency in the air.

Mrs. Tinsley had come down with a bad case of flu. Despite her exclamations that she should stay and work, she was being sent home by Miss Stewart.

"Really, Miss Stewart," she managed to croak, "I'm quite capable of—"

Notwithstanding her air of genteel diffidence, Miss Stewart wasn't having any of it. "Mrs. Tinsley, you're not well. You must go home and rest, so you may return as quickly as possible at full strength."

"London may be attacked at any moment, and—"

"Mrs. Tinsley, I must appeal to your common sense." Miss Stewart pulled out her trump card. "What if the P.M. became ill?"

Mrs. Tinsley paused to consider. Then she sneezed into her starched cambric handkerchief. "Oh, very well. But it's only for one evening." She stood up and put on her hat, stabbing it with long pearl-tipped pins. "I assure you," she declared as she made her way out the door, "I shall return tomorrow, first thing."

As the sound of Mrs. Tinsley's footsteps echoed down the hallway, Miss Stewart gave a gentle sigh and folded her tiny, plump hands. "Miss Hope?"

Maggie was typing a letter to one of the constituents. "Yes, Miss Stewart?"

"I think it's high time you worked with Mr. Churchill. Would you mind stepping in tonight?"

"Of course not, ma'am," Maggie replied. As nervous as she was, she wanted to get started.

"Very well, then, dear. Go into his study and wait. He'll be coming in from dinner and will be here shortly."

Maggie did as she was told and found herself in the Prime Minister's study. It was large, with dark wood paneling, a red Persian carpet, and several oil paintings of the seaside in ornate gilt frames, with *W. Churchill* signed in thick script.

Her heart was beating so loudly she was sure everyone in the building could hear it. With sweaty palms, she rolled the paper into the typewriter. She arranged and rearranged her fountain pens and thick, stubby pencils. She looked up at the black hands of the clock a half-dozen times. She waited. And waited.

And waited some more.

Nelson, Mr. Churchill's cat, came into the room and jumped on a cushioned window seat, sitting down and tucking his paws and tail under him.

Maggie looked out the window at the dying light. It was a glorious June evening—bright and warm in the waning sunshine, growing chilly in the shadows. She could hear the low chimes of Big Ben and then the lighter bells of the Horse Guards Parade strike the hour.

The fine weather was a blessing, because beneath the thin veneer of civility and pleasantries, England was a

nation bracing for the worst. Underneath their polite
façades, people were anxious, uneasy, depressed, fatalis-
tic. Children were being evacuated to the countryside.
Plans were proposed to relocate the royal family to
Canada. The contents of the Tate and the national museum had been put into storage. Dogs were being put
down. People were warned about fifth columnists, spies
living among them. A blackout was in effect night after
night.

The men, more than a million, who were too old, too
young, or too infirm to serve in the military, joined the
Home Guard. There were no guns for them, so they
armed themselves with hunting rifles, swords, billy
clubs, golf clubs, and pickaxes. Those without carried
broom handles or pepper—to throw in the face of the
enemy. It would be easy to laugh, Maggie thought, if it
weren't so desperate. And so very brave.

Maggie watched the country's preparations for invasion with a mixture of terror, disbelief, and admiration.
She remembered how, just a few years ago, occasionally
the newspaper would have an article or two about
Hitler and his growing power, or how then Minister of
Parliament Winston Churchill made speeches about the
growing Nazi threat in the House of Commons—only to
be ignored.

Just a year ago, when Neville Chamberlain was Prime
Minister, promising peace and offering appeasement,
Winston Churchill had been one of the few voices warning against the growing threat of Nazi Germany. In
speeches and articles, he'd said that Britain couldn't turn
a blind eye to Hitler's invasion of Poland the way she
had with Sudetenland and Czechoslovakia. England
must honor her treaty to back the Poles or else face dis-
grace. And England must rearm to defend herself or else
risk enslavement by the Nazis.

The audience booed and even threw papers at him, calling him crazy and worse.

Then Chamberlain declared war—and Winston Churchill became the new Prime Minister.

Without preamble, the man himself strode into the room.

The P.M. was in a rage. Fury seemed to radiate off his compact body. His brow was furrowed, and he paced the length of the room in apparent frustration. In turn, Maggie tried to make herself as invisible as possible.

It seemed to work, as he took no notice of her.

Mr. Churchill turned to the windows, where Maggie was better able to contemplate him in profile. He was shorter than she'd thought, with a stout and imposing physique. His face was rosy and plump, and his head was almost bald. He was wearing a navy-blue suit with a burgundy bow tie. From his waistcoat hung an engraved pocket watch. Gold-framed reading glasses perched at the end of his nose.

Without a glance in her direction, he began to speak, absorbed in the matter at hand: the problem of former King Edward VII now known as the Duke of Windsor. Since abdicating the throne to marry the American divorcée Mrs. Wallis Simpson, the Duke had set off for Madrid, then to Lisbon. Now he wanted to return to England.

"Sir, may I venture upon a word of serious counsel," the P.M. dictated. "Many sharp and unfriendly ears will be pricked up to catch any suggestion that your Royal Highness takes a view about the war, or about the Germans." As the words rolled from him, he paced the length of the carpet, hands clasped behind him. The cigar clamped in his mouth didn't help Maggie in understanding him. His delivery was far less distinct than it was for his speeches at the House of Commons or his BBC broadcasts.

"Even while you have been staying at Lisbon, conversations have been reported by telegraph through various channels which might have been used to your Royal Highness's disadvantage." And so on. But Maggie was able to catch what he was saying and keep up. She became almost hypnotized, engrossed in her task as he went on and on—she imagined herself not as a typist but as an extension of him, a link between himself and the page. They went on in this manner, with various letters, for almost an hour before he finally looked at her.

"You're not Mrs. Tinsley!" he exclaimed, looking aghast.

"No, sir," Maggie replied, heart racing.

"Where is she?" he barked.

*Oh, goodness.* "She's sick, sir."

"Sick?"

"Y-yes. Sick, sir."

He contemplated this for a moment and paced a bit, grimacing.

Then he glared at her over the frames of his glasses. "What's your name, girl?"

"Margaret Hope," she whispered.

"Holmes?"

"Hope," she blurted, her voice too loud in the quiet room. She reddened and fell silent.

"Yes, yes—Margaret Hope," he repeated, considering. His face lit up, and he broke into a beatific smile, unrecognizable from the stern figure of moments before. "We need some hope in this office," he muttered to himself.

"Yes, you may stay, Miss Hope," Mr. Churchill said, another pull on his cigar, watching the blue smoke rise, "while we see how you get on."

John passed Mr. Snodgrass in the hallway outside Winston Churchill's office. The older man beckoned the younger over.

"Yes, sir?" John asked.

"Miss Hope is in there. With the Boss. Alone."

"What are you insinuating, sir?"

"No, no—nothing of that sort, of course. But you know how sensitive these things are. I was against having her here as a private secretary—and I'm not convinced her working here as a typist is any better. But I suppose it's all the better to keep an eye on her."

Snodgrass set off down the corridor, and John followed, saying, "Surely, sir, you don't think she had anything to do with—"

"Of course not," Snodgrass snapped. "But she's here, and she's taking notes and writing memos on sensitive information."

"As do we all," John countered.

"As do we all," Snodgrass repeated, rounding a corner. "But not all of us have the family connections Miss Hope has."

"Miss Hope is unaware of her family connections."

Snodgrass stopped. "For now." He started again down the hall, quicker in his stride.

John easily caught up with him. "How's the investigation going?"

There was a pause as Snodgrass turned to descend a flight of stairs, his hand on the cold metal rail. "It seems we have a witness to Miss Snyder's murder."

"A witness? In the blackout?"

"Yes, apparently there was a waxing moon. One of Miss Snyder's flatmates was in and saw something out the window. Didn't think much of it at the time, but now that MI-Five is involved . . ."

"Can she identify a face?" John asked, jaw tense.

"The witness is being questioned today."

Because of the imminent threat of invasion, attendance at the Saturday Club's meetings was swelling. That week's gathering had adjourned, and a few of the members had taken their conversation to Malcolm Pierce's Cadogan Square flat. The parlor was papered in a faded gold japonaiserie print of geishas smiling coyly behind flowers and fans; the carved mahogany furniture was dark, and the brocades and silks were worn. Motheaten crimson velvet drapes were pulled over blackout curtains. The air was thick with cigarette smoke, and the gramophone played a recording of Kirsten Flagstad singing *Die Fledermaus.*

"What will happen if there's an invasion?" asked Mrs. Linney, her hands twisting her large diamond ring. Even though the evening was warm, she was wearing a tawny fox-fur collar. The fox's shiny black glass eyes looked crossed and slightly maniacal in the dim light.

"We'll be lined up and shot, I suppose," Pierce said with a serious face, then smiled, flashing his dimples.

Mrs. Linney's plump cheeks creased. "Oh, Malcolm."

"Look," he said, taking a sip of tea. The gold-rimmed cup was thin and fragile. "The press is largely under Jewish control, yes? So we're not truly getting the real story. Hitler will take care of Churchill and his Zionist gang, but as for people like us, well, once the dust settles and they know what we've been doing for their cause, they'll most likely give us medals."

"More tea?" Claire said, pot in hand. She'd made herself at home.

"Don't mind if I do, dear," Mrs. Linney said. Claire poured and then took a seat, crossing her legs at the ankles.

"The Jews brought it on themselves, you know," Pierce said. "Hitler's said again and again he wanted nothing—nothing from England. But then Chamberlain had to get involved after Poland. . . ."

"Hear, hear," said old Mr. Hodgeson, a Great War veteran in the corner. "We don't need English boys going to war again, just for the bloody Jews. Excuse my language."

"Poland and Czechoslovakia are Jewish interests, it's true," Pierce said. "That's the reason I'm adamant that we don't belong in this war. Look at this young woman," he said, nodding to Claire, who smiled back. "She's seeing a nice young chap, she tells me. Well, what happens when this nice young chap joins up with His Majesty's forces? What happens to her then? I'll tell you—he'll come home blind or maimed or worse, in a mattress cover secured with large horse-blanket safety pins. Slaughtered, just because Germany invaded Poland. And she becomes a widow—or ends up spending the rest of her life with a cripple. I've said it once, and I'll say it again—this is an unnecessary war."

There were tears in Claire's eyes that threatened to overflow. "But what can we *do*?" she said, her knee touching Pierce's.

"My dear," Pierce said, his leg pressing against hers. "I was hoping you'd ask."

# SIX

MI-5 WAS OFFICIALLY known as the Imperial Security Intelligence Service—but no one called it that. Headquartered in a small office building at 58 St. James's Street, MI-5's mission was counterintelligence. Protecting secrets. Catching spies.

And with the Prime Minister's blessing in wartime, at any cost, by any means necessary.

Down in smoke-filled windowless offices crammed with battered wooden desks, dented gray filing cabinets, and worn green carpeting, junior MI-5 agents toiled in obscurity.

"Mark, I need you on something."

Mark Standish, a youngish man with tortoiseshell spectacles, looked up from the piles of photographs on his desk with tired, red-rimmed eyes. He was dark-haired and doughy. "What is it?"

"I just spoke with one of our agents," Hugh Thompson said. "There's a high probability that someone from the watch list was spotted in London yesterday." Hugh was taller and slimmer, with a high forehead and deep-set green eyes. He had a tendency to stick his hands in his hair when he was frustrated, which was often, and so it stuck up at odd angles.

"Nazi?" Mark asked.

Hugh shook his head. "Bloody IRA. Suspected of coordinating several bombings, including the one at Euston."

"Euston, you say? Bad one, that." Mark shuffled through some papers. "Let's see. . . . Our agents in the field have picked up some leads in the last week about a possible attack by the IRA." Mark shuffled through some papers and picked one up. "Here it is, from Agent Dunham."

"What was the target?" Hugh asked.

"Saint Paul's Cathedral. But the time-and-date window passed."

"Passed?"

"Yes."

Hugh looked at the memo again. "What if the agents got the date wrong? Would be terrible if something happened to it. Change the skyline, terrify people, crush morale . . ."

Mark shrugged. "Don't know, old bean." He surveyed the mountains of papers and maps and photographs of suspects. "But I've got at least fifty IRA leads that are even more specific, and I suggest that's where we put our manpower. Most of them somehow connected with one Eammon Devlin."

"Fine," Hugh said. "But I'm taking this memo up to Frain."

As Hugh reached for it, Mark pulled it closer to himself. "I can take it to him," Mark said, smelling an opportunity.

Hugh snorted. "Why? I thought you had at least fifty leads that were more specific."

"You know, you're really a transparent bastard. Stop trying to brownnose Frain. He doesn't like it."

Hugh scratched his head, unwilling to push the matter. "Fine. Forget it, then." He snatched the memo back and jammed it underneath a towering stack of papers.

He sighed, unbuttoning his top button and loosening his tie. "Anything else?"

"Ah, here's something—that girl who was murdered in Pimlico." Mark picked up a piece of paper with a photograph clipped to it. He gave a low whistle. "Too bad—she was a real looker." He handed the photo to Hugh.

Hugh replied, "Thought that was a police matter. Open-and-shut case."

"Not when it's someone connected with the Prime Minister's office."

Hugh looked down at the photo again. The girl had a doelike quality to her. Not that it meant anything. "Think it was more than a murder, then?"

"Frain found a witness—one of the girl's flatmates caught a glimpse of a man lurking around. Didn't think much of it at the time."

"In the blackout?"

Mark leaned his bulk back in his chair. "There was a moon that night. Almost full. Said she got a decent look."

"Was she able to make an identification?"

"Not a conclusive one. She picked out a few men from photographs. The other two were decoys. But one was IRA—name of Michael Murphy."

"Murphy? That bastard's still in the country?" Murphy was implicated in a series of IRA bombings in London earlier in the year, which had killed almost fifty people.

"Apparently."

"But if it was Murphy, why her?" Hugh gave Diana's picture a hard look, as if she could somehow answer him. "And why now?"

At No. 10, Maggie was learning that Mr. Churchill could often be irritable, incensed, and sarcastic.

When she made a mistake—and she made plenty—her hearing, her education, and her country of origin were all called into question.

She single-spaced lines instead of doubling them. She typed *right* instead of *ripe, fretful* instead of *dreadful,* and *perverted* instead of *perfervid.* She made mistakes from anxiety, wanting to please so badly, and also from ignorance—making a mess of foreign names and places until she grew to know them.

Then there were just plain dumb errors. One day, in a move that reduced David to tears of laughter, she'd typed the Air Minister—as opposed to the Air *Ministry*—was "in a state of chaos from top to bottom." Needless to say, when the Prime Minister saw the memo, he roared his disapproval, kicking the wastebasket across the room and shouting, "I'll feed you to Rota!"—the lion from the London Zoo.

At least the rest of the staff thought it was funny.

Late one evening, he'd commanded, "Gimme klop!" Klop? *Klop?* Maggie panicked, not knowing what a "klop" was. After searching frantically, she brought in an entire series of books, written by Professor Kloppe, that she'd found in the library. No. Wrong. He'd meant the *klop*—the hole punch—as Mr. Churchill always required things punched and tagged instead of stapled or paper-clipped.

For "Gimme Prof!" Maggie was expected to know he meant Lord Cherwell, his science adviser. One night, in a vile humor, he bellowed, "Gimme Pug!" She thought he was going to take off her head when she brought in one of the small, wriggling pug dogs who freely roamed the halls of No. 10, along with Nelson, the cat, and a poodle named Rufus. No, no, no! She was a fool, she was an idiot, and he stamped his feet in frustration. No, by "Pug" he'd meant General Ismay, the link between

Churchill and the Chiefs of Staff Committee, whose face did have certain puggish qualities.

David watched in amusement as Maggie learned her way around No. 10, looking more like a decapitated fowl than a brilliant math scholar. While nothing could quite extinguish her looks, often her red hair would come free from her tortoiseshell clip, creating a halo of fuzzy curls. On the days when she wore makeup, a smudge of mascara would inevitably land on her cheek or flecks of red lipstick migrate to her teeth.

An order from the Old Man to "Gimme moon!" nearly sent Maggie over the edge.

"Why, good evening, Magster," David said in passing. Then, taking a closer look at her dark-shadowed eyes and slightly hysterical expression, "What's the Old Man got you running after tonight?"

"He wants the *moon*!" she whispered, biting her lip and trying not to wail in frustration.

"Ah, the moon, you say? Well, that's easy. I shall get you the moon, my dear Maggie—not to worry." And with that, he turned on his heel and left.

Maggie sat down at her desk and tried to organize the mountains of papers, with little result.

David returned. "Here you are," he said, handing her a sheet of paper. It was a schedule of the phases of the moon.

"The *moon*. Of course," she said, knowing that the phases of the moon were crucial for planning nighttime raids. "Thanks, David. I mean it."

Finally, late, late one evening after being roared at for more than ten minutes (and she watched the clock tick those minutes away as the Prime Minister shouted, stomped his feet, and kicked the wastebasket), Maggie had had enough.

Something in her face must have changed, for the P.M.

suddenly stopped. "What is it, girl?" he said, jabbing his cigar at her. "Cat got your tongue?"

Maggie was silent.

"Tell me!" the P.M. raged, kicking the wastebasket again, this time hard enough to knock it over. The sound reverberated through the room as papers spilled onto the carpet.

"Sir," she said, slowly and calmly, "with all due respect, I'm not the enemy. If you plan on treating me like a Soldaten of the Wehrmacht, I'd like to request a transfer." A pause. "Sir."

The P.M. blinked. Once, twice.

Three times.

None of the women who typed for him had ever spoken to him like this. How dare she! This, this—*girl*.

But . . .

Perhaps this was what Clemmie had warned him about in her letter, lecturing him on the danger of being "disliked by your colleagues and subordinates because of your rough sarcastic and overbearing manner."

His face softened. Perhaps he had been too hard on her. On the whole staff, for that matter.

"But I *need* Hope in my office," he said, his tone now wheedling, like a little boy's. "You can't leave. I simply won't allow it."

Maggie understood the risk she had taken in standing up to him—and also that this was as close to an apology as she was ever going to get. "Yes, Prime Minister."

"Keep Plodding On, Miss Hope. KPO," the P.M. intoned, making a stabbing motion at the typewriter with his cigar, referring to his motto. "That's what we do here—KPO."

\*   \*   \*

"Can't I just address the letter?" Claire asked, sitting at Pierce's long walnut desk in his Cadogan Square apartment's study.

"No, the handwriting inside the letter has to match the outside," Pierce replied. "Don't forget that all mail's opened and read now—we don't want anything to tip off the government censors."

Claire reread the words in front of her, then began copying, her handwriting decidedly feminine. "I don't understand. It just seems like a regular letter to me— the weather is good, the food is terrible, hope you're well. . . ."

"Ah, look carefully, my dear," Pierce said.

Claire read and then shrugged her shoulders.

He rose to his feet and came around behind her. "What do you see if you read down the left-hand margin?"

Claire scanned her eyes down the left side of the page. "It's in code!" she exclaimed. " 'Reinforcements for the enemy expected,' " she read slowly.

"Exactly," he said, placing his hand on her shoulder. "And this innocuous letter, in your charming handwriting, will go to some of our dear friends in France and let them know what's coming. They'll pass word on to Berlin."

"How did you get this information?" Claire asked, eyes wide, lips parted.

"Can't reveal my sources," said Pierce, stroking her hair. "Let's just say I have it on good authority."

David wanted Maggie to succeed at No. 10; after all, he was her friend, and also the one who got her the job. He felt a strange kinship with her. She was American, female, and a bit of a bluestocking. He was Jewish and slept with men—he knew he was tolerated because he kept his love life a secret, his Jewishness to himself, and had charm, wit, and style to spare.

David had also studied mathematics at university and, like Maggie, was fascinated by numbers, logic, and game theory. He was intrigued by Maggie's acceptance at M.I.T. for graduate work and asked endless questions. "So what about number theory?" he asked one late night in the office. "Do you know Alonzo Church's work? What about Wittgenstein's? Have you heard of Alan Turing? Brilliant fellow, from Cambridge. Wrote 'Systems of Logic Based on Ordinals.' "

Maggie, John, and David were in Mr. Churchill's study in the Annexe, a cozy, wood-paneled book-filled room that reeked of cigar smoke. The P.M. was preparing for another British foray into Norway, and much of the evening's discussion was about guns. After the debacle of the first Norwegian invasion, when the Royal Marines were proved unprepared, it was determined they needed rubber sheaths to protect their gun muzzles from the cold. A pharmaceutical company had developed and delivered the prototype, a sample of which John handed to the P.M. He picked it up and looked at it, then looked at the packaging, and then the box.

"No," he said, shaking his head. "Won't do. Won't do at all." John and David looked at each other in dismay. They'd worked hard to make sure everything was in order.

"Sir, what won't do?" John asked, his mouth tightening. "They're long enough for the muzzles, ten and a half inches, just as we discussed."

"Labels!" Mr. Churchill said, pounding his fist on the table.

"Labels?" David asked, looking confused.

"Yes, *labels*," the P.M. insisted. "I want a label for every box, every carton, every packet, saying 'British, size medium.' That will show the Nazis, if they ever re-cover any of them, who's the master race!"

Maggie raised one eyebrow. *Does he really mean . . . ?*

The P.M. cleared his throat. "My apologies, Miss Hope."

*He does, he does indeed.* She shot a look at John and was pleased to see that he'd colored slightly and was pretending to be engrossed in his notes. Nelson, who'd been curled in an unused chair, decided to roll over and clean his paws.

There was a knock at the door. It was Snodgrass, with his sloped shoulders and dusting of dandruff. "Sir, Mr. Frain is here to see you."

"Send him in!" roared the P.M.

In walked a tall man with black slicked-back hair and cold, gray eyes. He wore a carefully tailored yet under-stated suit. He was broad-shouldered and trim through the waist, and walked with a quick and confident stride.

"Good evening, Prime Minister," the man said. "I hope you remember me. We met at Chartwell a few times—"

"Damn it, man! Of course I remember you," the P.M. said. "Peter Frain, head of MI-Five. I hear that in your younger days at Cambridge, you were quite the chess player. Scotch?" he said, pouring himself a tumbler. "Macallan. Only twenty-two years but not bad."

"Neat," Frain replied, taking a seat opposite Mr. Churchill's large and imposing mahogany desk. "Yes, I used to play a bit."

"More than a bit, I heard," the P.M. continued. "Brilliant, cold-blooded, ruthless—that's how you're de-scribed."

Frain accepted his glass. "Before I became a professor at Cambridge. Although academia could be described by those words as well." Maggie's lip twitched as she re-membered Aunt Edith's battles for tenure.

"What was your field of expertise? Egyptology?"

Frain nodded before taking a sip. Mr. Churchill looked over to John, David, and Maggie. "Young men, that will be all for tonight. Miss Hope, I'll need you to take notes."

John and David left silently. Snodgrass followed, turning and closing the heavy door. As Maggie took a moment to unkink her neck before starting in with note-taking again, she noticed Frain looking at her. It wasn't a salacious look but instead the kind of look he might give a jigsaw-puzzle piece or a particularly interesting crossword clue.

"A chess player," the P.M. reiterated. "That's what we need in times like these. You know, the Lord God told Moses to spy in the land of Canaan. And He told Moses to recruit only the best and brightest. If that advice was good enough for God, it's good enough for me." He took a swallow of Scotch.

"But if you recall, sir," Frain said, "the intelligence gathered by Moses's spies wasn't used well. And so the Jews spent forty years wandering the desert."

"Touché." He reached for a fresh cigar, cut off the end, and lit it with a flourish. "What news?" he puffed.

"As you know, all of the mathematicians and the like have been gathered to crack German ciphers. We're recruiting more and more—Cambridge and Oxford men, to be sure—but we're also running crossword puzzles in the newspapers. The winners get more than the ten-quid prize—they get an all-expenses-paid trip to Bletchley Park."

"Good, good," the P.M. said. "What else?"

"Of course, there's the usual danger posed by spies and fifth columnists—not to mention our old friends the IRA. Our ministers of propaganda have been doing their best to alert the public to the threat."

"Yes, 'Keep mum—she's not so dumb'—good one,

that," the P.M. said, chewing on his cigar. The poster in question featured a blonde in a low-cut gown.

"And now local law enforcement agencies are being buried in reports of spy sightings—everyone wants to catch one. We're getting reports about hushed conversations in German, smoke signals, blinking shore lights. We even had one report of a Nazi parachuting right into a woman's victory garden."

"What happened with that one?" the P.M. asked.

"False alarm."

"Any truth to any of it?"

"No, sir," Frain replied. "We have yet to follow up on a credible threat. However, I do believe that they're out there. There are undoubtedly sleeper spies here in England, disguised as patriots, just waiting for that one message from Berlin to tell them their mission."

"Good hunting, Mr. Frain." They clinked glasses.

Frain cleared his throat, looking over at Maggie, working quietly in the corner.

"Ah, yes," the Prime Minister said. "Miss Hope—you may be excused."

Maggie gathered her papers and rose to leave. "Thank you, sir."

When the thick oak door had closed behind her, Churchill leaned forward. "Any news on that other matter?"

Frain sighed. "We have a witness to the murder of Diana Snyder. Her flatmate saw a man lurking outside the flat the day and approximate time of the murder."

"Who is he?"

"She didn't get a good look. It was night, and he was wearing a hat."

"Jesus Christ, man. All this and the goddamned Nazis, too." The P.M. pronounced the word in his own idiosyncratic way, *Nazzi*. He took another sip of Scotch and gestured to the door. "And Miss Hope?"

"So far, no IRA connection we can see. Although there *is* that matter . . . about her father."

"Doesn't know, does she?"

"Not a clue, sir."

"Well, let's keep it that way, then, shall we?" He raised his glass. "At least for the time being."

# SEVEN

THE P.M. OFTEN worked so late into the night that overnight shifts were required.

Bunking down in the Dock, the underground dormitory housing of the War Rooms set aside for junior staff working late, was one of Maggie's least favorite parts of her job. Lying on the hard, narrow cot, she covered herself with the rough, brown army blanket and looked at the little alarm clock she'd brought from home. It was nearly five in the morning, only two hours until she had to get up and start the whole routine over again. Listening to the dull roar of the subbasement's air-conditioning, she turned out her flashlight and tried to will her body into sleep. But she was still too keyed up after her marathon day. Her thoughts were racing.

She remembered about the classified paperwork she'd seen, the civilian casualties predicted, the hundreds of thousands of cardboard coffins the government had on standby that no one except the highest-ranking officials knew about. What would happen if the Germans invaded—would there be hand-to-hand combat in the streets? Would there be a secret police set up with tribunals and hangings? Would the prettier Englishwomen become the concubines of the conquerors, trading in their self-respect for better rations and safety?

She thought about the P.M.'s conversation with Frain. Would the war be lost because of a spy who'd managed to infiltrate some government office and obtain that one crucial piece of information that would change the course of history?

Maggie thought about numbers. Numbers weren't evil. Numbers, points, curves, fractions—they all existed independent of human thought and action.

She missed math. She loved the order, the cool logic, the joy of solving its inevitable steps. Now the numbers she saw were of the dead and wounded, of planes, ships, and U-boats downed. The black numbers against the white paper, once the source of so much pleasure for her, were now like tiny insects, signifying death. Sometimes she dreamed of numbers at night—dark, swarming digits flying with iridescent ebony wings. They'd swarm around her, nesting in her hair, crawling up her nose, into her eyes. She'd wake up in a cold, metallic sweat with the bedclothes in a pile at her feet.

The idea that this kind of violence and horror existed shook Maggie to her core. It was one thing to study war—it was another to live it. *What have I been thinking of my whole life?* Columns of equations had always made sense—that was what Maggie had always loved about them. Now that it was abundantly clear that there was no order, she felt empty. Cheated. Robbed.

The latest reports she'd read had turned her stomach. After invading a particular French town, Nazis had ordered the Jewish men to line up in front of their wives and children, then made them strip down and shave their private parts. A delousing program, or so it was called—really an exercise in power and humiliation. And they submitted. Because the alternative was being shipped off to one of the camps or being shot in the streets.

Learning all the sick and twisted details of the war, Maggie was starting to hate, hate with a ferocity she never knew she had within her. *Could I kill a Nazi?* she thought. Before, she would have said no. Or maybe— but only if she was in a kill-or-be-killed situation. But now she felt she could do it easily, with a song in her heart if it meant getting even. She could even picture drawing it out, adding to the suffering until they begged for it to stop, before she caught herself. *What's happening to me? Am I turning into a monster? One of* them?

Earlier that evening, David had taken her out to dinner, one of the government-sponsored British restaurants redolent with the odors of fried onions and oily fish. After the waiter brought their plates to the table, Maggie asked him what he thought. She was desperate for someone to pull her back to civilization. David seemed to be the best prospect.

"The nature of evil?" He'd laughed as he tucked into his corned beef hash. "Now, *that's* a festive topic of conversation!"

"I'm serious, David. You must have thought about it." Maggie played with her cutlery as her dry and tasteless bangers and mash became cold. She knew she needed some kind of rational perspective.

"My grandparents were German Jews and left for England in the late 1880s. But I have relatives who got out as late as 'thirty-seven—and they could only escape to somewhere like Shanghai. That's where they are now."

Maggie had no idea. "David. I'm so sorry—"

A muscle in his jaw twitched. "At least they're out of there and relatively safe."

She tried to imagine Aunt Edith, stripped of her life's work, wearing an armband with a pink triangle, confined to a ghetto. It was too much to envision. She reached over and took David's hand. "I'm glad they're safe. And I'm sorry it happened."

"Me, too," he said, his face inscrutable. "On both counts." The fate of his relatives must be weighing on David in a way that Maggie could never really know.

"But going back to your original question, no, I *don't* think Germans are inherently evil. However, I do think Hitler is, and he's surrounded himself with any number of madmen who probably grew up pulling wings off flies and drowning kittens for jollies. Like the Boss, I don't believe in so-called pariah nations. I see this as a war against Hitler and Nazism, not against the German people."

"But why?" Maggie insisted, images of the bombing—and now David's family—impossible to clear from her mind.

"The Germans must be made to feel they're not pariahs. They own and have produced much that's admired, and their former enemies must be willing to trust them and the new government they'll choose to elect. If this can be done, then I believe they'll respond in kind."

He finished his hash and put down his fork and knife. "Germany's given us Goethe's *Faust,* Beethoven's 'Ode to Joy,' Bach's Double Violin Concerto in D Minor, and, and"—he paused to think—"*sauerbraten* and Sacher torte . . . or is that Austrian?" He shook his head. "Regardless. It's just lost its way. For now."

Maggie considered what he said and wondered if he could be right. Maybe it was the only way to stop the cycle of violence and hatred. But it wouldn't be easy. "You *do* realize convincing other people—the French and the English, especially—this is the best way to go after the war will be difficult, if not downright impossible?"

"Oh, I do," he said, snagging one of the untouched, cold bangers from her plate.

"And you sincerely feel what you've described is the only way to spare future generations endlessly recurring wars?"

He grinned. "Have I convinced you?"

"I can see where you're going with it, but it requires a superhuman amount of compassion, don't you think?" Maggie looked at him. "I might just have to start calling you Saint David, if you keep this up."

"Still Jewish," he said sweetly. "Why does no one *ever* remember?"

The board outside read *Church of the Holy Apostles— Repent Ye, for Judgment Day May Be Close at Hand,* with the times of the Masses and confession in chipped gold-painted Roman lettering. Claire climbed the steep stone steps and pulled open the imposing iron-hinged doors.

The interior was silent, cavernous, and dimly lit, with banks of votives flickering, making shadows dance along the walls. A statue of the Virgin with a halo of gold and robes of forget-me-not blue presided over a side altar.

Claire dipped her fingers in holy water, made the sign of the cross, and genuflected to the carved wooden altar, then walked down the aisle, her heels clicking on the black marble tiles. She made her way past ruby, sapphire, amber, and emerald stained-glass windows to the dark wood confessional boxes that stood to one side. The sweet smell of smoky incense lingered in the air.

Besides Claire, the church was empty—not surprising, since confession was listed as hours away.

She resolutely made her way to the confessional farthest from the altar, went inside, and took a seat in the shadows.

Then waited in silence until she heard the grille slide open.

"Yes, my child?" she heard a low voice say.

"Bless me, Father, for I have sinned."

There was a long pause. Even though she had done this many, many times before, Claire held her breath.

Then she heard his voice.

"I'll say you have." The light switched on in the box.

"Michael!" she exclaimed, her face beaming.

"In the flesh, me love," the man replied.

Claire put her hand up to the grille, and Murphy covered it with his. They stared at each other a moment, and then she laughed.

"What?" he said, his dark eyes now stern.

"It's just—I can't get over the sight of you like that."

Murphy was dressed in a priest's black robes and white collar, with the traditional purple stole draped over his wiry shoulders. "What? Don't you like it?"

"It's just—don't you feel bad? Wearing the collar and not really being one?"

"I've done a lot worse in the name of our cause. And besides," he continued, "it makes the old birds happy—handsome priest listening to their petty little sins. I swear, some of the nuns stretch out their confessions just to sit in the dark and—"

"Michael!"

"That's Father Murphy to you, my child." His eyes became serious. "So, what news?"

Claire took a breath. "Well, I'm in. They had me write and address a letter. Oh, it was innocuous enough—the weather and the horrible food and all, but there was code in it. Code about troops moving into Norway."

"And, of course, you have a copy for me?"

"I memorized it and wrote it down as soon as I could after." She pulled a piece of paper out of her handbag and slipped it under the grille. "Here it is."

Murphy studied the paper intently. "Ah, I see it now. Good work. Devlin'll be pleased."

"Thank you," Claire said. "They're idiots, of course. Spoiled, pampered little Brits who think that glomming onto Fascism makes them more powerful. But after all . . ."

"The enemy of my enemy is my friend," they said in unison.

Murphy added, "Any friend of the Óglaigh na hÉireann is a friend indeed."

Claire smiled. "I always love hearing that. It sounds so much better than IRA."

"And we'll need the Nazis' help if we're going to achieve our ultimate goal," Murphy said. "The destruction of England."

# EIGHT

MAGGIE WALKED BACK up Regent Street, passing Oxford Street with all of the shops and the tall buildings with their uniform beaux arts façades, up to the less-fashionable Portland Place, just off Regent's Park. But she couldn't enjoy the scenery in the pearly morning light. She couldn't get the word *war* out of her mind.

She went over it again. FDR and Mrs. Roosevelt were in the White House. The Golden Gate Bridge was finally finished. The syncopated sounds of Glenn Miller were playing on the wireless, Picasso's cubism and Dalí's surrealism were causing a sensation worldwide, and most of the girls she knew back in Boston had a crush on Errol Flynn. How did war figure into that scenario? It didn't—and yet it was a reality. *The* reality. Any day now, the German Luftwaffe might turn its attentions from military to civilian targets. Meaning, of course, London.

Maggie tried to distract herself by noticing the contrast of the gray, almost monolithic buildings with their baroque architectural touches and the brilliant scarlet of the telephone booths and double-decker buses. She admired the easy elegance of the large black taxis and the colorful corner pubs. More than anything, though, she loved London's layers upon layers of history—a rich background of poetry and plays, politics and palaces.

She remembered, with a prickle of shame, how originally she'd never even considered the possibility of England's going to war. She was only dimly aware of Germany's annexing Austria and then Sudetenland. Instead, she'd been thinking of herself, absolutely panicked about changing her carefully made plans for graduate school.

It had felt absolutely wrong to be in London when she'd arrived in the summer of '37, instead of starting classes at M.I.T. It defied the very order of things, one of the reasons she was drawn to mathematics. "What is truth? What is beauty?" they were asked in English class—slippery, dangerous concepts. But in math, there was always an answer, and one could always be sure it was right. Truth was the correct answer, which could be proved. Beauty was in the elegance of the proof. As she worked through problem sets, numbers would arrange and rearrange themselves, unpacking their complexities, revealing their mysteries, until the final answer fell into place with the satisfying click of inevitability.

Math was elegant, logical, predictable—and preferable to the messy calculations of life. Through mathematics one could find harmony, stability, and order. And she desperately wanted that order. After all, her whole life had been forever changed when one car just happened to hit another on a random sunny afternoon, killing her parents instantly; it didn't take a Freudian to understand why she so loved math.

As Maggie approached the house, she was struck by its faded grandeur. She tried to imagine her father and Aunt Edith walking home on this same street. She tried to imagine her grandmother—who she was, what her life was like. She had sudden pictures of Christmases in London, of long letters with British stamps, of stories of her father and mother—all that was lost when Aunt Edith made her decision to cut off contact with Grandmother Hope. Then the image came of her dying alone, and Maggie felt angry, angry with Aunt Edith for all she'd inadvertently denied her. *Why had she?* Maggie thought, and not for the first time.

She recognized that it must have been strange for Aunt Edith—overwhelming, even—to suddenly find herself sharing her cramped faculty housing with a small infant; yet somehow she managed. As Maggie grew older, they became genuinely fond of each other, perhaps not in a mother-daughter way but as two kindred spirits, captivated by the quiet pursuit of knowledge. Aunt Edith encouraged Maggie in her studies, saying that with a degree and a career she'd be "free."

Edith had seemed relieved when Maggie took to math and science. It was something she could understand, as she herself preferred Bunsen burners, singed notepads, and periodic tables to the messy, uncontrolled variables of so-called real life. "At least if you blow things up in the lab, you know it's your own damned fault," she'd say with mock severity.

Maggie had always thought of Aunt Edith as Queen Elizabeth—powerful and alone, imperious and sad. As she grew up, she tried never to ask for things, tried to make as little disruption in Edith's life as possible. Other girls might have clamored for new clothes and complained about never going anywhere or having to cook dinner. Her peers embarrassed her. Didn't they know how much their very presence cost, both financially and emotionally? Didn't they ever worry that whoever took care of them just might have enough one day? Didn't they see how easy it would be for resentment to set in and grow?

What she did know was only the most basic of facts: Her father, Edmund Hope, was Aunt Edith's brother, a professor at the London School of Economics. Her mother, Clara, was his wife and an accomplished pianist. They had died in a car accident not long after she was born. "Just like newlyweds! Too busy kissing at the damned stoplight to pay any attention to the world around them," she'd overheard Aunt Edith say, with more tenderness than anything else. Still, she'd never known anything about her grandmother.

"I had a grandmother? And you neglected to tell me this for twenty-two years?" Maggie had asked, half joking. But Aunt Edith's face was resolved. This was no joke.

"We didn't speak. She disapproved of certain . . . choices I made in life," she said, picking imaginary lint off her skirt. They'd been in Edith's tidy, book-filled office in Science Hall at Wellesley, a crimson-brick building covered in glossy green ivy. "She—well, it's a long story. One that's long since closed."

Maggie was silent, thinking.

"Margaret, are you all right?" Even though Edith had lived in the States for almost thirty years, her accent was still clipped and British. Maggie sat in a straight-backed chair in front of Aunt Edith's desk. It was late June, and outside the window, high, lacy clouds moved quickly across the blue sky. *A grandmother,* she thought. Her hands felt cold and clammy.

"Was it because of Olive?" Olive Collins was one of the Wellesley economics professors; some people called Aunt Edith's relationship with her a "Boston marriage."

Aunt Edith ignored the question. "Your grandmother left everything to you. I've had Mr. Davis, our lawyer, go over the will, and it seems while there isn't much in the way of money, she did leave you the family house." Maggie must have looked blank. "In London."

"Well . . ." Maggie searched for the right words. Nothing. She was speechless.

"I think the best course of action is to sell the place and put the money into an account for your graduate studies. Mr. Davis has let me know the name of a reputable estate agent in London."

"You're going to London?" As shocking as the idea of a long-lost grandmother was, the idea of Aunt Edith in London was even more unnerving. She rarely left campus, let alone the town of Wellesley. Boston might as well have been oceans away. London was the equivalent of outer space.

"No," she said, her face tight. "*You* will go. The property is in your name, after all. I feel guilty sometimes that your life with me has been so narrow, that you know nothing of the place where your parents grew up. Spending some time in London will do you a world of good. Consider it your year abroad."

*A year? Defer my admission for a year?* And then it hit her. London. *England.* The homeland of Isaac Newton and Shakespeare, Big Ben and Buckingham Palace. It was somewhere she'd always wanted to go—but someday. Not now. Not for a year.

"I couldn't possibly go to London. I—I'm starting M.I.T. in the fall. You know how important that is." *A dead grandmother? No, no, no. This doesn't figure into my plans at all.*

"You'd only have to defer for a year at the very most, Margaret. Mr. Davis thinks it's important someone representing the family goes to appraise the property, clean out the house, and oversee the sale. I don't trust any agent to get the best possible price without someone around to represent the seller. I've already spoken with the dean himself. There won't be any problem with your matriculating next fall."

*Impossible. If this lawyer thinks it's so important, let him go himself.* But when Maggie looked into Edith's eyes, she realized there would be no use arguing. Maggie hated Aunt Edith for that moment.

"The truth is, Margaret, money is tight right now. Tighter than I've let on. I need—*you* need—the money from the sale of the house to help pay for M.I.T. I know it must be frustrating, but in a way, it's a godsend."

*Oh*. This was different. Since she'd been a faculty brat at Wellesley, the concept of tuition had never really surfaced. Of course, M.I.T. would be an entirely different situation. Maggie knew that she'd be ineligible for the few stipends and teaching-assistant positions that were available—they went to the men. But still—England? "I still don't understand why I have to go. Can't we just have this Mr.—"

"Davis. Mr. Davis."

"Mr. *Davis* just sell the place, then? Why do I need to be there at all?"

Aunt Edith sighed. That was never a good sign. "Maggie, as it turns out, there was a stipulation to your grandmother's will. It specified that should you decide to sell the house, you must oversee the sale. In person. I've done everything I can to try and get you out of it, but legally, it seems—"

"*You* were doing everything?" Maggie was struck with the obviousness of it. "You weren't going to tell me, were you? You were just going to arrange the sale and hand over the money, letting me think it was your money, never mind telling me that I had a grandmother, that she *just* died, and that she'd willed me her house!" She looked at Aunt Edith in shock. "I can't believe this!"

"Maggie, there's more history here than you can possibly appreciate. I just wanted to save you from this . . . unpleasantness."

" 'Unpleasantness'? That's how you're summing up this situation—an 'unpleasantness'? I think that Grandmother Hope made that condition in the will because she knew you would lie to me about her. And you did."

Edith looked down at her hands. They were thin, and in the late-afternoon sunlight, the veins ran blue under a scattering of freckles and age spots; she never was one for gloves. Maggie had a moment of sympathy for her but then reconsidered. She'd lied. She'd kept secret the knowledge that she'd had any family outside of herself. She lied about said grandmother's death. And if she could have, she would have lied about the inheritance.

"Look, I'm a college graduate now. Don't you think it's time to start treating me like an adult?"

"I'm well aware of your age, Margaret. And if you want me to treat you like a grown-up, you will need to behave like one. Unless you go to London and sell the house, you won't be able to go to M.I.T. I'm sorry, but there it is." She used her lecture-hall voice.

"All right." Maggie crossed her arms over her chest. "I'll see the house, pick up a teacup or two, and sell the place. You're sure M.I.T. will hold my place?"

"I have the dean's word."

She locked eyes with Aunt Edith. "Fine. I'll go."

And that was that.

But in London that year, as the elm trees had turned yellow and the house didn't sell, Maggie couldn't help worrying. The structure had fast become her albatross; under its cornices and cupolas, she'd felt herself reduced to duncelike immobility. Across the Atlantic, school, with its predictable rhythms and routines, had started without her for the first time. It was disconcerting. If she wasn't in a classroom, if she wasn't solving math problems, then who was she?

Of course she'd had to stay in London. She'd had no choice. And with war imminent and then declared, no one had been interested in buying such a large and old-fashioned place, with its outdated fixtures, rusty water pipes, and leaking roof. The heavy and hopelessly Victorian decor hadn't helped, nor the smoke-tinged wallpaper and dusty, moth-eaten silk draperies.

She'd been lonely that fall, rattling around the big house by herself. She kept the wireless on for company and haunted the postman for letters from home.

But she still couldn't help feeling sentimental about the place; it had been her grandmother's, and now—no matter how cruel and horrible she might have been to Aunt Edith—it was Maggie's. She'd found a few yellowed and crumbling letters her father had sent home to her grandmother during the war, even one where he described his first meeting with her mother—family history she otherwise never would have known about and was grateful to have. She couldn't help but look around and wonder what life would have been like if she'd grown up in London, with two parents and a grandmother, possibly a few brothers and sisters—as a proper English girl. The letters and house were her only link with that alternate existence.

But it had been rough going. The roof was the first thing to be fixed. It wasn't easy to watch the small amount of money she'd inherited from her parents, so prudently invested and guarded by Aunt Edith, dwindle away as the roof-repair project grew exponentially. Just as one spot was patched, another would spring a leak. Maggie reasoned she'd make it back and more when the house sold, but it was hard not to worry in the early hours of the morning.

She'd found the amenities to be old-fashioned compared to Aunt Edith's. In the evenings, Maggie read, wrote in her journal, or worked on a few problem sets in a soft circle of lamplight at the wooden kitchen table as she listened to *It's That Man Again* on the wireless.

The kitchen had been updated in the late twenties.

The floor was tiled with a checkerboard of blue and black squares, and the walls were painted lemon-yellow, stained and shadowed by years of smoke from the small stove in the corner. Flower-sprigged muslin curtains hung from windows that opened onto the back garden, overgrown with weeds and a tangle of red and pink tea-scented roses.

It had been in the kitchen that Maggie had begun to feel at home, waiting for her coffee to brew and listening to the wireless or eating supper and reading a book at the round, well-worn wooden table. The dining room was too intimidating for one person alone—although she'd been sure her grandmother would have been ap-palled at her casual American ways.

It was hard to believe, but she'd spent almost an entire year in London living alone. That was before Paige, who'd resigned from her job with Ambassador Kennedy, moved in with her. Chuck followed after, then the twins, and finally Sarah, who'd moved in last week.

Maggie took out the heavy iron key and let herself into Grandmother Hope's house, wiping her feet on the mat. The sight of the front hall still took her breath away. An ornate curved wooden staircase dominated the foyer, a grand dining room to the left, the parlor to the right. Sliding doors fitted with stained-glass pea-cocks in brilliant blues, emeralds, and violets divided the parlor in two.

Adjacent to the parlor was the library, two stories high with a stairway to the second level and a curved stepladder for reaching the higher shelves; each wall was lined floor-to-ceiling with dusty leather-bound books. A massive cherry desk stood in one corner, and various couches and chairs covered in protective sheets were scattered throughout. The rest of the house was crammed full of threadbare Persian and Chinese carpets, oil paintings of misty green English countrysides, and dusty Victorian bric-a-brac.

When she heard Maggie come in the door, Paige came running in her powder-blue quilted robe, giving her a peck on the cheek. "There, now, you must be exhausted!" Paige said, giving her a big hug, smelling of sleep and sugar.

Maggie set her battered leather valise down and allowed Paige to lead her into the kitchen, where the twins greeted her with enthusiasm. "You're too sweet," Maggie said to all three of them. "What would I do without you?" She slumped into a worn wooden chair with a sigh and looked around in gratitude. The delicious smell of baking hung in the air.

Just then, Sarah staggered through the door in her red-satin dressing gown.

When Sarah's flatmate had left the ballet after getting married and moving out of London, Sarah had moved in, choosing a small pink bedroom on the second floor between Maggie's and Paige's. Maggie hardly even knew she was there. She usually left for class early in the morning and then rehearsed all day, grabbed a quick bite, and then performed in the evenings, coming home well after midnight.

She hadn't brought much with her, just a suitcase jammed with clothes and a big bag of pink-satin toe shoes and silk seamed stockings. "I'm a gypsy, darling, what can I say?" she'd said, shrugging. Maggie really saw her only on Mondays, the company's day off.

"Maggie!" she said in her froggy voice, her face brightening. Her long brown hair was tangled, and there were black smudges under her eyes—remains of the previous evening's performance makeup. "Darling, you're back!"

"Just to wash out a few things in the bathroom sink

and pack up again, but it's good to see you. I've missed you all so much."

Paige said, "I'm making scones, and then there's the ubiquitous National Loaf—"

"Blech." Annabelle made a face.

"Forget bombs," Clarabelle added, "just drop a few loaves on the Germans."

"—and homemade strawberry jam, from our victory garden. There's some tea and—voilà!" Paige opened up the icebox with a flourish. "An egg! We all saved it for you." She carefully cracked it into a pot of boiling water.

"Thank you. And how are you doing, Sarah? How are things at the Wells?" Maggie asked, pouring a cup of weak tea. Still, it was hot.

"Fabulous—working on the *Swan Lake* act two pas de deux in case I get tapped for Odile anytime soon."

"How are you doing with the rationing? You must get so hungry doing all that dancing."

"Actually, it's the reverse; I feel as if I'm gaining weight. A lot of the dancers are used to doing a performance and then eating a nice steak or something. Well, of course we can't do that anymore. So we're eating a lot of bread and expanding a bit."

Paige poked at her own waist. "It's happening to me, too. I can feel it. My poor waistline—yet another casualty of war." She set a plate with the poached egg and a piece of toast in front of Maggie. The egg yolk was hot and runny, sprinkled liberally with salt and black pepper.

"And, Annabelle, Clarabelle—how have you two been doing?" Maggie asked.

"Keeping busy at the Queen's Theatre, as usual," Annabelle said. A play of Daphne du Maurier's *Rebecca* was running, with Owen Nares and Celia Johnson as the leads. Annabelle was playing the role of the young housemaid, while the shyer Clarabelle was the assistant to the costumer.

"Curtain's going up earlier—" Annabelle began.

"—so we have time to volunteer for the Red Cross—make tea and hand out Bath buns to the Saint Paul's Watch," Clarabelle finished. The St. Paul's Watch was a group of volunteer firemen, dedicated to saving St. Paul's Cathedral from any air attacks.

"*John* volunteers for the Saint Paul's Watch, you know," said Annabelle, twisting a lock of hair.

"Imagine that—with all he must have to do for the P.M.," Clarabelle added.

"We both think he's terribly handsome—" Annabelle began.

"—*if* a little serious," Clarabelle finished.

Maggie was annoyed. They barely knew John. Who were they to talk about him like that? Especially Annabelle. "The man needs a haircut," she said finally, biting into a piece of eggy toast.

"But, Maggie, *you're* the one working for the P.M.," Sarah said. "Tell us everything! It must be *so* exciting."

Maggie was at a loss for where to start. Certainly not with any statistics on coffin production or estimated civilian death tolls. Certainly not with any of the other classified documents she'd typed. "Well . . ."

Chuck wandered into the kitchen, yawning widely, pulling her flannel dressing gown around her large frame. Nigel, somewhat sheepishly, followed, buttoning his top button. "Good morning, girls!" Chuck boomed. Her attitude when war had been declared was carpe noctem, and Nigel had become a frequent overnight guest as his departure date loomed.

"Hello, ladies," Nigel added, a bit more subdued. Although they were all used to Nigel's spending the night when he was on leave, he always had a somewhat awkward manner when he ran into any of them, especially in the mornings. Perhaps he realized how thin the walls were, and how Chuck's . . . enthusiasm carried.

"Tea?" Clarabelle offered, her voice a bit chilly. She didn't approve of Nigel's overnight visits.

"Thanks," Nigel said, pouring mugs for Chuck and himself.

"So yes," Maggie continued. "The P.M.'s office. Scary and tedious and frustrating and—wonderful."

"So you like it there?" Sarah asked, spreading a tiny drop of strawberry jam thinly over her toast.

"I do."

"And you get to see everything?" Chuck asked, pouring more tea.

*If she only knew.* "There's no time to think when you're taking dictation. He just goes so fast, you're lucky just to keep up with him."

"But surely there must be something you've picked up, some indication of how things are going. . . . You know, troops, for example," Chuck asked. "The RAF?" She looked nervously over at Nigel, and he grasped her large-knuckled hand. Nigel had finished basic training and had begun flying missions from a military base not too far from London. He used his leave to get back to London to see Chuck whenever possible.

"Look, you know I can't tell you anything, right?" Maggie said, her voice soft.

"Maggie, I won't say anything, *le do thoil.*" Chuck crossed her heart and held up her hand.

"Well, I *can* tell you this—"

"Yes," Chuck said, leaning closer.

"It's top secret."

"What? What is it, woman? I'm dying to know!"

"It's . . . that Nelson—the Churchills' cat—is to play an integral role in breaking German ciphers."

The twins giggled. "Oh, *we* should get a cat!" Annabelle exclaimed.

"Two!" said Clarabelle. "They could be—"

"*Sisters!*" they both exclaimed.

Chuck ground her teeth in exasperation. "And just who's going to feed them and clean up their messes? Who's going to chase them around during an air raid, hmmm?"

"I loathe cats," Paige said. "And I'm allergic. By the way, he's lucky to have you. I hope he appreciates you."

"Nelson? Of course. The Churchills' pets are better fed than most Londoners these days."

Paige sniffed. "Mr. Churchill, silly. Because if he doesn't, I'll have to come down to Number Ten myself. And it won't be pretty."

Nigel grinned; he and Chuck exchanged a look. "Uh-oh, watch out," Nigel said.

"You're a good friend," Maggie said, patting Paige's hand, "but really, it won't be necessary. Not yet, anyway."

When breakfast was over, Chuck walked Nigel to the front door for a prolonged goodbye kiss, then disappeared upstairs. Paige and Sarah set to work on the dishes while the twins busied themselves with the newest *Tatler*.

Maggie went back to the front hall to look for her valise; it wasn't there. "Has anyone seen my suitcase?" she called into the kitchen. "I swear I left it at the door."

Her query was met with a resounding chorus of noes.

Puzzled, Maggie went upstairs. Hearing noises from Chuck's room, she opened the door. There was Chuck, opening the valise on the bed, rummaging through the contents.

"Oh, Maggie," Chuck said, her face reddening. "I just thought I could help out by doing your washing. I know you've had a tough time of it lately. . . ."

Maggie didn't have any important papers in her suit-case, but still. She went over and took the case.

"Thank you, Chuck," she said, feeling protective of her things and as though her privacy had been violated. "But it's really not necessary."

# NINE

Later that day Sarah invited Maggie to the Wells, to watch the company's class and a rehearsal. One by one, dancers wandered into a large, mirror-filled room with a hardwood floor. Maggie sat on a folding chair to one side. The not-unpleasant scent of fresh sweat and cologne hung in the air.

Looking at their lithe frames, she felt as clumsy and huge as Alice after she drank from the bottle in Wonderland. An older man sat down behind the battered-looking upright piano and began to play an accompaniment, while the teacher, a heavy-set woman with large, kohl-rimmed eyes and a black turban, surveyed the class and gave the count: "Five, six, seven, *and—*"

The girls were all ridiculously gorgeous, dressed in leotards and short skirts, their long legs bare, scuffed pink satin slippers on their feet. Sarah was wearing a darned black leotard and raggedy leg warmers. She'd tied back her hair with a striped grosgrain ribbon. There were just a few men, wearing black shorts, white shirts, and black dance slippers. All of the dancers held on to the barre; the motion of their feet became faster and faster, until Maggie became dizzy just watching them.

After adagio in the center, they began to cross the

floor in diagonals, running and leaping into the air in combinations of complex steps. Sarah ran and jumped with equal amounts of precision and abandon. What joy it was to watch them. Maggie could see how hard they worked, how demanding their art form was, and yet they looked so free.

When class was over, a tall, dark-eyed man with a long, thin face clapped his hands. "All right, then— who's staying for rehearsal? Margot and Michael, of course. The rest of you have the day off, unless you're in tonight's performance." Dancers ran to their dance bags, swinging them over their shoulders and talking and laughing as they left; the ones he'd asked to stay sat down on the floor or wandered to the barre to stretch their muscles.

Sarah walked over to Maggie; her gait, now that class was done, was more like a boxer's than a ballerina's. "So what do you think?" she asked as she opened her dance bag and took out a towel to blot sweat from her face.

"It was marvelous," Maggie said, "but I'd be in traction if I tried it."

"Nonsense," Sarah insisted.

"Miss Sanderson," the tall man called, looking down his long, aquiline nose. He was dressed in khaki and a white linen shirt, open at the collar. "Did you ask permission to bring a guest to rehearsal?"

Maggie immediately stood up, prepared to leave, but Sarah just laughed. "Oh, come on, Fred. This is my flatmate Maggie Hope. She's just curious as to what we dancers do all day."

The man walked over, and Maggie held out her hand to shake his. Instead, he drew it to his lips and kissed it. "Enchanté, Miss Hope. Frederick Ashton. Perhaps Sarah's mentioned me."

*Had she?* "Yes, well, of course."

He cleared his throat and glared at Sarah for her faux pas. "I am a choreographer," he said with a deep bow. "Choreography is my raison d'être."

"Too bad you can't make a living from it," one of the men called from the barre, and the rest of the dancers giggled.

"Silence!" Ashton shouted. The dancers all went back to stretching. "Today, Miss Hope, you will see art as it unfurls. What I do is first familiarize myself with the music—in this case, our own Constant Lambert's score. Then I break down the dramatic incidents and dances in relation to the music; I call it scaffolding."

"*We* like to call it Chinese water torture," Sarah muttered.

Ashton turned to her with just a hint of a smile. "Well, Miss Sanderson, since you have so much energy, why don't you demonstrate the choreographic process for your friend?" Sarah shrugged and walked back to the center of the room. The rest of the dancers put on leg warmers and sweaters, draping themselves languidly over the barre. "What I usually do is play the music for the dancer and then ask her to show me something."

As the pianist played a melody, Sarah began to move, trying out different steps. "I may indicate something, an image perhaps, such as a fountain, or a bird in flight." Sarah's steps took on a new dimension as she incorporated his words into her movements. He walked over to her and adjusted her arms, molding the dance on her in time to the music, as if he were a sculptor.

Although Sarah had begun the demonstration with an amused expression on her face, Maggie could tell she was now completely immersed. When the music was done, the dance might not have been finished, but something had definitely happened, something Ashton could draw from and refine. "It's not what you put into the dance, it's what you take out," he said, and called over a few of the other girls and had them repeat the steps with Sarah, editing as they went. The next thing she knew, not only had a dance been created but an entire hour had passed. Ashton clapped his hands. "All right, that's enough for today, girls. I'll work with Michael and Margot now."

Maggie had brought a camera with her, wanting to take some shots of Sarah during rehearsal. But as she observed Ashton work, she was too self-conscious to use it.

Sarah came over to Maggie when they were through, looking exhausted but happy. "I'll just be a minute," she said, and went to change. Maggie walked to the lobby and looked around, admiring captioned photographs of the dancers in costume—Alicia Markova partnered with a younger-looking Ashton, Margot Fonteyn dressed in a beautiful tutu and held aloft by Michael Somes.

Sarah emerged from the changing room looking like Katharine Hepburn in her gray flannel trousers and red cashmere sweater, dance bag thrown over her shoulder. "Want to walk through the park instead of taking the Tube home?"

"Sure." They made their way past King's Cross and St. Pancras to Regent's Park. The day was hot and clear, and the air smelled of fresh clover and rich earth. A slight breeze whispered its way through the green oak and elm leaves, causing them to flutter, showing their delicate silvery undersides.

There were a few people out strolling, an older couple with clasped hands, a man in a black bowler hat. As most of the dogs in London had been sent to the country or chloroformed—the barking of the dogs was considered too great a risk in case of invasion—even the usual walkers weren't around. The London Zoo's snakes and reptiles had also been killed, while the elephants and lions had been moved to a safer location.

Now, with war declared, the park felt so open, so exposed.

"Unbelievable, isn't it?" Sarah said, as they made their way over the bright green-and-gold fields. "It's such a gorgeous day. It should be raining, with a howling wind and thunderstorms, but no—it's the most ravishing summer on record. It's just too much to take in."

Maggie pulled out the camera to take some photos. "Pathetic fallacy," she said, trying to focus the camera on a silvery weeping willow alone in the field, holding back her hair to keep any stray strands from blowing into the shot.

"Sorry?"

"According to John Ruskin, *pathetic fallacy* describes when the weather corresponds to the emotions of the characters. You know, 'it was a dark and stormy night.' " Maggie snapped the picture, then walked closer to try for a better angle.

"See, you're just so smart, Maggie. I could never be as smart as you and Paige are; you went to university, after all. Here I am complaining about the weather, and you're quoting dead writers. It's positively intimidating sometimes."

*A smart woman, yes. So useful. Like a pretty gorilla.* "Are you joking? You're a dancer with the Sadler's Wells Ballet—an artist. And you're gorgeous! Believe me, I'd love to spin on my toes the way you do."

"It's overrated, but you're sweet to say. I started dancing when I was just a little thing, on doctor's orders. My mum didn't have the money for it, really, but I had weak knees and flat feet, and the doctor said I might have to wear leg irons. But he'd just been to the ballet and thought the exercises might do me some good."

Leg irons. Little Sarah in leg irons. "My goodness."

She smiled ruefully. "All I know is I heard the words *leg irons* and not only did my one class a week but practiced almost every waking hour. Pretty soon there was no more talk about leg irons, and the school took me on as a scholarship student. When the Vic-Wells Ballet played in Liverpool, my teacher wrote a note to Madame Ninette de Valois, who came to watch class. She said I could come to London and study at the Sadler's Wells School, on scholarship. I was fourteen, and became a member of the company at seventeen. So I just never had time for much school, or even family. Just ballet, really—all the time."

"But it must have been such an amazing experience, to find what you love and then have the opportunity to pursue it. The tutus, the roses, all those handsome men . . ."

"The tutus are sweat-stained and mended, the roses have thorns, and most of the men are big poofs, so there you go. It's the theater, it's illusion. None of it is real." They walked along in silence for a while. A bird on a high tree branch warbled and then fell silent. "There are a lot of sacrifices."

"Well, of course," Maggie said. "All that time you put in, the rehearsal schedule, the pressure of performing."

"And it's especially hard now, with everything that's happening," Sarah said, dropping down onto the soft, sweet-smelling grass under the boughs of the willow. "I mean, we're at war. The Nazis have taken Paris. Bombs could fall from the sky and we could be invaded at any moment. What does it matter if we're all dancing around, pretending to be swans or sylphs or whatever? It's all quite ridiculous, really."

At the edge of the park, they sat down near a particularly splendid old oak. They could see men removing the stately black fencing to be taken away and melted down for the war effort. Watching them, Sarah, with her long neck, looked particularly photogenic. When Maggie pointed the camera at her, she nodded, giving permission to shoot away.

"Look, Sarah, I understand how you feel," Maggie said, camera clicking. "And if you decide you want to make bullets or planes—or whatever—you know Paige and I will be right behind you. But what you do *is* important. You have a real gift, and unlike some people, you have the opportunity to use it. I mean, it's going to get ugly soon. And what you do—it's beautiful. Yes, it's an illusion, but there are going to be a lot of people who'll need to see that, to have a few hours where they can just get away. Me included."

"You think so?" Sarah said. "The things I've given up—sometimes I just don't know if they're worth it."

Maggie put down the camera and looked straight at her. "I do."

"What about you?" Sarah asked suddenly. "We live together, but I don't know the first thing about you, really—other than that you prefer coffee to tea and hog all the hot water. Are you a southern belle like Paige?"

"Goodness, no! Perish the thought," Maggie said, doing her best Paige impression. Sarah chortled. "I'm from New England, actually."

"Well, I'm glad you ended up in London, however it came about. Paige, too." Sarah rose and brushed off the bottom of her trousers. "And I like Chuck quite a bit. But those twins—"

"—can really get on your nerves?"

"Ha! Absolutely."

Then, "You know, today when I came in, I left my suitcase near the front door. After breakfast, Chuck had it in her room and was going through it. She said she wanted to do my washing." Maggie looked at Sarah. "Do you think I'm being paranoid?"

Sarah laughed. "Chuck? A spy? Hardly. She probably

just knew you'd been working hard and wanted to help out."

"It just seems very . . . personal. You know, going through my things."

"Maggie, you're an only child. People who grew up with siblings, well, we're not as precious about our belongings. If you don't mind my saying."

*She's probably right,* Maggie thought. Chuck grew up as the oldest of seven siblings; she was probably just used to playing mother hen.

"By the way, have you ever gone to see them?"

"See who?"

"Your parents." She took a moment to phrase the next words. "Their graves."

Maggie sighed. "I haven't. I know, I know—I've been meaning to. But somehow . . ."

"Seeing them will make it real?"

"Something like that. I don't remember them at all—but somehow I keep hoping that there was a mix-up—and that—" Maggie rose and dusted off her skirt. "Silly, isn't it?"

"Not at all," Sarah replied. "Should we head back now?" It was getting darker; they'd been warned that any attacks would most likely happen at night.

Sarah linked her arm through Maggie's as they walked quickly back to the house, eyes surveying the skies in uneasy silence.

"I don't like being played," Pierce said, his voice low, blending under the clattering of mismatched china and bent, tarnished cutlery in the Phoenix Café, a tiny, dark, and narrow tearoom just off Oxford Circus. Thick black tape in crosses on the windows obscured the scene outside and dimmed the light. "Not by you, Claire. And not by—"

Murphy gave his most dazzling grin. "Father Murphy," he said, fingering his collar.

"*Mr.* Murphy," Pierce said, the corners of his mouth pursing with annoyance. He took a sip of tea from a cup with a hairline fracture, painted with purple and gold pansies. "What you and the rest of your group have achieved since the IRA officially declared war on England is remarkable."

"The S-Plan," Claire said. "S for Sabotage. Devlin's idea."

"Right, right," said Pierce. "All those banks, Tube platforms, train stations, and post offices bombed, people panicking. Jolly good show, that. Good for Devlin."

Claire smiled. "Glad you think so. Now that you know who I am—who we are—let's talk about how we can work together. As we see it, the most dangerous development right now was Chamberlain's stepping down and Churchill taking over. Chamberlain would probably have broken if London was attacked, but Churchill—"

"Drunken sot," Pierce muttered.

"—isn't going to give up without a fight."

Pierce folded his hands neatly. "And how do you suggest we deal with Mr. Churchill?"

"Assassination. For starters." Murphy grinned. "And a few other tricks as well."

Pierce raised an eyebrow.

"And with my help and your resources, we have the perfect in," Claire said to Pierce.

"I know what the Saturday Club brings to the table," Pierce said. "But what can you offer?"

Claire leaned in close to Pierce and whispered in his ear, her breath warm and sweet, "We happen to have a connection to one of the Prime Minister's staff."

June 4, 1940. Maggie had finished her work typing copies of the Prime Minister's latest speech and was determined to watch him give it at the House of Commons.

She put on her hat and gloves and made her way from No. 10 to the House of Commons. Walking over the worn tile floor, she was conscious of how many men who decided the fate of England had walked these same steps. She made her way up to the Civil Servants' Gallery, behind the Speaker's chair, and took a seat next to David and John. As the pale men in dark suits assembled below, the benches crowded and the visitors' gallery overflowing, the room hummed with nerves and an undercurrent of fear.

There were the M.P.s, of course; there were the journalists, diplomats, the public. Maggie could see the face of Lord Halifax, Leader of the House of Lords and a long-standing Churchill critic, drawn and set. Former U.S. Ambassador to England Joseph Kennedy, another Churchill detractor and supporter of appeasement, had returned from the States and was in the Diplomatic Gallery, his long, thin face inscrutable.

Then the Prime Minister entered the room. He waited for the chamber to settle, scanning the audience, looking from one face to the next, acknowledging each.

Maggie had typed countless versions of the speech and knew it inside and out.

The P.M. began with defeat in Belgium, the disaster of France, and the "German scythe" that had cut down their armies. He talked about the desperate fighting in Boulogne and Calais, the alleged duplicity of King Leopold, the evacuation at Dunkirk.

He praised the bravery of the troops, the medics, the civilians. But while his words were thick with respect and gratitude, he was very clear on one point: "We must be very careful not to assign to this deliverance the attributes of a victory. Wars are not won by evacuations."

He sang the praises of the RAF: "May it not also be

that the cause of civilisation itself will be defended by the skill and devotion of a few thousand airmen? There never has been, I suppose, in all the world, in all the history of war, such an opportunity for youth. The Knights of the Round Table, the Crusaders, all fall back into the past: not only distant but prosaic; these young men, going forth every morn to guard their native land and all that we stand for, holding in their hands these instruments of colossal and shattering power, of whom it may be said that 'When every morn brought forth a noble chance,' 'And every chance brought forth a noble knight,' deserve our gratitude, as do all of the brave men who, in so many ways and on so many occasions, are ready, and continue ready, to give life and all for their native land."

Throughout the House, people began to stir, shouting, "Hear, hear!" in agreement.

Maggie looked over at John, whose face was grim. She nudged David. "Is he all right?" she whispered.

David shrugged, then whispered back, "A friend of his in the RAF was shot down over France. He sometimes feels that's where he should be, instead of Whitehall."

"Oh," Maggie said. *Well. That explains a lot.*

"We are told that Herr Hitler has a plan for invading the British Isles. This has often been thought of before. When Napoléon lay at Boulogne for a year with his flat-bottomed boats and his Grand Army, he was told by someone, 'There are bitter weeds in England.' There are certainly a great many more of them since the British Expeditionary Force returned."

There was a low rumble of laughter that traveled through the House, when minutes before it might have seemed impossible that anyone should ever laugh again. Maggie knew how the P.M. had written and rewritten those lines, and yet his delivery was so effortless. *Quin-*

*tessential British humor,* Maggie thought, *telling Herr Hitler to bugger off.*

The speech turned somber again. As the Prime Minister continued, Maggie could feel the temperature of the crowd changing. The crowd was utterly still, hanging on his every word, breathing as one. Every last man and woman would march with him, fight with him—they were ready to lie down and die with him.

For there was no question of where he would be—the front line.

"Even though large tracts of Europe and many old and famous States have fallen or may fall into the grip of the Gestapo and all the odious apparatus of Nazi rule, we shall not flag or fail. We shall go on to the end."

He didn't need his notes anymore. He flung them down and looked into the crowd, meeting their eyes. "We will go on to the end, we shall fight in France, we shall fight on the seas and oceans, we shall fight with growing confidence and growing strength in the air, we shall defend our island, whatever the cost may be."

Throughout the House, and doubtlessly all over England, chins raised and hearts beat faster. Maggie felt a shiver run through her, a shiver of fear, but somehow a powerful wave of ancient strength and honor as well.

The P.M.'s voice rose and rumbled with emotion. ". . . We shall fight on the beaches, we shall fight on the landing grounds, we shall fight in the fields and in the streets, we shall fight in the hills; we shall never surrender!"

The crowd roared its approval. Several M.P.s were in tears. Even Halifax and Kennedy had the grace to look moved. The majesty and grandeur of the English language, in the hands and on the lips of Winston Churchill, had power that even the threat of bombs couldn't subdue. Maggie's lips silently formed the words along with the Prime Minister, so many times had she typed them.

". . . And even if, which I do not for a moment believe, this island or a large part of it were subjugated and starving, then our Empire beyond the seas, armed and guarded by the British Fleet, would carry on the struggle, until, in God's good time, the New World, with all its power and might, steps forth to the rescue and the liberation of the old."

At the very back of the House, one M.P. rose from his seat and, slowly but loudly, began to clap. One by one, more people began to stand and join in, until finally the entire chamber shook with strength and power. Maggie, David, and John stood and clapped until their hands were sore and raw. Maggie's heart was bursting with pride, and there was a lump in her throat that made it hard to swallow.

When, finally, the Prime Minister had left and people began to file out, Maggie turned to David. "You were right," she said. "And I thank you from the bottom of my heart for helping me get this job."

# TEN

Claire and Murphy lay in his narrow bed, only a candle flickering in the darkness. The room was spartan, with yellowing wallpaper ripped and curling at the edge of the water-stained ceiling. The smell of that night's supper, turnip stew, seeped up from the kitchen.

"Father Murphy, where did you learn to do that?" Claire asked, her hand trailing down his smooth chest under the thin, worn sheet and scratchy gray blanket.

"Ah, the Lord works in mysterious ways, my love," he answered, stroking her hair.

They lay in silence for a moment, listening to a drunken couple make their way down the corridor outside.

When the couple had passed, Claire whispered in his ear, "You know, a lot of women would be scandalized, even by the thought of being with a man in a boarding-house room."

"I'm not just any man, I hope," Murphy said, pushing silky hair out of her eyes.

"No, of course not," Claire answered. "You're my sweet Mike."

"Glad to hear it," Murphy said. "It gets easier, doesn't it? Leading a double life, I mean."

Claire rolled onto her back and stretched. "I don't

know about that. When I'm with you, I feel alive. The cause, you, thinking of Ireland—it's so real. My other life is just going through the motions, really. That girl is a simpering fool."

"She's part of you."

Claire said, "Of course. I deliberately kept a lot of the basic facts of my life and hers the same. But I leave out the important details. My father, who spoke Gaelic. Witnessing countless atrocities against us. Hearing Jim O'Donovan speak and getting involved with the Óglaigh na hÉireann. Meeting you. Falling in love."

"But surely you must like being her."

Claire reached over him to the bedside table, where there was a pack of cigarettes. She took one out, lit it with a mother-of-pearl-inlaid lighter, inhaled, and then blew out the smoke slowly. "I did. I mean, at first it was easy." She took another drag. "But then things changed. Chamberlain declared war. And that awful, awful man became Prime Minister."

"In some ways it's been a godsend."

"Yes," Claire agreed, lazily stretching the hand with the cigarette over to the ashtray, where she tapped off the ashes. "Churchill's dead set on leading England into this foolish war. But foolish for them, not for us. Ireland's still neutral, and we have a fantastic opportunity to help England's enemies."

Murphy sighed and took the cigarette from her, taking his own slow drag. "It's too bad you couldn't have gotten the typist's job in Churchill's office. Would have made all this a bit easier."

"I know, darling. But look, our plan is good—great, even. It will succeed. And we *will* bring down this corrupt government."

"Amen, my child," he said, grinding the cigarette into the ashtray. Then he leaned in and kissed her deeply. "And now, where were we?"

\*    \*    \*

"I spoke the other day of the colossal military disaster which occurred when the French High Command failed to withdraw the northern Armies from Belgium at the moment when they knew that the French front was decisively broken at Sedan and on the Meuse," the P.M. intoned, pacing back and forth on the Persian carpet in front of his desk in his office at No. 10. He was squinting, as though picturing the phrases in his mind's eye, as Maggie struggled to type them.

". . . The disastrous military events which have happened during the past fortnight have not come to me with any sense of surprise. Indeed, I indicated a fortnight ago as clearly as I could to the House that the worst possibilities were open; and I made it perfectly clear then that whatever happened in France would make no difference to the resolve of Britain and the British Empire to fight on, if necessary for years, if necessary alone."

As he dictated, he paced the length of his office. Words were rolling off his tongue, and Maggie kept up as best she could.

". . . There remains, of course, the danger of bombing attacks, which will certainly be made very soon upon us by the bomber forces of the enemy. It is true that the German bomber force is superior in numbers to ours; but we have a very large bomber force also, which we shall use to strike at military targets in Germany without intermission. I do not at all underrate the severity of the ordeal which lies before us; but I believe our countrymen will show themselves capable of standing up to it, like the brave men of Barcelona, and will be able to stand up to it, and carry on in spite of it, at least as well as any other people in the world. Much will depend upon this; every man and every woman will have the chance to show the finest qualities of their race, and ren-

der the highest service to their cause. For all of us, at this
time, whatever our sphere, our station, our occupation
or our duties, it will be a help to remember the famous
lines:

> " 'He nothing common did or mean,
> Upon that memorable scene.' "

The Prime Minister stopped at the window. ". . . We
must not forget that from the moment when we declared
war on the 3rd September it was always possible for
Germany to turn all her Air Force upon this country, together with any other devices of invasion she might con-
ceive, and that France could have done little or nothing
to prevent her doing so. We have, therefore, lived under
this danger, in principle and in a slightly modified form,
during all these months. In the meanwhile, however, we
have enormously improved our methods of defense, and
we have learned what we had no right to assume at the
beginning, namely, that the individual aircraft and
the individual British pilot have a sure and definite supe-
riority.

"Therefore, in casting up this dread balance sheet and
contemplating our dangers with a disillusioned eye, I see
great reason for intense vigilance and exertion, but none
whatever for panic or despair."

At that, Maggie looked up. Did he really believe that?
Or was truth just another casualty of war—the war of
rhetoric he was waging for the British spirit?

And at this point, did it even matter?

". . . What General Weygand called the Battle of
France is over. I expect that the Battle of Britain is about
to begin. Upon this battle depends the survival of Christian civilisation. Upon it depends our own British life,
and the long continuity of our institutions and our

Empire. The whole fury and might of the enemy must very soon be turned on us.

"Hitler knows that he will have to break us in this Island or lose the war. If we can stand up to him, all Europe may be free and the life of the world may move forward into broad, sunlit uplands. But if we fail, then the whole world, including the United States, including all that we have known and cared for, will sink into the abyss of a new Dark Age made more sinister, and perhaps more protracted, by the lights of perverted science."

He turned back to face the room and stabbed each word with his cigar for emphasis. " '*This* was their finest hour.' "

After these words, he slumped down at his desk, head in hand.

"Go and type for your life," he said, without glancing in her direction.

"Yes, sir." Tears stinging her eyes, she ran to get copies of the speech ready.

Later, much later, Maggie looked up from the papers and folders covering her wooden desk as Nelson wound his way around her ankles. "Your calculations are off," she said to John as he dropped off a memo in the underground typists' office. It was not without satisfaction. It helped her forget all of the thoughts she'd been having. Thoughts about bombs. About war. About her parents.

John had been working in the War Rooms for days without respite. His dark suit was looking rumpled and wrinkled, as though he'd slept in it—which he probably had. His face was pale, and his thick, curly hair stood out at odd angles from his head. His eyes were sunken and haunted.

"I beg your pardon?" He sat down and rubbed his temples, his face beginning to turn crimson. In his opinion, Maggie was one of the most beautiful women he'd ever seen. And she was different—so very different—from any other woman he'd known. She was smart—brilliant, really—and wasn't afraid to speak her mind. Especially to him. From the moment he'd met her, she had unknowingly broken down most of the defenses he'd long held in place, and when she was present, no one else seemed to matter.

John didn't think war was the time for romance, and the office was certainly not the place. And then there was the fact that he knew more about Maggie and her place in the scheme of things than he was allowed to let on.

So all he could do was watch in mute appreciation as Maggie slowly made herself at home at No. 10 and the War Rooms over the summer, her red hair glinting gold in the fluorescent light, leaving a trail of violet perfume everywhere she went.

But Maggie had other things on her mind. She'd noted and studied all the mentions of Radio Direction Finding in Mr. Churchill's memos intently. From what she could glean, RDF—radio direction finder—was a warning system, using radio waves to detect enemy aircraft, also known as radar. This way the RAF knew exactly when the German fighters would arrive and exactly where they would be.

The mathematician in Maggie was drawn to the descriptions of how the device worked. Using the transmission of radio waves, it was possible to measure the length of the interval between the emission of a radio pulse and the return of its "echo," as charted by an oscillograph. When aircraft were in the sky, the radio emissions would bounce off them, showing their positions. RAF planes had special identifying signals on them, allowing air force commanders to differentiate between friendly and enemy aircraft.

"*You* know about RDF?" John said.

"I type all of Mr. Churchill's memos and letters—I'd have to be insensible not to. I also know queuing theory, differential equations, and cryptography," she said with a smile.

She was gratified to see John's eyes widen.

John sat looking at Maggie for some time, head cocked to one side. "Do Mrs. Tinsley and Miss Stewart know?"

"With all due respect, Mrs. Tinsley and Miss Stewart don't have degrees in mathematics."

John was silent. Then, "Really? My calculations are off?"

"Look, it's simple, really," Maggie said in her best Aunt Edith lecture tone, pulling out a piece of scrap paper to illustrate the point. "If you're using the radar equation, all the variables must be in place before solving for the position of the German planes."

"Yes, yes, I *know* that," he said, getting up and beginning to pace. Maggie could tell he was reworking the problem in his head. "So then why are the numbers off?"

"There's an additional step. You've assumed that $F$ equals 1, which means that you're calculating in a vacuum. You see, it's not just an abstract problem, you're also dealing with the real world, where things get a little more complicated."

"Is that a fact?"

Maggie ignored him. "You need to figure in a few additional variables to calculate $F$: the bend of the earth's surface and the density of the refraction due to air layers at different altitudes. You also need to know the plane's ground speed—which is different from airspeed, or what appears on a pilot's gauge—as well as the wind speed and direction, the relative humidity, and altitude at sea level."

"Oh," he said, stopping his pacing. He scratched his head. "Ah."

"You can just compensate for the additional factors. For example, if you assumed that density decreased linearly with height, and used the arc of a circle from London to Berlin . . ." Maggie went back to the scratch paper, pulling out her beloved Faber-Castell slide rule from the desk drawer, and made a few calculations.

"You've got one of those?" John whistled between his teeth. "That's a beauty."

*What did he think I used? My fingers?* "Graduation present." Of course, Maggie never thought when Aunt Edith gave it to her at commencement that she'd be using it to figure out enemy plane trajectories.

"That's quite impressive." He pulled up a wooden chair, the legs scraping over the linoleum floor, and sat down again. He leaned in to look at it, giving off the faint scent of shaving soap and wool.

"Thank you." It took her a few minutes to look up various numbers and make calculations. "And voilà! A corrected answer."

He put his finger to the side of his forehead and started to massage his temple. It was clear that he was out of his depth. "I've got to get this in by the end of the day. I'm hopelessly behind." He looked at Maggie with trepidation. "I studied classics at university—don't actually remember much maths. I—I don't suppose you'd, ah—"

"I'd be delighted." Maggie picked up his memo. "Look, everything else in the report is fine; I'll just redo the calculations, and you'll be set."

"Thank you, Maggie."

*You'd* better *thank me,* she thought, inordinately pleased, as he went out the door. But she was soon absorbed in the sheer joy of math again as she worked through the problems. How she'd missed it.

An hour or so later, Maggie was outside John's office, about to drop off his corrected memo as well as a data table for him to use in the future, when she heard voices. "Says she knows about RDF?" It was Snodgrass.

"She *does* know about RDF, sir. And about queuing, cryptography, you name it."

"She does, does she?"

Maggie strode into the office, chin high. "Mr. Sterling. I wanted to drop this off for you. The numbers we discussed," Maggie said, looking directly at Snodgrass. He sat in the chair across from John's desk, a cigarette in one hand and legs crossed at the knees.

John stood up and reached out for the papers she offered. "Thank you, Miss Hope." He looked at the calculations. "Mr. Snodgrass, this is what I was talking about," he said, handing the papers over.

"Good, good," Snodgrass said without looking at them. "Better get some of your maths books out and refresh that memory of yours, old boy!"

John looked at Maggie, then back at Snodgrass. "I believe Miss Hope would be able to assist Mr. Greene in these calculations far better than I."

"That may be," he said, leaning back in his chair, gesturing toward Maggie with his cigarette. "Miss Hope may be clever."

Maggie held her tongue, but she could feel her jaw clench and a pulse begin to beat behind one eye. *Dim-witted fop*, she thought.

"You're a smart girl," Snodgrass said to her, "and that's good. You'll have intelligent children. But isn't it more important to worry about your appearance and not calculations? Let the boys like John here take care of it. Stick to the typing, please."

John had the grace to look ashamed. "I really think, sir, that in this case—" he began.

"No!" Snodgrass roared. Both Maggie and John jumped a little. "No," he amended, softer this time.

"But I *can* help," Maggie said. "I *can* help—and you're not letting me."

"I'm sorry, Miss Hope, I really am," Snodgrass said quietly. He took a long drag on his cigarette and exhaled. For a fraction of a second, Maggie swore she could feel real regret emanating from the man. Then he extinguished the butt into the ashtray.

"Sorry?" Maggie said. "You're *sorry*? Then why are you acting like this? Why are you refusing a perfectly valid offer of assistance? Why do you think we're fighting this war, anyway?"

"I'm not sure—" Snodgrass began.

"For goodness' sake, Mary Wollstonecraft was British!" Maggie exploded. "*A Vindication of the Rights of Woman*? Have you even read it?"

"Maggie—" John said.

"No, I've held my tongue for a long while, and now I'm going to have my say. Why are we fighting this war?"

She glared at the two men, hands shaking with anger. "I'll tell you. It's because if Hitler has his way, we'll all be slaves—and, as an American, with our shameful history of slavery, let me tell you how monstrously horrible that would be. We're fighting for the right to be free citizens. It's a *privilege* that the Americans and British have—no matter if you're rich or poor, you're born free—and you can express your opinion and vote. And work. And this doesn't just apply to men. Women are slowly but surely making strides—the vote, higher education, laws that protect our money and property. But this treatment of women—middle- and upper-class women—as though we're children or goddesses or precious objets d'art—well, that's a kind of slavery. So, you may want to keep me in the drawing room, or the kitchen, or the nursery—or the typing pool—but it's simply another form of tyranny—one that we're *supposedly* fighting against."

Without waiting to hear more, Maggie turned and walked out into the hallway, heart beating quickly, blood pounding in her head. She made her way to the ladies' loo, locking the door behind her.

Ignoring the sickening chemical smell, she leaned against the wall, taking in deep breaths, until she was sure she wasn't going to hit anything—or anyone. She washed her face and hands, and returned to the typists' office. *A pretty gorilla. A bridge-playing dog. With everything women are doing for the war effort, is that all we are in the opinion of men?* She understood why Aunt Edith had been so bitter—and appreciated the lines on the side of her mouth from where she pursed her lips. *I hate Dicky Snodgrass. Hate, hate, hate.*

She went back to her desk in the typists' office, slamming a few things around. She was alone, so Mrs. Tinsley wouldn't snap and Miss Stewart wouldn't wince. Then she attacked her stack of typing with a vengeance.

"Sorry about that." It was John, in the doorway, running his hands through his dark hair.

"Don't give it a second thought," Maggie said tightly, fingers still moving over the keys.

"It's just—well, there are more things in play than you know."

"Of course," Maggie said, stopping and looking up at him. "And there are more things in heaven and earth than are dreamt of in my philosophy. Or something like that."

John took a few steps into the typists' office. "You know it's not personal—it's not *you*."

"Really? Well, Snodgrass certainly had me fooled, then."

John took a few more steps toward Maggie's desk. "Politics . . ." he said. "Politics isn't like equations. It's a nasty and dangerous business."

Maggie's eyes opened wide. "Dangerous? I can't believe that my helping with RDF calculations could possibly be dangerous. Oh—perhaps I might get a paper cut. Heavens!"

John came around the desk and knelt in front of her. He grasped her hand. "I—I can't say, Maggie. I wish to God I could, but I can't. But trust me. Would you, please?" Maggie looked at him, her irritation momentarily forgotten as she wondered at this abrupt display of emotion and uncharacteristic appeal.

Suddenly, they heard a door down the hall slam, and John pulled away. As he rose to his feet, Maggie looked at him in shock.

"Just trust me, all right?" he said, turning on his heel and leaving.

When Maggie looked down, she realized that her hands were shaking. *I don't have time for this.* She jammed a fresh piece of paper into the typewriter and began to attack the keys with renewed vigor.

"Are you all right, dear?" It was Miss Stewart, powdered and curled, coming in for the evening shift. She took off her straw hat with pink silk roses and smoothed down her hair absently in the mirror. "What did Mr. Sterling want?"

"I really don't know, Miss Stewart," Maggie said in a voice sounding strange and distant even to her own ears. "I really don't know."

# ELEVEN

CLAIRE LEFT MURPHY at the boardinghouse shortly before five a.m., a cold drizzle falling through the morning light. Pigeons cooed under the building's eaves. Across the street, a statue of Lord Nelson wept tears of soot.

She paused at the building's entrance and knotted a silk scarf under her chin, then opened her umbrella. It was a quiet morning, and traffic was thin and the shops were still closed.

Only the café across the street was open. A balding man in a blue seersucker suit sat at the window, reading a paper and drinking a cup of tea. He looked up for an instant, then looked down and turned the page.

Claire flipped up the collar of her gabardine coat. She'd been warned about MI-5, but she'd been careful and always felt anonymous. Suddenly, she sensed prying eyes everywhere.

Outside the café, a few people were queuing up for the bus. Claire looked at them and had the uncomfortable feeling she'd seen one of the faces before—maybe at the hotel, maybe on the Tube.

Maybe in the park.

She looked up at the flats across the street, the windows with taped diamonds and blackout curtains making blind eyes. *If they're watching you, they'll do it from a fixed position,* Murphy had told her. From an upper room or a restaurant or shop.

Claire scanned the windows and rooftops, looking for anyone's gaze. There was no one watching. She detected no movement.

With another quick glance around, she pulled on her gloves and began to make her way through the streets in the rain.

Maggie couldn't make Snodgrass give her more responsibility at work. And she wouldn't even *try* to figure out what was going on with John. But there was, she realized, one thing she could do. Needed to do.

And that was, finally, to pay her respects to her parents.

She'd meant to do it for a long time but had put it off—after all, seeing the headstones would make it seem that much more real. And she didn't want it to be real.

But Sarah's asking, plus a growing fear that somehow Highgate Cemetery might be destroyed in any and all upcoming attacks, made her realize she needed to do it. Now.

"What would you like, miss?" the flower seller near Regent's Park asked, his hands tough and leathery enough that he didn't need to wear protective gloves.

"I'll take that bunch of violets, thank you," she replied. Simple and somber, the purple blooms seemed appropriate for her mission to the cemetery. As did her plain cotton dress, straw hat, and lightweight coat.

"Right you are, miss. Party?"

"Highgate." *Yes, I'm going to Highgate Cemetery,* Maggie thought. *I've put it off, in denial, but it was just prolonging the inevitable. I must go.*

"Ah," he said. "Newspaper all right, or do you want them wrapped special?" he asked as he plucked the violets from their bucket, water from the stems dripping down his hands like tears.

"Wrapped special. Please."

Maggie took the Underground to the Archway station, then walked up winding and woody Swain's Lane to Highgate Cemetery.

It was a rambling, tree-shrouded wilderness filled with Victorian Gothic gravestones, tombs, catacombs, and mounds. Maggie found its beauty surprisingly comforting on her solemn mission.

She walked through rows and rows of monuments and carved angels with unfurled wings—some as cherubs looking heavenward, some in the form of pretty young girls with eyes cast demurely down, and some as goddesses draped languorously across mausoleums. Some headstones were smooth white marble with fresh flowers in vases, others dark and crumbling, covered in green moss and olive lichen.

*Here lies Mary Pyne, wife of Victor, after a long illness, rest in peace,* read one limestone headstone with elaborately carved clasped hands, nearly obscured by glossy ivy. *Henry David Atwood, 1870–1873, beloved baby boy* was etched in pocked black marble above an engraved broken rosebud. On another, a serpent swallowed his tail in an endless circle while the moss-covered stone proclaimed, *In memory of Robertson Worth, dearly loved husband and father. You are in our hearts always.*

She was using a map she'd found at Highgate's entrance. After a few false starts, missed turns, and tripping over some gnarled ancient tree roots, she found herself at the grave she sought.

She saw her mother's name and dates with engraved wings on the gray marble headstone: *Clara Louise Hope 1892–1916.* She knelt down on the grass and touched the etched letters with her gloved fingers for a long moment. *Hello, Mother,* she thought. *I'm here. Your daughter is here.*

After wiping away her tears and giving her nose a good blow with her handkerchief, Maggie busied herself by emptying water from the vase and throwing some long-dead roses into the compost pile, then filling the vase with fresh water from a nearby fountain. She returned to the grave, arranged the dark purple violets in the vase, then knelt down once again on the grass.

*It hurts to be here,* Maggie thought. *It hurts to see her name on the stone. Lord, how it hurts.*

And then, *Who's been here and leaving flowers on her grave?*

She rose to her feet, then looked around. And where was her father's grave? Surely they were buried together? Or at least near each other?

She looked and looked but to no avail.

In the distance was a cemetery worker, a stooped man with ruddy sunburned cheeks and brown-splotched hands, pushing a red wheelbarrow.

"Lovely flowers, those, miss," he said, releasing the wheelbarrow and touching his hand to his felt cap.

"Yes," she replied. "Thank you."

"Nice to see someone tending to that one," he went on. "It's been a while."

"Are you familiar with all the graves? There are so many."

"Been 'ere since just after the war—back in 'eighteen. Lots of friends 'ere, died over in France. Work every day except Sunday, miss."

"I'm wondering if you could help me, then. That grave over there, Clara Hope, is my mother's. But I can't find my father's."

"What's 'is name?"

"Edmund Hope. Edmund Charles Hope."

The man took off his cap. "No one 'ere by that name, miss. And I'd know."

*It can't be. He has to be here,* Maggie thought. *And yet . . .* Even though the day was warm, she felt a chill as the stillness of the cemetery permeated her skin.

It felt like a warning.

"There were dried flowers on my—on Clara Hope's grave when I got here. Do you know who left them?"

"Gentleman used to come 'ere regular. Used to leave white roses." The man rubbed his whiskered jaw with his large hand. "But I ain't seen him 'ere in a long while."

The old gardener again touched his hand to his hat, then picked up the handles of his wheelbarrow. "I'd best be getting on, miss."

"Of course," Maggie replied quickly, mind whirring. "Thank you."

Maggie returned home, mind racing, heart pounding. First, a phone call.

"Margaret! What's wrong?" Aunt Edith's voice on the other side of the transatlantic call sounded tinny and faint.

"I have a question for you."

There was a pause. "Of course."

"Where is my father buried?"

A longer pause. "Oh, Margaret—I never thought . . ."

"You never thought what? That I'd ever go looking for their graves? Well, I did. And I found my mother's. But not my father's. So where is he?" Maggie clutched the receiver tightly.

Silence.

"Well?"

"Margaret, do you have to—why can't you just let the past alone?"

"Why won't you answer the question?"

Edith sighed. "Some things, well, it's just easier if you let them be."

*Why isn't she answering me? What's going on?*

There was static crackling over the line.

"Margaret, I think our call is breaking up—" There was silence and a click, then the broad whine of the dial tone.

Professor Edith Hope sat in her large, comfortable office in ivy-covered Science Hall. It was mid-June, and she was catching up on some of the endless administrative paperwork she had to do. Outside, red-breasted robins were chirping and the lush grass sparkled in the sunshine. She looked, unseeing, out the lead-glass windows over Wellesley's vast lawns at the neo-Gothic spires of Green Hall's immense bell tower and contemplated her last phone call with Maggie.

*Of course the infernal girl is asking questions. She's a rational girl, a scientific girl, a logical girl—and with her staying in London, it was just a matter of time before she began piecing things together.*

*However,* Edith thought, rubbing her stiff hands against the chill in the air before turning to her typewriter, *there's time. There's still time.*

*Wellesley, Massachusetts*

*Margaret—*

*I must insist that you come home immediately.*

*Did I not do enough for you when you were a child? I know I wasn't a real mother at all, let alone a good mother. But I did feel—and still do—that I have a responsibility to Edmund to keep you safe.*

*We never pretended, you and I, that I was your mother, not even your adopted one. I didn't think it would be fair to poor Clara; it also simply wasn't in*

*my nature, I'm afraid. But I do know we have a spe-
cial rapport, brought on by our mutual interests.*

*Please don't allow your anger at me to keep you
from what promises to be a stunning career and a
happy, productive life. I've worked too hard for that.
You've worked too hard for that.*

*Please come home. There's still time.*

*Edith*

What she really wanted to write but somehow couldn't
was: *Everything I did, I did for you.*

"Let's go over this again."

Pierce was meeting with Claire and Murphy in Queen
Mary's Gardens in Regent's Park. The day was foggy
and overcast, the grass beaded with the morning's rain.
The roses—scarlet, pink, gold, and ivory—were in full
bloom, nearly glowing against the dark clouds. The air
was fragrant with their spicy perfume, and plush bum-
blebees bobbled and buzzed, drunk on the golden
pollen.

Besides the occasional pedestrian and plump pigeon,
they had the wooden bench in the rose garden to themselves, knowing there was no way their conversation
could be overheard. Claire sat between the two men.

"While the Tube bombings have been effective in
causing a certain amount of panic and hysteria," Claire
said, "we're agreed we need to damage the British capacity for waging war."

Murphy added, "Working together, we can launch a
three-pronged attack."

"Right—Claire will take care of the assassination,
you're responsible for the bombing, and I'm in charge of
the kidnapping. I'll get word to Berlin about moving forward," Pierce said. "The details will appear in tomorrow's *Times*."

"You can't just radio them?" Murphy asked.

"No, I can receive incoming radio messages, but sending one out would be too dangerous."

Claire pushed her hair behind her ears. "Don't you worry about being caught, though? Working with the Saturday Club and all?"

"Ah, I subscribe to the theory of 'hide in plain sight,' my dear," he said. "Rather Like Poe's 'Purloined Letter,' you know." It was obvious from his tone that he didn't think she did.

"*Un dessein si funeste, S'il n'est digne d'Atrée, est digne de Thyeste,* Malcolm?" Claire said.

Murphy blinked. "What's that, now?"

"Literally translated, it means, 'If such a sinister design isn't worthy of Atreus, it is worthy of Thyestes.' " Claire said. "It's what Dupin tells the narrator at the end of the story."

Pierce blinked at her, his lips curling into a smile. "Brava, my dear, *bravissima,*" Pierce said, looking at her with new eyes. "Quite right, quite right. I'm hiding in plain sight. Which is why we've been working in codes." He handed over the advert. "And this one, my friends, is a beauty."

"I love it!" Claire exclaimed, taking in the innocuous line drawing of three women swathed in chic clothing. A squirrel reared up on his hind legs in alarm, then scurried up a tree. "All over England, women will be looking at what they think is the latest in ladies' fashion. Genius, really. Just genius." She and Pierce looked at each other, and each held the other's gaze.

"And you're ready for your part?" Murphy asked, laying a hand protectively over Claire's.

"Of course," she replied. "I was born for this mission. And you?"

"I'll be at Saint Paul's, of course."

*     *     *

They each went their separate ways in the park, with Claire walking down the long paths to make her way to the street.

A young man, pink-cheeked and barely old enough to shave, sat on a long park bench reading *The Times* and dropped a section. A stout woman in gray twill and sensible shoes disappeared behind a cluster of oak trees.

And as Claire walked out of the park and put her arm up for a taxi, one pulled right up in front of her. What was it Michael had said about the watchers of MI-5? That they would pass you in the street and you'd never even give them a second look.

"Where to, miss?" asked the grizzled cabbie through the open window.

"Changed my mind," she said, turning on her heel.

She went back into the park, following a footpath that led to an Italianate garden filled with blossoms of crimson, ginger, white, and gold. She stopped to admire one of the weathered stone statues, surreptitiously looking around.

There was no one else in sight.

She retraced her steps.

Nothing and no one.

When she reached the street, she walked quickly to the Great Portland Street Tube station instead of taking a cab. At the station she bought a ticket for Oxford Street. The train was just about to close its doors when she pushed her way in, ignoring the disapproving stares of the other passengers.

She quickly composed her features and found a seat.

Mark Standish and Hugh Thompson met Peter Frain at his club, housed in a three-story white-brick mansion with Romanesque columns. At the glossy black door, they showed their identification to an unsmiling British soldier holding a Sten gun.

The guard waved them into the marble-and-gilt entrance hall and pointed to two etched-glass doors. "Jesus," Standish breathed.

"Nice to know how the other half lives, eh?" Thompson replied.

Through the doors was a gigantic, high-ceilinged room that housed a swimming pool. The walls were covered in blue, cream, beige, and dark-brown tiles in mosaics of ancient Babylonian archers. Inside, the air was hot and moist. Men, pasty and middle-aged, did the crawl or backstroke in the lanes.

Frain finished his lap, then swam over to the men, incongruous and awkward in their suits. "What happened?" he asked, climbing out of the pool and receiving a fresh towel from one of the attendants.

"She went into the Tube station, sir," answered Standish, nervous and trying not to stare at his nearly naked boss, who had the wiry build of a rower. "We sent an agent after her, but she made it onto a train before he could reach her."

"Damn it," Frain muttered, trying to get water out of his ears. "How long were they in the park?"

"About fifteen minutes," Thompson replied. His face was getting moist in the damp heat, and his temples were beading with drops of sweat.

"Plenty of time to exchange information."

"Yes, sir."

"Sir, she's an amateur. At some point she's going to make a mistake. And we'll be there to catch it," Standish said. "I'll get one of the girls to type all this up in a report for you. Then you can bring it to Mr. Churchill."

Richard Snodgrass, a slight figure in a pinstriped suit, appeared in the doorway and made his way over the gleaming tiled floor to Frain and his two men. "We're moving forward, then? We *are* moving forward?"

"A pleasant day to you, Mr. Snodgrass," Frain said,

wrapping the towel around his waist. "And most assuredly, we're moving forward."

"And, about—Miss Hope, still—?"

"No," Frain said, heading toward the dressing room. "As far as we know, she still has no idea at all."

# TWELVE

As much as Maggie wanted to tear the island apart to look for her father, ordinary life went on with work at No. 10 and all its other commitments and responsibilities. Including hosting a party for Chuck's upcoming birthday.

As Paige was working as a driver at all hours and the twins couldn't really be counted on for anything involving cleaning, one weekend Sarah and Maggie together uncovered the furniture in the parlor, dining room, and library, beat the dust from the rugs with large wooden paddles, polished the floors with lemon-scented wax, and washed the crystal. Finally, sweaty and aching, they surveyed their handiwork with pride.

The pipes might have been crumbling and the roof ready to cave in, but there was no denying that the house looked exquisite. The chandeliers sparkled, the brass gleamed, the wood glowed. "The furniture does look a little shabby," Maggie admitted, poking at a moth hole in a velvet chair.

"Don't even think about it," Sarah rejoined. "No one will notice in the lamplight. It's going to be fantastic. You wait and see."

There was a noise from the kitchen. Maggie and Sarah looked at each other. Were any other of the girls home?

As they walked through the kitchen door, they heard a whispered, "Yes, yes, I'll be there," and saw Chuck hurriedly replace the telephone receiver.

"Oh, I didn't know you were still home," Maggie said.

"Just . . . had to make a call," Chuck said quickly. "Can I help with anything?"

"I think we're all set," Sarah said.

"Great!" Chuck said, backing out of the kitchen.

"Well, that was strange," Maggie said to Sarah.

"Quite."

The guests began to arrive just after seven o'clock. Maggie, Paige, Chuck, and the twins were at the door to greet them, dressed in their best summer frocks.

"Why, look at you, Chuck," Paige said, taking in her silk dress, along with the pin-curled hair and hint of lipstick. "We'll have to call you Charlotte tonight."

"Not if you want to live," Chuck deadpanned. The twins giggled.

They were to be eleven: the six girls; John and David, of course; plus Simon; and also Dimitri, Sarah's frequent ballet partner. And Nigel was coming from the barracks on leave.

The tall wax tapers were lit, the table was set, and dinner was in the oven. Thanks to Sarah, a surprisingly good cook, delicious aromas wafted through the house.

"Jolly good show, ladies," Nigel said as he arrived with the other boys. He looked smart in his dress uniform, and they splendid in their dinner jackets. "The place looks wonderful, as do all of you." He grabbed Chuck around the waist, spun her in a circle, and gave her a kiss on the cheek. "You, especially, my dear."

"Why, thank you, kind sir," Chuck replied, dropping into a mock curtsey. John looked away. He had circles underneath his eyes, and his cheekbones looked sharper than ever.

"Oh, please," Maggie said to John. "Don't you *ever* have any fun?"

"Occasionally. But this is England, after all. Fun's considered to be in poor taste."

Maggie gave him a half-smile.

"Don't mind him," David said, kissing Maggie's cheek. "He's still in a filthy mood over Hitler's tour of Paris." She caught a whiff of gin on his breath.

"And you?" she asked, trying not to glare at Annabelle and Clarabelle's fussing over John.

"Oh, I've had too much to drink to be in a filthy mood about anything."

That left Simon Paul, John and David's friend from Oxford, whom they'd met at the Blue Moon. Maggie offered her hand, which he took and kissed. "Welcome," she said.

"Thank you," he replied. Then, to Paige, "Why, Scarlett O'Hara, you're ravishing!"

Dimitri arrived last; he was tall, dark, and slim, with a gallant air about him.

Finally, with theatrical timing, Sarah entered at the top of the staircase, wearing a daringly low-cut gold lamé dress. "Everyone," she said, raising her arms in a commanding gesture, "thank you so much for coming for Chuck's birthday." After she made her grand entrance down the staircase, she said, "This is Dimitri Zakharov, my favorite partner. Dimitri—meet everyone."

Dimitri looked at the assembled group and smiled. "*Milo mi poznac.* Pleased to meet you." He clicked his heels together and bowed to Sarah, offering her his arm.

Simon offered his to Paige. "Charmed, I'm sure," Paige cooed, obviously won over. She took his arm and led everyone into the library for cocktails.

Once everyone had taken their seats, Paige mixed a

pitcher of martinis, using what was left of Grandmother Hope's liquor cabinet. "You look just like Myrna Loy," Simon said, as he watched her put ice in the silver shaker, slick with beads of condensation.

Paige laughed and tossed her hair. "Well, it's not the American Bar at the Savoy," she said, handing him a glass, "but everything's cold, and as you can see, the vermouth's been kept to a minimum. Now, tell me all about your club at Oxford."

After a few drinks, the group sat down at the table, set with Grandmother Hope's good china and crystal. Nearly everything was from their victory garden. There was a thyme-scented vegetable soup to start, then carrot soufflé, peas with mint, glazed turnips. David had somehow procured some red wine, which they used to toast Chuck's birthday. Although Maggie had been nervous about pulling it off, the dinner was excellent. Dimitri was funny and charming and, as it turned out, Polish, not Russian.

"Public likes Russian dancers," he said over weak tea and birthday cake with white icing and tiny pink fondant roses; Chuck, Paige, and Maggie had all saved their sugar, butter, and egg rations for a month for it. "My real name? Stanislaw Wilecki." They all laughed. "Dimitri" just seemed more dashing, somehow. "And Alicia Markova? Really Lilian Alicia Marks. English."

"*No!*" Annabelle exclaimed.

"It's true," Sarah replied, licking buttercream frosting off her fork. "And the great Margot Fonteyn is really little Peggy Hookham from Surrey. I thought about changing my name myself, except then all my friends from Liverpool would never learn when I become rich and famous."

"What are you working on these days, Sarah?" John asked. "I don't have as much time as I'd like to get to the ballet." *Really? Does being patronizing and moody keep you on a tight schedule?* Maggie thought.

"*Swan Lake*—music by Tchaikovsky, choreography by Petipa, staged for us by Nicholas Sergeyev, former regisseur for the Mariinsky Theatre. You should see Dimitri in it, David," Sarah said, taking a sip of her tea. "He's learning the role of Prince Siegfried."

"I'd like that," David replied, reaching for yet another petit four.

"*David!*" Paige said, giving his knuckles a rap.

"What?" said David. "Carpe diem! Or carpe cake, I suppose."

"Of course," Dimitri said, "Michael Somes is lead, but I am understudy. So maybe perhaps I go on someday as lead."

Simon smiled. "Fairy tales. Perfect for tutus."

Sarah smiled tightly. "It's a tragedy, actually. The story of *Swan Lake* is about two girls, Odette and Odile, who resemble each other so closely they can easily be mistaken for the other. Odette is the innocent maiden turned into a white-swan queen by an evil sorcerer. The prince falls in love with her and tries to save her. But the sorcerer deceives him—and tricks the prince with a black swan, Odile, who impersonates Odette. The prince confuses the two, and poor Odette is doomed to remain a swan forever."

"Ah," said Simon. "Freud's old Madonna-whore dichotomy."

"What's interesting," Sarah continued, "is that the same dancer performs both roles. Odile goes undercover as Odette, as it were. Conniving bitch," she said, laughing.

"First of all," said Chuck, "Freud's a horse's ass. Second, Sarah, that's wonderful. I can certainly see you in both roles."

Annabelle interjected, "Is it hard to go back and

forth?" She smiled. "I only have one role in *Rebecca,* and it's hard enough—what's it like to do two?"

"It is a challenge," Sarah replied. "There are the technical demands, of course—but then there's the fact that one character's very soft and vulnerable, while the other's quite steely and very sexy—but imitating the first. So it's a balancing act."

Dimitri turned to David. "When do you come to performance?" There was a silence that went on a bit too long.

Maggie could feel David's discomfort at Dimitri's public attentions and rushed in, changing the subject. "Well, with our schedules, who can? Anyway, that reminds me of a joke—well, it's really more of a logic problem—called 'The Liar and the Truth Teller.' "

"Oh no," Nigel groaned. "Reminds me of Eton."

"It's not hard, if you think it through," Maggie said. "All right, so there are two soldiers at a crossroads. One always lies, and one always tells the truth, but you don't know which is which. You need to find out whether the left or right path leads to safety but can only ask one of them a single question. What should you ask? And what should you do, depending on what they answer?"

"Easy," Annabelle said. "No matter what answer either gives you, take the *other* path."

Maggie was surprised.

"I don't understand," Chuck moaned, shaking her head. She'd had too much wine to think clearly.

"Well, if you ask the truth teller," Maggie said, "he'll tell you which path the liar will tell you to take."

"And if you ask the liar," John said, "he'll know which path the truth-telling soldier will tell you to take. However, since he's a liar, he'll point you in the wrong direction. So just take the other path."

"Bravo!" Maggie said. *All right, so maybe he is smart.*

*But he doesn't have to be so very condescending at the office about it.*

Chuck looked heavenward. "*This* is why I became a nurse."

John looked over at Nigel. "So when do you push off, old sod?" Nigel was being sent to a secret location and wouldn't be in contact with anyone, not to mention Chuck, for an indefinite period of time.

"About a fortnight," Nigel replied, leaning over and giving Chuck's thigh a squeeze through her dress. "Can't say I want to leave my gorgeous girl here alone, but now that I've decided, it seems like it's time to get on with it."

"We know you'll do splendidly," Sarah said. "You'll come back a hero, all decorated with medals and—little ribbons."

*Little ribbons?* Maggie mouthed at her. Sarah shrugged.

"I don't care what I come back with, it's what I'm coming back to," Nigel said, looking at Chuck. They could all tell she was trying hard not to cry.

"Good Lord, I didn't mean to do this now, and at the dinner table, of all places, but here goes." He took a deep sigh and suddenly got down on one knee, taking her hand. "Charlotte, my dearest Chuck, would you do me the incredible honor of—becoming my wife?"

Chuck looked stunned. Everyone at the table was dumbfounded.

"Ooooooh!" the twins exclaimed together, eyes wide.

Chuck blushed furiously. But without hesitating, she threw her arms around his neck and kissed him long and hard, causing everyone at the table to clap.

"Yes, yes, *yes*! I would *love* to be Mrs. Nigel Ludlow," she declared, holding his ruddy perspiring face between her hands, laughing and crying at the same time.

As Nigel and Chuck turned back to each other for another kiss, Maggie led everyone in a round of "For He's a Jolly Good Fellow," and David refilled everyone's glass.

"I'm sorry, but I don't have a ring yet, sweetheart," Nigel said as he sat down and pulled Chuck onto his lap.

"It's fine," she murmured, her lips against his collar. "Don't need any goddamned ring. I'm not some gold-digging debutante."

"Good gracious," Annabelle said, taken aback.

"No ring?" Clarabelle added.

"I don't care about any ring," Chuck said to Nigel, burying her face in his shoulder. "I just care about you."

"Well, you'll have one by the time I get back from my first leave—and then we'll start planning the wedding. What do you say, my love?"

Chuck considered. "Will your parents have to come?"

"Well, that *is* traditional, darling."

A pause. "Why don't we just elope?"

Nigel laughed. "Ah, that's my girl," he said as he wiped his red face with his handkerchief.

Later in the evening, as they left the table to relax in the parlor, Maggie realized why ladies and gentlemen were encouraged to separate after dinner. The men clustered around the fireplace, drinking brandy and engrossed in yet another political argument. At least David didn't join in; instead, he played "Mad About the Boy" on the piano.

Maggie wandered over to David. "Sounds wonderful," she said, suddenly conscious that the piano was out of tune and missing an F string. "Or at least as wonderful as possible on this old thing. You're very talented."

"Thanks, Magster," David said. He moved over on

the bench to make room for her, then launched into a
Noël Coward medley. Maggie took the opportunity to
study his long and graceful fingers as they moved across
the keys. He had a lovely tenor voice and was perfectly
at ease at the keyboard as he launched into a sprightly
melody:

*"The Stately Homes of England we proudly
     represent,*
*We only keep them up for Americans to rent,*
*Though the pipes that supply the bathroom burst*
*And the lavatory makes you fear the worst,*
*It was used by Charles the First, quite informally,*
*And later by George the Fourth on a journey north.*
*The State Apartments keep their historical renown,*
*It's wiser not to sleep there in case they tumble down*
*But still if they ever catch on fire, which, with any
     luck, they might*
*We'll fight for the Stately Homes of England!"*

As he segued into "Mad Dogs and Englishmen," he
said, "Lovely dinner party."

"Thank you. I'm so glad it turned out all right—"

But Simon and John's discussion was quickly turning
into an argument. John's voice was getting louder.
"Look, it's like the Old Man said—the way you all
wanted it, if Saint George had tried to save the fair
maiden from the dragon, he'd have been accompanied
by a delegation instead of a horse—and had a secretary,
not a lance. Then, after signing some sort of meaningless
agreement with said dragon, the maiden's release would
be referred to the League of Nations. Then, finally, Saint
George would be photographed with the dragon, and it
would have run on the front page of *The Times*.

"But when all was said and done, the damned dragon
would have kept the damned maiden—and Saint George,

his secretary, the Round Table, the agreement, the entire blasted League of blasted Nations—all would have been burned to a crisp."

"That's hardly what I was proposing, John, and you know it," Simon said, his voice turning menacing. "We were all there for the King-and-Country debate. I signed it, you signed it, David and Nigel signed it—"

"We were young, ignorant," John exploded. "We didn't know what was happening in Germany. We didn't know anything about *anything,* for that matter."

"Look, John," said Simon, "here's what *is* happening—when the government goes to war, it commits mass murder on a huge scale. Our side, their side. It's all murder."

John countered, "In a world with madmen like Hitler, war's most definitely inevitable. Don't you think he must have laughed when he heard about King and Country? Realized that without a strong military, England would be ripe for the taking? And look at us now. Germans have invaded Paris, we were beaten at Dunkirk and barely escaped, now they're poised to invade at any moment. . . ."

"No, no, no!" Simon said, slamming a fist down on the mantel. "It's inevitable because the government knows it has a ready supply of young men, willing to go out and die for their country—and who won't ask questions. Well, I asked questions! I'm *still* asking questions! I'm disgusted with past wars for King and Country, disgusted with England's treatment of Ireland, of India, of Palestine—and in my opinion, the jury's still out on this war, too."

"The IRA's a bunch of murderers and thugs," John said through clenched teeth. "And anyone who suggests otherwise is a traitor."

Maggie stood up. "Stop it!" she cried, unable to take any more. "Stop it! Both of you!" she said, hands on hips. "To fight or not to fight? We're *all* in this war. As

John says, invasion is imminent. I really don't see how political parties matter anymore. When we've won this war—and I do believe we will—there'll be time enough for philosophical arguments and debates. Until then, we're all in England, we're all in the same boat, we've all got a common enemy, and, and—Nigel and Chuck are getting married. Now, please, for King and Country, just *shut up*!"

As everyone took a moment to regroup, David selected the record *Me and My Girl*. He put it on the phonograph, starting the turntable and carefully placing the needle in the groove. As it popped and crackled, beginning "The Lambeth Walk," he said, "I don't suppose there's any more cake?"

# THIRTEEN

AND THEN, FINALLY, after months of anticipation and dread, the Luftwaffe attacked London.

Maggie was making copies of the P.M.'s letters in the Annexe office with Mrs. Tinsley and Miss Stewart when the air-raid siren began its low wail. This was no drill.

As they made their way down to the protected underground War Rooms, they could hear the roar of the aircraft engines. *Ours? Theirs?* Maggie thought. She threw open a window to look. There were hundreds—*thousands*, it seemed—of planes circling overhead, black insects against the sky, leaving silvery vapor trails against the blood-red clouds, darkening in the setting sun.

"Air raid, please. Air raid, please," they heard Mr. Rance, the overseer of the War Rooms, call. It didn't surprise Maggie that at a time like this he was using the word *please*. At No. 10, one said please for everything. She could just as easily imagine him saying, "The Four Horsemen of the Apocalypse, please. Four Horsemen of the Apocalypse, please."

As they heard the antiaircraft guns rumble and saw the aircraft break formation to dive into dogfights, Miss Stewart placed her hand gently on Maggie's shoulder. "There's nothing you can do by watching, my dear."

Maggie nodded, yet she was unable to tear her eyes

away from the spectacle in the sky, frozen with fear, fascination, admiration, and anger.

"Come along, Miss Hope," Mrs. Tinsley said, leading the way downstairs.

Maggie took a moment to scoop Nelson up from on top of her desk to take him with them. "Coming."

Below, an argument was brewing.

"I shall," the P.M. stated emphatically. "I *shall* go up and watch. It's my city, damn it. And you"—he waggled his finger at General Ismay—"shan't stop me."

"Sir," General Ismay began, yet again, "as your adviser, I hardly think it prudent—"

" 'Prudent'? *'Prudent'*?" Churchill spluttered. "We're at war, man. There's nothing prudent about it."

General Ismay sighed. "Then please, sir. Only for a few moments."

Mr. Churchill looked around at the gathered staff. "Who's in?" he said with his cherubic smile, as though inviting them to cocktails.

Maggie raised her hand. John and David raised theirs. The senior staff—General Ismay, Mr. Attlee, and Mr. Eden—decided to go as well. The P.M.'s ever-present shadow, Detective Inspector Walter Thompson, followed the P.M. with a grim face.

"Don't panic—remember, we're British," David joked as they went up the stairs in the shadows, but no one laughed. From their vantage point on the roof, it looked as though all of London was burning. The entire horizon of the city glowed orange-red in the dark.

Sirens wailed and Messerschmitts screamed overhead. They could hear the great thudding boom of bombs ripping buildings apart, and could feel the answering shake from British gunfire. The building rocked and swayed in response; it was all so close. The savagery and destruction happening were almost too much to bear. A terrible tremor went through Maggie, and she involuntarily took a step backward, right into John. He put his hands on her shoulders for a moment to steady her; she was surprised and flustered by his touch. As John dropped his hands, David took her arm to give her a reassuring squeeze.

But David didn't turn his eyes from the horizon. None of them could. The very air tasted of death—acrid, bitter, and metallic—and as Maggie looked up into the sky, she could imagine the souls of the newly dead hovering over them.

New waves of planes flew over them in two-minute intervals. Their motors ground and growled in vicious anticipation of dropping their cargo. Batches of incendiary bombs, clusters of lights called chandeliers, fell into the blackness, flashing with brilliance before burning down to pinpoints of dazzling white. They watched most of them go out, one by one, as firemen extinguished the blazes before they could rage out of control. But some burned on, and soon a yellow flame leapt up from the white center. Yet another building was engulfed in flames.

Above the fires, the sky seethed red. Overhead, making a ceiling in the vast heavens, was a cloud of pink smoke. Up in that shrouding were tiny, brilliant specks of flashing light—antiaircraft shells bursting. The barrage balloons stood in clear relief against the burning horizon, glowing crimson. Maggie was suddenly glad Aunt Edith wasn't there to witness such an event.

They were silent in the face of such savagery, except for David, who let out a soft whistle as one particularly gorgeous chandelier exploded. It was the most beautiful and horrific sight Maggie had ever witnessed. She could feel the wetness of her sweat seeping from her armpits, pooling between her breasts, and running down her back, even in the cold.

As her thoughts went to her flatmates, out there, vulnerable, in that vast expanse of darkness, she could feel her shell of denial begin to crack. Fear had become a real person standing too close and pressing against her, hard and crude, daring her to cry out in panic.

"You all right?" John whispered.

She pulled herself up and stood straight. "Yes, I'm all right." She was. She would get through this. They would all get through this. "And you?"

His voice was steely. "I'm getting back to work."

Yes, work. Work was the only thing they could do.

The next morning, Maggie walked around bombed-out London. According to the BBC, the raids had been perpetrated by three hundred bombers, escorted by six hundred fighters. In just one night, more than four hundred people had been killed. Not to mention the bomb damage and resulting fires, including a huge one on the London docks. And the bombers were going to keep coming—night after night after night.

She walked past cats peering out from boarded-up windows, past houses with balconies, turrets, and Palladian windows. Past chimneys and church towers pointing accusing fingers up to heaven. Many of the once-proud houses were next to mountains of rubble or the skeletons of buildings. Maggie felt shock, disbelief, and overwhelming sadness at the violence and ruin and waste of it all.

As night after night of bombing went by, Maggie was beginning to feel, even amid the grief and loss, a sense of defiance emerging, a fierce solidarity that overrode the fear, and a wicked sense of black humor that outsiders might not understand. Bombed-out shops were open for business, regardless of damage sustained.

"More open than usual?" Maggie joked with one grocer whose front windows had shattered in the raids.

The man grinned back at her. "Right you are, miss, right you are."

Another open store displayed the sign: *They can smash our windows but they can't beat our furnishing values.* Even the police station posted: *Be good—we're still cops.*

As the days turned to weeks, everyone in London learned to live with it. They learned to live with the dread and the fear, the sleepless nights and their churning, sour stomachs. They learned to get up and run to the flimsy corrugated-steel Anderson shelter in the dark without tripping and falling. They learned to live with the glow from fires burning in the East End and to live with the smell—the stench of thick, black smoke and an underlying scent of things best not discussed. Many people, more than 170,000 by some accounts, learned to live underground in at least eighty different Tube stations, sleeping on the floor, cooking over small grills, and using buckets for toilets.

They became used to seeing the endless processions of people dressed in black, coming to or from the constant funerals and memorial services.

They learned to read the morning papers without weeping.

But there were some things they couldn't get used to. Didn't want to. When yet another bomb dropped on their block, Maggie, Paige, and Sarah saw bodies—bodies of their friends and neighbors—pulled out from the rubble. Those weren't the kinds of things they could forget.

But they could go on. They had to. They all went to work, ate their meals, spoke to one another in the shops, went on as though they were people in one of those classic British plays—always polite, terribly formal, occasionally stiff. It was almost comical sometimes.

There was really nothing else to do.

*     *     *

The ad ran in *The Times* as planned, an innocuous line drawing advertising the latest in women's fashion: day dresses with skirts ending just below the knee, wrist-covering gloves, straw boater hats, and spectator pumps.

But crosshatched into the drawing where the stitching was were hundreds upon hundreds of minuscule dots and dashes. Put together, they spelled out a message for anyone who knew where to look.

Pierce was pleased to see its placement—some pages in, bottom left-hand corner, beneath the cricket scores, next to the crossword puzzle—easily glanced over and dismissed.

Except for those who were waiting for it.

At his desk, he clipped it carefully from the paper with small, sharp scissors and put it away for Claire to include in her next letter to Norway. "Bloody idiots," he muttered to himself as he stirred his tea with satisfaction. "They'll never see it coming."

There was a knock at the door. He rose to his feet and opened it. There was Claire.

He smiled, and their eyes locked. "I was hoping you'd come," he said.

She pressed herself against him and circled his neck with her hands. "I know," she said. "I thought we should celebrate."

His body began to respond. "What about Michael?" he managed finally, his voice thick with desire.

Her hand started at his shirtfront and found its way to his belt. "Let's not talk about him right now."

Despite the bombing, which barraged London night after night, Maggie decided to return her attention to finding out more information about her father.

*An odd mission indeed,* she thought distractedly as

she got ready to leave, pinning on her brown straw derby hat with lilac ribbons and adjusting it in the mirror before leaving the house.

One fact she knew about her father was that he'd been a professor working with the Operational Research Group in the Department of Discrete and Applied Mathematics at the London School of Economics. It seemed like a good place to start.

Samuel Barstow, the department chair, allowed her into his office, crammed full of books, papers, and files in no discernible order. On the wall was a reproduction of Escher's woodcut *Day and Night*. The air was thick with dust and cigarette smoke, while a spiky aspidistra kept vigil on the window ledge.

Barstow was in his mid-sixties, sported a striped bow tie, and had a pale, papery look to him, as if he rarely if ever saw the light of day. "I don't have much time, Miss—"

"Hope. Maggie Hope," she said, offering her hand.

He rose and clasped it, leaving ink smudges on her beige gloves. "Pleasure. What may I do for you, Miss Hope?"

"I was wondering if you might answer a few questions for me."

"About the final?" he said, pushing back woolly gray hair. "We covered all of that in class. Just find someone and get the notes—"

"No, Professor Barstow. Actually, I was wondering if you could tell me anything about my father—Edmund Hope. He was a professor here from 1906 to 1916, working in this department."

Samuel Barstow sat down suddenly, as though deflated. He gestured to the dark-green leather chair opposite his desk. "Oh, my dear, my dear."

Maggie moved a stack of blue books to the floor and perched on the edge of the seat.

"Edmund Hope. I haven't heard that name in, well—forgive me, it's been a while." He took out a heavy silver lighter and lit his cigarette, drawing in the smoke and then exhaling a blue cloud with a sigh.

"I realize that," she said, leaning forward.

He stared at the tip, which smoldered red in the office's gloomy light, then closed his eyes. As he did, she noticed the deep lines around them, the bruiselike purple shadows beneath, and the creases on his forehead. *He's about the same age my father would have been,* she thought. *Would be. My father would have the same wrinkles by now.*

Professor Barstow took a long drag on his cigarette, then exhaled. "Miss Hope . . ."

"Maggie. Please."

"Maggie," he repeated thoughtfully. "It's so very good to meet you, Maggie. You're without a doubt your father's daughter, but with aspects of your mother as well, of course. I only met her once or twice, but your father always had a photograph of her on his desk. We used to tease him no end about it—how he'd managed to persuade such a pretty girl to marry him."

Maggie wanted to hear more—she wanted to hear everything—but she knew she had to bring the conversation back to the topic at hand.

"Did you go to his funeral?"

"Did I—" His moist eyes looked shocked.

"You see, I was wondering if you did, or if you know of anyone who did."

"What on earth would make you ask that? Of course I went to your mother's funeral."

"My mother's?" she asked. "No, this is about my father's. I—"

"My dear child," he said, leaning forward. "I never went to your father's funeral."

She folded her hands tightly together. "Why not?"

"Because—to the best of my knowledge—your father is still alive."

Maggie gasped.

"I know he was living alone, not coming in to work, and drinking a bit more than prudent," Barstow said. "We were all terribly worried about him. His sister was taking care of you, and he—well, one day, he just disappeared."

" 'Disappeared'?" Maggie said, unclenching her hands. "No one can just disappear."

"That's what it seemed like. He became increasingly isolated and delusional—and the next thing we knew, he was gone."

"Yes, but gone *where*?"

"My dear, I wish I could say. But there was the trench war, you know. Your father and I were friends, and it gives me great pain to say this. I assumed he'd gone to the country or something like that—to get his head back together. But the months went by, and then the years—and he just never came back."

*He didn't die?* Maggie felt the hairs on the back of her neck rise. *This is what Aunt Edith was trying to keep from me? But why?* "So he could be out there? Alive?"

"It's a distinct possibility," Barstow said. "Although, I suppose, any number of things could have happened to him over the years."

"Do you have any idea where he might have gone?" she pressed. "Did he have a favorite place outside of London?"

Barstow sighed and scratched his head. "It was so long ago. . . ."

"Please," she implored.

"Well, I do remember that he spoke quite often of his time at Cambridge. Loved the place. Always had a warm spot in his heart for his days at university. That's all I can think of."

*Cambridge. Yes, he'd done his undergraduate and doctoral work at Trinity,* Maggie thought. It was better than nothing. "Thank you, Professor Barstow." She opened her handbag and took out a fountain pen and a small notebook. She scribbled something down, ripped it out, and handed the paper to him. "Here's my number, if you remember anything more." She rose to leave.

"You know," he said slowly. "Sometimes people don't want to be found."

Maggie was struck by his candor. "I realize that," she said over her shoulder. "But if there's a chance, even just a chance—I have to try."

# FOURTEEN

Even with nightly air attacks, life went on.

"We have tickets! We have tickets!" Paige called up the stairs.

Anything to do with Sarah and her dancing career—with *glamour* in a drab wartime world—left Paige giddy with delight. She danced into the bedroom just as Maggie was drawing her bath. Although she applied Odo-Ro-No under her arms, sprinkled with bicarbonate of soda and splashed with violette eau de toilette, like most of her fellow Londoners, she needed a bath.

"Tickets to what?" Maggie grumbled through the bathroom door, feeling annoyed as she stepped out of her dressing gown and into her allotted five inches of lukewarm water. She'd just returned from LSE and wanted to sort through everything Professor Barstow had told her in peace and quiet.

"The ballet, silly. They're performing again, you know, although curtain time is earlier, because of the air raids. Sarah just called—she's dancing the lead in *Swan Lake*! Margot's sprained her ankle, and Sarah's going on for her! She's leaving tickets for us at the box office. We need to pick them up at half past six for the seven-o'clock performance, which leaves us just an hour to get ready. Come on—chop, chop!"

Maggie sighed, did a quick scrub, and reluctantly got out of the bath. Whatever she could do to find her father she couldn't do tonight, after all.

Even with blackout curtains in place, the theater appeared a world removed from the city at war, a city being bombed from above almost nightly. The lobby overflowed with golden light, magnified by the many chandeliers, spilling over the glossy marble floors. Paige took care of the tickets and then led the way to the orchestra section. "Oooh, good seats," she exclaimed, clapping her hands.

Maggie looked at the chairs covered in crimson velvet, the elaborately carved ceiling with its chandeliers and murals, the gold curtain masking the stage. It was gorgeous. As they were handed programs and moved into their row, she saw that John and David were already there.

They rose to their feet, John spilling sections of newspaper all over the floor. The headline read, "Battle of Britain: RAF on the Offensive!"

"Long time no see, Magster," David said as he took off his glasses to wipe them with his handkerchief. He put them back on and then leaned past John to take a closer look. "Quite the posh frock you have there. Mainbocher, 'thirty-seven?"

"Paige's, back of the closet."

"Well, you look divine. Doesn't she, John?"

"She looks all right at the office," John said, bending to pick up his newspapers. Ah, that was the charming John that Maggie knew. Although she had to admit that both he and David did look elegant in their black bow ties and dinner jackets. She opened her program: *At tonight's performance, the role of Odette/Odile will be played by Sarah Sanderson.* John had finished gathering up his fallen tabloid and was attempting to straighten the sections. The rustling of the papers was excruciatingly loud.

"Do you enjoy ballet, John?" she asked, as John gave up folding the papers and tucked the mess under his seat.

"I don't know much about it, really."

"You grew up in London. You must have seen a few."

"A few," he admitted. "Yes."

"I saw Martha Graham and her dancers in concert before I left," Maggie said, "which was beautiful, in an angular sort of way. Something you'd need to see more than once, though, to appreciate. And I went to New York with a group of friends years ago; we saw the American Ballet do some amazing dances set to the music of Igor Stravinsky. The choreographer was Russian, a man named Balanchine, I think. It wasn't what you'd expect at all—there were no tutus, no princes and princesses, just the music. What music looks like."

"So you like modern music, then? I'm an Igor man myself." Why was she not surprised John liked Stravinsky?

"Oh, I don't pretend to understand it. It's not as though you walk out humming it, the way you do with Tchaikovsky. But it was an evening I'll never forget. There was one ballet, *Apollo*—"

She blushed, realizing John was looking at her intently.

"Go on," he said.

"Well, it's just that—oh, look, it's starting."

The lights dimmed, and they applauded as the conductor came out and bowed, then raised his baton to cue the overture. As the music swirled around them, Maggie forgot the late nights at the office, the Dock, the daily trials of slimy slivers of soap and worn-down toothbrushes, of rationing and the dreaded National Loaf, and was transported to a fairy-tale realm where a prince could fall in love with a woman turned into a swan by a horrible curse.

Maggie knew Sarah was good, and worked so hard, but she felt a prickle of excitement when she took the stage. She was dressed in a white tutu, her hair pulled back with white feathers. But when she moved, she wasn't just a dancer in a beautiful costume, she was an enchanted swan. Her movements, light as thistledown, spoke of Odette's plight—her captivity, her straining for release from the spell. There was a yearning, a sense the prince might somehow be able to free her, and also a resignation, an admission of the sorcerer's power.

As they filed out of the theater to the lobby for intermission, Simon caught up with them. He must have come on his own, or perhaps Chuck or the twins had invited him. "You hated it," he said to Maggie and Paige, lighting a cigarette and inhaling.

"Hardly," Paige said, tossing her golden curls.

"I'm joking, Scarlett. I could see you adored it." Chuck and Nigel were sharing a romantic moment in the corner, while David and John were involved in an intense discussion with some men at the bar—politics, of course. Maggie saw the twins approach them. *The Ding-belles,* she thought as they approached John, with Annabelle leaning in so he could light her cigarette. *And look down her dress.*

Simon leaned in. "That's quite some frock you have on, Scarlett," he said to Paige, looking her up and down and brushing his hand down her back. Maggie stiffened. After the party, she just didn't like him. Didn't trust him.

Paige was her usual flirtatious self. "Why, thank you, kind sir," she said in her southern drawl.

"It's you. It suits you," he murmured. Suddenly, John was right beside them, his face tight and his eyes unreadable. He and Simon glared at each other for a moment. "Ah, yes, John. How did you like the dancing girls?" Simon asked.

"I think it's time to go back to our seats," he said evenly.

Simon winked at Paige. "Very well, then. I look forward to your official memo on the performance."

John didn't flinch.

"We'll continue after the show. What do you say, Paige?"

Maggie was trying to figure out John's sudden interest in Paige and Simon, when Annabelle sauntered up and took his arm possessively, with a high-pitched giggle.

"Why, I'd love to," Paige said, and Maggie was puzzled to see John's brow furrow. Was it because of Paige and Simon, or Annabelle?

Maggie thought Acts III and IV were even more wonderful. As Odile, the black swan and counterfeit version of the heroine Odette, the white swan, Sarah was magnificent. Perfection was the moment when she, as Odile, most obviously imitated Odette, rippling her arms and traveling on pointe in vulnerable, tender white-swan-like fashion toward the duped Prince Siegfried.

When the final curtain lowered, Paige and Maggie jumped to their feet, applauding madly, as Sarah took curtain call after curtain call.

"Let's go backstage," Maggie said as the crowd began to disperse. "We're friends of the prima ballerina, after all." She took Paige's arm. "Come on!" The group headed back to the stage door, which was unlocked and unguarded.

They wandered backstage, a dim, cavernous space with long racks of costumes and boxes full of broken rosin to keep toe shoes from slipping, looking for Sarah. The smell of sweat and cigarette smoke hung in the air. As stagehands put props away, they could overhear snippets of conversation: "Terrific show, darling!" "Oh, but did you see the Russian section?" "*Merde,* I fell off pointe, can you believe?"

They walked past throngs of sweaty half-dressed dancers in heavy stage makeup, towels and sweaters thrown over their shoulders, and asked where Sarah's dressing room was. Inside, they found Sarah, slight and glistening with sweat, wrapped in her red silk robe. She was gingerly pulling off false eyelashes.

"Hello, kittens!" she called, getting up to kiss everyone. She appeared almost ridiculously tiny offstage and so funny with her heavy white makeup and drooping eyelashes that Maggie had to laugh.

"So what did you think? Did you like it?" she asked.

"You have the best legs I've ever seen," Simon said. "I could have looked at them all night. Oh, wait, I did."

Sarah rolled her eyes. "Let me talk to the grown-ups. What did you think?"

"Exquisite," Paige said, checking her makeup in the mirror and touching up her nose with some of Sarah's powder.

"First-rate," Nigel added, gazing at Paige.

"I loved it," Maggie said, giving Sarah a kiss on the cheek. "You were amazing!"

"You were like moonlight," John said. Maggie looked at him, surprised. His comment was beautiful; she never realized he had a poetic streak.

"Sweet Johnny, I'm sure you say that to all the swans. And now I, for one, would like to celebrate!" she continued, taking off her makeup.

"The only place to celebrate the newest Tchaikovsky Swan Queen is the bar at the Langham hotel, of course," David said. "Vodka for everyone!"

"Ooooh," Annabelle and Clarabelle cooed together. "We just *love* the Langham!"

"Right-o," Simon added. "Russian vodka—what are we waiting for?"

They entered the Langham hotel through tall columns and porticos and proceeded into the lobby, the shining floor designed in circles of black, green, burgundy, and white marble.

"Very *Grand Hotel*," Paige said, savoring the elegance.

"Very Victoria Train Station," Simon stage-whispered back, obviously not impressed.

Annabelle had slipped her arm through John's, while Clarabelle walked with David. Maggie's feelings for the twins usually alternated between exasperation and tolerance, but she was suddenly extremely annoyed with them.

The group made its way through the lobby to the bar, dark and smoky, with mahogany paneling and maroon leather chairs, and filled with the sound of clinking glasses and high-pitched girlish laughter. They all took seats around a long table—John, Annabelle, Sarah, Nigel, and Chuck on one side, and Maggie, Simon, Clarabelle, David, and Paige on the other. The waiter approached. "We'll have a few bottles of champagne," David said, waving down the length of the table. "While the British pound is still worth something."

"And I'd like a Romeo y Julieta cigar," Simon said. "That's what the P.M. smokes, isn't it, Red?" he said to Maggie. "Should make you feel at home."

The waiter went to the humidor at the corner of the bar to pick out Simon's cigar, then brought it back to the table, where there was an elaborate ritual of cutting the ends and lighting it. Finally, taking a long puff, Simon leaned back, satisfied, jutting out his chin in an all-too-familiar pose.

The champagne was opened and set in a silver bucket

at David's right elbow, along with widemouthed coupes etched with flowers. David shooed the waiter away, then filled each glass. "Champagne," he proclaimed, standing, "the perfect drink to toast Miss Sarah Sanderson, prima ballerina assoluta." He bowed his head.

"To Sarah," they all chimed in, clinking glasses. "Cheers!"

After the toast, Sarah spied Dimitri at the bar and rose to join some of her fellow dancers; apparently, the bar was quite the gathering place for homesick Eastern Europeans. She took David along with her.

"More drinks, then?" Simon said, refilling Maggie's glass and then Paige's, then laying his hand on Paige's silk-clad thigh under the table. Just as Maggie was about to comment, she caught a glimpse of Annabelle whispering something in John's ear and changed her mind. After all, Paige was a grown woman—and he'd probably been practicing the move for years.

As Maggie looked down the table, she saw that Chuck was a bit tipsy; she and Nigel were rubbing noses. The conversation at their end had turned to Edward and Mrs. Simpson.

"But it's just so *romantic*!" Paige thumped the table with her dainty fist.

"Well, of course, Scarlett; you're American," Simon said. "You don't realize the monarchy has nothing to do with the princes and princesses of fairy tales."

"Oh, but what was it he said after he gave up the throne?" Paige closed her eyes to think. "That he couldn't go on as King without—what?"

" '—the help and support of the woman I love,' " John finished. *Who knew he had such a romantic side?* Maggie thought, finishing her glass of champagne and letting David pour her another. *Or at least a good memory. It must be remarkable champagne.*

As the singer started a slow rendition of "I Get Along

Without You Very Well," Annabelle turned to John. "I *adore* this song," she cooed, jumping to her feet. "You simply *must* dance with me. Come on," she entreated, grabbing his hand and pulling him to his feet before he had a chance to refuse.

*For such a skinny little thing, she's certainly pushy,* Maggie thought through the golden haze of champagne bubbles.

As they got up to dance, Maggie's eyes followed them. Simon pounced. "Dance with me, Scarlett?"

Paige smiled. "Of course."

Maggie saw Simon and Paige dance together, then leave the dance floor to go—where? Sarah was suddenly at Maggie's side. "We have to stop them," she said, her face pale.

"Stop them?" Maggie said, surprised. "You mean . . . But surely Paige deserves to have some . . . fun. It's not any of our business, after all." Maggie was taken aback. Sarah always seemed so bohemian—why this sudden puritanical streak?

"I—I can't say. But I need to talk to her."

Maggie looked at Sarah's face. She was dead serious. "All right, then—let's go."

"Would you like to see Wallie Simpson's suite?" Simon said to Paige. He reached into his pocket and pulled out a set of keys. "The concierge is a good friend of mine," he said, his fingers stroking her back. "Come on, what do you say?"

"Why, yes, Simon," she said, looking up at him through her eyelashes. "I'd love to see it. It's a place of . . . historical interest, after all." She strolled with Simon to the lobby, where they took an elevator with intricate inlaid wooden panels upstairs.

"Here we are," he said, walking in as though he owned the place. "The infamous Mrs. Simpson Suite."

The walls were an ivory-colored watered silk, the drapes a heavy blue-and-gold brocade, which nearly hid the blackout curtains. A powder-blue silk sofa was flanked by two end tables, topped by Chinese vases.

"It's not as though Edward and Mrs. Simpson were the only lovers at the hotel," Simon continued, the scent of alcohol on his breath. "Oscar Wilde brought any number of young lads here. They say Antonín Dvořák stayed here regularly with his grown-up daughter—if you know what I mean." He gave a chuckle. "But I tell you, we Brits are a lot less prim and proper than you Americans seem to think."

Paige smiled grimly; after years in London, she was under no illusions of English politesse.

He swept open a door. "And here, my dear, is the bedroom," he murmured, putting his arm around Paige and turning her toward him.

Without warning, there was a loud knock on the suite's door. "Oh, damn it all to hell," he said. As he bent to try to kiss Paige again, there was another knock, followed by loud and steady pounding.

"Jesus Christ," he said, going to the door and opening it.

"You?" he exclaimed when he saw Sarah and Maggie, his face reddening.

Sarah quickly walked over to Paige. "Are you all right?" she asked.

"I'm fine," Paige said, looking confused.

"Paige, there's something you should know," Sarah continued evenly.

"Why don't you two"—Simon spluttered—"*meddling bitches* mind your own goddamned bloody business!"

And then the air-raid siren began its low moan of warning.

The four looked at one another and froze.

The forlorn tone of the siren rang out again, and they heard scrambling and doors slamming as people evacuated their rooms.

"There's a bomb shelter in the basement," Sarah said. Without another word, they all filed out of the room and down the stairs.

Down in the basement, it looked as if the party had simply moved. People had brought their bottles and glasses with them, and the hotel staff had set up groups of tables and folding chairs. The candlelight from long wax tapers lent the proceedings a falsely festive air. A large family, sleepy-eyed and in their pajamas, were applauded as they made their appearance.

Maggie spied Chuck, Nigel, David, and the twins huddled at a table in the corner and led the way over to them. Maggie noticed John wasn't with them.

"There you are! We were wondering what happened to you," Chuck said, pulling Maggie down next to her and Nigel.

"No matter how many times we go through this, it's still just horrible," David said, sighing. "More champagne?"

Maggie and Sarah looked to Simon, but he'd noticed a man in the throng. He went to meet him, and they shook hands with vigor, obviously old friends. Paige's face was inscrutable.

"John went to Saint Paul's—he's one of the Watch, you know," David said as Maggie observed Paige's face, looking after him. "Helps keep the damn cathedral from burning down."

With a tap on the shoulder, Sarah pulled Paige and Maggie aside. As they walked to a small empty table, she said, "Paige, love, I know Simon's charming and handsome—but he's just not good enough for you. He doesn't think much of women. Sure, he's fun to flirt with. But believe me, he's like a child in a toy store, always wanting the newest and shiniest bauble. You can do better. Believe me, I know." She gazed in Simon's direction, her face etched with regret.

"You—and Simon?" Paige asked.

"Long time ago." She laughed. The sound was bitter and hard. "Didn't quite work out." She laid a hand on Paige's arm. "Look, he only wants what he can't have. And once it's done, he's on to the next conquest." She took a sharp intake of breath. "When I was with Simon, we—I—" She dropped her eyes. "He raped me, and I got pregnant. I was so ashamed, somehow got it in my head that it was all my fault. When he heard through the grapevine, he gave me some money and told me to take care of it."

*Sarah? Simon?* Maggie thought, finally putting the pieces together. *Simon's a rapist?*

"I knew I couldn't support a baby on my own. I'd ruin my body and my career. If I came forward and accused him of rape, no one would believe me—it would be my word against his. And as an unwed mother, I'd be a leper. I don't even know if my mum, my own mum, would have forgiven me if she knew. Going home to Liverpool was out of the question. So I took the money and did what I had to do." Sarah raised her head, and her eyes challenged Paige and Maggie to pity her.

Maggie didn't. "That must have been an incredibly hard decision."

"What made it better was that I had friends who stood by me. David and John. They found a doctor—a good one, not one of these back-alley butchers. He had an office in Knightsbridge. They took time off work to go with me. Went with me to the appointment, helped me home afterward, got me hot soup and fresh flowers. Let me cry. They both wanted to kill Simon, but I managed to talk them out of it."

"Ah," said Maggie. She looked at Sarah. Above the red rose in her décolletage, her shoulders were narrow, her collarbones sharp and fragile.

"Oh, Sarah," Paige said. "I had no idea. I'm so sorry—"

"Pssh, I'm fine," she said, brushing off any concern. "I don't hate him; he's not a monster. But I wouldn't do that again. And I wouldn't want to see any of my friends go down that road, either." Sarah sighed. "They were close before, at university, but I don't think John ever forgave him."

"Well, thank you, Sarah," Paige said.

Maggie put her arms around Paige and Sarah, hearing the muffled sounds of bombing overhead. She realized that slowly but surely, she was getting used to the fact that people simply weren't like numbers. Just when you thought you had an answer, they'd go and surprise you all over again.

# FIFTEEN

THE NEXT DAY in the underground typists' office, Maggie sorted through all the memos on her desk stamped *Action This Day* to give to the P.M. when he awoke from his midday nap.

Nelson jumped onto her desk, surprising her. The papers slid through her hands and landed on the floor in a mess. "Oh, Nelson, for goodness' sake . . ." she muttered, getting down on her hands and knees on the dusty brown linoleum to gather them. She noticed a fresh run in her stocking. *Perfect. Just perfect.*

Nelson jumped down and gazed at Maggie intently with large, green eyes from under Mrs. Tinsley's desk.

"Careful, Nelson," Maggie said to him, cleaning up the papers. "Not everyone likes cats as much as Miss Stewart and I do. Don't let the Tinzer catch you here." The Churchills' pets roamed the offices with impunity. While everyone tolerated them, some, like Mrs. Tinsley, weren't pleased.

A few of the sections had flipped open. There was the crossword-puzzle page, with the ubiquitous clothing adverts. Demure day dresses with silk flowers at the neck, straw hats with ribbons, and strappy shoes. *Good Lord, is that what we're going to be wearing? If we have enough rations to spare, that is. "Make do and mend" is more like it,* she thought, contemplating her own brown cotton dress with the white piping. It was old and not in the least fashionable, but it was relatively clean and freshly pressed.

Maggie looked at the advert, then looked again, closer this time. She blinked. Those weren't stitches—at least, they weren't just stitches. Those tiny little thread marks on the hems of the skirts were dots and dashes. Or were they?

*Code?*

*No, of course not. That would be insane.*

She closed the section and pushed it away.

Murphy went back to his boardinghouse to change into his priest's robes once again. Granted, they were the robes of a Catholic priest, not Anglican, but he doubted anyone would notice.

He made his way to St. Paul's Cathedral. "Good afternoon, Father," two matronly women said as they passed him on the marble stairs leading up to the magnificent Baroque structure. Wren's immense classical dome, with its golden cross, was held aloft by two tiers of double Corinthian columns, set between two Renaissance-inspired towers.

He tipped his hat and gave a charming grin. "Good afternoon, ladies."

The very size of the cathedral was always a shock. He made his way down the soaring space of the nave, padding softly over the black-and-white diamond-shaped marble tiles. Most of the windows had been boarded up for safety during bombings, leaving the atmosphere dimmer, softer, and cooler.

He walked past the elaborately carved choir benches, past the elevated murals of saints and prophets, beneath gold, bronze, and indigo Byzantine-style mosaics of angels of the dome, and beyond the enormous Gibbons organ, to the crypts' entrance.

Checking carefully that he wasn't being watched, he went down a flight of steep and dark stairs, down and down, until he reached a large hallway. He took a series of turns until he found himself in a small room, dank and dimly lit. There, he pulled out a golden watch from a deep pocket.

It was the last component of the bomb he had so assiduously built and smuggled into St. Paul's piece by piece underneath his robes. Potassium chloride, sulfuric acid, wires, gelignite, detonator . . . It was all in place now.

As he wired in the watch, which would serve as the bomb's timer, he hummed to himself, an old Irish ditty his grandmother used to sing.

> *"Never till the latest day shall the memory pass*
>    *away,*
> *Of the gallant lives thus given for our land;*
> *But on the cause must go, amidst joy and weal and*
>    *woe,*
> *Till we make our Isle a nation free and grand.*
> *'God save Ireland!' said the heroes;*
> *'God save Ireland' said they all.*
> *Whether on the scaffold high*
> *Or the battlefield we die,*
> *Oh, what matter when for Erin dear we fall!"*

*Gran, you'd be so proud,* he thought, surveying his work. *And using Da's watch, too—that's the perfect touch.*

Before he could stop it, his thoughts returned to the night that the British had burned down his house, killing his mother. He'd hidden in the shed and finally crept out and saw the Black and Tans beating his father to the ground, then giving his lifeless form another savage kick before divesting him of his wedding ring and pocket watch.

As he hid behind the corner of the house to observe them go, eyes blank with shock, he heard one of the men. "Look, there's a little one!"

The other men looked, ready for another fight. "Should we get him?" one asked, not eager to leave any witnesses behind.

"Nah, he's not worth it, after all," the first man said. "Here, lad. Catch!" And he threw the pocket watch through the air.

Without thinking, Murphy's hand reached up into the air, and he caught it before hitting the dirt path, hard. The watch was solid and warm in his small hand.

"Something to remember your dear dad by," the man said, cackling.

His companions laughed. "And us, too!" one shouted as they made their way off into the darkness.

Looping the last green, white, and orange wires around the pocket watch, he thought, *This is for you, Da,* and then he gave the screw a final twist.

The day went on—there were letters to write, dictation to take, filing to do. But still Maggie couldn't shake the unsettled feeling that she had almost seen something. As though out of the corner of her eye.

*Could it be?* she thought, reaching for the newspaper again.

*No.*

*No, no, no.*

Her hands found the paper, flipping it open again to the page with the advert. She couldn't take her eyes from the stitching, the dots and dashes.

Nelson meowed, loud and long, and came over to her. He rubbed against her ankles, purring.

She ran her hands through her hair. "Nelson, quiet! I'm trying to think."

Abwehr was the German intelligence agency—the counterpart to MI-5 and MI-6. It had three distinct types of spies operating in Britain. The first, known as the S-Chain, consisted of agents who entered the country with false British identities and engaged in spying. R-Chain agents were third-country nationals—neither British nor German—who entered Britain legally, collected intelligence, and reported their findings back to Hamburg or Berlin. Then there were the V-Chain agents—sleeper agents who melted seamlessly into English life, waiting to be contacted and activated.

Malcolm Pierce had been waiting for years.

In the bedroom of his apartment, he double-checked to make sure his blackout curtains were completely closed. Then he locked the bedroom door.

To the casual observer, the bedroom looked unremarkable. There was striped green paper on the walls, a mahogany four-poster bed, and gold-framed paintings of foxes and hounds. There were no personal mementos or photographs. A large bay window provided an excellent lookout onto the street below. And in the closet, hidden underneath piles and piles of merino and cashmere sweaters wrapped in tissue, was a suitcase radio.

Pierce had been living in London under an assumed name for almost a decade, but he still found himself longing for the strong black coffee and *baumkuchen* of his childhood. He shook off the thought and took down the suitcase, placing it next to the window for optimal reception. He opened the lid and switched it on.

Every week, on Monday nights at ten, he switched on the radio and listened for fifteen minutes. If the higher-ups in Berlin had orders for him, that's how they'd contact him.

Every Monday night for ten years he'd opened his suitcase by the window and listened. Every Monday night he had pen, paper, and codebook ready, just in case. And nearly every Monday night, all he'd heard was this empty hiss of the airwaves. The communiqués he did receive were always short and sporadic.

Tonight, however, would be different. The message had been placed in the newspaper advert. Claire had clipped it and sent it to the contact in Norway, who'd posted it on to Berlin. And tonight he would receive his orders.

After what seemed like an interminable wait, the radio sputtered to life.

The operator in Hamburg typed out code, fast and staccato. Pierce wrote it down, then asked the operator to repeat the message, standard protocol. She did, and he acknowledged and signed off.

It took Pierce several more minutes with the codebook to decode the message.

When he did, he held it in shaking hands and stared at it in incredulity and wonder.

*Bedienhandlung die Zuversicht.*

Translated, it read: Execute Operation Hope.

"John?"

John looked up from the pool of light from his green-glass banker's lamp, which illuminated the neat stack of papers on his wooden desk in the private secretaries' underground office.

There was a large black-and-white sign admonishing *Quiet, please,* propped up against a metal pipe. Next to it hung a gas mask. David's desk, on the other side of the room, was a mess, covered with a paper proclaiming in large block-print letters, *For the love of GOD and COUNTRY, do NOT TOUCH.* A clock with a white face and black Roman numerals ticked off the seconds loudly, while a tiny metal fan recirculated the stale, warm air.

"Yes?" he said, his angular face breaking into a smile.

Maggie looked down at the scrap of newspaper in her hand, then back at John's desk. He had a cubby with shelves marked *The Prime Minister, Air Ministry, Secret, Most Secret,* and *The King.*

She looked back down at the clipping in her hand, ink coming off on her fingers. *A women's fashion advertisement, no less. It's preposterous,* she thought. She could just picture Snodgrass's reaction.

"Maggie?"

"Nothing," she said. "Just . . ."

"Yes?"

She turned back around and sighed. She trusted John—she did. He'd stuck up for her in front of Snodgrass, after all. She walked a few steps forward and handed him the newspaper clipping.

John's eyebrows drew together. He had to remind himself to breathe naturally with her so close. "Are ladies' skirts shorter this year?"

"No, no," Maggie said impatiently. "Look at it. Really look."

"I don't—"

"Look!"

John did. "I see . . . I see a newspaper clipping. It's a clipping of an advertisement for ladies' fashion." He looked closer. "I see . . . drawings of women in dresses and hats."

"Ah!" Maggie said. "You're getting closer now. Look more closely at those lines."

John squinted. "The drawings are comprised of lines. Lines and crosshatching. And dots—"

"Yes!" *Ding, ding, ding! A Kewpie doll for the private secretary!*

John shrugged. "It looks like any other newspaper advert."

"But—don't you see? Dots and dashes." *Do I have to hit him over the head with it?* "It could be code!"

John gave a heavy sigh. "Look, Maggie, I appreciate your enthusiasm, I do. And I know you've been taking notes for the Boss and Mr. Frain, so it's no wonder you've got spies on your mind. But I think this is a bit of a reach."

Maggie set her jaw. "I'll have you know, steganography is the practice of writing code in plain sight. The word comes from the Greek for 'concealed writing.' The first recorded example of its use is Herodotus in 440 B.C., when Demaratus sent a warning about a proposed attack on Greece by writing it directly on the wooden back of a wax tablet before applying the beeswax."

"Yes, but—"

"And Herodotus tells us about a warning about a Persian invasion of Greece tattooed on the head of a slave. The hair grew in so no one could see it—and then the Greeks got the message when they shaved the slave's head."

"Maggie, I—"

"There's a grand historic tradition of messages hidden in ordinary places," she said in clipped tones. "So you won't mind if I have a go?"

"Suit yourself," John said with an inscrutable look.

"I'll need a Morse-code book."

John got up, pulled one down from the shelf, and handed it to her.

She turned on her heel to leave.

"Maggie," he called after her, gently, "why don't you leave it here with me? I'll take a look and then show it to Snodgrass."

"No, no. I'll keep it," she shot back at him over her shoulder. "Thanks, anyway."

"Maggie!" he called after her. She stopped and turned. "There's a lecture tonight at LSE. Anthony Eden's speaking. Tonight at seven. The Peacock Theatre on Portugal Street."

"So?" Maggie said, still annoyed.

"Meet me there. We can talk."

# SIXTEEN

MAGGIE WAS LATE.

She ran through the cold mist for the Regent Street bus, getting to LSE after seven. John was waiting in the chilly, smoke-filled lobby, leaning against a magnolia-painted Ionic column, hands stuffed in his jacket pockets.

"Ah," he said, his angular face softening for a moment. "There you are." He looked tired and wan; his eyes had dark circles.

"Hello, John," she said. *Well, at least the lecture's starting—we don't have to talk anymore.* "Then shall we go in?"

He gave a courtly bow. "After you."

They found two seats together in the back of the crowded auditorium filled with chattering students who called to one another, smelling of smoke and wet wool, wrapped in their purple-and-yellow-striped school scarves. Maggie felt a sharp pang as she looked around at them all. *This is where I might have studied,* she thought. *At least Aunt Edith would approve of the evening's outing. And it's where my father once taught, after all.*

They sat together in what was growing to be an uncomfortable silence.

The lights in the auditorium soon dimmed, and

Anthony Eden walked onto the stage. Maggie recognized him from the office, medium build, with a thick black mustache, black eyes, and a square jaw. As his speech on the importance of keeping up morals while under attack came to an end, she shrugged back into her light coat.

John asked, "There's a nice café nearby. Er, would you like to get a cup of coffee?"

"Are we going to discuss—that matter?"

"Of course."

At the café they sat on rickety wooden chairs. John leaned down and put a matchbook under the marble-topped table to steady it. Maggie glanced around. The walls were papered with faded pink roses and blue hydrangea, and the waitresses looked tired and harried. Maggie and John ordered two cups of coffee.

Maggie stirred a splash of what was passing for milk into the thick, red ceramic mug to make the watery brown water drinkable. "Brownian motion," she said, warming her hands on the cup. "When you stir in the milk it swirls around and disperses, but if you stir backward, it will never come together again. You can't stir things apart."

"God's a Newtonian, then?"

"I believe in free will, actually."

"But you're a mathematician!"

"They're not mutually exclusive concepts." She took a sip. "I really do miss American coffee."

He looked wounded. "British coffee's good."

"No, it's not. Come on, you're all so particular about your tea. Surely you could take the same care with coffee. It's delicious when it's done right—all dark and rich."

He drew himself up. "Well, I'm sorry it's not to your liking. There's a war on, you know."

"It's fine, John." They sat in strained silence for a while. *Obviously, this was a terrible idea.*

"You know, Americans can't make proper tea."

*Oh, for God's sake.* She stared, incredulous.

He looked vaguely flustered. "I just meant that the coffee . . ." Then, off her look, "This isn't about coffee, it's that you can't go around criticizing other countries when you're a guest there. Here."

"John," Maggie said. "Taste the coffee. I mean, really. It's terrible. This is not about national pride. Bad coffee is bad coffee is bad coffee. Besides, not only am I a citizen, but I'm a homeowner. And a taxpayer. And I work for the *Prime Minister.*"

"Oh, forget it." He took a big gulp of the muck and tried not to grimace. "So what did you think of Eden's speech?"

*All right, let's try again.* "Interesting. But I have to admit I was still thinking about the . . . puzzle."

His dark brows drew together.

She lowered her voice. "The code. You know, the one in the advert? I've been working on it all afternoon."

"Right. And?"

She sighed. "And . . . well . . . nothing. Nothing yet, that is."

"Maggie—do you actually think there's a possibility . . ."

"Yes?"

"A possibility . . . well, that you're seeing things that aren't there? After all, there are censors—people trained to pick up that kind of information."

"Oh, you mean the Oxbridge men?" she snorted. Then, "Look, I'm working on my own time, so I don't see what business it is of yours."

There was a long silence, and Maggie checked her watch. "Do you need to get back to the office?" she asked, finishing the last of her coffee and blotting her lips with the napkin, leaving a faint red kiss. "Or do you have Saint Paul's Watch tonight?"

"No. I mean . . ." John took a deep breath. "Maggie, I—" There was an odd gesture, a stiffened shoulder and then the rolling of one hand into the other.

*Oh, dear Lord.* She found herself blushing furiously. "Is this your idea of a *date*?"

John looked down into his coffee.

"I don't even see why you'd want to go on a date with someone like me, anyway," she said. "You don't even take me seriously when I bring up the possibility of there being—" She lowered her voice. "You don't take me seriously about anything."

"I do too take you seriously. I said I'd look into it and pass it on to Snodgrass. I lent you the codebook, for God's sake. You're the one who didn't leave the clipping with me."

"You thought I was getting carried away because I'm sitting in on meetings with Frain. Just because you're not in on it . . . "

Maggie rose as majestically as she could manage, shrugged on her coat, grabbed her pocketbook, and started for the door.

"That's not it at all," he said, getting up. He gave a few coins to the waitress and followed.

Maggie would have walked faster, but her skirt was too tight around the knees. *Stupid skirt.* "And if you followed your seriously misguided logic to its inevitable conclusion," she snapped, tromping through mud puddles to the bus stop, shrouded in the growing darkness of the London blackout, "you'd see anyone with eyes and a brain can break codes. Not just spoiled, rich Oxford graduates who've never actually had to work for anything a day in their lives!"

"Is that how you see me?" John said, keeping pace with her easily with his long legs. The evening traffic gave them just enough light to navigate. "Spoiled and rich?" He shook his head. "Typical."

Having reached the bus stop, Maggie turned to face him, hands on her hips. "Well, aren't you? You and David. And Snodgrass. And Frain, for that matter. You're all upper-class men who've had every advantage, every door opened for you. It's no wonder you want to preserve the system that created you."

In the dim light from the traffic, John's face looked flushed. The evening was now a complete and utter disaster. To top it off, it was beginning to rain again. Big, cold drops splashed on them, but it didn't stop them from glaring at each other.

Just then, the red bus pulled up beside them, its shuttered headlights cutting through the gloom, windshield wipers whispering softly.

"This has been the most disagreeable evening ever," Maggie said in her best Aunt Edith tone, as she waited in line behind an older man to board. She knew she was being petulant and childish, and she didn't care.

John was silent.

Without warning, the air-raid siren began its keening wail. Maggie's stomach lurched into a fast descent, and instinctively John grasped her arm. They looked at each other, argument forgotten. Around them, people scrambled for shelter.

"Let's go back to the café," she said. "There's bound to be a basement."

"Lead the way."

They made their way through the thick darkness as quickly as they could as the drone of planes grew louder. There must have been hundreds of them circling overhead in formation. Finally, finally, they made it back to the café.

"Come on, ducks—in you go," said the waitress, recognizing them from earlier, even with wet hair. "Door in the back on the right goes down to the basement." They ran through the shop to the door and then down the tiny, narrow stairs.

Then the bombs began to drop.

They could hear the screams of the bombs as they came down and feel the vibrations as each one hit nearby. Maggie worried that the building above would collapse, falling in on the basement. *Is there a bomb up there with our names on it?*

Down in the damp-smelling cellar, people had brought their cups and saucers with them, and the staff was moving the furniture. Thin yellow beams of light from various people's flashlights lent the proceedings a spooky, haunted air.

John and Maggie sat down on a bench against the wall. An elegant older man in a cravat and monocle took out a small silver flask from his coat pocket and held it out to Maggie. "Want some, darling? Gin. In case of emergencies."

"Don't mind if I do," she said, and the man passed her the bottle. She unscrewed the cap and took a swig. It didn't help. John shook his head no, so she gave it back to the man. "Thanks," she said, trying to keep her tone light.

"You're welcome, luv," he said, taking a long pull. "I think it's going to be a long night."

The sounds of the bombs and their jolts on impact were getting stronger. They could now smell the smoke from above seeping in through the closed doors and windows, harsh and pungent, as the bombs continued their death drops.

"They're getting closer," she whispered, and John put his arm around her. Their thighs and knees were pressed together so tightly that Maggie could feel his bones and muscles beneath his wool trousers. She could feel his warmth and smell his neck.

Bombs pounded down. They could only imagine the horror and the damage. Maggie squeezed her eyes shut and wondered what it felt like to be dying on this damp night. *Would it be quick? Oh, please, God, just let it be quick.*

For what felt like days they sat there, pressed together, the impact from the bombs bruising their bones. *We're going to be stiff and sore tomorrow,* Maggie thought, then caught herself. *If there even is a tomorrow.* For distraction, she tried making patterns with numbers, starting with the Fibonacci series, as far as she could go.

Far more comforting was John's arm around her shoulders.

There was a wild crash, as if the sun itself had exploded. Maggie clapped her hands over her ears as her heart threatened to escape her chest. John must have sensed what was happening, for he threw her down on the floor, covering her body with his.

As the blast hit the building above with a deafening roar, the room filled with thick clouds of dust. All of the air seemed to have been sucked out of the room. Maggie choked and heard people around her coughing and retching.

She suddenly realized that John was lying on top of her, his cheek against hers, his breath ragged in her ear, their hearts pounding together.

John struggled to speak. "Are you all right?" he said, his body pressing against hers.

"I'm fine," she said, voice shaking. Then, realizing the incongruity of their position and their conversation, she broke into a smile. "And you?"

"Fine," he said, stroking her hair and looking down at her. "Just fine."

Without warning, the bombing let up, like a storm that had passed. They heard the noise from the planes become more distant and then, finally, disappear. They waited, and waited, and waited—and then came the all-clear siren. Awkwardly, John rolled off Maggie, and they edged away from each other, getting to their feet and shaking off the dust and debris.

They stumbled from the café into the darkness of the street. There was thick, black, bitter-smelling smoke everywhere. Their eyes watered and stung. As they made their way down the street, they could hear the drone of fire-engine sirens wailing and the tinkle of broken glass being swept from the street by the ARP workers. The café seemed all right, although many of the windows had broken and there was broken glass scattered over the front walkway. In the crimson glow of the fire, the shards sparkled like crushed diamonds. Maggie mused how pretty they looked, even as she realized the inanity of the thought. *Broken glass. Pretty.*

The brick house across from them had been hit; an orange-and-blue fire was tearing through it. Papers, books, pillows, and children's toys littered the street, blown from the house by the impact of the blast. A pink-satin dancing shoe, somehow still pale and pristine, had landed right in the middle of the road. At least the family was all right. The five of them—mother, father, a gangly teenage girl, and small twin boys—huddled together in their nightclothes, watching their home burn.

John approached them. "What can I do?" he said.

The father shrugged. "Not much to do right now. Fire department should be here soon."

"If you need a place to stay—"

"Thank you," the father said. "But Mother and Father live nearby. They'll be happy to take us in."

The wife rolled her eyes in mock horror and gave a wan smile. "Don't know what's worse—the Blitz or the prospect of living with my in-laws."

The man gave her a kiss on the cheek. "It'll be fine, darling."

John turned back to Maggie. "Look, about earlier—"

"Don't even think about it. I was awful."

"Not at all." Then, "May I at least walk you home?"

Maggie looked around, at the fires and the bombed-out buildings. "Thank you," she said, taking his offered arm and holding it tightly. "I'd appreciate that."

As they made their way up Regent Street in the grayish early-morning gloom, the air was pungent with smoke. It had been a heavy night of bombing, to be sure; the street was full of broken glass and debris. A dead sparrow, wings spread, lay in the middle of the road. As they walked up Portland Place, Maggie slowly began to realize that while she'd been at LSE, her own neighborhood had been hard-hit.

She began to walk faster, breaking away from John. Her hands became icy, and she could hear the blood rush in her head. She was nearly running now, heart in her throat. *All right, just calm down. It's fine, it's fine, there's no reason to—*

Sarah and Chuck were sitting on the front steps of the house, still as statues. The twins were a stair beneath, their arms around each other, faces hidden. At the sound of footsteps, they all lifted their heads. As soon as Maggie saw their tearstained faces, she knew.

Paige was dead.

# SEVENTEEN

"SHE WAS DRIVING back to the base when the car must have overturned in the raid," Chuck said.

They sat together on the steps, numbly watching the sky turn a milky gray at the horizon, John sitting on a stair below. "The gas tank must have ignited—" Sarah's eyes overflowed again. "Oh, hell."

With shaking fingers, Chuck rummaged through her handbag and pulled out her battered cigarette case. She pulled one out and tried to light it, but her hands were shaking so badly that she couldn't. John took the lighter and cigarette gently from her hands. He rolled the wheel slowly down on the flint. A blue-and-orange flame erupted, and he held the cigarette tip in it and inhaled. When it was lit, he returned it, and the lighter, to Chuck.

"Thanks," she said, taking a deep drag.

"When?" Maggie asked.

"Early tonight," Annabelle said. "Police came by around midnight."

"It was an accident?" John asked.

"An accident," Clarabelle said.

Sarah blew her nose. "The cop said that it looked like she must have hit a fallen tree. Must have hit it and flipped." She drew in a ragged breath. "The car flipped." She couldn't speak for a moment. "Then it caught on fire."

Maggie tried not to picture a car engulfed in flames, Paige inside, trying to get out.

"I know," Chuck said, as if reading her thoughts. Her usually booming voice was uncharacteristically small and tight.

They all sat on the steps in silence for a long time. The morning faded in and out as time stopped and started in bursts.

*Paige is dead*, Maggie thought over and over again. It just wasn't sinking in.

Paige would come walking up the street or waltz through the door at any minute, scolding them for being late, asking about their day, showing off her newly made-over dress. Paige giggling over tea in the kitchen, Paige dancing, Paige in Latin class, at the dining hall at Claflin.

It was impossible that she was dead.

"Her mother—"

"Said we'd call her. We just couldn't, though," Annabelle said, looking over at Chuck, who shook her head.

"Besides, it's only, what, one in the morning in Virginia?" Clarabelle added.

"We can call her in a few hours," Maggie said. "Let her sleep. It's going to be the last night of rest she'll have for a while."

"Yeah." Chuck took a long drag on her cigarette. Maggie struggled to piece together practical details.

"What about her body?" John asked.

Sarah blinked. Hard. "No body. Nothing recovered."

"Oh my God," Maggie said. "Oh, please, no."

"Maggie . . ." John said, sitting down on the step beside her.

But it was true: Paige was gone. And there was nothing left of her. And nothing for the three of them to do except wait for dawn in Virginia to make the phone call.

Just before they left for the service, Maggie stood at the doorway of Paige's room. They'd packed all of her belongings in a domed wooden steamer trunk to send back to her mother in Virginia. She told the girls they could keep what they wanted. Maggie had decided to keep Paige's heavy, square glass bottle of Joy with the golden cap, nearly empty. Just a whiff of the sweet rose-and-jasmine fragrance would conjure up memories. Sarah kept one of Paige's blue-satin hair ribbons.

"Come on, Maggie." She could hear Sarah calling her from the front hall as well as the twins' subdued murmurings. It was time to go.

"Coming," she called. Chuck looked in. "Chuck!" Maggie exclaimed, taking in her friend's changed appearance. "You're—you're wearing a *dress*. And *lipstick*."

"Well," Chuck said, smoothing down the skirt with gloved hands, "Paige would've liked it, now, wouldn't she?" Paige was always trying to get Chuck to wear skirts and dresses and lipstick and perfume. All of the things she thought were life's necessities.

"Yes. Yes, she would." And when Maggie left, she closed the door softly.

The memorial was held in a small, dimly lit church in the neighborhood. The altar was decorated with fall flowers: late-blooming red roses, yellow-and-white chrysanthemums, bittersweet.

In the long, dark pews, they stood with their heads bowed. Maggie bit the inside of her lower lip until it bled, and thought about the possibilities for code in the ad, in a desperate attempt not to scream. Glancing around, she could see everyone was beaten down by grief. *When did we all start to look so old?*

Maggie glanced at John, standing so stiffly upright in his best black suit, wishing she could reach out and take his hand. The fine lines around his eyes were more pronounced, and his face was even more angular, if possible. As the priest led them in prayer, he swayed the slightest bit.

It was time. It took forever for Maggie to reach the podium, her footsteps an endless series of clicks on the hard, unforgiving floor.

"I—I decided to read a poem by Henry Scott Holland." Her voice was uneven, and she took a breath and tried to steady it. "I think Paige would have liked this. And I think she would want us to think of her in this way.

> *"Death is nothing at all,*
> *I have only slipped into the next room*
> *I am I and you are you*
> *Whatever we were to each other,*
> *That we are still.*
> *Call me by my old familiar name,*
> *Speak to me in the easy way you always used*
> *Put no difference into your tone,*
> *Wear no forced air of solemnity or sorrow*
> *Laugh as we always laughed*
> *At the little jokes we enjoyed together.*
> *Play, smile, think of me, pray for me.*
> *Let my name be ever the household word that it*
>     *always was,*
> *Let it be spoken without effort,*
> *Without the ghost of a shadow on it.*
> *Life means all that it ever meant.*
> *It is the same as it ever was,*
> *There is absolute unbroken continuity.*

*Why should I be out of mind*
*Because I am out of sight?*
*I am waiting for you, for an interval,*
*Somewhere very near,*
*Just around the corner.*
*All is well."*

When Maggie returned to her seat, Sarah put an arm around her and Chuck gave her a hard squeeze. The twins both reached over to pat her hand. She bent her head. Hot tears ran down her cheeks, dripping on the black-marble tiles. Sarah handed Maggie her embroidered handkerchief, and she took it, wiping her face and stifling her sobs, concentrating on picking lint off her skirt.

A thread hung from the bottom, and she pulled at it, finding a grim satisfaction in watching the stitching begin to unravel. She knew her real mourning would be saved for when she was alone, with the door closed, running water in the tub to drown out the noise. She was afraid if she let her emotions go in the polished marble silence, there would be no way to go on, this day or any other.

Afterward, they went for drinks. There didn't seem to be anything else to do.

"How are you holding up?" John asked at the Rose and Crown, making room for Maggie to slide in next to him in the booth. He smiled, though he looked as terrible as she felt.

"I'm fine, John, thank you," she said, sitting down next to him and then making room for Sarah, who put her arm around her. Clarabelle and Annabelle went to the bar to fetch the drinks.

Maggie barely registered anything beyond numbness. She was completely exhausted, and when she looked at Sarah, she looked just as drained. As did Chuck, whose red lipstick, worn in Paige's honor, had smeared a bit on her front teeth. Even the twins were uncharacteristically quiet when they returned with the glasses. The girls sat together and held one another up, as everyone told stories about Paige, little things she'd done or said, some poignant, some hilarious.

It was Maggie's turn. "I remember—" The problem was that she remembered too much. Even looking around the pub brought back too many memories: the first time they'd ventured out to get a drink, the first time Paige introduced her to David and John, how they'd argued politics and mocked her various beaux . . . Her throat closed up, and she couldn't speak. "Sorry. Maybe later," she finally got out.

She could feel John's eyes on her and wanted to meet them but couldn't quite manage it.

"To Paige," they toasted. And they drank.

# EIGHTEEN

Back in the private secretaries' office at No. 10, John took a few moments over his chipped mug of lukewarm tea to look at the clipping he'd found in another edition of the paper, the same one Maggie had shown him. Dots and dashes, to be sure. He scanned his shelf and took out another book of Morse code and tried to decode.

*Nothing, nothing. Just gibberish.*

John pushed it aside and sighed.

Another dead end.

He was sorry, for it meant he would have to tell Maggie.

John was only twenty-six years old, but he already had deep furrows between his brows. Long ago, or so it seemed, at Oxford and then at No. 10, he'd had a few short-lived love affairs with women, and did so in a way that nothing became messy and no one was hurt. But among the women he'd known, there was no single great love. With Maggie, though, things were different. He was drawn to her—her face and body but also her intellect, her sense of humor.

But now, since the war had started, everything had changed. He went about his work keenly aware that other able-bodied men were serving in the RAF and army and Royal Navy. What was he doing with a desk job when they were out there, putting their lives on the line? He'd already lost two friends in the RAF, shot down by German Messerschmitts. He pictured them plummeting to their death over the English countryside. He felt in some way that by working in an office, even if it was for the Prime Minister, he was letting them down. Letting their memories down.

A few years ago, when war still seemed an impossibility, he would have charmed Maggie, made her smile and then laugh, taken her to dinner. There would have been no awkwardness, no fiasco at LSE, no hesitation. But that was then, and this, alas, was now. They worked together. This was wartime. And everything was different.

*It's not to be,* John thought. *And next time I see her, I'll tell her that sometimes an advert is just an advert.*

David walked into their spartan War Rooms office. "Mooning again, old boy?" he said, sitting down to a pile of paperwork.

"Hmph," John said, looking up from the tight glow of light from the lamp, embarrassed at being caught at just that.

"Well, don't wait too long," David said, pulling out a manila folder and flipping through the pages inside. "She's smart and pretty—and far too good for the likes of you."

"No time for that sort of nonsense," John said. "If you haven't noticed—"

David rolled his eyes.

"—there's a war on."

David grinned. "My point exactly."

After work, back at home, Maggie rang David, who was still working late at the office.

"I have a favor to ask," she said.

"Your wish is my command," David replied, sitting down at his desk chair.

"Feel like getting out of the city?"

David pushed aside a pile of papers. "And get away from the bombing? Always."

"Road trip to Cambridge?"

"Cambridge? What's there?"

Maggie was silent for a moment. What did she actually expect to find? "I don't know, really. Ghosts, maybe? With luck, an answer or two." She nervously twisted the coiled black telephone cord. "Interested?"

"An answer or two about what, Maggie?"

"It's about my father," she said. "I think—well, I think there's a possibility that he might be alive."

"Alive?" David said.

"I don't know. Maybe. I at least want to investigate the possibility. Ask some questions. And Trinity College at Cambridge seems like a logical next place to go."

David looked up at the clock. "Give me a couple of hours to finish," he said. "I'll pick you up at your place."

"You're a wonderful, *wonderful* man," Maggie exclaimed. "You really are."

"I know. See you soon."

When David replaced the black receiver, John looked over. "Was that Maggie?"

"You know it was, old boy." David leaned toward him and smirked. "Jealous?"

John snorted. "Hardly. So"—he stood up from his desk chair and came around to sit on the edge of David's desk—"you're going to Cambridge, then?"

"Indeed, old boy," David said. "Why she doesn't want to go to Oxford is beyond me, but—"

"What's in Cambridge?"

"Why, what do you care?" David said. "It's not like you're *mooning*, is it?"

"David—this is important. Why does Maggie want to go to Cambridge?"

David sighed. "It's something about her father. Probably nothing. But if it helps her feel better . . ."

John jumped to his feet and walked quickly to the door.

"Where are you off to?" David called after him.

"Just remembered something," John called back. "Go on."

"Great bloody Odin, is everyone losing his bleeding mind?" David muttered, turning back to his notes. Men and women. He'd *never* understand them.

John burst into Snodgrass's office.

"She knows!"

Looking up from the files on his large oak desk, Mr. Snodgrass said mildly, "Mr. Sterling, would you kindly remember to knock first, please?"

John shut the door behind him and then said, in a lower tone, "She knows."

"Who knows?" Snodgrass said. "Who knows what?"

"Maggie. She knows."

"What exactly *does* she know?"

"I'm not sure. But she's on her way to Cambridge."

"All right, then." Snodgrass lowered his pen, smoothed his comb-over, and picked up the green telephone receiver. "Then we have work to do."

"Nice car," Maggie said, settling into the smooth leather seat of David's Citroën as the car purred through blacked-out London.

"My poor baby," David said. "The rubbish that passes for petrol these days will be the death of her." He was dressed casually in a white open-neck shirt, navy jacket, and gray-flannel trousers.

There was a comfortable silence as they drove in the

silky black—only the moon and the dim light peeking through the slotted headlight covers provided illumination.

"It really was good of you to drive me to Cambridge tonight. By staying over, you're using one of your only days off."

David patted Maggie's hand. "As you are, Magster. Glad to do it. Besides, it's raising my profile at the office, you know—escorting a pretty girl . . ."

She punched his arm.

"Ouch!"

"Love tap," she said. "Now, we need a plan for when we get to Cambridge. Settle into the rooms at the University Arms hotel, then head for Trinity."

"If your father's still in the area, he'll at least have shown his face at the High Table once in a while."

"Sounds like a good place to start."

Maggie must have found him by now, Edith realized. And if she hadn't, she would soon; she was too smart not to. The game was over. Now all Edith could do was explain herself and hope—pray—that Margaret would understand. After all, Edmund had gone insane, undoubtedly still was. Surely what she'd done was forgivable.

*Wellesley, Massachusetts*

*Dear Margaret,*
  *I write this letter with a heavy heart.*
  *As you may have ascertained, I had quite an unusual childhood. Not only did I show an aptitude for the sciences, believed to be quite rare for a young girl, but I also went to university, one of the few young women who did in the late 1800s. Being such a fish out of water at Cambridge, especially in graduate*

*school, it seemed as though no one understood me and my place in the world.*

*Except one other graduate student. She was doing advanced work in economics, and soon we became best friends. As time passed, I fell in love with her, and she with me. I asked her back to London with me for Christmas holiday and, well, your grandmother must have guessed the true nature of our feelings for each other. She called me "unnatural" and worse. My friend never spoke to me again; the experience had somehow tainted what we had. What was pure and loving and tender had become twisted and perverted when exposed to the outside world.*

*It became impossible for me to continue on, either denying who I was or living a life I couldn't share with the rest of my family. It was impossible to reconcile what I felt—who I was—with what was expected of me. I had to leave. Otherwise, it would have destroyed me.*

*When Clara died and Edmund, well, had what we referred to as "the incident," of course I took care of you. Edmund and I had discussed it when he'd drawn up his will—that I would be the one to look after you, should anything happen to him and your mother— your grandmother would be too old to look after a young child. Although we planned for the eventuality, it was always in the abstract; we never thought it would ever happen, let alone while you were a baby.*

*The circumstances were just so unusual—to say the least. Edmund had just lost his wife.*

*At first I thought he was entitled to go a bit mad.*

*But as time went on, he didn't seem to be getting any better.*

*And despite the fact that I'd never even liked babies or children—well, I fell in love. With you. You weren't just any baby. You were Margaret—with your serious eyes and shocking red hair that indicated an inner fire. As you contemplated your chubby little fingers and toes with such wonder, I knew that I could never let you go. And even though he was your father, I realized Edmund wasn't up to the task.*

*When I came to collect you, your grandmother had to mention my "lack of moral rectitude," intimating my home would not be a proper environment for a child, and so on. I was once again cast out by my own mother, and suddenly the brave new world that I had created for myself was falling apart. And yet I had to pull myself together and take responsibility for this little life that had come into mine.*

*When I finally got my Ph.D. from Cambridge, I sent my c.v. to various women's colleges in the States that were hiring women faculty. When Wellesley made me an offer, I jumped at the opportunity. It was a chance to start over, as myself, in a place where I had no family, no roots, no responsibilities to anyone but myself. America seemed not just the new world but a place for new beginnings. My new beginning. At Wellesley, I was able to live the life of the mind I so desired, while I was still able to be the person I was in my private life. With an ocean between us, there was no way your grandmother could sully my feelings or make me feel any less of a human being for having them.*

*And so we went to the United States, you and I. I needed to get away from my mother's judgments. And I truly didn't think Edmund would ever recover.*

*The situation was complicated. I'm not making excuses, but it was just easier when you were younger to say that both your parents had passed. I always meant to tell you the truth, but as years went by, it just . . . never seemed to be the right time.*

*I hope you can find it in your heart to at least try to*

understand my position, if not forgive me. I am, by the way, very proud of you for staying in London, even though I still hate it and worry myself sick about your safety every single day. Since Mother's passing, I've also tried to understand her position, and although I still don't, I have—at least most of the time—learned to forgive her.

   I do love you.

    *Always,*

    *Edith*

# NINETEEN

THE NEXT DAY, after a breakfast of powdered eggs and brackish tea at the University Arms, Maggie and David set out for Trinity College. Even with the wartime indignities—stripped metal off staircases, ad hoc vegetable gardens, air-raid shelters, and boarded-up windows—Cambridge was a beautiful place. The sky overhead was a pale blue worthy of John Constable, with wispy, cirrus clouds. The warm wind smelled fresh and loamy. All of the oxygen went to Maggie's brain, making her feel light-headed and invigorated.

"The Wren Library," David said, pointing at a building with soaring proportions that looked to be carved from ivory.

"How do you know? I thought you were an Oxford man!"

"Brief fling with a Cambridge coxswain. Travesty, I know."

"Ah," she said, realizing what David was confirming. "Yes."

"I thought maybe you'd guessed, but I wasn't sure."

"When did you first realize your"—*How does one phrase this?*—"your preference?"

They were strolling alone in a Trinity courtyard; the only company was a burbling marble fountain and two tiny brown sparrows, who twittered and preened in the water.

"I believe the current term is 'like that.' " He looked at her and smiled, letting her know it was all right to have asked. "For example, when did you know you were 'like that'? And just for the record, I always knew."

"My aunt Edith is"—she'd never said it out loud before—" 'like that,' too. She's had someone special in her life for years, another professor."

"Ah." David processed the information. "Was it strange at all?"

"No, not really. I mean, yes, it was strange, but only because I was raised by my aunt, who's more or less a mad scientist, and not my parents. Not because of anything else. And just for the record, I knew about your . . . preference."

"Really?" David cocked an eyebrow.

"Sarah mentioned she wanted to set you up with someone in the company—Dimitri, I think."

"Ah, yes, Sarah," he said. "Sarah's always trying to find me dates—men from the Sadler's Wells, usually."

"And Paige knew," Maggie said.

"Paige," he said, shaking his head. "Paige certainly loved to flirt. And I was around and, well, safe, I suppose you'd say. Not that I minded, of course."

"Yes, Paige certainly loved to be the center of attention." They were silent, remembering. It was still raw.

"And John?"

"Yes, John knows. He's my best friend, after all."

"And there's never been . . ." Maggie didn't think so, but she just wanted to make sure.

"No, John likes girls, all right. Just doesn't put too much time and effort into it. Too busy with work these days."

Maggie decided not to mention the awkward evening at LSE and the night in the café's basement—the night that had been overshadowed by Paige's death.

Instead, she changed the subject. "So, how does it . . . I mean, is there someone in your life now?"

David made puppy eyes behind his glasses. "No, I'm all on my lonesome these days, I'm afraid. Although there was, at one time, a very nice chap from the Treasury department."

Maggie's eyebrows shot up. "Fred Gibson?"

"Freddie," David said with a wry smile. "Freddie, Freddie . . . Didn't work out, though." David sighed with mock drama. "And now, poor me, I'm all alone."

"But how do you . . . meet?"

"My dear Maggie, do you think I only ever see you lot? Please!" He grinned. "I'm quite the man about town, you know."

She laughed and shook her head. *Of course.* "And you always knew?"

"Always. I always knew. And my parents, bless their hearts, have always had enough sense to look the other way. They don't ask too many questions, the dears." David's face quickly became serious. "But, Maggie, it's not as though the age of Oscar Wilde is really so long ago." Even though they were alone in the courtyard, his voice dropped to a low whisper. "It's still considered a crime, and people are still being sent to prison. Or mental institutions, where they're dosed with hormone injections. And since I'm working in Whitehall, of all places, it's not exactly something I'll ever be able to shout from the rooftops."

Maggie patted his back. "Not right now. But maybe someday."

"Maybe," he said, and pushed up his glasses. But he didn't sound convinced.

\*     \*     \*

They walked into the bracing wind along the empty cobblestone paths, through Trinity College's quadrangles
and bijoux buildings, over vast expanses of rough green
lawn and victory gardens. They passed two lines of pale-
faced slender young choristers in snowy white ruffs,
their red gowns flapping in the breeze. Finally, they
reached Neville's Court—the dining hall.

As they passed through the doors into the cavernous
wood-paneled space with the long tables, Maggie suddenly felt very small, gauche, and shabby. She looked up
into the soaring rafters and let out a sigh. After all, this
was where Sir Isaac Newton dined.

"Just a dining hall. With the same horrible English
food as everywhere else. They build it big to be intimidating—don't let it get to you," David stage-whispered.
Maggie thought she could smell that day's luncheon:
shepherd's pie and sour-apple custard.

The hall was empty—most men were part of the war
effort, after all—but at the end of the hall was a small
dais, the High Table, where wizened dons in black robes
were beginning to disperse after their meal. Maggie tried
to walk lightly, to stop her heels from tapping so loudly
on the floor.

"Sir, pardon me," Maggie said, going to the don with
the kindest eyes. "My name is Maggie Hope, and this is
David Greene. I'm trying to locate someone."

A few eyebrows raised, but the don stopped and
looked down through his horn-rimmed glasses. "Most
of the boys are off serving King and Country, my dear,"
he said with a twinkle. He had thinning silver hair and
rosacea across his cheeks and nose.

"No, it's not that," she spluttered, "it's—"

"We're looking for Professor Edmund Hope," David
cut in gracefully. "A colleague said he might have re-

turned to Trinity. Would you happen to have seen him recently?"

"Edmund Hope," the don said slowly. "Edmund Hope. That's a name I seem to be hearing quite a bit these days."

He looked at David and Maggie as they exchanged glances. The eyes weren't twinkling now; instead, they looked steely and hard. "Follow me," he said. "We need to speak in private."

Don Anthony Collier's office was dignified and imposing. A stained-glass window picturing St. George and the dragon was crisscrossed by heavy black tape, and a reproduction of William Blake's *The Good and Evil Angels* hung behind the large golden oak desk.

"Please have a seat, Miss Hope, Mr. Greene," he said, gesturing toward two brown-leather chairs.

Maggie and David took their seats, and he did the same, behind the desk.

"Edmund Hope was a student here before the war. The other war. Brilliant, as I recall."

"He was my father," Maggie said.

Don Collier folded large liver-spotted hands. "I see."

David cleared his throat. "Miss Hope has been under the assumption that her father passed away in 1916— in a car accident. But she has reason to believe that he might still be alive. One of his colleagues suggested he might have returned here, sir."

The don knit his fingers together and regarded them from under bushy eyebrows. Maggie's hands shook slightly, and she folded them firmly in her lap, to keep them still. After an interminable wait, he said, "And you both—who are you? What is it you do?"

"I—I work for the Prime Minister, sir. I'm one of the typists."

"And I'm a private secretary to the P.M."

Don Collier swiveled in his desk chair. "I'll need a moment," he said, waving them out. "Just wait outside. Shan't be long."

David and Maggie shared a look, then went out into the hall, leaning against wood-paneled walls. "What do you think it all means?" Maggie whispered.

"Don't know," David replied. "But surely he must know something—otherwise, he'd have sent us on our way at once."

Maggie felt light-headed.

Finally, the door opened.

"Well, I called over to some friends in Whitehall, and it seems that a certain Miss Hope and Mr. Greene are indeed gainfully employed by the office of the Prime Minister. However, the powers that be would like you to give up this goose chase and return to your duties."

*That's what you're saying, but what's really going on?* Maggie thought, a prickle of adrenaline running through her. *Obviously, we're onto something. And not only are we onto something, but there are some higher-ups who don't want us to get any further and find out anything more. But—why?* "Sir, does that mean that my father's alive?"

"Your father is dead, Miss Hope," Don Collier said. "I'm dreadfully sorry for your loss, my dear. It's time for you to move on."

Michael Murphy lit a cigarette and blew three smoke rings into the air, each smaller than the last. It was the first time he'd ever been allowed over. Claire would never have let him, except he had a shared bath at the boardinghouse, and with all they had to do, they couldn't afford anyone seeing her make her transformation. So she sneaked Murphy in through the back garden and then up what had once been the servants' staircase. She knew the others were at work.

Claire was sitting in front of a white vanity with a blue-taffeta ruffle and a tarnished mirror with etched roses. An opened package of red hair dye lay on the shelf, along with a bag of cosmetics—a silver tube of eye shadow, a worn-down cake of black mascara, a stubby scarlet lipstick. For her hair there were Kirby grips and sugar-and-water setting lotion.

She felt a surge of excitement as she completed her toilette, almost as if she were an actress in a play, about to go on on opening night. *It's time,* she thought. *It's finally time. We're really about to pull this off.*

Maggie and David walked slowly back to his car.

"Bastard!" Maggie said, fuming and fighting the urge to kick the tires in frustration. "He knows. He *knows,* and he's just not saying. . . ."

"Maggie," David said gently, "it's not his fault. There's a war on, you know. Everything's a secret these days. Information doled out in little crumbs . . ."

"War," Maggie said, stopping suddenly. "That's it—war!" She hugged David and gave him a kiss on the cheek. "War! Oh, you brilliant, *brilliant* man!"

"Well, yes, of course," David said, pleased. "But what are you getting at, Magster?"

"You just said it—there's a war on."

"Common knowledge."

"And if my father is alive, and evidence certainly suggests it, he'll most likely be doing his part for the war effort."

David's eyes widened. "You think he's a soldier?"

"Not in the way you're thinking. You know about Bletchley Park, of course."

"Bletchley? Certainly. That's where all of the mathematicians and the like have been gathered. . . ." His eyes widened. "Suffering Shukra—you think he's a cryptographer?"

"I think it's probable," Maggie said. "Given his expertise in mathematics. How far is Bletchley from here?"

"Bletchley." David stared off. "Small town on the Varsity line, halfway between Cambridge and Oxford. Right on the A-Five to London. Used to pass it on my way to see Wesley." He looked at Maggie. "Uh, you know. The rower."

"How long do you think it will take?"

"Not much more than a few hours, probably." He squinted at his watch. "We'll have the afternoon and evening there, but then . . ."

"We have to get back by tomorrow morning, bright and early, I know," she said, picturing the look of disapproval on Mrs. Tinsley's face.

"But it's an absolutely brilliant idea," David said. "And if he's there, we'll find him!"

Maggie had her doubts. "You're awfully optimistic," she said. "There's probably all kinds of security that even we can't get past."

"You'll see," he said. "Just wait."

Claire contemplated her reflection in the mirror. The red hair really didn't do much for her complexion, but it looked fine. More than fine. She could really pass for Maggie—especially in a hat with a veil.

*Poor Maggie,* she thought. *She's so earnest, so well intentioned. She thinks so damned hard about everything. Thank goodness she's gone off to Oxford or Cambridge or wherever. The timing's perfect.*

She looked around, feeling suddenly wistful. They'd had good times here, it was true. What had started out as an accidental meeting, and a friendship of convenience, had turned into something more. Half the time, Claire had forgotten she'd been playing a role. She'd even felt a pang of guilt when she and Murphy had faked her death. *Maggie's a sweet girl,* she realized, feeling more than a touch of shame over her deception. *A sincere girl. Loyal to a fault.* She sighed. *Still, she'll get over it. Someday.* Who was she trying to fool? *Well, maybe not, but the deed will be done, regardless.*

And there was a job to do. She put a final dab of powder on her nose, then rose to her feet and spun around. "Ta-da!" she sang, hands on hips.

"It's good," Murphy said. "Very good. But of course I miss your hair."

"Don't you like the red, darling?" Claire reached up to pat her waves of hair, held back with a carved tortoiseshell barrette. "There's not much to do with it. She doesn't care much about her hair, after all." She looked down at her hands, stripped of polish and cut straight across. "Or her hands."

Murphy gestured to the brown straw hat on the bed. "Try it with that."

Claire put on the hat and stabbed it with a pearl-tipped pin. Slowly she lowered the net veil down over her eyes, then dropped them and gazed demurely at the floor.

"What do you think?"

"Dead ringer," he said with a low whistle. "Congratulations, my dear. Are you ready?"

Claire gave a sigh and then looked at her reflection in the mirror once again. "Ready as I'll—"

They both started at a noise from below, then froze. Claire put her finger to her lips.

David and Maggie drove through an autumn countryside of copses and hedges beginning to turn yellow and brown, orchards with trees laden with tiny red apples, fields dotted white with grazing sheep. They motored past thatch-roofed pubs and over-wrought Victorian rail-way stations, the heavenward-pointed spires of Gothic churches, and the occasional Romanesque Norman tower with narrow arrow slits in its thick, heavy walls.

*It's enough to make you want to sing "Rule Britan-nia!,"* Maggie thought, rolling down the window and letting the fresh fall air blow over her. She was trying not to get overly excited about something that could turn out to be just a dead end. *I only hope Robin Hood and his Merry Men don't accost us before we get there.*

Bletchley was a small Victorian railway town, with brick homes and shops with cheerfully colored awnings built up alongside the train tracks. The air was punctu-ated with the sound of locomotives chugging, clanking, and then letting off low, mournful steam whistles and belches of steam and soot.

David navigated his way through town and, after a few wrong turns, pulled up in front of the Eight Cups.

"Is this really time for a pint?" Maggie managed.

"We can both do with a bit of lunch," David replied with a grin. "And before we do anything else, I have to make a phone call."

"A phone call? To whom? Why?"

"Just give me a few minutes."

Murphy and Claire heard the sounds—a bag dropped down, a coat hung up. Then the light tread of feet on the stairs.

"Hello?" They heard a low and raspy voice call. "Anyone home?"

The door suddenly swung open. "Hello? Maggie?"

She'd taken a step into the room when Murphy came at her, swinging a milky-glass bedside table lamp at her head. There was a sickeningly loud thump on impact, the glass shattering and raining down. The young woman crumpled to the floor like a broken doll.

Claire took one look at the figure on the floor, arms flung open and legs akimbo, blood gushing from the wound on the head and starting to puddle in her hair.

"Oh my God, Michael!" she cried, falling to her knees, mindless of the shards of broken glass. She looked up at him. "What have you done?"

It was one thing to assassinate the Prime Minister to further their cause. It was another to just, well, murder someone. Someone who hadn't done anything, really. Her thoughts flashed to Diana Snyder, and she shook her head as though to force them out.

"What I needed to. What we needed to. Now let's get up and get moving."

Claire's shoulders slumped, and she buried her face in her hands, the grim reality setting in. "Is she dead? Really dead?" Diana Snyder was different—Claire hadn't known her. But this wasn't the same. This was someone she knew. This was someone, she realized, she loved.

Murphy felt at the prone girl's neck for a pulse. "If not now, she will be soon." Then, "For Christ's sake, pull yourself together, Claire," he said, taking the powder-blue silk quilt from the bed and throwing it over the girl's slight, still form.

Claire looked at him, tears in her eyes. "You didn't have to kill her."

"Yes, I did. Because you didn't have the courage to kill her yourself." He gently but firmly put his hands on her upper arms and gave her his most charming grin. "Besides, you, my dear girl, have an appointment with the Prime Minister."

With a long last glance down at the girl's body, Claire

wiped tears from her eyes and squared her shoulders. She took a deep breath. "You're right. I do."

Maggie sat down in the smoky, dim dining room of the Eight Cups, which boasted burgundy flowered wallpaper, lace curtains covering the ubiquitous blackout tape, and spindly dark-wood tables and chairs. From the blowsy blond waitress, she ordered the fish of the day for both of them—an unidentified sea creature covered in a gummy sauce. Maggie toyed with hers in silence while David used the telephone in the back. In the distance, she heard a church bell toll five times, its solemn chime reverberating through the air.

*All right,* Maggie thought as she waited, pulling out the newspaper clipping and the codebook for company. Around her she could hear the low rumble of conversation, the clink of silver and china, and the wireless playing "A Nightingale Sang in Berkeley Square."

She took a deep breath and then released it, letting her mind go still. What was it she needed to see? No, wait, maybe if she didn't try to look so closely . . .

Nothing.

*Oh, hell,* she thought crossly, pushing it aside.

As she walked the gravel paths of St. James's Park in the cool fall air, passing the lake and plots of dying victory gardens, ducks and geese honked overhead as if in warning. Claire adjusted her hat and arranged the waves of newly red hair to conceal as much of her face as possible. She flipped up the collar of her coat against the bracing breeze and steeled herself as she reached the sandbagged Whitehall and the government buildings, making her way to the Treasury—and the entrance to the War Rooms.

*This is it,* she thought. *This is really it.*

Head down and eyes lowered, she passed by the two marines standing duty and presented her identity cards. One looked at her papers and motioned her along. The other spent considerable time looking them over.

Claire took a deep breath and forced her face to relax. Finally, he handed her back her papers. "Thank you," she said as he opened a large metal door, which gave a terrific creak as it swung open. She went down a narrow spiral staircase into the bowels of the building.

Michael Murphy and Malcolm Pierce were engaged in an intense conversation in the shadows of the Black Horse pub. Pierce looked at his watch. "Must have happened by now."

"Claire's a good agent. She won't let us down. And she'll get herself out, too. That's part of the plan." Murphy twisted his Claddagh ring, then motioned to the waitress for another round. "Besides, it's not as if Churchill's office would send out a press release to the BBC. They'd keep it quiet. We won't know for days, most likely. Weeks, even."

"You're right," Pierce said, quieting for a moment as the bartender put down two more pints in front of them. "Although most likely your girl's a goner, isn't she?" he continued in a low voice. "Poor thing; such a looker, too. You'd think they'd use an ugly girl for that kind of mission."

"Your goal is Germany's winning the war," Murphy said, shrugging. "Ours is a united Ireland. Claire knew what she was up against."

"You'd blow up the Pope if you thought it would help, wouldn't you?" Pierce gave an admiring whistle through his teeth.

"Look, I've set off a few bombs in my day—Tube stations, women, kiddies. . . . The higher-ups thought it was bad publicity, ultimately. And the bigwigs put a stop to it." He shook his head. "Shame. We were just getting started, really shaking them up."

"That's why, when we had this opportunity with Claire—and Maggie Hope—"

"Speaking of Miss Hope, what ever happened to her?" Pierce asked suddenly.

"She's away—some sort of trip, Claire said. Seemed like the perfect timing."

"Perfect, until she comes back."

Murphy swigged the rest of his beer. "What—you're saying we need to . . . ?"

"My friend—" He paused delicately. "I would take care of the situation."

Murphy got to his feet and stood for a moment and thought. Why should that bitch Maggie Hope get to live when Claire, love of his life Claire, probably wouldn't? He'd take care of Maggie. But first things first.

"Sorry, mate," he said, putting a few coins down on the table for the beer. "I've got an appointment with our friend Paul."

"Very well, then," Pierce said. "We'll each be on our separate ways." *With our separate memories of the same woman,* he thought.

"*Go n-éirí an t-ádh leat,*" Murphy said.

"Good luck to you, too."

Just as the waitress brought more hot water for the tea, something clicked.

*There. There it is. It's code, Morse code.*

*But it doesn't* translate.

"Want anything else, love?" the waitress asked. "We have strawberry cobbler—not bad, even if we don't have enough sugar. . . ."

"No," Maggie said, not even looking up. "Thanks, though."

Maggie set her jaw in frustration.

*It just doesn't translate.*

*Maybe . . . Maybe it's super-enciphered? One code within another? Scrambled once, then again? All right, let's try that. . . .*

# TWENTY

THE AIR UNDERGROUND was cold and damp, and had the watery smell of concrete and chemical toilets. Claire's heels clicked loudly on the cement floor as she walked down a long hallway with low whitewashed ceilings and hoses looped against the wall with red fire buckets, passing men with clipped mustaches and somber faces. She walked quickly and kept her eyes averted.

She and Murphy had been over stolen blueprints of the Treasury and the War Rooms, but walking the steep stairs and cinder-block corridors was altogether different. Nonetheless, Claire kept her pace brisk and her head down as she made her way to the P.M.'s underground office.

Her hands were shaking as she found it, room 65A, next door to the Map Room and across the hall from the Transatlantic Telephone Room. She knocked, and when no one replied, she eased the door open and found herself inside.

The P.M.'s tiny private chamber had all the trappings of a senior officer—camp bed made up with a quilted silk duvet, plush red Persian carpet, large wooden desk. Microphones for his BBC broadcasts. A humidor for his cigars.

She felt light-headed, and flashes of light danced around the periphery of her vision as she sat down at the P.M.'s desk and removed the pistol from her handbag. With a series of quick clicks, the ammunition was loaded and the silencer attached.

Maggie refused to give up believing the code to be super-enciphered, a code within a code. *All right,* she thought, scratching her head, *what if . . . What if it's written backward? What then?*

And so --- .-. --.- ...- ... .- ...- -. .- --.- -.-- .... .- - / -- .... .. .-. . ..-. ...- .--. .. - --. / --- .-. --.- ...- ... .- ...- -. .- --.- -.-- .... .- - / .- -. .. / ..-. .-. .-. -... ... ... ...- -- ...- .-. . / --- .-. --.- ...- ... .- ...- -. .. ...- .- ...- -. .. .- --.- -.- - .... .- - / -.-. -. .... -.-- in Morse code became Orqvsavnaqyhat Mhirefvpug Orqvsavnaqyhat Are Frrbssvmvre Orqvsavnaqyhat Cnhy.

*Bugger, bugger, bugger,* Maggie thought, rubbing her temples and biting her lower lip.

Murphy and Claire had no illusions about the mission she was to perform. Her goal was to assassinate Winston Churchill and thus topple the British war machine. Everything else was secondary.

Claire would do the deed and then get out as quickly as possible, before the assassination was even discovered. Then into Michael's waiting arms.

But a more likely scenario was that she would be apprehended and hanged as a traitor to the empire. Or she could be killed by marines on the spot. In any case, they both knew her chance of survival was low. In a sense, she was already a ghost.

But she wasn't thinking about her own death as she waited, loaded pistol pointed at the door. She was gathering her courage, her hatred. She remembered the targets she had practiced on, the rabbits and then the deer. How it felt to see them panic and run, then the hit and the huge recoil in her arm, and then how their eyes became glassy and still just as they began to fall. She remembered her first real kill, the British officer in Dublin who'd harassed her mother, then followed them back to their house. She'd fired a shot through one ear and out the other while he was raping her mother on the dining-room table. With Murphy's help, she'd disposed of the body, driving to the sea and taking out a small fishing skiff.

Then the door opened.

It was hopeless, just hopeless. Maggie felt the beginnings of a headache coming on, like an ice pick behind her right eye. *I've already wasted so much time. . . .*

She looked for David. *Probably still at the telephone.*

Her eyes kept going back. *All right, you annoying, miserable, pathetic bunch of dots. But what about, say . . . half-reversed alphabet?*

Then the code read: O R Q V S A V N A Q Y H A T / M H I R E F V P U G / O R Q V S A V N A Q Y H A T / Q R E / F R R B S S V M V R E / O R Q V S A V N A Q Y H A T / C N H Y

*Damn, damn, damn.* She pushed her hair back again and stared at the ceiling. A tiny black insect buzzed by her, and she batted at it, absently.

As she yawned and stretched, it came to her—and the hairs on the back of her neck prickled with excitement. *But . . . what about . . . in German . . . ?* She felt cold and gripped the pencil hard, her heart beating fast. She could practically smell success.

Translated, the code transformed into: *Bedienhandlung die Zuversicht / Bedienhandlung der Seeoffizier / Bedienhandlung Paul.*

*Jesus,* Maggie thought, shivers going up her spine. *Jesus, Jesus, oh, sweet Jesus.*

It took her a few moments, but she translated the German to English.

The broken code read: *Operation Hope. Operation Naval Person. Operation Paul.* Maggie copied it out in her notebook, breathing faster.

*What the . . . Operation Hope? Could that . . .* She'd almost let herself think, *Could that have something to do with* me? She nearly laughed aloud. *But that's ridiculous. I'm just a tiny cog in a very, very, very big machine.* She gave a grim smile. *And apparently a narcissistic cog at that.*

She turned her attention back to the notebook.

*Operation Paul.* Simon *Paul? After all, he's made no secret of the fact that he opposes the war. He works for Lord Halifax, a well-known Appeasement supporter. . . .*

*But Operation Naval Person?* Maggie took a ragged breath. Naval Person was Mr. Churchill's code name, a reference to his stint as First Sea Lord. Could it be . . . an attempt on his life?

She put some money down on the table and ran to the short, dark-haired, and haggard bartender. "The phone, please?" she asked breathlessly.

"That way, miss," he said, pointing to a dim hallway behind him.

Maggie found the phone booths and went to one a few down from David. She groped in her handbag for some change, inserted the coins, then dialed a sequence of numbers. She waited, chewing her lip and tapping her foot. "Westminster double-three four nine," she said to the operator.

There was a series of short clicks and a pause, while a crackle of static danced across the line.

"John Sterling, please. Of course I'll hold. Yes, this is urgent. . . ." Maggie wound the thick black cord around her wrist. "Hello, John? It's Maggie. No, no, I'm fine—" She listened and then interrupted, her voice soft and inaudible to anyone else in the room. "Look, John, that code? It's for real. It's in German, and it's backward, in half-reverse alphabet. If you translate it, it says Operation Hope, Operation Naval Person, and Operation Paul. Not sure about the other two, but Operation Naval Person must have something to do with Mr. Churchill."

"Maggie, where are you?"

"John, this information is far more important than—"

"Are you still at Cambridge?"

Maggie could see David finish his call, replace the receiver, and head back to the table.

"I'll call back later," she whispered behind a cupped hand. "But please look into it. It's imperative!"

When Maggie returned to the table, David's face was unreadable. "Made a few calls," he said. "Pulled in some favors."

"Yes?" Maggie wasn't sure if she should tell David about the code or not. But technically John was ranked higher than David and had a higher clearance.

David laid his hand on hers. It was cold. "Maggie, you were right. Your father's alive. And working at Bletchley."

She was silent for a moment, letting the news sink in. *Alive. My father is alive.* Suddenly, a possible secret code didn't seem so important. "But why—"

"It's a little complicated," David continued.

"Complicated?" *How can this be more complicated?* "But where is he? I want to see him!" Her hands were shaking. "I *need* to see him."

"And you will," David said. "But first you'll have to prepare yourself."

*Is he joking?* she thought. *How can anyone prepare for such a meeting?*

"It's not going to be what you expect."

At No. 10, John replaced the glossy green receiver with a loud click and then rummaged through the piles of papers on his desk, trying to find the clipping. On top of David's in-box, Nelson blinked his eyes and then got up and stretched, his back hunching in an arch.

"Why she feels the need to go running off—with everything else that's going on . . ." he muttered. Nelson jumped to the floor, landing lightly on small black paws.

As John sorted, he saw the newspaper clipping fall to the floor. "Gods." He sighed, getting down on his hands and knees to retrieve the fallen scrap of paper.

Suddenly, he blinked. Once, twice.

Three times.

He scrambled to get a Morse-code book down from the shelf and started to transcribe the dots and dashes. Then reverse them. Then unscramble by using reverse half-alphabet. And then transcribe the German into English.

"Bloody hell," he said. "Bloody *hell*! She's right. It's backward. Bloody, bloody, bleeding Germans . . ."

He'd felt his skin prickle as he began the decryption, but he didn't allow it to stop him until he'd finished. As he looked at the decrypted message, he felt the roar of blood fill his ears. Nelson meowed, but John ignored him.

"The Boss," John managed, struggling to his feet. "I've got to tell the Boss."

The door opened. It was John, carrying a newspaper clipping and his notes. "Maggie? But we just spoke on the telephone—"

Claire had worked through a multitude of scenarios in her mind, but this one had never occurred to her.

John fell silent as he looked. He stared, not trusting his eyes. "Paige?" he said in a whisper. Then, *"Paige?"*

"Oh, John. I'm sorry. I'm so, so sorry."

## TWENTY-ONE

THE BLETCHLEY ESTATE, a Victorian Tudor-style mansion surrounded by high fences, was guarded by marines. When David showed their identification papers, the guards waved them through.

As David and Maggie drove up to the imposing red-brick house, they could hear the cacophony of a construction crew and the honking of ducks and geese. Overhead, the sky was a glossy enameled azure and the fall afternoon sun was warm. Maggie felt her underarms start to perspire and had the sudden thought that she should have worn something lighter than her brown poplin suit.

"Victorian monstrosity," David muttered as he pulled in and parked. The place bustled with men and women in uniform as well as civilians, mostly men, in baggy wrinkled trousers with worn linen jackets. The estate's lawns were patchy and worn from all of the foot and bicycle traffic to makeshift huts and office buildings. The gardens were overgrown and shabby. A fat duck with an iridescent green head waddled across the parking lot.

"So *this* is Bletchley." Maggie looked around in amazement as they walked to the front door. She imagined how it must have been at one time, before the war. She half closed her eyes and saw it. A smooth, green lawn. Children in flowered cotton dresses and sailor suits running back and forth with kites, while nannies in starched white aprons looked on approvingly. Ladies in silk afternoon gowns—rose and daffodil and mint— sipped tea and ate meringues with tiny ripe strawberries, while men in blue seersucker suits and straw boaters drank amber sherry.

"Officially, it's the Government Code and Cypher School," David said. "I secured our clearance. But first we need to jump through some hoops."

They went in and were taken through dusty halls and up an ornate wooden staircase, now scratched and scraped. In an upstairs room was a long table covered with a gray army blanket. Outside the window Maggie could make out several magnolia trees and an assortment of huts and buildings, surrounded by a security fence of upright metal laths topped with swaths of barbed wire.

"Miss Hope," one of the officers said, and led her into the hall. He was short and round, with buck teeth and a shadow of stubble. He held up his hand to David. "I'm taking you to meet Dr. Edmund Hope, your father." He said to David, "You'll wait here."

"But—" David began.

"Sorry. Orders," the officer said.

"It's all right," Maggie assured him, and herself as well. "It's fine."

David gave a quick wink and a pat on the back. "I'll be waiting for you."

Maggie and the officer went down the long hallway, their footsteps echoing on the scuffed wood.

"In you go," the officer said, gesturing at a door.

For a few seconds, she stood there in front of the door, unblinking. Once the thick oak door was opened, nothing would be the same ever again.

She grasped the white ceramic knob and turned; the

door opened with a click and a creak. The room was cool and dim; drawn shades diffused the light.

It took a while for her eyes to get used to the half-light. When they did, she could make out the slumped figure of a man behind a battered wooden desk. He reached to a lamp and turned it on. "There, that's better," he mumbled.

Then, to Maggie, "Who are you?"

"Kneel!" Claire hissed.

"No," he said, not believing his eyes.

"Shut up."

John did as she directed, dropping the clipping and his papers and falling to his knees, hands on his head. But he kept his eyes on her face. "Paige," he said, finally accepting the figure in front of him.

"I'm not Paige!" she cried, her hand shaking. "My name is Claire."

"Paige—Claire," he said. "Don't do this. Whatever's going on, just put down the gun and we can talk about it."

She was silent, lips pressed tightly together, while one hand wrested the case off the P.M.'s bed pillow. She threw the pillowcase at him. "Put this over your head. Then turn around."

"If you're going to murder me," John said slowly, pillowcase in hand, "at least have the courage to look me in the eye."

She did not.

"Paige. Put down the gun." John stood up very slowly, lowered his arms, and took a step toward her.

"Stay where you are!" Claire said shrilly. She caught a glimpse of the clipping that had fallen. "What—what's that?" she cried. "Where did you get that?"

"The advert?" John asked softly. "Why? Did you have something to do with that? Operation Naval Person?"

Claire blanched, and John knew that Maggie had been right. He took another step forward. "It's over, Paige."

"No," she whispered. Her hand was shaking.

"Yes," he countered.

"I'm afraid it *is* over, Miss Kelly," echoed Snodgrass from the doorway.

## TWENTY-TWO

"Who are you?" the man repeated. Their eyes locked, and Maggie felt a shudder of recognition.

She tried not to stare. "My name—" she began in a small voice. Then, stronger, "My name is Margaret Hope."

"Margaret Hope," the man said, leaning back in his army-issued metal folding chair. "Margaret Hope, Margaret Hope, like the Pope, Pope, Pope, is a joke, is a joke, is a joke, joke, joke!"

She stared in disbelief. The features were the same ones she knew from photographs—the man had the same high forehead, aquiline nose, and strong jaw. He was older now, of course, and laugh lines, forehead creases, and silver hair at his temples had changed his appearance. But not too much.

There was no mistake. This was her father.

And there was something terribly wrong with him.

"Pope, joke, antelope," he muttered, gazing off to an unseen point. "Lope, rope, billy goat!"

"Father?" she said softly. "Daddy?"

The door creaked open. "Ah, Miss Hope, Professor Hope," a high-pitched nasal voice said. Maggie turned to find a tall, thin man with a receding hairline and small yellow teeth. He was dressed in a gabardine jacket and slacks. "My name is Kenneth Easton. Pleased to meet you, Miss Hope."

He walked in and turned on an overhead light. "I must apologize," he said. "I meant to be here when you arrived, to make introductions."

Grasping Easton's outstretched hand for support, her father rose to his feet. Although he was wearing a shirt and tie and jacket, when he shuffled from behind the desk, it became clear that he was also wearing blue-striped cotton pajama pants and scuffed leather slippers.

"Edmund," he said to the man, "this is your daughter, Margaret Hope. Miss Hope, this is your father."

The man who was her father continued to mutter and mumble, his eyes unfocused.

"All right, Edmund," Easton said, not unkindly, "let's get you back, shall we?" He wrapped a coat around her father's shoulders and placed a red-plaid tea cozy on his head. "Won't wear a hat," he said to Maggie, a note of apology in his voice.

A white-clad nurse arrived at the door, the edges of her hat curled upward like wings. "Professor Hope," she said in a stern voice, "time for your medicine." Before he shuffled off with her, he looked back in Maggie's direction. "Grand, band, shake her hand," he said in a monotone.

"Let's be on our way, Professor Hope," the nurse said.

"Shake hand! Shake hand!" he insisted.

Mr. Easton sighed. "Miss Hope, would you oblige?"

She extended her hand, and her father clasped it with both of his. The grip was weak, and the flesh was cold.

And then, like a wraith, he was gone.

"Mr. Easton," she managed finally, "how—how do you know my father?"

Kenneth Easton gestured to another metal folding chair and took the one behind the desk that Maggie's father had vacated. "Miss Hope, please sit down."

When she did, she realized how shaky her legs were.

"May I offer you a cup of tea?"

*Goddamned stupid British and their goddamned constant need for tea!* "No. Thank you. But I would like some answers."

"Of course you would," he said, folding his hands. "I know that you've signed the Official Secrets Act, so you know that any and all information you learn you must protect—upon pain of death. Hanging, specifically . . ."

"Yes, yes," she said brusquely, waving a hand. "Please. "

"Let's start at the beginning, shall we? When your parents were in the car accident, your mother died instantly," he said, voice gentle now. "But your father was alive. Barely, but alive. He was in a coma for quite some time, and then had a long and arduous road to recovery."

Mr. Easton made a steeple with his fingers. "Apparently, you were taken to America by your father's sister, a Miss Edith Hope. Because of the precarious state of his physical, and especially mental, health, she made the decision not to tell you he was still alive. She asked him to honor that decision, which he has."

A horrible, awful, and unforgivable decision.

"But—"

"It was a most difficult situation. You see, your father recovered to a certain extent, but he never fully regained his faculties. He was able to function—at an exceptionally high level—as a professor at LSE. But he was almost, how shall I put this? An idiot savant—gifted in his subject but unable to form any sort of connection with the people around him."

*My God.*

"As time went on, even that was taken away from him. By the time the war began, he'd already left LSE and was living in Cambridge, cared for by some of the old guard at Trinity."

"If he's so ill," Maggie said slowly, "why is he here?"

"Your father may be mentally ill, but he's still a genius. And we are in desperate need of geniuses at Bletchley—or Station X, as we call it. Established in 'thirty-nine by the Government Code and Cypher School to intercept—"

"Yes. Where you're breaking German ciphers."

Easton looked shocked.

"I work for the Prime Minister," Maggie explained. "I know what's going on at Bletchley."

Easton took Maggie's measure. Finally, he said, "Well, then you must know that we've recruited some of the most brilliant minds Britain has to offer. Alan Turing is here, of course. Has been from the beginning. But there are other remarkable people working here as well—mathematicians, cryptologists, Egyptologists, chess champions, crossword experts, polyglots—"

"And my father."

"Yes, your father."

"But he's still . . . ?"

"Mad as a hatter. But harmless, absolutely harmless. And brilliant. Can't go into the particulars, of course, but there are some codes we never would have even touched if not for him. He's doing hero's work, you know."

"I see." She didn't really, not yet. But what else was there to say?

"I know this is extraordinary news. But given the circumstances, and the fact that you're working for the P.M., Snodgrass thought you should know."

She blinked. "Snodgrass? He's responsible for this?"

"Well, yes, of course," Mr. Easton said. "Thinks quite highly of you, you know. Pulled a lot of strings for this meeting to happen."

It was just too much to take in.

"I think I'll take that cup of tea now, Mr. Easton."


"Claire Paige Kelly," Snodgrass said. "Fancy meeting you here."

In a series of quick and fluid movements, Snodgrass crossed over to her, twisted one arm behind her back, and took the gun from her other hand.

She whimpered while he held on to her.

He nodded to John, who went for the telephone. "Yes, a situation. In the P.M.'s War Room office. Thank you."

John turned to Snodgrass, impressed and relieved. "Sir? You—you know her?"

"Miss Kelly has been on the MI-Five watch list for some time, Mr. Sterling. She's American, true, but has strong IRA connections. Let's just say that we had more than enough reason to keep tabs on her."

John slumped over and grabbed onto the back of a wooden chair. "Why didn't you tell me?"

Two marines in full dress uniforms walked quickly into the room and assessed the situation. Snodgrass nodded to them. "Take her to the cell," he said. He turned back to John. "And spoil all the fun?" The marines deftly snapped steel handcuffs around Claire's wrists and began to lead her away.

John looked back to the clipping. "Sir," he said, bending down to retrieve it.

"John," Claire whispered, her eyes welling with tears.

"No?" he said, rising up, clipping in hand. He turned to Snodgrass and handed it to him. "This advert contains code, sir. In the stitches. Decrypted, it says execute Operation Naval Person, Operation Paul, and Operation Hope. This . . . she . . . ?" He gestured to Claire, who was now on her way out the door. "This attempted assassination was most likely Operation Naval Person."

"Let me see that," Snodgrass said. He scanned the advert. "You're sure?" he said.

"Yes," John replied. "Also, Maggie—Miss Hope—is at Bletchley. Asking questions. And starting to get answers."

"I know," Snodgrass replied. "We have it under control. For now."

After the drive back and a desultory dinner, which neither one ate, Maggie and David went back to the hotel. In her room, David tried to fill the silence with chitchat as he lounged in a pistachio-green tufted chair. "Great Ganesh, did you see the way that desk clerk looked at us? Yes, we have two rooms, but you could just tell he thought there would be lots of"—he gave a significant pause—"sneaking back and forth during the night."

"Well, you *are* in my room now," Maggie said, lying on the eiderdown quilt, looking at the corner where the toile wallpaper met the ceiling, trying to process everything Mr. Easton had told her. "And you *will* have to sneak back."

David slipped off his black-leather shoes and put his feet up on the bed. "Don't suppose I could get a foot rub first?"

"You have a hole in your sock."

David lifted up his foot and inspected it. His pink big toe poked through the black sock, with a few pieces of lint attached. "Nefarious Neptune."

"Try stockings," she snorted. She looked down. Hers already had a small run at the heel.

"Have, actually. None too comfortable."

There was a silence. "Look, do you—do you want to talk about it?" David ventured finally.

"It's just . . . Oh, I don't know." She was unsure how to put it into words. "I mean, my father's alive. But he's not really . . . there. I'm proud that he's able to help the war effort, but—"

"Does it feel like losing him all over again?"

"In a way. I had all of these . . . expectations, and they're all dashed now. And I had quite a few things to say to Aunt Edith, and now I only feel sorry for her. Maybe I wouldn't have done the same thing in her shoes, but I'm beginning to understand why she did it." She could see Aunt Edith, younger, with her whole future ahead of her, with a dead sister-in-law, an insane brother, and a small infant. "Maybe it's best not to know everything."

David sighed. "Maybe so."

"And yet we just can't help ourselves, can we?"

David had fallen asleep in the chair, mouth slightly agape, snoring lightly. Maggie didn't want to leave him alone at the hotel in the middle of the night. But she knew they were due back to No. 10 first thing in the morning—and this night might be the last chance she'd ever have to see her father again.

She exchanged her suit for a heavy cardigan and brown corduroy trousers, and her linen pumps for thick-soled shoes. Then she found her coat and, pocketing her keys and ID, let herself out as silently as possible.

*As if anything short of an air-raid siren would rouse David from his snoring.*

"Rather late for a walk, don't you think?" said the fat, balding, shiny-faced man at the front desk.

"Insomnia," she said. "Need a bit of fresh air."

"Don't go too far," the man cautioned. "Not a girl alone." He gave her a lascivious look. "Unless you're meeting someone."

Maggie gave him a conspiratorial look. "Actually, now that you mention it . . . Is there a back door I could use?"

"Down that hall there and through the kitchen. Can't miss it." A broad wink. "Good luck, then, with your . . . meeting."

*If he only knew.*

After Maggie left, the desk clerk picked up the telephone and dialed. "Yes, sir. She just left the hotel."

The blackout was in full effect, of course, but the moon was a crescent, silvery and high in the shadowy sky. The wind blew through the trees, and they rustled in the dark. The cool air smelled of earth and wood smoke. Overhead, the stars glimmered and gleamed—Ursa Minor and Polaris, Pegasus and Pisces, Cassiopeia and the diffused glow of the Milky Way.

In her hand she had the piece of paper her father had slipped to her when they'd shaken hands as he left.

It had taken quite the effort not to look surprised, and then to keep it hidden from Mr. Easton until she could hide it in her purse. It was even harder to wait until David and she had returned to the hotel and she'd been able to lock herself in the loo and read it:

13012113031852519161520202575
1017215514191916152118201815014
23514554201520011211

*The numeric ramblings of a crazy man?* At this point, Maggie doubted it. *A code. Vigenère Cipher, most likely. But what's the key? Usually both parties have a key of some sort. . . .*

Maggie thought. *All right, what's the one piece of information we both know, even after all these years, not knowing anything about each other?* After a few false starts, Maggie hit on it: her birthday, March 1, 1916.

And so, written numerically, the birthday became the key: 01/03/1916, which began the series of numbers:

01/03/1916/4/5/6/7/8/9/10/11/12/13/14/15/16/17/18/
19/20/21/22/23/24/25/26/

And then, by substituting 01 = 1, 03 = 2 and 1916 = 3:

1/2/3/4/5/6/7/8/9/10/11/12/13/14/15/16/17/18/19/20/
21/22/23/24/25/26

. . . which then became letters in sequence:

a/b/c/d/e/f/g/h/i/j/k/l/m/n/o/p/q/r/s/t/u/v/w/x/y/z/

And so,

1301211303185251916152020575
1017215514191916152118201815014
23514554201520011211

. . . became:

131211331852531520201175
10172155141931521182018 1514
23514554201520 11211

. . . which then became:

13/1/21/13/3/18/5/25  3/15/20/20/1/7/5
10/17/21/5/5/14/19  3/15/21/18/20  18/15/1/4
23/5/14/5/5/4/  20/15  20/1/12/11

And, finally,

**MAUMBREY COTTAGE
10 QUEEN'S COURT ROAD
WE NEED TO TALK**

## TWENTY-THREE

MAGGIE PICKED HER way carefully through the streets of the town, narrowly avoiding being hit by a bicyclist. "Watch it, lady!" he called through the darkness.

"I'll try," she muttered. She passed closed-up shops, a restaurant, a pub—shutters dark, but the strains of "Roll Out the Barrel" still managed to penetrate. She gave a wry smile. Even in the midst of the blackout and war, people still found it in themselves to sing.

As she passed out of town, still moving cautiously, the darkness began to feel thick. She could have been anywhere. But still, after a few wrong turns and a stumble that left her ankle sore, she found herself on Queen's Court Road.

Maumbrey Cottage was fashioned from round, gray stones and covered in ivy and hawthorn. By the light of the moon and stars, it looked like something out of a fairy tale. *No seven little men or big bad wolf to meet me,* Maggie thought. *Just the Mad Hatter.* She switched off her blackout torch, a slim pencil of fragile light piercing the darkness, and took a deep breath. She knocked at the door.

After a few heart-wrenching seconds, she heard footsteps and then the squeak of the door as the man she recognized as her father answered. "Come in," he said in a surprisingly reasonable voice. "May I take your coat?"

Dumbly, she walked into the light, shrugged off her coat, and looked around. There was a small parlor with low beams and a kitchen beyond, and a steep staircase with dark Tudor woodwork. The room was cozy from a roaring fire.

"Please sit down," he said. "Tea? Or perhaps something stronger? I think I might have some brandy around still."

"Brandy. Please," Maggie said, sitting down gingerly on the moth-eaten velvet sofa. *Who is this man?* He seemed perfectly fine now. His eyes had lost the glazed expression they'd had at Bletchley and now seemed warm and sane. He poured amber liquid into the two snifters and gestured to the couch.

There was a silence. Then he began, "You broke the cipher. I thought you would. And now I suppose you're wondering—"

The hour, the lack of sleep, and the shocks of the last few days were starting to make Maggie feel frayed at the edges. "Why, yes," she said. "I am." She took a sip of the brandy. It felt hot going down her throat.

"Margaret," he began. "I know this is difficult. Before we begin, I want to show you something."

He got up and went to a large cardboard box on the small table. "All of this," he said, putting the box down next to her on the sofa, "was for you. Is. If you'll still have it."

He sat back down, and she turned toward the box.

Gingerly, she lifted the lid.

Inside were presents. Lots of presents, some wrapped in pink paper, some in silver-and-blue tissue. Some of the wrapping paper was old and yellowing, while some looked brand-new.

Maggie picked up one of the packages. It was small and wrapped with faded butterfly paper.

"Open it," her father instructed. "Please."

She tore off the paper, and inside was a small, white stuffed lamb with a yellow-satin bow and a tiny silver bell around its neck.

"Ah, the lamb," he said. "That was for your third birthday."

She put it down and stared at it. "Well, you're a little late," she said, trying unsuccessfully to hide the bitterness.

"I know," he said. "I want to try to explain. When your mother died, I thought I would lose my mind. I did, actually, for a while. Was hospitalized for a year or so. When I finally came out, Edith had already taken you to America. I was in no shape to care for a child."

"So why these?" She gestured at the pile of gifts. *Does he really think that these will make up for everything I've gone through? Growing up without a father? Thinking he was dead all this time? The lies? The deceit?*

"Oh, Margaret," he said. "I never stopped thinking about you. I thought of you every day. And I bought those presents for your every birthday. But Edith said that you'd been through enough. And my grip on reality was precarious enough that I let myself be convinced that you were better off not knowing me."

"And do you think that's true? Or do you think that was easiest for you?"

Edmund looked at his hands.

"Why didn't you stay and fight for me?"

"I tried. I did the best I could."

"Why didn't you try harder? You just *left*."

"Maggie . . . Is there anything you need? Anything at

all?" he asked. "Money? I have money. God knows I don't spend any of it myself. . . ."

"No," Maggie said finally. "I don't need anything from you."

There was an uncomfortable silence, which Maggie finally broke. "And so, how did you end up here? At Bletchley?"

"Once I was well enough that I didn't need to be in hospital, I didn't know where to go or what to do. London reminded me too much of your mother. I knew I had to leave. And several of the dons at Cambridge were kind enough to let me stay with them, teach the odd class."

"Ah," Maggie said. "That's how I found you. I went to LSE, and Samuel Barstow said that not only were you alive but that he thought you might have gone back to Cambridge. It was there that I put it together with Bletchley."

Edmund blinked. "How do you know about Bletchley?"

"I work for the Prime Minister, as a typist. Privy to a lot of classified information."

Edmund took a moment to process what Maggie had just told him. "Samuel . . . Good Lord, yes, Samuel Barstow . . . Well, there were lots of 'madmen' at Cambridge in those days. And a lot of us are here now, at Bletchley."

"Cryptanalytic work," she said. "Yes, although I wasn't briefed on the specifics, I know that much."

"Cryptography, yes."

"But why the act?" she pressed. "You seem perfectly fine here and now."

"Ah, that," he said, rubbing his chin. "You see, I was a known quantity. Everyone knew that I'd had a break of sorts, and that I'd been a little wobbly on my pins ever since. It made it easy to pretend to be a mad genius to the rest of the cryptographers."

It was almost too much to comprehend. "But—but why?"

"MI-Five came to me and suggested it. It's suspected that there's a leak. A secret agent, if you will. Because I'm in many ways disregarded, it's my job to keep an eye on the rest of the boffins. See if anyone slips up."

Maggie took a sip of brandy. A large one. "So they agreed to let me see you—*if* you kept up the charade," she said.

"I never expected to see you, not after the war broke out. Why would a girl from America be in London? Especially with a war on. But when Richard Snodgrass called—"

"Snodgrass?" Again, that *man*. He was everywhere, it seemed.

"Mr. Snodgrass knew that you were trying to find me. He also knew about my position and its sensitive nature. So yes, I agreed to the charade. But I couldn't let the opportunity to meet with you pass by."

"How did Snodgrass know I was trying to find you?"

"We're all under surveillance," Edmund said. "I've been undercover for years, and we're getting very close to catching our spy. Peter Frain is the head of the operation, but when you became involved, I'm sure Mr. Snodgrass—"

"But I'm just a typist. Why would he be interested in someone like me?"

"An excellent question, my dear," said a man stepping out of the shadows. "A most excellent question."

Back in his office, Snodgrass looked once again at the clipping, blinking rapidly. "Mr. Sterling, are you absolutely certain?"

"It's in code, sir. It's Morse code, German and backward. Half-alphabet. It mentions three operations. Operation Naval Person must refer to the fact that Mr. Churchill used to be the First Sea Lord—"

"Which means that although we have our assassin in custody, there are still two other scenarios in play." Snodgrass picked up a red Bakelite receiver. "Yes, get me MI-Five. Peter Frain. It's urgent."

While they waited, Snodgrass put his hand over the mouthpiece. "By the way, good work, Sterling, very good work." Then Snodgrass was speaking to Frain. "Don't have much time. There's been an attempt on the P.M.'s life. We have the would-be assassin, Claire Kelly, in custody."

A silence on Snodgrass's end, and then, "But there's more. According to what we've uncovered, it's only the beginning. Something about Operation Hope—"

Snodgrass's slight shoulders slumped. "Yes, that's what I feared, too. And Operation Paul."

John shuffled impatiently. "And Miss Hope?"

Snodgrass gave him a stern look. "Miss Hope is in Bletchley. Although our 'madman' played his role convincingly." Snodgrass said into the phone, "We'll be off directly, then, to collect her."

He hung up the phone and headed for the door. "Well, Mr. Sterling, what are you waiting for? First we need to find Miss Hope and Mr. Greene and just pray they haven't done anything else stupid. Then we'll find Professor Hope and take him into protective custody."

John looked at him, speechless.

Snodgrass was already walking down the hallway at a fast clip. "Come along, Mr. Sterling."

"Who the hell are you?" Edmund Hope asked, face tense.

The white-haired man stepped toward them. "Name's Malcolm Pierce. How do you do? Professor Hope, I presume," he said in a civilized voice, as though they were at high tea.

Maggie found her voice. "What are you doing here?"

He ignored her. "There are a number of people who'd be quite interested in what you're working on, Professor Hope. We know you know there's a spy at Bletchley. And we know you're the decoy to catch him. So by kidnapping you, we keep our agent safe and also gain a treasure trove of information on England's capacity to break German code."

"I'm not telling anyone anything," Edmund said.

"You will if you want your precious daughter to stay alive," Pierce said, walking closer to Maggie. Cold sweat dripped down her back, and everything seemed to be moving in slow motion.

"Now, this is what is going to happen," he said in a soothing voice, pulling a coil of rope from his jacket pocket. "Slowly and quietly we're going to leave. There's a car waiting in front. Professor Hope, you will drive, whilst I keep your daughter company in the backseat. You will do exactly as I say. Do you understand?" He handed the rope to Edmund.

Edmund swallowed. "Dearest Margaret, I'm so sorry," he said as he tied her hands together with rope.

"That should keep you out of trouble, Miss Hope," Pierce said. The narrow cord was rough and cut into her flesh. "Very good," Pierce said, as Edmund tied the last knot.

"Now, let's be on our way, shall we?"

"*Bedienhandlung die Zuversicht,*" Maggie said suddenly, realizing.

"What?" Both Edmund and Pierce looked shocked

"*Bedienhandlung die Zuversicht,*" she said slowly,

piecing it together. "Operation Hope. This is what the code in the advert meant by Operation Hope, isn't it? Kidnap Edmund Hope, one of England's best code breakers. Before he can identify the German spy."

"What code?" Edmund said. "What advert?"

"There was an advert in the paper," Maggie explained. "Ladies' fashion. But there was Morse code embedded in the stitching of the dresses."

Pierce finally found his voice. "So you figured it out. But it's too late now." Then, "Does anyone else know?"

"No," she whispered. "No, just me. No one believed me."

Pierce smiled, dimples flashing. "Good."

*Not if John puts it all together, too,* Maggie thought. *And quickly.*

In his office at MI-5, Peter Frain slammed down the telephone receiver. He was seething.

"Goddamn it!" he thundered. He shouted to his secretary, a stout woman with large, capable hands. "Get me Mark Standish and Hugh Thompson. Now!"

"Yes, Mr. Frain. Right away, Mr. Frain," she called back, dialing their extension.

"And get me a copy of last Friday's newspaper! At once!"

The secretary finished her call and then bustled about, trying to find a copy of the paper. Minutes later, Standish and Thompson appeared, eyes wary.

Frain paced back and forth on the Persian carpet in front of his desk. He turned to face the younger men.

"There's been an attempt on the Prime Minister's life," he said. "IRA agent Claire Kelly is in custody, being held at the War Rooms. Richard Snodgrass interceded in time. He and one of his associates are going to Bletchley. But it now looks as though there's going to be another attack somewhere. So for the love of God and England and all that is holy—what else have you two idiots neglected to share? Anything to do with a Paul?"

Hugh pushed back his sandy hair. "Someone named Paul, sir? I'll check, but not that I can think—"

"Don't think! Go! Put it all in a file," Frain yelled after him, getting his coat and hat. "I'm on my way to Downing Street." Under his breath, he muttered, "The head rolling shall commence when I return."

"Where is she?"

Snodgrass and John were at the University Arms hotel, having driven the last few miles on a flat tire. They'd convinced the man at the desk to give them a key, then bolted upstairs.

John shook David awake, none too gently. "Where's Maggie?"

"John?" David said sleepily. "What are you . . . ?" Then, as he grabbed for his eyeglasses and staggered to his feet, "Oh, good Lord!" He managed to arrange the wire frames on his face. "Beneficent Buddha! Tell me this is some kind of nightmare—and that Richard Snodgrass is not in my room!"

"This is supposed to be Maggie's room," John said. "Where is she?"

David looked around, blinking. "She was here—we were talking, and then I must have fallen asleep—"

Snodgrass looked heavenward. "God help us all." He turned to David. "Get your coat and hat. We have to get Miss Hope." Then, "Perhaps we should have tied a bell on her."

David shrugged on his jacket. "She's all right, though? Isn't she? I mean, where would she go? And at this hour? It's—what—just past midnight?" He looked at John and Snodgrass, suddenly realizing. "And why are you two here?"

"When we get back, remind me to fire both of you," Snodgrass said. "But in the meantime—move!"

# TWENTY-FOUR

It was impenetrably dark. Only the dribble of yellow light from the shuttered headlights and the sliver of moon permitted Pierce to see into the gloom. They passed through bleak, deserted villages and over grassy hills. Edmund drove uncomfortably fast, the car shuddering and shaking around some of the tighter corners.

"Nearly there, nearly there," Pierce said, consulting an old road map. "Now turn right. Yes, right here. Into the drive."

An ornate sign proclaimed *Westmore Place,* but the rusty black gates and grass-tufted drive belied the elegance of the name. Edmund and Maggie exchanged a look in the rearview mirror as the car headed up a steep rise and pulled in front of a rambling timber-framed brick house. Some of the stonework was crumbling, and the shrubbery was overgrown. Ivy obscured the windows. An owl shrieked through the silence.

They went up a cobblestone walkway, Pierce with his gun to Maggie's back. They reached the front door, once painted a glossy black, now dull and peeling. Pierce reached out to the bellpull, which made a low, mournful chime.

After a pause, the door was opened by a large-boned

woman. Her coarse salt-and-pepper hair was pulled back into a tight bun. She was dressed in a brown twill skirt, cashmere cardigan, and sensible lace-up oxfords. A triple strand of gray pearls encircled her neck. The dim light from within spilled out in a corona around her.

Behind her was a red-cheeked, snowy-haired man with an enormous white handlebar mustache, wearing plaid trousers and a brown hunting jacket.

"Mrs. Leticia Barron? And Mr. Roger Barron?" Pierce asked.

"Yes, of course," Leticia said, her eyes taking in the ropes on Maggie's wrists and Pierce's gun. "Please do come in."

Roger made a few grunting sounds.

They had a few moments to get their bearings. Two enormous black dogs with coarse and dusty fur were lying in front of a stone fireplace. The walls were covered in dark wood paneling that had seen better days, while moth-eaten stags with glassy black eyes, trophies of the chase, kept watch from above. Worn Persian rugs with large holes covered the stone floor. The windows were shrouded by blackout fabric, making the walls seem gloomy and close. The room smelled of wood smoke, mothballs, and wet dog.

One dog opened one dark, watchful eye, then closed it and went back to sleep. The other didn't stir. "Linus and Mortimer," Leticia cordially said to the three.

"I'm Malcolm Pierce, as you know. Henry Hodgeson from the London Saturday Club was kind enough to set this meeting up."

"How absolutely wonderful to have you here," Leticia trilled, extending a soft, white hand. Her eyes were bright. "Of course, when Henry told me the circumstances I was delighted to offer our humble home. Let's go into the kitchen, shall we? Oh, it's been so long since we've had guests!"

Maggie realized Leticia saw no irony in this.

The kitchen was large, with high ceilings and a black-and-white tile floor. Dirty dishes filled the sink. The smell of fried offal and overflowing rubbish bins soured the air.

"Please sit down," Leticia said, gesturing to the scarred wooden table. Even though her armpits were damp with fear, Maggie nearly let out a hysterical giggle when Leticia followed up with a genial, "Tea?"

Pierce gestured to the floor. "Sit down there, please." It was awkward with her hands tied, but she and Edmund complied. Pierce sat down at one of the black Windsor chairs but kept the gun trained on them.

"No tea, Mrs.—"

"Leticia."

"Thank you. Leticia. We still have a lot of work to do tonight."

She took a seat next to Pierce at the table, while Roger hung back near the door. Her eyes danced with excitement. "I can't tell you how thrilling this all is. We're just glad to be able, in our small way, to help."

"An enormous help," Pierce said. "The Führer will be most grateful."

"You know him?" she said, hand to heart. "What's he like?"

"A god among men," Pierce said. "He saved Germany. Gave her order and strength and discipline."

"How amazing," Leticia said, leaning in. "People here just don't understand it. That drunken fool Churchill certainly doesn't.

"And they—" Leticia gestured to Edmund and Maggie.

"One of Britain's premier code breakers and one of the drunken bastard's secretaries. Invaluable sources of information, the both of them. Which is why we need to get them to Berlin." He took a moment to smile at his captives, dimple flashing. "Tonight."

"And that's where we come in," Leticia said, fingering the silvery pearls around her neck. "I knew it was dangerous to keep that old Airco in the barn. But I knew it might come in handy someday."

Maggie tensed. *A plane?*

Leticia stopped suddenly, her brow furrowed.

"What?" Pierce prodded.

"It's just that—"

"Yes?"

Roger leaned up against the door frame. "Plane's a two-seater. There's only room for two."

"Damn it," Snodgrass said.

Maumbrey Cottage was still and silent; only the two half-full brandy snifters gave the illusion that the place was still inhabited.

"Damn it. We're too late."

"No!" John was vehement. "We must go after them."

Snodgrass rubbed his chin, looking around for signs of a struggle.

"Can someone please explain to me what exactly's going on?" David asked.

John gave him a grave look. "Paige never died," he said. "She's an IRA sleeper agent who faked her death. She tried to use Maggie to get classified information on Churchill. When that didn't work, she infiltrated Number Ten and tried to assassinate the Old Man. Posed as Maggie to get in. Nearly worked, too."

"Hardly," Snodgrass snorted, still looking for clues. "We were watching closely. Of course we did a background check when Miss Hope was hired. We were already keeping a watch on Miss Kelly. The fact that she and Miss Hope were friends was a red flag. I didn't want her hired at all, if you recall."

David gave a slow nod.

"And certainly not as a private secretary." Snodgrass sighed. "You may recall that Miss Kelly worked for Ambassador Kennedy before he returned to the U.S."

John strode to the door. "I don't know about you two, but I'm not going to just sit around and wait. We have the addresses of the Saturday Club's safe house. I say we go. Who's with me?"

"That's where we met her," David said, hurrying after John. "At one of those cocktail parties Joe Kennedy was always giving. Nigel would always invite us— he was trying to win over Chuck."

"Yes," Snodgrass said as they made their way to David's car, and got into the passenger seat. "Miss Kelly made sure to connect with you. And when the tide turned and Chamberlain stepped down, she became even closer, didn't she?"

John got into the backseat. "That's why she suggested Maggie for the typist's job," he said, connecting the dots. "She wanted to get a friend into Number Ten, when she couldn't get the job herself."

"And that's why you didn't want Maggie to work as a private secretary," David realized, sliding behind the wheel. "Too much classified information."

Snodgrass gave a nod as David turned the key in the lock and the engine turned over. "I didn't want her working at Number Ten at all. But then Mr. Frain convinced me it was safer. We could keep an eye on her."

The car pulled out of the driveway in the darkness. "So she really could have been a private secretary, not a typist," David realized.

"Good Lord, yes," Snodgrass said. "That girl's smarter than the two of you put together. I would've been lucky to get her! But by that time we were suspicious that Miss Kelly and her handler were planning something big. It was easier to keep Miss Hope close but not let her know too much. Why do you think I was so distressed at her learning about RDF?"

"Ah," said John, putting the pieces together.

"And what about her father?" David asked, straining to see the road ahead.

"Miss Hope believed he passed away in 'sixteen. We were concerned that if she found out he was still alive, she'd compromise his cover. Or that *he'd* compromise his cover—which, of course, he did." He looked at David. "Once I found out what sort of a fool's errand you and Miss Hope were on, I realized that I needed to make a few calls."

"So he's not really insane?" David said.

Snodgrass shrugged. "It was necessary—is necessary. There's a spy at Bletchley. That's how the Germans know to keep changing the rotator wheels for their ciphers once we manage to break them. And with Professor Hope considered brilliant but mad, we hoped that the spy would slip up and reveal himself."

"Has he?" David asked.

"Not yet," Snodgrass replied. "But we're close. Very close."

"But what about Maggie? And her father?" John said.

"Professor Hope must have, somehow, secretly asked Miss Hope to meet with him. It was inevitable, really— he hadn't seen her for years, and having her think he was mad proved too much for him. We knew there was a chance that he'd attempt to reveal more."

"But what *happened* to them?" David asked.

"He's close to finding out who the German spy at Bletchley is. Or, failing that, by their removing him from the equation, our ability to break German ciphers would be seriously diminished. I'm afraid that's the significance of Operation Hope."

David's tone was grim, and his hands tightened on the wheel. "So they're going to either break him or kill him?"

Snodgrass tilted his head. "Most likely break him, then kill him."

John started. "And what about Maggie?"

"Hope probably wouldn't break himself," Snodgrass said. "But if . . ." He trailed off delicately.

"If his daughter's in danger, he just might," David finished, pressing harder on the gas pedal.

Roger watched Maggie and her father while Pierce went to the car for his radio. There was an uncomfortable silence.

"Rather awkward, what?" Roger offered up.

Edmund looked away, pretending to be interested in a row of chipped crockery on the shelf.

"Indeed," Maggie replied lightly. "My name is Maggie Hope, and this is my father, Edmund," she said, giving them names, trying to humanize them in the eyes of their captors. "How do you do?" Maggie said to Leticia, giving her the most winning smile she could muster.

Pierce entered with his suitcase radio. "Shut up," he snapped to Maggie, setting it down on the table and opening it. Leticia helped set up the aerials for transmission and then waited, nearly giddy with anticipation, as they heard the empty hiss of the airwaves.

Pierce typed out his code slowly and carefully. "It's been a while," he said, almost apologetically.

On the other end, there was an explosion of typing. Pierce copied it down, then asked for a repeat.

"Is that really Berlin?" Leticia breathed.

"Hamburg, actually."

From his bag he procured his codebook. It took him several minutes to decrypt the message.

Finally, he looked up. "I have confirmation that they want me to break you both and then take the remaining one to Berlin," he said.

## TWENTY-FIVE

"CAN'T YOU GO any faster?" John called from the cramped backseat.

"Mr. Sterling," Snodgrass barked from the passenger seat. "Mr. Greene is driving an ancient car, with watered-down petrol, in the midst of a blackout. Perhaps you'd like to take over?"

"She's not old," David said from the driver's seat, pushing up his glasses and then patting the leather-covered dashboard. "She's vintage. Like a fine Bordeaux. And since yours blew a tire in Bletchley, she's all we've got."

"Maggie needs us. Her father needs us," John said.

Snodgrass looked in the mirror back toward John, and his face softened for a moment. "And we'll get there. Hang on, old boy."

"You're sure we're going the right way?" David insisted.

"Mr. Frain has had men watching Malcolm Pierce. He believes Pierce will be going from Bletchley to a safe house before trying to leave the country. Apparently, one of the London Saturday Club's members has a contact nearby, and that's where Mr. Frain thinks Pierce will take Maggie and her father. At some point, somehow, they'll probably try to leave the country."

"Leave the country?" David said, surprised.

"It's possible," Snodgrass said. "A boat to Ireland. Boat with a predetermined submarine pickup. Perhaps a plane flying under the radar to France, then another to Germany."

They all took a moment to consider the possibilities.

"By the way," Snodgrass said to John, catching his eye in the rearview mirror, "good work breaking that code."

"Sir, it wasn't me," John said from the backseat. "It was Maggie. Maggie broke it."

Snodgrass permitted himself a smile. "She did? Good for her."

"Maggie?" David said.

"Yes. She noticed the code embedded in the advert a few days ago and showed it to me. To tell the truth, at the time I didn't think it was anything. She called me around five today saying she'd broken it. That's when I realized Mr. Churchill was in danger and went down to his office—"

"Where Claire had a gun on you," Snodgrass said.

David started. "Who's Claire?"

"Paige," John answered.

"Paige?" David turned in his seat to face John. "No, Claire."

"Paige is Claire."

"No, Paige is Paige."

John sighed. "Paige is really Claire."

"Holy Hera." David looked into the blackness out the window and considered. "And Maggie figured it out? And didn't tell *me*?"

"No. I mean yes. She figured out the assassination attempt but doesn't have any idea that it was Paige. Claire, I mean. Or that Paige is Claire."

"*If* you two are finished," Snodgrass thundered, "we still have the matter at hand to take care of!"

"Well, then, who's Malcolm Pierce?" David asked meekly, eyes on the road. "Besides an undercover agent."

"We've identified him as Albrecht von Leyen," Snodgrass said. "He was born at the London Hospital in Whitechapel in 1901 to Wolfgang von Leyen, a diplomat and wealthy Prussian aristocrat. His mother, Emily Ainsworth, was an English debutante. The family lived in London until the Great War, then moved back to Berlin. The mother died of lung cancer in Prussia in 1920. Meanwhile, Wolfgang and young Albrecht moved around quite a bit after the war, including another stint in London. In 1937, von Leyen vanished. We can only speculate what happened—that he underwent Abwehr training and was sent back to London under an assumed name, Malcolm Pierce."

"And he's able to pass for British," David said, tapping the brakes and swerving to avoid a deer stopped in the road.

"Von Leyen allegedly died in a hiking accident in the Alps," John said. "His body was never recovered. Meanwhile, a man named Malcolm Pierce dies alone and destitute at Bethlem Royal Hospital. Von Leyen assumed his identity and became Malcolm Pierce, ordinary British citizen. Of course, he joined that Fascist group, the Saturday Club, in order to make connections with like-minded British citizens."

"That's how we found him," Snodgrass added. "And that's how he was able to make contact with Miss Kelly and her handler. He's working with them to coordinate their attacks."

David turned back to look at John. "How the hell do you know that?"

"I have clearance," John said, looking out the window and not meeting David's eyes.

"So do I."

"Mine's higher-level than yours."

"Prat," David said, swerving to avoid a fallen tree branch.

"Boys, this isn't some sort of Oxbridge club where everything is debated over port and cigars," Snodgrass snapped. "We all work for the Prime Minister. We all handle sensitive information on a need-to-know basis."

"And apparently John needs to know more than I do," David said, sniffing, looking at John in the rearview mirror.

Snodgrass sighed. "Britain is doomed."

"Almost ready," Pierce said, stoking the red-and-orange fire with a heavy iron poker.

Edmund struggled in his bonds, but Roger had tied them too well. Pierce continued to poke at the fire with one hand while keeping his drawn pistol pointed at Edmund with the other. "Roger," he said. "Tend to the girl."

Roger came up behind Maggie and placed both hands on her shoulders. Then, stroking the back of her neck, said, "Now, you be a good little thing and we won't have any trouble." Her flesh crawled at his touch.

"Roger!" Leticia hissed.

"Sorry," he said, dropping his hands. "Getting into the spirit is all."

"Leave her alone," Edmund said. "Look, take me— I'll tell you anything—everything. But let her stay; let her live. She's no threat to you."

"Why do you care so much about me?" Maggie snapped. "It's not like you know me. It's not as though you've ever acted like a father before this."

"Margaret!" Edmund whispered. "This is not the time."

"Ah, family reunions," Pierce said, his eye on the poker that was slowly but surely heating up. "But I'm afraid she already knows too much. Besides, she probably has quite a few tidbits of information worth hearing."

"She could identify us," Roger said, worried.

"So I'll have to die," Maggie said slowly to Leticia, whose eyes widened in sudden understanding. "That will make you murderers." She gave Leticia a hard look, sensing a moment's hesitation. "Are you sure you can live with yourself—as a murderer?"

"Not before she can tell us when the Americans will join the war." Roger looked her in the eyes. "Surely, as Mr. Churchill's secretary, you must have typed innumerable missives to President Roosevelt and filed any number from him. Is America joining in the fight or not? And when? What are they bringing to the table?"

The truth was that she had typed what felt like hundreds of letters from Mr. Churchill to President Roosevelt. And seen a number of his responses. The United States was sending food and arms, as well as planes, submarines, and ships. Although there was no official commitment from the United States yet, it was very close to entering the war.

*But they don't need to know that.*

"Mr. Churchill and President Roosevelt have limited contact," Maggie said, turning back to Roger. "And when they do communicate, it's by scrambled telephone line. In private. I don't know anything else," she lied.

Maggie had a sudden and fierce longing to see Aunt Edith. *Don't let the bastards get you down,* she used to say. As she felt the horror of the situation closing in on her, she clung to Edith's words.

"That's too bad," Pierce said. "All right, Professor Hope, now let's try you. Where are you boys in relation to code breaking? What do you know?"

Edmund blinked hard, and a muscle twitched in his cheek. "We haven't gotten very far," he said in a conciliatory voice. "As you must know by now, we're receiving German decrypts. We only have one key. Takes too long to decode—and so not much practical use, I'm afraid. . . ."

What he wasn't saying, what he couldn't say, was that the key to British intelligence was something the Germans had never counted on. Bletchley didn't use human beings. At least, not in the way the Germans expected. It was using Alan Turing's calculating machines, based on the work of the Polish cryptographer Marian Rejewski. Nazi ciphers were slowly but surely being broken by these British machines—hundreds and thousands of times faster than any human could possibly do it. Although they were still at the very beginning and had a long way yet to go, espionage was entering a new age.

"Really?" Pierce said. "Somehow I doubt either one of you is telling the truth." He gave the fire one last stab with the poker. "Here's the way this is going to work. Do you see this poker? It's nice and hot now. Well, I'm going to burn your daughter with it until one of you tells me what I need to know. She's a pretty thing—too bad she won't be when I get through with her."

He walked toward Maggie with the red-tipped poker. She fought in her restraints, but Roger held her arms down. The poker came at her face, and she could feel the heat it was giving off. Her heart felt as though it would explode.

The poker touched her hair, and she could hear the sizzle and then smell the stink of burning.

"You bastard," Edmund rasped between clenched teeth.

"It's all right," Maggie managed to get out. "Done worse with my curling iron."

Leticia gave a chortle, then clapped a hand over her mouth. Once again, Maggie locked eyes with her.

Pierce heated the poker again and then touched it to

the wooden kitchen table. There was a hiss and a wisp of smoke. From the corner of her eye, Maggie could see Leticia jump. From the panic in her eyes, Maggie could see that Leticia had never expected things to get this out of hand.

"Mr. Pierce," Leticia began, "surely you don't need to—"

"Shut. Up."

The words struck Leticia like a slap in the face. She cowered and seemed to shrink a few inches.

Pierce started toward Maggie with the poker again. This time, he touched it to the shoulder of her cardigan, which smoked and smoldered before burning out. The smell of scorched cotton filled the room, and she could see Leticia's nostrils flare.

Pierce touched the poker to her shoulder again, and this time pressed it into the flesh.

Maggie cried out as the burning metal seared her arm. The stench of charred flesh filled the room. Unbidden tears filled her eyes. She turned once again to Leticia, deliberately allowing the tears to run down her face. Maggie saw Leticia blanch.

"All right! All right!" Edmund said. "I'll tell you. Everything. Just stop."

All eyes turned to him.

"As you know, we're aware you're sending encrypted messages," Edmund said.

The poker waved in front of Maggie. "Tell me something I don't already know," Pierce said.

Maggie could see Leticia begin to inch around the kitchen, unnoticed by the men.

"We know that you communicate with each other using ciphers generated from five rotator wheels."

Leticia was now at the kitchen sink.

"Yes, I *know* that already," Pierce said, impatient.

Leticia picked up a large, black cast-iron skillet. Maggie could see remnants of scrambled eggs—that day's supper?—coating the bottom.

"Leticia!" Roger called.

*Yes!* Maggie thought. *Leticia, you* do *have a moral compass, after all.*

As if in slow motion, Pierce turned to her. "Mrs. Barron? What on earth do you think you're—"

The heavy pan hit Pierce at the base of his skull. He crumpled to the floor.

Roger gasped at Leticia. "You stupid bitch! What have you *done?*"

Murphy wasn't impressed by the symmetry and elegance of the soaring interior of St. Paul's Cathedral. *Too bloody Protestant,* he muttered, as he made his way down a side aisle, his tread soft on the black-and-white marble tiles. He avoided looking at the altar and any depictions of Jesus.

He permitted himself to light one candle in the chapel of St. Dunstan for Claire and her mission before moving on. Claire was surely dead by now, he knew. But if she had accomplished her mission—to assassinate that bastard—then it was worth it.

It had to be.

An elderly woman with an elegant gray chignon, holding a Bible in trembling, blue-veined hands, gave Murphy a sideways look.

"Eh, sorry, ma'am," he said, suddenly realizing he still had his hat on his head. He snatched it off and covered his heart with it, affecting a pious posture as he made his way down the long aisle.

When he could see that no one was looking, he let himself through one door and then another, taking a few flights of stairs down to the crypt. From there, he made his way in the dark to a place he'd come to know quite well.

The place where, slowly, night after night, he'd been building the bomb.

"Hey there, darlin'," Murphy said, running his hands along the bomb's edges. He'd spent many hours down in the darkness crafting this beauty. Between destroying Winston Churchill and then St. Paul's Cathedral—the spirit of London to so many of the bloody Brits—he and Claire would bring England to her knees. With no firm leadership and a panic-stricken public, the Germans would have no trouble finishing the country off.

"All right, baby," he cooed to the machine, twisting a wire here and tweaking one there. "It's almost time."

Above him, mothers prayed for their sons in the military, widows prayed for their dead husbands, and even a few atheists clasped hands and looked heavenward in hope. None of these people were in Murphy's thoughts as he set the timer on his bomb.

In the darkness, the gold pocket watch began a slow ticking countdown.

## TWENTY-SIX

"ROGER!" LETICIA HISSED, still holding the heavy skillet that had taken down Malcolm Pierce.

Roger's eyes bulged as he took in Pierce's prone form. "Christ, woman! Are you daft? What did you do that for?"

"I didn't sign on for murder! Pierce said Hitler would bring order and stability." She wrinkled her nose. "Not torture in my kitchen!"

The dogs barked in the background, excited by the noise, their claws scraping on the locked kitchen door.

"But you believe in the cause?"

"Y-yes," she answered. "I'm just not keen on the idea of burning people with hot pokers." She clicked her tongue. "Not at all seemly."

"Sorry to hear that," Roger said. "Going ahead anyway."

Maggie and Edmund exchanged a look. Pierce's gun was on the floor. If there was some way one of them could get to it, they'd at least have a chance.

"Roger!" she said. "You'll do no such thing!"

"I don't think you understand. In for a penny, in for a pound, what? These two people can identify us. And people in Berlin are waiting for a prisoner to be delivered."

"They're waiting for *Mr. Pierce*. Not you."

"Don't really think they give a damn about Pierce, long as they get what they want. Which is why I'm going to be flying one of them in the Airco to Berlin myself."

"You haven't flown in years," Leticia protested.

"Just like riding a bicycle." He shook his head. "Never thought I'd be flying in another war."

"Roger! You can't just take one and leave the other one here. And what about me? What am *I* supposed to do?"

"It's fine," he said reassuringly, moving toward her. "Everything's fine."

Her mouth made a perfect round O of surprise before she slumped to the floor beside Pierce.

Roger turned back to Maggie and Edmund. "Now, let's get on with it, shall we?"


Claire was being held in one of the underground conference rooms of the War Rooms, seated on a gray metal folding chair with her arms handcuffed behind her back and her feet tied to the chair's legs. The only other furniture in the room was a battered wooden table and another folding chair. The room was lit from above by a naked fluorescent bulb. The air, silent except for the rumble of air-conditioning, was still and stale.

She started when she heard the click of the lock and then the scrape of the door in front of her. Then she saw the man enter, carrying a black leather briefcase.

"Miss Kelly," he said, setting down his briefcase. "I am Peter Frain, Director General of MI-Five."

She trained her eyes on the table in front of her.

Frain removed his Anthony Eden hat with its upturned brim and his trench coat. He sat down opposite her, then unlocked his briefcase and pulled out a file.

"I want to call the American embassy," she said, finally. "I'm a U.S. citizen. I have rights."

"Sarah Sanderson had rights, too." He called through the open door, "Bring her in."

Two police officers wheeled in a metal gurney. On top was a large black zippered bag. They wheeled it next to Claire and then unzipped it, revealing a face. Inside, there was a woman, a beautiful woman. Dead. Her eyes were closed. She looked pale and peaceful.

Claire looked away, her eyes shining with tears. "You sick, sick bastard," she whispered finally.

He motioned the men to take the body away. "We didn't kill her, Miss Kelly," he said. "You did."

"No! It wasn't me!" Claire swallowed. "Besides, there's . . . collateral damage . . . in any war." Even to Claire, the words sounded weak.

" 'Collateral damage' named Sarah Sanderson."

Claire slumped in her chair. "I'm not even supposed to be alive," she said.

"Yes," Frain said. "We gathered that the plan was to assassinate the Prime Minister, then kill yourself. However, it didn't quite pan out that way, did it?"

Claire was silent. A vein throbbed in her temple.

"I highly doubt that you could kill yourself, let alone another human being. Why else would John Sterling still be alive? Any assassin worth the name would have taken him out immediately. Your only chance to survive now is to tell us everything you know."

Once again, Claire was silent.

Frain opened the manila folder on the desk and began to read from the pages inside. "Let's see—Claire Paige Kelly. Born July second, 1916, in Richmond, Virginia. Father is Francis Xavier Kelly, linguist. Mother is Imelda Mary Donovan Kelly. Educated at Miss Porter's School and Wellesley College. Came to London in 'thirty-eight to work for Joseph Kennedy, U.S. Ambassador to England. Principal interests, though, are boys and booze. When war broke out and Ambassador Kennedy returned to the States, applied for the Women's Auxiliary. Recommended by Ambassador Kennedy. Interviewed March fifth. Accepted. Cleared. Started work the following week. So far, so good?" He raised one eyebrow. "Care to add anything?"

Claire said nothing.

"Not exactly a rigorous process of selection. But then again, you're a U.S. citizen, and there's a war on. And you do come from a rather rich American family and have a reference from the Ambassador."

Frain looked back down at his notes. "Summers in the family home, located just outside Belfast. That wasn't enough to be a red flag initially, but when you applied for the position as the Prime Minister's secretary, we thought it was worth investigating. Ultimately, along with your U.S. passport, it was enough to keep you from the position."

Claire didn't move, but the color drained from her face.

"We discovered you were an avid churchgoer, Miss Kelly. Especially during off-hours. A Catholic church."

"There's nothing wrong with that."

"At first we thought it was just an affair with a priest. But of course, it was more complicated than that."

"I want a lawyer."

"And I want the lion to lie down with the lamb," Frain said. "But neither of us is going to get what we want, are we? Especially Diana Snyder."

There was a sharp intake of breath from Claire.

"Ah, I see you remember. We have a witness placing a Michael Murphy at the scene of the crime, but you were there, too, weren't you?"

Claire said nothing, but a muscle beneath her eye started to twitch.

"That's your—what do you call it in the States? Fifth Amendment right, I suppose. We don't have that here.

And besides, you and I both know you might as well have murdered her, that poor young girl. You lured her in somehow, set it up for Murphy. You're just as guilty as if you stabbed her yourself."

Claire bit her lip, hard, to keep from crying out.

"You tried for the job with the P.M.—what a coup that would have been! But alas, you had too many red flags attached to your personnel file already."

Frain looked at her. "But that didn't stop you from suggesting an old college friend, a Miss Margaret Hope, for the job, did it? And you anticipated that as Miss Hope's best friend and flatmate, you'd get important information from her."

Claire still said nothing.

"Meanwhile, Miss Kelly, we were also monitoring the Saturday Club. When you got involved with them, we started to dig a bit deeper. At first we thought that perhaps Miss Hope was in on the plot as well. But then we realized that the parish priest you met at odd hours was actually Michael Murphy. We were able to connect you with both the IRA and Abwehr."

Claire looked up. "I want a deal," she spat.

"You're going to hang unless you convince me otherwise."

Frain pulled a cigarette from a monogrammed silver case, lit it, and inhaled deeply.

"What about the life of Michael Murphy?" he asked conversationally. "Is he also 'collateral damage'? Like Diana and Sarah?"

"Michael?" Claire blinked. "You have Michael?"

"As I said, we've been tailing you and Mr. Murphy for some time now. Our men have already taken him into custody."

"Michael won't negotiate," Claire said flatly.

"Probably not. Which is why, in order to save him, you'll have to."

When Claire blinked, Frain knew he'd read her correctly. She wouldn't talk to save herself, but she could be convinced to protect her lover.

"What are you offering?"

"We are prepared to offer you this—your life and Mr. Murphy's. In exchange for information."

"I—I can't."

"You tried to assassinate the Prime Minister of England, and you failed, Miss Kelly. Failed. Now tell us what we want to know and we'll let you and your Mick boyfriend live."

Maggie and Edmund took in Leticia's unmoving body on the floor next to Pierce's. His gun was still on the floor next to him. Roger still had his pistol pointed at the two prisoners. The barrel moved unsteadily between Maggie and her father, as though he couldn't figure out which one to shoot first.

Maggie grimaced and tried not to cry out in pain as her arm continued to throb.

Outside the kitchen, the dogs snarled and whined.

"Quiet!" Roger shouted. The dogs gave a few low whines, but then whimpered and padded off.

"Why don't you undo these ties and we'll have a nice chat," Maggie gasped between waves of pain. "That's what you want, isn't it?"

"And look how well that worked," Roger said. He walked behind Maggie. She could smell his cologne—vetiver mixed with sweat and fear. He began working on the ropes around her hands. She bit her lip, refusing to show him how much it hurt her arm.

"You're taking me?" she managed. He'd put the gun down next to him, on the floor.

"You're smaller, female, easier to control," Roger said as he worked. "And you probably had access to more high-level information than you're letting on here. I'm sure the gestapo will have a number of techniques to get you to talk."

"And what about you?" *Just keep him talking,* she thought, *keep him distracted, and maybe we have a prayer.* "Your wife is dead, your contact is out cold. You're going to start over with a new life in Berlin?"

"Here I'm nothing—no one," he said, working at the ropes around her wrists. Red and raw waves of pain shot down her arm like hot currents of electricity. "See this house? We used to have servants, horses, hunting parties. Now it's gone, all gone. There's nothing left for me here. In Berlin, I'll be a hero."

The ropes fell away, and Maggie was free. She rubbed her wrists, trying to get the circulation back, then slowly lifted her arm to look at the wound on her shoulder. Gingerly, she tried to raise the fabric of the blouse and sweater away from the charred flesh—bad idea. She winced and set her teeth.

Roger pressed the gun into her temple and grabbed her elbow, forcing her to her feet. "Now, don't get any ideas, my dear," he said.

He took the gun from Maggie's head and pointed it at Edmund.

He cocked the gun and, distracted by Edmund, relaxed his hold on Maggie's arm.

She knew this was her only chance.

"Goodbye, Professor Hope," he said.

As he did, Maggie used her last ounce of energy to spin around and dive for Pierce's gun, still on the kitchen floor.

In a single move, she grabbed it and pointed it at Roger. It was bigger and heavier than she expected, and her shoulder throbbed in protest, but it fit into the soft palm of her hand with surprising ease.

"I believe we have what's called a stalemate, Miss Hope," Roger said, looking at her with an expression of genuine surprise.

Suddenly the door behind him burst open. There stood Snodgrass, flanked by David and John.

"Ah, Miss Hope," Snodgrass said. "I see you have things well in hand. However, I hope you don't mind a little backup."

Roger realized he was outnumbered.

"Please drop your weapon, sir," Snodgrass said in a neutral tone. Maggie had never thought she'd be so glad to see his stringy hair and sloping shoulders in her life. Not to mention John and David.

"Blast it all!" Roger said.

"I must insist," Snodgrass said.

Roger could see that he was out of options. Slowly, he knelt down and placed the gun on the floor. With his right hand, Snodgrass kept the gun on Roger. With the left, he pulled out a pair of handcuffs and tossed them to David, who caught them in one hand. "Will you do the honors, Mr. Greene?"

David went over to Roger and cuffed his hands behind his back, none too gently.

"You too, Miss Hope," Snodgrass said. Maggie lowered her arm.

John strode to Maggie. "Are you all right?" he said, offering his hand.

She took it. It was large and warm and comforting. *Of course he figured it out. Of course he came.* She stood up and handed the gun over to Snodgrass, who clicked on the safety. "Fine, thank you. Although it's been"— she looked over to Edmund and gave a wry smile— "quite the evening."

"And night," John said. "What were you thinking? Gallivanting all over the countryside? Making people worry . . . ?"

"And *you*," David said to Edmund, pointing his finger. "Aren't you supposed to be crazy?"

Edmund shrugged. "It's a long story."

"Once MI-Five picks this one up," Snodgrass said, indicating Roger, "we'll have plenty of time to chat."

# TWENTY-SEVEN

PETER FRAIN DROPPED his cigarette to the floor, grinding it beneath his heel. "I want you to tell me who's still out there."

Claire pressed her lips together and looked off into space.

"We know the only reason you're even considering helping us is because of Mr. Murphy," Frain continued. "But believe me, it's not too late for us to change our minds about how we treat him."

Claire looked at him and blinked. *Good,* he thought, *let her chew on that.*

"There were a few men I heard Michael talking about," she ventured finally. "But I don't know where they are or how to get in contact with them."

Frain rose to his feet and walked around the table until he was behind Claire. "Who's Eammon Devlin?" he whispered hoarsely in her ear. He already knew who Eammon Devlin was—one of London's biggest and most successful underground figures. Devlin provided "protection," ran several brothels, and since the start of the war, maintained a thriving black-market business specializing in sugar, cigarettes, petrol, and stockings. He was always suspected of IRA ties, but so far they'd been impossible to prove.

"I heard Michael speak of him a few times, but I never met him. He's one of the higher-ups; that's all I know."

Frain straightened up. "That's not good enough."

"It's going to have to be."

Without warning, Frain tipped her chair over. Claire, with her arms and legs still cuffed, hit the cement floor with a resounding bang. Claire screamed in shock and agony.

A guard appeared at the door. "Everything all right, Mr. Frain?"

"Perfectly fine, thank you," Frain said, bending over Claire's form on the floor. Her face twitched in alarm and pain.

The guard left, closing the door softly behind him.

"Let's try this again," he said mildly. "Tell me about Eammon Devlin."

"I already told you!" Claire moaned.

"You said you never met him."

"I haven't."

Frain brought the chair, with Claire in it, to its upright position once again. "Unless you tell me the whole truth right now, that deal to save your lover is off the table. And he'll hang for treason."

"But you said—"

"Do you think the Prime Minister will really honor that agreement? For the duo who tried to kill him? Michael Murphy—and you—will be executed for war crimes. But first you'll go to prison while you wait for your trial. And let me tell you, I know a little something about prison in wartime. These murderers and rapists— they're all criminals, but they're British criminals. Get that? And we'll let it be known exactly what you're in for."

Frain knelt down in front of the girl, pupils large and black in his gray eyes. "And know this: I'll give you about two weeks before you attempt suicide. Six weeks until you succeed. Mr. Murphy may hold out a little longer, but not before he's suffered . . . unspeakable acts."

Frain let the words sink in. Then he rose to his feet and turned, as though to leave the room.

"Wait!"

Frain stopped but didn't look at her.

"Eammon Devlin is the man we reported to. We took our orders from him—but he never contacted us directly. Or at least he never contacted me directly. I received my orders through Michael."

Frain turned around slowly. "What about the bomb at Saint Paul's?"

"Michael is the one who smuggled the pieces in, and he assembled it. But Devlin designed and built it. He's an engineer originally—he knows how it works. And he's the only one who can stop it."

"Where is he?"

She blinked. "I don't know."

"Miss Kelly, must I remind you—"

Claire met his eyes. "I wish to God that I did. But I don't. I don't know!"

Back at No. 10, the mood was tense. It was morning, and a baleful red sun illuminated the horizon through pearly gray clouds. They didn't have much time left. Less than four hours, to be precise.

Edmund, David, John, and Maggie were sitting at one end of the large, dark-wood rectangular table in the Cabinet Room, on William Kent red damask chairs with ornate gilded frames. The room was light and airy, with ecru walls and wainscoting the color of clotted cream. The grandfather clock ticked loudly, while in the distance, Big Ben chimed the hour with a slow and steady gong. There was a small vase of purple heather on the ornate white-marble fireplace mantel. The attached note read, "To the Prime Minister. For luck."

*We'll need it,* Maggie thought. Her arm still throbbed. To take her mind off it, she thought of the upcoming day's schedule and when the P.M. would take a meeting with the rest of the cabinet. Then she turned to John, looking at his profile in the light from the windows. He caught her glance and smiled.

Snodgrass entered the room, followed by Frain, who closed the heavy door behind him. But not before Nelson padded in, leaping gracefully onto a side chair and settling in, purring loudly.

"Professor Hope," Snodgrass began, gesturing at the man in the somber suit, "this is Peter Frain, head of MI-Five. Mr. Frain, why don't you bring everyone up to speed?"

"Thank you, Mr. Snodgrass." He looked at the assembled group. "Let's not waste time with the Official Secrets Acts you've signed, yes? Since the beginning of the war, MI-Five has been tracing the actions of various individuals we believe dangerous to England. We were aware of Malcolm Pierce as a homegrown Fascist, and one of the leaders of the so-called Saturday Club. As you well know," he said, with a nod to Edmund and Maggie, "he turned out to be much more dangerous. Albrecht von Leyen was a sleeper agent for Abwehr. His goal was to kidnap Professor Edmund Hope, who was about to uncover one of *their* sleeper agents. Thanks to those here, that plan was thwarted."

"What happened to him?" Maggie asked. "And Roger and Leticia?"

"Malcolm Pierce and Roger Barron have been taken into custody, where they will be debriefed," he said. "Leticia Barron is dead."

"But what *happened,*" she pressed, remembering how Leticia had ended up saving their lives.

"The police called a disposal team, which took her body to a crematorium in North London," Frain said. "However, the official story is that the Barrons were called away to assist a sick aunt in Edinburgh."

*Disposal team. Crematorium. All right, then.* Maggie was silent.

Frain said, "But that's not all that happened."

John looked at Maggie with concern.

"Yesterday, there was an attempt to assassinate the Prime Minister." Snodgrass, David, and John looked on impassively. But Edmund started and Maggie gasped.

Frain held up one hand. "The assassination was thwarted, thanks to the quick action on the part of Richard Snodgrass and John Sterling. The perpetrator was one Claire Kelly, also known as Paige Kelly—"

*Paige?*

"—a colleague of Malcolm Pierce and also the IRA."

"Maggie," John said. "I'm so sorry."

*Paige?*

"Miss Hope, it pains me to have to tell you this, but you need to know that in order to carry off the assassination, Miss Kelly disguised herself as you to gain entrance to the War Rooms. You also must know that to secure her cover, she and her companion, an IRA agent by the name of Michael Murphy, killed a young woman named Sarah Sanderson, who'd discovered Claire in her disguise as she was leaving."

The room was stunned and silent—apparently, not even Snodgrass and John had known this detail.

*Paige?*

*And Sarah?*

"Sarah," Maggie managed finally. *"Sarah?"*

Edmund patted Maggie's hand awkwardly. Still, it was a comfort.

John looked pale as well.

"I wish that were all," Frain said.

"You mean there's more?" Maggie said bitterly. Surely there was a limit to how much one could take. Nelson jumped down from the chair, then wound himself around her ankle. She absently reached down to pet him.

"I'm afraid so." He looked at the group. "The attempted assassination of Mr. Churchill and the attempted kidnapping of Professor Hope were part of their plot. We've thwarted both those plans. However, there's still one more we need to defuse."

"Operation Paul," Maggie said.

"Yes," Frain replied.

Maggie processed his new information as a way to distract herself from the other revelations—Paige was alive and Sarah was not. Paige was a traitor named Claire. Sarah was dead. Paige—or Claire—was alive. It was somehow easier to think about Paul.

Whoever he was.

Frain entered Claire Kelly's interrogation room once again. It looked the same, only Claire was more distraught and disheveled. Her lipstick had worn off, leaving a red stain, and she had dark, bruiselike shadows underneath her eyes.

"Can I please get something to eat?" Claire said in a weak voice.

Frain didn't answer; instead, he pushed a photograph in front of her.

"Do you recognize this man?"

Claire looked at the photograph of a man with a receding hairline, beaky nose, and intense black eyes. "No."

"He's connected to Michael Murphy."

"I don't know him."

"His name is Joseph McCormack. He's a physics teacher at the London Oratory School."

Claire looked up at Frain. "You know more about him than I do, then."

"He's also our only way to reach Eammon Devlin. And we can't do that without your help."

"Why should I help you? I've already gotten all I'm going to get for cooperating."

Frain's demeanor gentled. "That's not necessarily true," he said, sitting down at the desk and leaning in closer to Claire. "I know you love Michael. You've already shown me that today. But unless you help us get to Devlin, you'll never see him again."

Another knock at the door. "Come in," Frain called.

A tall man in a black MI-5 uniform entered. "Our teams are in place, sir."

"Thank you," Frain said. "Have them stand by."

The man nodded and left. Frain rose, clasping his hands behind his back. He looked down at the girl.

"I'm offering you your life, Claire. You and Mr. Murphy will be extradited to Ireland, where even non–IRA sympathizers will be much more lenient with you than we. This is what you told me you wanted. I'm offering you a life with Murphy, instead of hanging for treason. Right now the only question is—which do you want?"

Claire was silent.

Frain turned to leave.

Without looking at him, Claire said, "What do you need me to do?"

Frain turned around to face her. "Go to Joseph McCormack and tell him that you need to speak to Devlin."

Claire snorted. "He won't let me through his front door, let alone get near Devlin."

"He will when you tell him that you've got a hostage who can help him."

Claire's eyes widened. "A hostage? Who?"

Frain permitted himself a small smile. "We'll let you know when it's time."

## TWENTY-EIGHT

MAGGIE HAD A plan.

"You want to do *what*?" John was pacing back and forth in the Cabinet Room while Maggie sat on one of the carved mahogany chairs, Nelson purring contentedly on her lap.

"The cover story goes like this," she said. "MI-Five will transport"—it was hard to say the name, but she managed—"Claire to the detention center. The vehicle has an accident. During the ensuing chaos, she secures one of the weapons and takes me hostage. She'll take me to McCormack. Then he'll lead us to Devlin."

David was trying to get the facts straight. "And when you get to Devlin—what? You ask nicely for the override key?"

"Yes," Edmund interjected. "Please enlighten us on this point."

"All of Devlin's bombs in the past have had override keys," Frain said. "That's the way he designs them—this way, he keeps ultimate control over the bomb and it can't be used against him. Miss Kelly will use Miss Hope as the pretext for getting inside and then will"—he cleared his throat—"ingratiate herself in order to find the key, which is always on his person. Now, about the mission—we're going to handle this passively."

John started. "What the hell does that mean?" Then, to Maggie, "Sorry."

*As though* swearing *would offend me at this point,* she thought.

"It means that we'll have undercover MI-Five in every car, in every store, in every window, in the area. We're not sending Miss Hope there alone."

"No, she's going with the woman who stole her identity, killed Sarah, and tried to assassinate the Prime Minister," John said.

Snodgrass sniffed. "Yes, and what about Miss Kelly? You think she'll be able to play her role convincingly?"

Frain shrugged. "Well, she's managed to live here in London for most of the past three years while part of an IRA terrorist cell and remain undetected. She fooled her employers, her colleagues, and her friends. Yes, I think we can all rest easy that she's an expert at deception."

Maggie looked over at John. "Right now this is our best and only chance to find Devlin, get the key, and save Saint Paul's."

"How do we know she'll play along?" John asked.

Frain folded his hands. "No matter how well we fabricate this story, Miss Hope will be in extreme and immediate danger. Which is why we'll move in at the first sign of trouble." He looked at Maggie. "Are you absolutely sure this is something you're willing to do?"

Edmund touched her hand. "You don't have to, Margaret," he said in a low voice. "Everyone will understand if you don't."

"It's dangerous, to be sure," David added.

John simply looked at her, waiting.

*My decision. It's my decision,* Maggie thought. But all she could see was the lovely, graceful dome of St. Paul's, which had already survived so much.

Nelson gazed up at her with his inscrutable green eyes.

"I'm doing it," she said.

Everyone turned toward Frain. "Right, then. You'll be briefed on the mission with Miss Kelly, and then both of you will head out directly. Thank you, Miss Hope."

Edmund looked at her and gave a resigned sigh. "Well, in any case, you should have your arm taken care of before you leave."

"I'll do it," John offered. Then, at David's look, "I *do* know first aid."

"Right," David said, taking off his glasses to give them a quick polish. "Go on, then."

"We have the first-aid kit in the office. Do you want me to bring it here?" he asked.

"I can make it," Maggie said, trying to keep her tone light. "I think."

When she tried to stand, it felt as though every muscle in her body seized up, every single nerve ending protested, *No more. Please, no more.* Nelson gave a sharp meow as he was dislodged to the floor, then concentrated on cleaning his fur.

John held out his arm without comment, and Maggie took it.

In the private secretaries' office, John offered Maggie his desk chair. He removed his jacket and rolled up his shirtsleeves, busying himself with the bandages and ointments.

"If you could, er—"

"Take off the sweater?" Maggie unbuttoned the cardigan and tried to pull it off. The dried blood had fused the cotton fibers to the wound. "Damn," she said as the sweater came off. "Damn, damn, damn."

John smiled in spite of everything that was happening. "Good to know you don't mince words."

Maggie closed her eyes against the fresh waves of pain. "I think I'm going to have a lot more to say when this is all over."

"Now, if you could just, um, unbutton?" John asked.

Gingerly, Maggie did as he asked, wincing again as the fabric pulled from the wound, which was revealed to be an ugly gash, black from clotted blood, now oozing.

"Not as bad as I thought."

Despite the pain, Maggie had to give a weak smile. "Ah, that trademark British understatement."

"Stiff upper lip, don't you know. We don't believe in drama."

"I've noticed."

As John gently cleaned the burn with antiseptic, Maggie started shivering. "You're in shock." He put his arms around her. "It's going to be all right."

Maggie grasped his forearm; the part of her mind not distracted by pain noticed that John smelled of soap. "Really?" she said. "Because I'm starting to wonder."

He went back to bandaging, laying clean gauze over the wound and then taping it up. "I believe in you," he said, meeting her eyes. "And you have all of us—me— right behind you."

"Thank you, John," Maggie said.

Maggie rolled down her sleeve and put her sweater back on. She would have loved to change her clothes— how long had she been in them?—but she and Frain had agreed that it would look more realistic for her to wear the same outfit.

"Don't mention it," he replied lightly. "By the way, you were right."

"Right?" Maggie didn't know what to say. She was suddenly quite conscious of his proximity.

"If you hadn't figured it out, Paige—Claire—might

have gotten to the P.M., and your father might be on his way to Berlin. So—"

Maggie gave a grim smile. "Two down, one to go."

Claire looked at Maggie when she entered the holding cell but didn't speak.

Which was a good thing. The sight of Claire—wearing her clothes, although now wrinkled and stained, her hair dyed garish red—was almost too much for Maggie to bear. But they were going to have to work together, Maggie realized, so she needed to put aside her feelings. *For the moment.*

"Paige," Maggie ventured finally. "Although I hear it's Claire now."

"Maggie, I'm so, so sorry," she began, "I never meant to—"

"Claire, Paige—whoever you are. I don't want to hear it." She took a deep breath. "We're going to go through with this mission. We're going to find Devlin. And we're going to get the override key so that we can save Saint Paul's from blowing up. And that. Is. All."

Claire's eyes filled with tears. "Maggie, please—"

"I'm afraid that we don't have time for this, Miss Kelly," Frain said from the doorway. "In fact, we have less than two hours now." He walked toward Claire with an iron key, then used it to unlock her handcuffs.

As Claire rubbed her wrists, Maggie turned to Frain. "What's next?"

"We've already created the fake accident site, in case McCormack or Devlin wants to check your story."

"Fine," Maggie said.

"Fine," Claire echoed softly.

"The thanks and praise of a grateful nation will be yours, Miss Hope," Frain said.

"A dry martini will do nicely."

Frain's lip twitched, and he nearly smiled. "I think

that can be arranged," he said. "Good hunting. To both of you."

From the backseat of Frain's car at the accident scene, they heard ambulances wailing and saw crashed cars with broken windshields and people covered in what looked to be blood being wheeled away on gurneys by emergency service workers.

Maggie looked around at the scenario of destruction in disbelief. "And this is all staged?" she said to Frain.

"Absolutely," he replied. "Now, let's review," he said to Claire and her. "You two were involved in the accident. Claire was being transported to a women's prison, awaiting trial, and Miss Hope was accompanying her to provide a deposition. And now I must do something I already regret."

Without warning, he backhanded Maggie.

The slap reverberated in the small space of the car. She swayed under the force of the blow, the sting seeping into her face. Frain's handprint was hot on her cheek.

"What the—" Claire started.

"—hell was that for?" Maggie finished, raising her hand to her face, which was already starting to swell. "My dead father is alive—and sane. I haven't slept. I've been kidnapped. I've been held at gunpoint. I was burned by a hot poker. I just learned that my dead best friend is actually a live traitor. So I ask you, Mr. Frain— just what the bloody *hell* was that for?"

"Again, Miss Hope," Frain said, "I apologize profusely. But you need to look like you've been injured in a car accident."

"And you couldn't have hit *her*?" Maggie said, rubbing her face.

"Now, remember," Frain said, "our agents have covered the surrounding area." He took out a pistol and loaded it, then handed it to Claire. "Take this gun," he instructed. "This has to look as convincing as possible."

Slowly, with disbelief in her eyes, Claire accepted the pistol. She looked at Maggie. Then she looked at Frain.

"You know you won't use it," Frain said calmly. "Because you know you're surrounded by agents. And because of Mr. Murphy." He looked at Maggie. "Are you ready?"

Maggie raised one eyebrow. "Ready as I'll ever be."

Maggie and Claire didn't speak as they made their way to McCormack's apartment. The building was remarkably nondescript, with red-brown bricks and lined by dusty shrubs.

At the door, Claire grabbed Maggie's good arm. Her other was in her coat pocket, clutching the butt of the pistol for reassurance. "What if McCormack doesn't believe us?" she said.

Maggie removed Claire's hand from her arm. "First of all, don't touch me," she hissed. "Second, it's our job to make him believe us. And you're the expert at that, aren't you?"

Claire had the grace to drop her eyes and look slightly ashamed of herself.

It almost made Maggie feel better. Almost.

Claire knocked at the door.

No response.

She knocked again, louder this time.

No response.

She put her ear up to the door. "I can hear his wireless," she said. She knocked for a third time. "Look, we know you're in there," she called. "Open the door."

Slowly, the door opened and they saw a slight man, hair gray at the temples, wearing a white button-down shirt, brown cardigan, and corduroy trousers. His face had a mild, sheeplike quality beneath heavy black spectacles. In the background, they could hear the BBC broadcast ". . . *as people were evacuating the accident site. We have no word about the number of fatalities and injured, but reports are that more than a hundred people were affected . . .*"

"Who are you?" he asked, eyes darting from Claire's face to Maggie's.

"Claire Kelly," she responded.

*The name sounds so strange from her,* Maggie thought.

"Who?"

"Claire Kelly. I'm a friend. I know Michael Murphy. He's been compromised."

McCormack's eyes widened, and his nostrils flared. "I don't know what you're talking about," he said finally, closing the door.

Claire stopped it with her hand. "I need to speak to Devlin."

"I don't know anyone named Devlin."

"Yes, you do."

"Go away," McCormack said. "Before I call the police."

Claire took a step forward into the apartment. "You won't call the police. And we both know why."

McCormack tensed for a moment. "What do you want?"

"I have a hostage," she said, indicating the gun in her coat pocket, pointed at Maggie. "Someone Devlin will want. Her name is Margaret Hope. She works with Churchill at Number Ten. Now, please, let me in before someone sees me."

McCormack stepped aside and let the two girls in. The flat was neat and tidy. Stacks of student papers covered the rickety wooden kitchen table next to a mug of steaming tea and a plate of half-eaten toast and jam. A pair of vivid green budgies preened in an antique Victorian birdcage near the window.

He closed the door. "How did you find me?"

"Michael. Michael Murphy."

"I don't know any Michael Murphy."

"He knows you." Claire took a breath. "Michael and I were working together. I was supposed to take out Churchill. But I was arrested. They were transporting me to a holding cell, and there was a car accident. Everyone was killed or injured. I managed to get a gun and then decided to take this one as a hostage. She's Churchill's secretary—too valuable to kill—at least without pumping her for information first."

McCormack's forehead creased with thought. "The accident I heard about on the wireless." He said abruptly, "Don't move."

He went to the telephone, picked up the heavy receiver, and dialed some numbers.

"This is McCormack. A woman named Claire Kelly is at my flat."

There was a short silence. "She claims a man named Michael Murphy told her."

Another silence. "She has an asset. Someone who works for Churchill."

Maggie held her breath, waiting.

"Yes, I understand," he said finally. He hung up the receiver.

"Devlin will see you."

## TWENTY-NINE

In McCormack's car, a black Vauxhall, there was an uneasy silence. Ambulances from the staged accident keened in the background. Claire was driving, and McCormack and Maggie were in the backseat. He had the gun poking into her ribs.

"How far are we going?" Claire asked.

"Not far," he said.

Claire looked at McCormack's reflection in the rearview mirror. "You seem nervous."

"What do you expect?"

"Look," she said, "I wouldn't have contacted you if I felt I had a choice."

"And as a result, I have no choice."

"We do whatever we need to for the cause, so what's the problem?"

"There is no problem."

In the backseat, Maggie kept going over the plan. This was their only chance to stop the bomb, she knew. And something, a number of things—anything—could go wrong. *Too many variables . . .*

The car made its way through the rubble and debris of the East End—until the war, it had been the largest and most important port on the face of the earth—and pulled up, finally, in front of a large gray warehouse. It stood intact amid the surrounding destruction, arrogant and alone. Large lorries rumbled in and out, and a few men in dirt-stained sweaters loaded heavy-looking boxes into an unmarked truck.

McCormack pointed. "Go through those doors and to the right. He's expecting you." Maggie and Claire got out of the car. As they walked toward the entrance, they suddenly heard the car's engine rev behind them. They turned to see McCormack speeding away.

Claire looked at Maggie. Maggie looked at Claire.

They knew there had to be MI-5 agents getting into place—behind mountains of rubble, hidden by the few brick-and-mortar walls still left standing—but she couldn't see them. Were they really there?

"This is it, I guess," Maggie said finally.

Claire gave a quick nod.

There was a black gate with an electronic buzzer for deliveries. Claire pressed the button, and a shrill ring reverberated throughout the building.

Nothing.

She pressed it again, longer this time.

After an interminable pause, the door clicked open. They walked through and took a small freight elevator to the second floor.

Eammon Devlin was sitting behind a teak desk, flanked by two muscled flunkies. He was in the early part of middle age and remarkably pleasant-looking, with regular, even features and light brown hair parted neatly on the side and glossed with Brylcreem. He was dressed in an innocuous brown twill suit and looked like an accountant or perhaps a librarian. Behind him, the blackout curtains were raised, giving him a view of the boats working on the leaden Thames in the morning light.

He looked at Claire and Maggie, and smiled pleasantly. Despite his warm affect, Maggie felt a shudder of fear run through her. She thought, *"O villain, villain, smiling, damned villain! / My tables—meet it is I set it down / That one may smile, and smile, and be a villain."*

"Look at what the Germans have done to this place," he said, indicating all of the East End. "Used to be one of the glories of England. And now? Destroyed. Pity." He smiled once again, like a kind uncle.

"You've caused me a lot of trouble," he said mildly to the two young women. "Miss Kelly . . ."

"I didn't have a choice!" Claire cried. "They had me in custody and were taking me to be hanged. The accident was my only chance—and I didn't know where else to go—"

Devlin poured some coffee into a cup. "We've received word that Murphy was picked up and is now in custody. He's a good man." A pause, as he put the pot back down. "They'll hang him, you know."

"Yes," Claire said. Her face was impenetrable.

"You're a good liar, Claire Kelly," he said, adding a sugar cube with tiny silver tongs.

Claire looked up sharply. "What?"

Devlin stirred the sugar into the coffee. Then he picked up the cup and saucer, took a sip, and sighed with pleasure. "Nothing like a good cup of coffee."

"Mr. Devlin, please believe me. I did not betray you."

Devlin looked at Claire, then at Maggie.

He went around to the desk's drawers, pulled out a small gun with a delicate ivory inlay from the top drawer, and then handed it to Claire.

"Prove it to me," he said, with the same pleasant expression.

This scenario had not been part of the plan. Maggie could feel her armpits dampen and sweat bead on her top lip and lower back.

Claire took an endless moment and looked at Maggie. A muscle in her jaw twitched.

*This is it,* Maggie thought. *This is really it.* That was all she had time to process.

Then Claire said, "This is a waste."

"What?" Devlin said, surprised.

"She's one of Churchill's key secretaries," Claire said. "The information she knows could be invaluable to us. To you."

"I asked you to kill her," Devlin said pleasantly. "Now, do it."

Claire lowered the gun and checked to see if it was loaded.

That brief act of delay provoked an avuncular look of disappointment on Devlin's face. "Oh, Miss Kelly," he said, sighing and shaking his head, "I expected so much more from you."

Then, to the other two men, "Please show our guests downstairs. I'll see them again after Saint Paul's."

"They've been in there too long," Snodgrass said, drumming his short, bony fingers on the Cabinet Room table. Edmund, John, and David looked on, tense and pale. Frain was on the phone, standing with his back to the other men.

There was a tap at the door. "Excuse me?" It was Mrs. Tinsley.

"What!" Snodgrass exclaimed, rising to his feet.

"May I—may I be of any assistance?"

"You may be of assistance, Mrs. Tinsley, by carrying on with your duties," he said sharply.

Mrs. Tinsley took a step backward, hands to her pearls. "Of course, Mr. Snodgrass," she said. "I only meant . . ."

"As far as we know, she's all right," he said, his voice softer now. "We'll let you know when there's news."

"Thank you," Mrs. Tinsley said. She turned and closed the door behind her.

"What's going on at Saint Paul's?" Edmund asked Snodgrass. "Has the bomb squad made any progress?"

"Some," Snodgrass said. "But not enough. Not with only an hour left." He ran his hands through what was left of his hair. "We need the damn override key."

Frain replaced the receiver and turned around. "MI-Five has lost visual confirmation on both Miss Hope and Miss Kelly. But they also state that no shots have been fired."

"What now?" John asked, his face gray.

"Now we wait."

"You can wait," Edmund said. "I have an idea."

Devlin's men tied Maggie and Claire to a water pipe in the basement. They stood, back to back, their hands bound with wide adhesive tape and attached to the pole in the oily gloom from slatted windows high up near the ground. The large room was filled with towers and towers of cardboard boxes, and the air smelled of dampness, mildew, and mouse droppings.

Without speaking, the men left, their footsteps on the stained cement floor fading into the darkness.

"Well, you must be happy now," Maggie said when the footsteps died away. She pulled away as much as she could in her bond, not wanting to touch. Her arm burned and throbbed.

"Hardly," Claire muttered.

"Let's see if I got all this straight—you fooled all of us, you were a secret IRA agent conspiring with Nazis, you killed Sarah, you took my identity, you tried to assassinate the Prime Minister."

"*Michael* killed Sarah," she said in a quiet voice. "Not me."

"Well, that makes it all better, now, doesn't it?" Maggie snapped. "I'm sure it was a great comfort to Sarah."

Claire was silent for a moment. "I don't suppose you can appreciate what I did back there. I could have killed you—should have killed you—when Devlin handed me that gun."

"And why didn't you?"

Claire gave a deep sigh. Just when Maggie thought she'd never speak, she said in a small voice, "Because I can't kill anymore. I didn't—I didn't know what it would be like. The toll it would take."

" 'The toll'?"

"I killed one man. And he deserved to die. But I've been part of other plots, Diana Snyder, now . . ." She could barely bring herself to say the name. ". . . Sarah . . . ."

"Ah," Maggie said. "It's different when it's someone you know, is it?"

"I didn't do it—but I was there."

"And then you were going to kill the P.M.? Mr. Churchill?"

Claire squirmed in the darkness. "John—John got to me first. And again, I couldn't pull the damned trigger. I know John—knew him—I just couldn't shoot him point-blank. I couldn't make my hand do it."

Maggie took a moment to absorb what Claire had told her. Then she snorted in the darkness. "So your hand's your conscience? Good for your hand, then."

"It saved you back there, so don't be snippy about it."

But Maggie wasn't through. "And now—*if* we live— since you cooperated with Frain, you and your boyfriend will probably just get extradited to Ireland, where they'll no doubt celebrate you as heroes."

"No. They won't," Claire said in a low voice. "Most Irish don't condone the actions of the IRA."

"Really?"

"Yes, really. Think of the Irish flag—green, white, and orange stripes, yes? The green is for Gaelic tradition. The orange represents the supporters of William of Orange—in other words, the Protestants. The white in the center is supposed to signify peace between the two."

"Sounds promising—peace, that is."

"There can be no truce," Claire spit out, "not while they want to wipe out the Catholics."

"Still," Maggie said, "you'll have it better there than you would here."

Claire was very still.

Maggie tried to hold back, but she couldn't. It had been a very long, very bad day. "Were you laughing at us the whole time? I mean, when you pretended to be Paige . . . Were you just thinking what idiots we all are and how easy we were to fool with your charming-blonde act?"

Claire was silent for a moment. "I don't expect you to understand, Maggie."

"Well, do enlighten me. We're not going anywhere soon. And you owe me that much."

She sighed. "Paige isn't a lie—at least, not in the way you think. Paige is who I'd be if I grew up in Virginia, an all-American girl, blissfully ignorant of what's really happening in the world."

Maggie wasn't expecting this.

"But that's not what happened. I spent my summers in Ireland. And there I saw the most horrible forms of injustice. There was the Home Rule Act. Have you ever even heard of it?"

She hadn't. "No."

"The Irish wanted to rule themselves. The Brits didn't agree. It's—say, the Irish are the American colonists in the 1700s and the British are, well, the British. Imposing heavy taxes and arbitrary rules."

"I'm still not seeing why you'd get involved."

"The British executed the leaders of the IRA after the Great War. One person described it as 'watching blood seep from behind a closed door.' It was guerrilla warfare from then on. We were fighting to preserve our language, our culture, and our freedom."

Claire drew in a ragged breath. "In Belfast, where we lived in the summers, there was horrifying violence. The Protestants were vicious. They'd pull people out of their homes and execute them on their front steps, and then they'd burn the houses down. Then the British sent their Great War vets—Black and Tans we called them, because of their uniforms—and they were even worse. I can't—I can't tell you how bad it was," she said. "But I can tell you that it continued—continues—to this day. I—saw my mother raped. By a British officer. And my father, who wasn't doing anything except trying to keep the Celtic language from falling into oblivion, was shot."

Well. That certainly explained a lot. "But even so," Maggie said, not wanting to give too much, "why bomb London? Why try to assassinate Winston Churchill? There's a much bigger war going on right now."

"Depends on how you look at it."

"And you really believe that? I mean, the Blitz? Sarah and John and David . . . Are they really the enemy? Am I?"

"You're not the enemy, but you support the enemy. With your taxes, with your ignorance, your passivity . . ." There was a pause. "You can't help but be who you are. But neither can I. I don't expect you to understand."

*What was there to say?* "I still don't understand, I admit," Maggie said slowly. "And I can't—*ever*— forgive you." *But.* "But I can see that you've gone through a lot. Unspeakable things."

And so they stood, back to back, in the darkness, until Claire started singing, her soprano voice thick and trembling but then gaining strength:

*"In Mountjoy jail one Monday morning*
*High upon the gallows tree,*
*Kevin Barry gave his young life*
*For the cause of liberty.*
*But a lad of eighteen summers,*
*Still there's no one can deny,*
*As he walked to death that morning,*
*He proudly held his head on high.*
*Just before he faced the hangman*
*In his dreary prison cell*
*The Black and Tans tortured Barry*
*Just because he wouldn't tell*
*The names of his brave comrades,*
*And other things they wished to know.*
*'Turn informer and we'll free you!'*
*Kevin Barry answered, 'No.'*
*Shoot me like a soldier.*
*Do not hang me like a dog,*
*For I fought to free old Ireland. . . ."*

# THIRTY

St. Paul's and the surrounding area had been evacuated. "Gas leak!" undercover MI-5 agents in coveralls told churchgoers and clergy. "Sorry! Everyone must evacuate. So sorry. We'll take care of it as soon as possible. Sorry—so sorry."

Frain and Edmund pulled in front of the church and sprinted up the marble steps to the soaring Corinthian columns and the huge doors. The lanky, boyish agent keeping watch said, "Go right in, sir."

They made their way down the nave and past the altar, then down one narrow staircase and another and another, into the stuffy dimness of the crypts. The air was chill.

The bomb squad worked on dismantling the explosive with quiet efficiency. Frain looked to Arthur Hurley, the agent in charge. "What news?" he asked.

"Not much, sir," Hurley admitted, rubbing the gray stubble on his chin. That and the black circles under his eyes were testament to the amount of time he'd been working on the bomb. "If we take her apart, she'll blow. If we don't take her apart, she'll blow." He gave a nearly imperceptible shrug. "And we can't move her without taking her apart." Only the tension in his jaw belied his light tone.

"Would it be possible for me to take a look?" Edmund said.

"Suit yourself, sir," Hurley replied. "We've got our best men on it, but maybe a fresh set of eyes . . ."

Frain and Edmund walked into the crypt where the bomb was. It was larger than Edmund had expected. The two agents working on it rose when they saw them. "We're working on it, sir," the taller one said. "But so far, she's unbreachable."

"I think," Maggie said, wiggling her wrists, "I think if I can just pull up the end of this tape . . ." Her fingers worked at the wide black adhesive tape, picking and pulling.

"I think you're right," Claire said, also working at the tape.

"Too bad you cut your talons," Maggie said. "Would have helped."

"Well," Claire said, under her breath, "I was trying to look like you. Right down to your chewed-on little fingers."

"Better than the hair. Red's a hard color to pull off."

"Would you just be quiet and let me work?"

"I'm just saying."

They were silent. The only noise in the dark was their fingers scraping at the tape. "I've got it!" Maggie said finally. "Got the end! I've pulled it as far as I can—can you reach it?"

Claire wiggled her wrists and fingers. "Let's see." She explored, using her fingertips. "All right, I've found it. . . . I'm pulling. . . ."

"It's working," Maggie said. "Let's just keep going. We've got it now."

It took them a while, but eventually they got their wrists free. Once they did that, it was a snap to undo their ankles. There was a moment, a short and fleeting moment, where the two smiled at each other in the gloom and it felt, almost, like old times.

Almost.

"Come on," Maggie said. "Let's get out of here."

Maggie and Claire headed for the stairs, tiptoeing their way up. As they did, they heard shouting. They peered around the door. Ten MI-5 agents had guns trained on Devlin, who was wearing a trench coat, carrying a briefcase, and had his back to the door. "Please hand over the override key," the lead agent said, almost amicably.

"I think not." Devlin smiled, his affable face now a death's-head grimace. "If you kill me, you'll all die."

"But then—you will, too," the agent said, uncomprehending.

"Exactly," Devlin said, his mild eyes unblinking. "A hero's death. A martyr to the cause."

"Professor Hope?" Frain said, gesturing to the device on the crypt floor.

"Please, call me Edmund."

He knelt down by the bomb and peered at it intently.

"We tried to bypass the remote current with the battery," the shorter, stouter agent said to them. "But it was too unstable. We didn't want to risk it. There's enough juice here to bring down the whole church and a few city blocks."

"Is there a trip wire?" Edmund said, now down on all fours.

"Jesus Christ, Sherlock," the taller agent snapped. "Of *course* there's a bloody trip wire."

"All right, all right, just asking," Edmund said.

Frain motioned for the two to step back, which they did, reluctantly. He, too, stepped back but never took his eyes off Edmund. "Anything?"

The agents were getting impatient. And nervous, because Frain was blocking their view.

"I don't know," he replied. "There are a few options. But any one of them could be a trick."

"That's what we were saying, sir," the taller agent said. "It basically comes down to green, white, or orange. If we cut the correct one, the bomb will be disabled. If we cut the wrong one . . ."

"Kaboom," the shorter agent finished. "There's enough dynamite down here to take down the whole bloody cathedral. He must have smuggled it all in, stick by stick."

"Thank you," Frain said drily. "Professor Hope?"

He glanced up at Frain and got to his feet, wiping his hands on his trousers. "We could use that override key. Have one yet?"

All eyes fixed on the ticking gold pocket watch. Then Frain said, "No. And we now have exactly twenty-four minutes."

From the crack between the door and the wall, Maggie and Claire took in the scene before them. Maggie whispered, "If he blows us all up, there'll be no stopping the bomb at Saint Paul's. . . ."

Claire knew what she had to do. "I'm sorry, Maggie," she said softly. "I'm sorry about everything, especially about Sarah."

Without warning, she opened the door wide enough to walk into the room. There was a long moment as the seconds ticked and Devlin and his men saw and acknowledged her presence.

Things began to happen more or less at once. As Devlin made his move, Claire grabbed a chair, raised it over her head, and ran to Devlin. He spun to face her and fired a single shot.

She staggered for a moment under the impact, making a high-pitched keening moan, but then continued on, side-swiping him with the chair.

Devlin staggered from the impact but didn't fall. He looked more shocked than anything else. "Miss Kelly," he said, putting his hand to the wound. "You shouldn't—"

Claire slumped to the floor, her blouse slowly staining crimson.

In what looked to be slow-motion choreography, one agent dove for the briefcase and threw it to another, who began to open it, while yet another agent shot Devlin through the head, which exploded, leaving nothing but blood and tissue. When he'd fallen, two agents ripped the gun from his hands, then began to search his body for the key.

Time began to progress normally again.

"Claire?" Maggie cried, running to the girl. Although blood continued to pump from the wound in her chest, Claire's body was still and her eyes glassy. "Paige?"

The closest agent examined Claire's body, then lowered her eyelids. "She's dead," he said impassively.

The agents searching Devlin's body began to panic. "There's no key!" one cried. "There's no key!"

Maggie got to her feet. Her shoulder protested at the abuse and gave a renewed white-hot throb of pain.

"But—" But there was Paige. Claire. Lying in an ever-widening pool of her own blood.

"Place might be rigged," the agent said. "We've got to move out."

"But—" Maggie said.

"We have to go."

They made it to an unmarked black van parked in the warehouse's lot and climbed in. A few other men in the van moved aside to make room for them to sit on the floor, and one closed the sliding door with an ear-splitting bang. With a screech of the tires, the van sped off.

"You were pretty brave back there, miss," one of the men said. He was blond, almost white-haired, with kind eyes.

"Thanks," Maggie managed.

He gave her hand a quick pat. "Sorry about your friend." He looked around at his comrades, who nodded.

"Name's Will," he said. "Will Archer."

"Maggie," she said, on autopilot.

"Maggie, nice to meet you, although under unusual circumstances."

"Likewise."

"Are you all right? You look a little green around the edges," he said.

"I think—I think I need to not talk right now," she said, feeling a sudden pressure rising beneath her ribs and a wave of nausea. For a brief moment, she thought she was going to vomit. Then, mercifully, the urge subsided, but she could feel her legs and hands start to shake.

She felt light-headed and bent over, trying not to faint.

She exhaled explosively and then began to sob in long, racking silent cries. Her hands clenched and unclenched, her body admitting what her mind couldn't yet process.

Will Archer patted her back awkwardly as she sobbed silently.

"I'm sorry," she said finally, sitting up and taking large gulps of air.

"Not to worry," he said, taking a large linen handkerchief from his pocket and passing it to her. "Clean. On my honor."

"Thank you," she said, dabbing her eyes and then

blowing her nose with a good, loud honk. "Thank you very much." Then, "So now what?"

Archer spread his hands helplessly and shook his head. "I wish I knew."

Maggie raised her chin. "How far are we from Saint Paul's?"

## THIRTY-ONE

THE VAN PULLED up a few blocks from the cathedral, and the men jumped out. There was a barricade manned by bobbies in uniform. "So sorry," they solemnly informed the milling, muttering crowd. "So terribly sorry. Everything's closed. Come back tomorrow. Sorry for the inconvenience."

The agents sprinted to the barricade and jumped over.

"What the—?" the bobby yelled. He had red cheeks, a double chin, and bulging, buggy eyes.

One turned around. "MI-Five!"

"Right," the cop muttered. "Here to save the bloody day." He saw the crowd's reaction to the agents and said, "Gas leak! Not to worry! It's all under control."

Maggie tried to follow.

"Oh, no, you don't, miss," the bobby said, suddenly joined by another. "It's off-limits; you can't go in there."

"But I'm with them!"

The officer took in her bruised face, dirty hands, and ripped and burned sweater, and slowly shook his head. "Right, miss," he said, trying not to laugh. "Sure, you're a secret agent." He elbowed his friend, laughing. "Looks like we have our very own Mata Hari here."

"She's with us," Archer shouted from the stairs.

"Yes, sir. Of course, sir," he said, begrudgingly letting Maggie by.

Together, Archer and Maggie sprinted up into the cathedral, down the endless nave, and down to the crypt, dark and dank as a dragon's lair. Breathless, they met up with Frain, Edmund, Snodgrass, and the other agents in the gloom.

"Miss Hope, this is highly—" Frain began.

"It's not safe, Margaret. Get out," her father continued.

Archer ignored them. "There's no key, sir." He said to Frain, "No actual key, at least. Not like his other bombs."

As the other agents groaned, one exclaimed, "Damn!"

Maggie thought for a moment. "No *actual* key . . . no literal key," she said, as though to herself. She turned to her father. "What does the bomb look like?"

"Do you think," he began, "even absent father that I was, that I would *ever* allow you to—"

"*I'll* take you," Archer said. Frain nodded his approval and followed them into the heart of the crypt, where the bomb softly ticked like a beating heart.

Maggie and Archer circled the bomb, taking its measure—all of the dynamite wrapped in different-colored wires. "What's this?" Maggie said, pointing to the gold watch.

"Timer," one of the agents on the bomb squad said curtly.

"But why a pocket watch? Is there any significance?" He shrugged. "Damned if I know."

"And look," Maggie continued. "The wires."

"What about them?" Frain asked.

As though in a dream, Maggie recalled her last conversation with Claire. *"The white in the center is supposed to signify peace between the two."* It reminded her of something, but she couldn't quite place it.

Frain grimaced. "You say one needs to be cut?" he asked the head of the bomb squad, who nodded.

"Cutting one will shut down the whole system. But it's impossible to know, from the configuration, which one it is."

*What is it?* Maggie thought, trying to remember. *Something about the Irish flag . . .*

"Five minutes, Mr. Frain," said an agent, over the ticking.

Maggie furrowed her brow. *Something about green . . .*

"Sir! She's gonna blow!"

"Yes, yes." Frain waved at him impatiently. "Go ahead, get out. Get all the men out, including Professor Hope."

Maggie and Archer looked at each other and then at Frain. "No, we've come too far now," she said. Archer nodded.

As the other agents exited, pulling Edmund with them, Maggie, Archer, and Frain stared back down at the wiring.

"I doubt that he would ever let the green wire be cut," Maggie began, knowing what it symbolized, what it had meant to Claire.

"So then it's white or orange—fifty-fifty chance."

"Cutting orange is like cutting the Protestants," Archer mused.

"But cutting the white is destroying the truce, such as it is," Frain said.

"Orange or white, then?" Maggie said, heart in her throat, hot sweat beading on her upper lip and lower back.

"That *is* the question," Frain muttered.

Then it came to her. It was Chuck—Chuck in the pub, on Maggie's first day of work at No. 10, so long ago. What had she said? *"I love Ireland and her green, white, and orange flag with all my heart, but the IRA makes me ashamed to be Irish. That's the point of the goddamned flag, you know. Green for the Gaels, orange for the Protestants—and white for the peace between them.*"

"What if it were a British and Nazi flag!" Maggie blurted suddenly.

Frain and Archer looked at her.

"No, really—blue for Britain, white for truce, black for Nazism. If we'd made the bomb, which one would be cut?"

"Black," Frain said unequivocally.

"Black," Archer seconded.

"Me, too. I'd cut the black wire, too," Maggie said. "So then—it has to be orange. We need to cut the orange wire."

"Fifty-fifty chance at this point," Archer shrugged.

"Well, Mr. Archer?" Frain said, looking at the golden pocket watch, with less than a minute to go. "Will you do the honors?"

Archer picked up a pair of slender wire cutters and took a deep breath.

He snipped the orange wire.

The ticking stopped.

"Oh, gods," Maggie muttered, hearing a ringing in her ears. *It's the end. After all this, it's finally the end.*

A few moments went by, and the three stood, still as statues, as though afraid their tiniest movement would set the ticking in motion again.

Finally, Frain turned toward Maggie and Archer. "Well, Mr. Archer, Miss Hope," he said. "Well done."

In the dim light, Archer's face looked unusually moist. "I—I think I need to sit down."

"Me, too," Maggie echoed, the enormity of what had almost happened pressing upon her for the first time. "Me, too." Then she found herself adding, "I don't suppose anyone has any tea?"

\*  \*  \*

David and John were in the crowd outside, and they rushed over to Maggie when they saw her emerge from the cathedral and walk down the steps with Frain and Archer. "Maggie, are you all right?" John asked, his brows knit with concern.

"You look like the devil," David offered.

John shot him a look.

"Well, she does," he mumbled.

"I'm fine," Maggie said. In a low voice, she added, "We found McCormack; he brought us to Devlin. There was no override key, so we had to choose which wire to cut. . . ."

Maggie looked up at the dome of St. Paul's with its colonnaded drum, stone lantern, and golden ball and cross, soaring high above them. In the middle distance it shimmered against the brilliantly blue morning sky.

People walked past Maggie, John, and David, talking and joking and laughing. Oblivious to what had almost happened.

The dome, more than two hundred years old, stood silent and steady.

Spent from anxiety and worry, they leaned against the wooden barricades. A few men in dark double-breasted suits, long umbrellas tucked firmly under their arms, walked by quickly. Housewives in flowered dresses, lips red with lipstick, carrying woven willow baskets, came from the shops with short steps. An exhausted-looking mother reached inside a pram and gave her wailing baby back his pacifier, while a young girl, her glossy auburn hair in soft pin curls, took a soldier's arm. A few gray pigeons flapped and pecked.

Traffic passed by, and a black taxi beeped in annoyance at a couple who'd stopped to kiss in the middle of the crosswalk. An older woman with perfect posture in a russet felt hat stood still and averted her eyes as her well-groomed corgi relieved himself against a car tire.

Maggie wanted to climb atop the barricade and shout, "Don't you realize what almost happened today?"

And then she thought about Sarah and Paige and Claire and her father—and even Richard Snodgrass, who was a far better man than she'd ever given him credit for being.

*This—this is the world we're fighting for.*

John said, as though reading her mind, "And they'll never know."

"And that's as it should be," Maggie said. People had enough to worry about, what with the war and being bombed most nights and wondering and waiting to find out if their loved ones in the military would return or not. They didn't need to know about every near miss.

"So what happened?" David asked.

"Obviously, nothing," Frain replied.

"And you—you're all right?" Maggie asked her father. It was a little early to be hugging.

Or so she thought.

He suddenly enveloped her in a tight embrace. "I'm fine, just fine. And you?"

"Ouch!"

He looked at Maggie with concern.

"Arm's still a bit sore," Maggie said. "But I'm just fine. More than fine," she said lightly, surprised but pleased by the hug.

"Well, at least Saint Paul's will be standing tomorrow," John said. "And the evildoers are taken care of."

"For now. We've got tabs on at least thirty other suspicious groups," Frain said. "Not to spoil the moment."

"But today, at least, we saved the world," David said. "I say, let's have a drink."

Snodgrass grimaced. "A tad early, even for you—isn't it, Mr. Greene?"

As they followed Frain and the others to the cars,

Snodgrass piped up: "Do I need to remind you that we all must return to the office? There's—"

"—a war on, you know," David, John, and Maggie chimed in without turning around.

Frain stopped abruptly and then turned, causing the group behind him to stop as well. He glared at them all. "While I'm certainly aware there's a war on, and do commend your work ethic, I believe you are all in a state of shock. Therefore, I suggest at least taking the rest of today off to recuperate. Then you may return to work. Professor Hope, your absence from Bletchley can be covered. We'll return you to your post after you've had a chance to rest."

"Fine," Snodgrass amended. "You may have today off. But don't expect *me* to tell Mrs. Tinsley."

He walked past Frain, muttering, "That woman scares me."

Murphy had eluded the agents tracking him yet again, and was enjoying a congratulatory cup of tea in a café not far from St. Paul's. *The better to get a good view,* he thought as he slipped into a table by the window, which afforded a vista of the dome rising over the main streets leading from St. Paul's. The tea in the dimpled white cup was as thick and brown as shoe polish.

"Would you like anything else?" the waitress asked.

"I'm fine, love," he replied. "Just the bill, when you have a minute."

He looked at his watch.

The wireless was on—bloody cricket scores.

He drummed his fingers on the table. There should be something by now. Some news over the wireless of the Prime Minister's demise. Civilians running in fear from the destruction of St. Paul's.

But the dome still stood. Inspiring. Comforting. Infuriating.

As his watch ticked out the minutes, there was nothing. The minutes turned to ten and then an hour and then more.

The earth still spun on its axis. People went about their business. Mothers pushed babies in prams, an old grizzled gentleman walked an even more grizzled dog. A young boy holding a chocolate bar sprinted by at full speed, arms pumping, while a middle-aged shopkeeper with a round belly and short legs tried to catch him.

"God damn it," Murphy muttered, and left some coins on the table. Did he dare make his way back to St. Paul's?

He slipped out the door, examining faces as he did. No one familiar. He went up the street, then doubled back, trying to see if anyone was following.

Without warning, he ducked into a narrow and dark back alleyway. He ran a few paces, then let himself in one of the shop's unlocked back doors.

Two agents in plainclothes burst into the alley, then looked around in confusion. "Bloody hell!" the taller one said. "Where'd he go now?"

The shorter one pulled out his gun as he looked behind some rubbish bins. "Damned if I know."

Before she could join John and David in a car, Edmund pulled Maggie aside. "Margaret—"

"Maggie," she said. "My friends call me Maggie."

"Maggie. There's something more you need to know."
*More?* "Yes?" *What fresh hell is this?*

Frain stepped up to them. "Miss Hope, what your father is trying to say is that your home is now a crime scene." He cleared his throat. "Miss Sanderson was in Miss Kelly's bedroom. Apparently, she'd happened unexpectedly upon Miss Kelly and Mr. Murphy as they were adjusting her disguise."

"So . . ." Maggie said slowly, realizing. "That's why Sarah died."

"Oh, right." Frain looked just the slightest bit flustered. "Actually, she *didn't* die."

There was a collective gasp from the assembly. "What?" Maggie whispered.

Frain had the grace to let a shadow of guilt cross his face before hardening it into a professional mask again. "I let Claire think that—to humanize the death and destruction she was intent on causing. I believe that's why she ultimately turned against Devlin."

"So Sarah's . . . alive?" Maggie's cheeks turned crimson in anger, and her eyes filled with hot tears. "And you couldn't have told *me* that? Here I was, after *everything* that's happened, thinking Sarah was dead—"

"Claire Kelly had to believe she murdered her friend. And quite frankly, we didn't know how good of an actress you were. I could take no chances with such a delicate situation." Frain took a deep breath. "I must offer my profound apologies, Miss Hope."

Maggie blinked. *Was the man a monster? Was he born without a heart?* Then she wiped at the tears leaking down her face. "I really don't know what to say," she finally replied. "How is Sarah? Where is she?"

"Miss Sanderson is recovering nicely, not to worry."

"Thank God," Maggie said. *Sarah,* she thought. *Sarah's all right. Oh, thank you, God.*

Frain took a spotless cambric handkerchief from his jacket pocket and handed it to Maggie. "By the way, I took the liberty of having one of the officers pack up some of your things. Not only is the place, for the moment, a crime scene and off limits to anyone but the police, but I thought—"

"That I probably wouldn't want to go back." Maggie nodded. "Yes, you're right." *Bunking down in the Dock,* she thought. *Oh, well.*

"Margaret, Mr. Frain is putting us up at the Savoy."

Frain cleared his throat again. "Mr. Churchill, actually, is footing the bill. In gratitude for everything you've done. Your father, until he returns to Bletchley, and you, until you can make other arrangements."

They looked at her. "The Savoy." A bath. With hot water. Clean sheets. Room service.

It took her a moment, but finally Maggie responded: "What are we waiting for?"

After Maggie had a long, hot, luxurious bath—deliberately ignoring the five-inch water mark until glistening iridescent soap suds nearly ran over the tub's sides—she had an enormous meal that contained nothing but black-market delicacies. Then she took a long, deep sleep that lasted for hours.

She was awakened by a sharp rap at the door. Then another. Then pounding.

In a fog of sleep, she got out of bed, threw on a bathrobe, went to the door, and peered out the peephole.

It was Mr. Churchill, flanked by marines in uniform and shadowed by the ever-present Detective Sergeant Walter Thompson.

*Good Lord*, she thought. *Mr. Churchill! And I'm in my dressing gown!* She slowly opened the door.

"Miss Hope!" he said, removing his hat to reveal his pink, bald head. "I'd like a word with you."

Maggie startled. "Yes? Er, sir?"

He stood in front of her, expectant.

"Oh. Yes, sir," she said, suddenly aware of her ratty tartan bathrobe, her uncombed hair, and the circles she knew were under her eyes. She winced inwardly, to be caught in such a state—and by the Prime Minister, no less. "Of course. Please come in, sir," she said finally, opening the door wider and stepping aside.

He gave her a piercing look as he strode in. Then, without ado, he sat down on the burgundy brocade wing chair near the room's window and took out a fat cigar and a monogrammed lighter. "Mr. Frain and Mr. Snodgrass have kept me informed of everything that's been happening. Quite a busy few days for you, what?"

That was one way to put it. "Yes, sir." What else could possibly be said in response?

"Sit! Sit down!" he thundered at her. Maggie did as she was told, sitting on the chair opposite.

He lit the cigar, drawing the air through, making the tip burn bright orange. "I'm sorry to hear what you've been through, Miss Hope." He took a deep puff on the cigar and exhaled.

Maggie took a gulp of smoke-filled air and nearly choked. "Thank you, sir," she managed.

"Taking it hard, are you?" he asked, not without sympathy.

Maggie cleared her throat and drew her robe tighter around her. "I'm—I'm fine, sir."

"Fine. Yes, yes—of course you're fine. We're all fine, aren't we?" He turned to the window and looked out at the view of the Strand below, chewing on the end of his cigar as the smoke rose around his head. "Sometimes . . . when I'm feeling the weight of these times . . . I paint," he said. "I paint, Miss Hope! Did you know that?"

"Yes, sir." How could she not? Some of Mr. Churchill's paintings were hung in the Annexe. They were lovely—sunny Mediterranean landscapes and jewel-toned still lifes of ripe fruit and flowers, even a portrait of Mrs. Churchill in her younger days.

"Whenever I'm followed by the Black Dog, I paint. Do *you* paint, Miss Hope?"

Maggie was at a loss. Was Winston Churchill, the Prime Minister of England, really sitting in her hotel room, asking her about her artistic abilities?

"No, sir." She was sure he didn't want to hear about her problem sets and crossword puzzles.

"You should. 'Happy are the painters, for they shall not be lonely,' I always say."

She was silent, listening. What was he getting at?

"Painting," he continued, leaning back and pulling on his cigar, "is a friend in times of need. Do you understand me, Miss Hope?"

"I think so, sir."

"It doesn't have to be painting. It could be cooking, music. Photography. Doesn't matter. The important thing is to KPO. Do you know what KPO means, Miss Hope?"

Of course. "Keep Plodding On, sir."

"Absolutely right. KPO. That's what we do, keep plodding on."

Abruptly, he rose, gave a quick bow. Then he gestured with his cigar and walked out of the room. Maggie scrambled to her feet and followed.

"And, Miss Hope?" he said at the doorway.

"Yes?"

"Meet your new roommate."

*What now?* Maggie thought. *Who else gets to see me in all my bathrobed glory?* But as Mr. Churchill walked away, a tall, slender figure entered the room.

"*Sarah!*" Maggie shrieked, reaching out to hug her. "Sarah!"

"*Ooof,*" Sarah said, nearly knocked over by Maggie's attack. "Careful, love."

"Oh, sorry, sorry," Maggie said, releasing the girl from her embrace. "Are you all right? How are you? Good Lord, Sarah."

"Can't complain." She gingerly reached up to her head and patted it through a white gauze bandage. "Better than the alternative, you know."

Maggie shook her head in disbelief as she closed the

door. "Come, sit down, now," she said, leading Sarah over to the chair the P.M. had just vacated, and sitting down opposite. "You know, that bastard Frain let us think you were dead."

"Well, it was touch-and-go for a while there," Sarah said, removing her hat and setting it on the walnut side table. "But as you know, we dancers may look pretty, but we're strong as steel on the inside. I wasn't going to let a little bump on the head finish me off. Not when I might be dancing Odile again."

Maggie took a deep breath. She had to ask. "Do you remember . . . I mean, did you see . . ."

Sarah knew what she was asking. "No, I don't remember anything," she said. "And probably a good thing, too. Although Mr. Frain filled me in on the details."

"Mr. Frain?"

"Came to see me at the hospital. Convinced me to play dead for Paige—Claire—that bitch—in the interrogation room. My best role to date. Juliet's death scene will be nothing after this!" Sarah spoke in a strong voice, but Maggie could see her hands worrying at each other.

"It was quite the—"

"Yes," Sarah said quietly.

Maggie reached over and took her hand. "Yes. Yes, indeed."

## THIRTY-TWO

THE PHONE RANG. It was David. "Hullo, Maggie. How're you holding up?"

"Doing pretty well," Maggie said, "considering. By the way, you'll never guess who's with me."

"We know—Sarah," David said smugly. "Yes, Snodgrass and Frain have taken me into their confidence. Finally. I know all about Sarah's part. . . ."

Maggie rolled her eyes at Sarah, across the room. "*David,*" she mouthed and Sarah nodded.

"So anyway," David continued, "we're all going to the Blue Moon Club tonight. Good band playing and all."

"The Blue Moon?" Maggie said, jolted. "At a time like this?" She still felt shaky and weak. Surely Sarah couldn't be up for it, strong as she sounded.

"Well, I say, Magster—we saved London. I do think we're entitled to a few drinks and dancing."

"I don't know. . . ."

Walking over to Maggie and the telephone, Sarah said, "Here, give me that." She took the receiver. "Right. What time? Yes, we'll be there. With the proverbial bells on."

She hung up the phone, and Maggie looked at her.

"I nearly died, love," she said simply. "It's time to live."

The agents, whoever they were, had taken all of their not-too-vast wardrobes. Sitting in their room at the Savoy in her bathrobe, Maggie let Sarah style her hair in red ringlets and apply lipstick and powder.

Sarah burned a bobby pin over a candle to rub the black on Maggie's lashes and smudged some iridescent aquamarine shadow from a carefully preserved tube over her eyelids. "So this is how you do things at the Sadler's Wells?" Maggie asked.

"Ha!" Sarah laughed. "If you were going onstage you'd need at least three more inches of pancake, scarlet cheeks, and false eyelashes. I'm going for something a little more natural for you."

She'd done her own face already, and her shining black hair fell in perfect finger waves to her shoulders. She wore a black-silk confection with red-satin roses on the shoulders, very Spanish and seductive.

Then she took a look in the closet. "Hmmm, I think this should do nicely," she said, pulling out a long dress of white silk and holding it against Maggie.

The dress, while exquisite, was low in front and even lower in the back. Cut on the bias, it would skim the body so closely as to leave very little to the imagination.

"Um, I don't think so," Maggie stammered, pulling her tattered flannel robe around her. There was having a glamorous evening, but there was also such a thing as modesty.

"I know it's very spring 'thirty-eight, but really, it's not as though anyone else—"

"No, no, no! It's not outdated—it's gorgeous—but, um, don't you think it'll be a little long? And tight?"

"Oh, darling, this one was always a little too short on

me. And there's plenty of room through the hips. Now, shake a leg, we only have a few minutes."

Maggie hesitated. *Hips?* she thought, about to lodge a retort. Then she remembered that Sarah had almost died—and thought the better of it.

" 'Beauty for duty,' Maggie, remember?" Sarah said. "Are you going to shirk?" she demanded, holding out a pair of silver high-heeled evening slippers.

They were going to be too small, Maggie could tell, but she jammed her feet in nonetheless. If she was going to do this, she was going to do it right. "No, indeed."

"Well, then, get dressed!"

Later, looking at her reflection, Maggie wasn't displeased. The dress was gorgeous—the gleaming fabric was heavy and cool to the touch. A sea-green wrap covered her bandaged arm nicely. There were circles under her eyes, to be sure, but she was young, and they weren't that dark. She was perhaps a bit thinner than she'd been a few months ago, but it wasn't that obvious. There were no sudden lines or wrinkles, no wiry white hairs.

And yet she felt different. She was not the same person she was before.

Suddenly she stuck her tongue out at her reflection in the mirror and picked up her beaded handbag, ready to go downstairs.

Maggie and Sarah walked through the oak-paneled lobby with its urns of fresh roses and scent of floor polish to the American Bar, a clubby little hideaway in the Savoy in the same flat, geometric, elegant deco style as the lobby. Only the fire extinguishers and signs pointing to the nearest air-raid shelters indicated that there was a war on.

Photographs of Hollywood stars—Bette Davis, Greta Garbo, Marlene Dietrich, Errol Flynn, and Clark Gable—looked down from the walls. The room was hazy with smoke; the tinkle of Gershwin on the piano competed with the low murmur of conversation, mostly from men with gray hair accompanied by young women. Who were *not* their daughters, Maggie noted.

Frain was already there, at a side table a little removed, with a good view of the room. He immediately stood and pulled out a burgundy velvet-covered chair for Sarah and then for Maggie. "Are you feeling better now?" he asked. "Not that you have to feel better, of course. But sometimes a hot bath and some sleep can work wonders."

"Yes, indeed," Maggie said. Everything still felt a bit surreal and as though it were moving too fast. She was glad Sarah was there beside her.

A tall and slender waiter appeared at their table. "What may I get for you?" he asked, putting down a gleaming silver bowl of salted almonds.

"I believe I owe you a martini, Miss Hope." He turned to Maggie. "Would that suit?"

*Would it?* "Of course."

"Miss Sanderson?"

"Same, thanks," she said.

"Three martinis, dry, straight up," Frain replied.

*Apparently, rationing doesn't exist here,* Maggie thought. When the waiter left, she said, "And call me Maggie, please."

"Then you must call me Peter, both of you. After all, we've been through quite the ordeal together."

The waiter returned silently with the drinks. Drops of water beaded on the glasses.

"An understatement . . . Peter," Sarah said as they clinked glasses. They sipped their drinks. The martinis were cold and medicinal.

"Miss Sanderson," Frain said, "if you don't mind . . . I have something I'd like to speak to . . . Maggie about."

"Of course. Excuse me, won't you?" Sarah asked, rising to her feet. "I need to powder my nose."

"Thank you," Frain said, also rising to his feet. He and Maggie watched Sarah as she made her way gracefully through the bar.

"I don't know if this is the right time to bring it up," Frain said, "but the truth is, there's not always the time that we'd like."

"What do you mean?"

"When the agents were at your flat picking up your things, they happened to notice your diploma, summa cum laude in mathematics. Your Phi Beta Kappa key. Newton's *Principia Mathematica*." He raised one eyebrow. "Most impressive."

*Goodness gracious,* she thought. *What else did they see? Did I make the bed? Were there stockings and pants and brassieres hanging in the bath?* Although it seemed like several lifetimes ago when such things were important, she suddenly felt mortified. "Guilty as charged," she said, taking another sip.

"Mr. Snodgrass said you're a mathematician. Handy with allocation, queuing, trajectories, that sort of thing. He also said that you're the one who broke the code contained in the newspaper advert."

Maggie had to smile. *Did he, now? I'll have to have a chat with my new pal Dicky.*

"And the agents saw lots of books, too. Books in French and German. Do you just read those languages, or can you speak them as well?"

"Oh, my aunt Edith made sure I learned to read, write, and speak several languages at an early age. German is required for any mathematician, of course. And I'm fluent in French as well."

"*Sprechen Sie Deutsch?*" he asked softly.

"*Clar,*" she replied without thinking, slipping into

German easily. "How else could one discuss the life and work of Johann Carl Friedrich Gauss?"

"Who taught you?" he asked. His accent was perfect.

"One of the German professors at Wellesley," she replied. "My aunt Edith wanted me to learn, and Frauline Drengenberg missed Berlin and speaking German—so it worked out well."

Maggie smiled. Mr. Frain—Peter—was right. A hot bath and a drink really did work wonders; she hadn't felt this relaxed in, well, a long time. She took another sip.

He switched back into English. "The reason I ask is that I'd like you to come work for me."

This revelation brought her up short, causing her to slosh her drink. "Work for *you*?"

"Yes. At MI-Five."

Her mind was working remarkably slowly. "At MI-Five? Me?"

"The Prime Minister can get anyone to type, but we're always on the lookout for smart recruits."

"Really?"

"Yes. You proved you can work well under pressure. You're smart. You speak French and German fluently. And the fact that you're, well . . ."

"What?" she asked, eyeing him warily.

"The fact that you're an attractive young woman is a plus in this line of work," he said formally.

Maggie arched one eyebrow. "You want me to become a spy?" She found the idea at once ridiculous and strangely appealing.

"Why, yes," Frain said. "Maggie, we'd like you to join MI-Five and train to be a spy." He took a sip of his martini, then put down the glass. "Would you consider it?"

An MI-5 agent. A spy.

Was Frain—Peter—playing with her? Did he get some sort of erotic thrill from approaching young women with this offer? Did he do it to make himself look glamorous and powerful? Was he trying to get her to sleep with him?

Maggie took his measure, looking into his flinty gray eyes. Somehow, she didn't think so.

"Of course, you'll have a lot of questions," Frain said.

*Do I ever.*

"And so I'll set up a meeting tomorrow morning so we can discuss them."

"What about Mr. Churchill?"

"While you've distinguished yourself in your position as typist, I believe your considerable talents might be put to better use elsewhere. MI-Five might be just the place for you."

"I've led a rather quiet life," Maggie said. "I'm not sure—"

"The world is turvy-topsy these days, isn't it? You don't have to decide tonight," he said. "But do think about it."

Sarah returned to the table, and the three finished their cocktails. Frain caught the waiter's eye, and silently the glasses were cleared and the bill slipped onto the table. He took care of it in a practiced motion.

"And about that offer," Maggie said. "I'll think about it."

"Good," he said, rising and holding out one arm to Maggie and one to Sarah. "And now, shall we be off?"

# THIRTY-THREE

At the Blue Moon Club, the sound of trumpets and clarinets cut through the clouds of smoke and dim light as Maggie, Sarah, and Frain crowded into a small velvet banquette already occupied by David, John, Edmund, and Snodgrass. The twins were both on the dance floor, cutting the rug with two soldiers on leave. She was gratified to see John raise his eyebrows, just a touch, at the sight of her in the white-satin dress.

"You do clean up well, Magster," David said, as Will Archer and a few other agents joined the group.

As the Moonbeam Orchestra played a cover of Duke Ellington's "In the Mood," Frain ordered a bottle of champagne, which the waiter brought on a silver tray. First they toasted to Will Archer. Then to the whole MI-5 team. Then to Edmund. Then to Frain. Then to David, for driving. Then to John, for driving, too. Then to Sarah. And then to Maggie.

"To Mr. Snodgrass," Maggie said, lifting her glass.

"Why, thank you, Miss Hope," Snodgrass said, reddening slightly but looking pleased nonetheless. "I hope now you'll forgive me for the private-secretary matter. . . ."

"Of course," Maggie said.

"Let's not forget poor Diana Snyder," David said.

And she was toasted as well.

Suddenly, Maggie spotted a sparkle on Chuck's left hand. "What's this?" she asked, pulling it into the light.

"Nigel got me a ring," Chuck said, surveying the huge cushion-cut diamond set in filigree. "I was thinking maybe a plain gold band, but he had to get *this*. . . ."

"And the wedding?" Maggie asked, her voice squeaking in excitement.

"This Christmas, in Leeds—if he can get leave. God help me," she said, rolling her eyes.

The twins, breathless, joined the group. "The ring!" Annabelle said. "Isn't it just—"

"—beautiful?" Clarabelle finished.

"It is, indeed. To Chuck and Nigel," Maggie said, lifting her glass.

"Chuck and Nigel," the table intoned.

Chuck blushed. "And to the Belles," she said, raising her own glass.

"Really?" Maggie said. "Fill me in?"

"We're going on tour," Annabelle said. "It's a great opportunity. We'll be able to get out of London—"

"—and we've both been promoted," Clarabelle added. "Annabelle's going to be playing Rebecca and I'm going to be in charge of costumes."

"Well, congratulations, girls," Maggie said. "To you and the tour of *Rebecca*!"

When the song changed to "Bugle Call Rag," Chuck and the twins left to dance once again.

"And what about Claire?" Maggie asked. It was easier, she found, to refer to Paige as Claire.

"What *about* her?" Chuck asked, her face dark. She'd only just been brought up to speed after signing her own Official Secrets Act. They'd all had to, even the twins.

"Should we toast to her?" Maggie really didn't know anymore. "She died helping us find the key."

"Her boyfriend built the bomb!" Will said, and took a swig.

"I understand she was your flatmate?" Edmund asked. "And that you were at school together?"

"Yes," Maggie said. "You think you know someone . . ."

"And then they surprise you," Edmund said with a wry smile. "I'm sorry to have been such a surprise, Maggie."

"Of course," she replied. "I'm just glad it all turned out all right in the end." Then, "Well, mostly all right."

"Miss Hope," Snodgrass said. "I've been speaking to Mr. Frain about your new position—"

Maggie held up her hand. "I haven't decided anything yet, sir."

"You're leaving?" John asked, face falling.

"Weren't cleared for that piece of news, were you?" David muttered. John glared at him.

Maggie looked at John and smiled. "Nothing's been decided. Besides, it's not as though I'd be leaving London—"

"Well, good, then," John said. *He wants me to stay,* she thought with a sudden thrill of happiness.

Edmund cleared his throat. "Working with Mr. Frain sounds dangerous. . . ."

"Working at Bletchley isn't?" She had him there.

"Not the same thing," he said solemnly. "Now that I've found you again, I'd hate to lose you."

"Come on, all of you, this is getting much too serious," Maggie said. "We'll work it all out tomorrow. In the meantime, I'd like to dance." She looked at her father and held out her hand.

"My dear," he said, as he led her onto the floor and into the dim, smoky haze. "It would be an honor."

Out on the dance floor, under the muted glow of the chandeliers, Edmund held Maggie easily, as though he'd taught her to dance when she was young. As though she'd made her debut on his arm.

"Are you going to take Frain up on his offer?" Edmund asked.

"I really don't know," Maggie said coldly. Maggie felt angry, resentful. Who was he—this man, this stranger— to suddenly appear in her life?

"I know I have no right to ask . . . no right to know. . . ."

"No, you don't," she said. "You—you took the easy way out. Even when you got better, you still took the easy way."

"Yes, you're right," he said. "It was wrong. And I'm sorry. I'm going to try to make it up to you if it takes the rest of my life."

The conversation was awkward, painful, but Maggie was filled with a sudden need to talk. "I'm going to need you to talk about . . . my mother."

"Clara?" Edmund said with great effort. "Maggie, those were—dark days. Best forgotten."

"No," she said forcefully, causing a nearby couple to stare. "I need to know. I need you to tell me." Then, quietly but still intently, "Don't you think you ought to talk about it? Get it out? Isn't that what Freud would say?"

"Freud . . ." Edmund said. "Freud was not British."

Maggie was silent.

"But yes, yes, you're right. You deserve to know. And I need to tell you."

There was another silence but less tense this time.

Edmund cleared his throat. "I do . . . I do want you to know how proud I am of you. And I know I've given up all rights to be your father. But perhaps we can be friends?"

" 'Friends'?"

Suddenly, Edmund's self-control broke and he smothered a racking sob. "Friends. Anything. I'll take anything. Oh, Maggie, I just want to be part of your life, while we still have this chance. While there's still time. I know I was wrong. And I want, more than anything, to make things up to you. As best I can."

In a desperate voice he added, "My dear girl, can you ever forgive me?"

"Maybe not tonight," she said finally, blinking back her own hot tears. "But someday. Maybe someday."

"I'll take that," Edmund responded. "Thank you."

David and Chuck were dancing, Chuck a full head taller and David with his head on her impressive bosom. Together they turned to watch John thread his way through the couples on the dance floor. "May I cut in?" John asked.

Maggie looked up at him and nodded.

"Of course," Edmund said, relinquishing his place and returning to the banquette.

John took Maggie's hand and drew her toward him. As the blond singer, her peachy flesh spilling out of a tight red-satin dress, segued into a slow rendition of "I Get Along Without You Very Well," he drew her into him, and they began to dance.

"This is all very strange," Maggie said, leaning her head against his chest, smelling his bay rum cologne.

"Which part?"

Maggie considered. So much was strange these days.

"What are your parents like?" she asked instead.

"My parents?" John laughed. "My father, Archibald Sterling, flew Sopwith Camels and Bristol F-Two-Bs in the Great War. Now he lives in Derbyshire and is a crotchety old M.P. in the House of Commons. And my mother, Jane Sterling, writes children's stories. Naughty puppies, bluebirds who talk, fluffy chicks who lose their way—that sort of thing."

Maggie gave a wistful smile. "So they didn't fake their own deaths?"

John twirled Maggie around and then drew her in again. "Listen, Maggie. You know, parents—all parents—have secret lives. If they didn't, they wouldn't be parents after all."

"So you think I should forgive him?"

"I think—I think you should give it some time."

The song came to an end, but John didn't release her. As the blond chanteuse relinquished the microphone, the orchestra began to play "Bewitched, Bothered and Bewildered," the lush melody carried by a golden trumpet.

Maggie looked up at John, her arms still tight around his neck. "Do you *like* your father?"

"I suppose. I don't really *know* my father. He was always in the office or away in London when I was growing up." Then, "But, nonetheless, I'd have to say that I do love him."

"Well," Maggie said. "I don't know if I love my father."

"That's understandable."

"He left me. He lied to me." Maggie stopped dancing in the middle of the floor. "My father's a liar."

John stopped as well. Together, they stood in the middle of the floor as the other dancers slowly spun around them.

"It's hard to trust someone who's abandoned you."

"Am I terrible for not wanting to let myself care about my own father?"

John sighed. "He might do something tomorrow that might hurt you. How would you—will you—deal with that?"

"I don't know," she said. "Does that make me a bad daughter?"

John put his arms around her, and together they began to dance once again. "You're a good person," he replied, and kissed the top of her head. "And you'll fig-ure it out. You'll see."

Much, much later, John walked Maggie to the door of the Blue Moon. They stood in the silver-papered en-trance hall, while men in dark jackets and women in low-cut dresses made their way past them. They stepped out onto the sidewalk, into the bruised blue of the evening. The light from the passing traffic was dim, and a cool breeze had begun to blow, whispering through the tree leaves. The air smelled of damp and petrol fumes.

"I'm fine, really," she said, pulling her wrap more tightly around her. "I'll just take a taxi back to the hotel." It was late, she was exhausted, and her arm was starting to throb again.

"Are you sure?" he said. "I can go with you. I mean, as an escort." He put his hand up and started to rub the back of his neck. "What I mean is, to escort you to your room—and leave you there. To go to bed. Er, I mean, get some sleep."

"Poor John," David said, walking up to the duo. "Just kiss him and get it over with, won't you?"

Maggie put her hand on his arm. "I'm fine, really." She lifted up onto tiptoes and gave him a quick kiss on the cheek. "I'll see you tomorrow, all right?"

A shiny black cab pulled up. "This is my ride," she said.

John opened the door. "You're sure?"

"I'm sure," she said firmly. "But thank you, just the same."

Maggie smiled and got into the backseat of the taxi. John closed the door. "To the Savoy, please," she said to the driver. Then she let her head lean onto the seatback. It felt so good to finally rest, to be still, if just for a mo-ment. . . .

As the cab pulled out and headed on its way, she felt a crawling sensation on her skin, as though someone was watching her. She opened her eyes and looked up to the rearview mirror. The driver was staring at her.

"Hello, Miss Hope," the man said, with a charming grin. "Fancy meeting you here."

"Just like that?" Back at their banquette, Frain was incensed. "You let her get into a taxi that pulled up"—he snapped his fingers—"just like that?"

"She insisted she was fine, sir," John said.

Chuck wasn't about to let someone like Frain intimidate her. "Maggie's a big girl now—she can take care of herself." Then, to Edmund, "Er, sorry."

"What's going on?" Edmund asked.

"Our brilliant friend here just let Maggie get into a taxi. Alone," Frain said.

David considered. "Well, it's not *that* late. I do think she'll—"

"You don't understand," Frain said, rising to his feet. "Michael Murphy is still at large."

"What happened to Claire?" the driver asked, his eyes in the rearview window wild. "What happened at Saint Paul's?"

"Claire's . . . in custody," Maggie managed.

"Liar!" he spat. "They've probably already hanged her, haven't they? My dear, sweet Claire . . ."

Even through her fear, one corner of her mind kept working. *This is the man Claire was in love with? God help us.*

Without warning, the low wail of the siren began.

"Oh, Christ," he muttered. "Fucking raid."

Then, without further preamble, bombs began to drop.

There was a terrible crash as they passed alongside a

building as it was hit. The glass of the front windows shattered, and dazzling orange-and-blue flames began to devour the structure. The taxi was caught in the rain of broken glass, papers, and books. A pink knit baby bootie landed on the windshield.

The vehicle lurched and swerved, and crashed into a metal streetlight post with a resounding crunch. The car's hood was suddenly folded like an accordion. Metal rubbish bins fell over, clattering on the pavement, and a dog began barking in the distance.

Maggie's head hit the seat in front of her, and she blinked, several times, trying to think. Her hands worked at the door handle, now seemingly stuck. "Come on, come on, come on," she muttered.

All she saw was Michael Murphy's fist coming at her face, and then everything went black.

Maggie turned over and groaned, waves of pain and nausea washing over her. As she blinked her eyes open, she realized she was in complete darkness. She rolled over and started to feel her way around. Hard-packed dirt floor, a few cigarette butts, a bunk bed, low curved aluminum roof—she realized he must have knocked her out and then dragged her into the house's Anderson shelter.

The raid seemed to be over, for the moment.

Of course, she now had bigger problems to worry about.

"You're not going to get away with this," she heard him muttering outside the shelter's door.

She groped around in the dark to see if there was anything handy to use as a weapon.

Nothing.

She tried the door. It was locked. There was no way out. The air suddenly felt hot and suffocating. She took a ragged breath in.

"Dear Maggie—what have they done with Claire?" His voice was coming from overhead. He must be sitting on top of the Anderson.

"I told you already."

"I'll let you out when you tell me where Claire is."

"That's all right," she said, knowing that he wouldn't like the truth and it would be pointless to lie. "I'll just stay right here, thanks."

She heard Murphy's footsteps, then the sound of liquid hitting the Anderson's steel roof. Then there was the smell of gasoline, sharp and heady.

"You want to know something about Claire, Maggie Hope? She was ready to die for her cause. But she's not going to die in a British prison. I won't let her! Where is she?" He screamed into the night, "Where is Claire?"

Maggie was frantically trying to dig a hole in the dirt underneath the Anderson large enough to fit through. It was an impossible task, and her hands were scratched and filthy, but she continued digging, flinging the dirt behind her.

"Where is she, Maggie?" he called. "Where's Claire?"

She bit her tongue and kept digging at a furious pace.

Maggie jumped when she heard a crack and felt the shell of the Anderson shudder and shake. He must have punched it.

"She didn't get to Churchill. It was all for nothing. Well, I'll tell you, Maggie Hope, I'm not going to let you—and her—ruin everything I've worked for."

"She's in a women's prison, just outside of Sheffield. Just go away. Please." She kept digging.

From the distance, she heard John's voice calling, "Maggie! Maggie!"

"Here!" she yelled, as loud as she could. "I'm here!"

John followed the muffled sound of Maggie's voice and sprinted around the side of the house.

Michael Murphy heard him coming. He hid himself behind a rubbish bin, let him pass, and then jumped him from behind.

The two men wrestled on the ground, knocking over metal lawn chairs that crashed in the darkness. Murphy kicked John in the groin, then got him into a headlock.

"So you're the boyfriend, huh? Pierce didn't get you? Guess I'll have to finish the job. But first," he said, administering several vicious blows to John's face, "I'm going to take care of your girl."

John lay, writhing in agony, as Murphy took a packet of matches from his inside front pocket and lit one, throwing it onto the Anderson.

It made a sparkling red arc as it flew. The Anderson ignited with a whoosh of air. Bright orange flames crackled merrily on the curved roof.

"She's in there, mate." He knelt down to John and whispered in his ear, "Now we'll both have girls who died for the cause, won't we?"

Through the aluminum roof of the Anderson, Maggie heard the fire catch and then ignite with a dull roar. Instantly, heat started permeating the shelter. She kept throwing the weight of her body against the back wall, until the metal gave from the fastenings and there was enough room to force her body through.

She wriggled out from the Anderson, choking and coughing, her white dress tattered and covered in dirt, just as the flames engulfed it. Her lungs cried out for oxygen, and her hands were scratched and bleeding. She rolled as fast and as far away as she could, the heat still radiating onto her skin. She retched into the grass, and as she wiped her mouth she realized she wasn't dead after all.

She crawled blindly on her hands and knees, dress torn and dirty. She saw John lying on the ground a few feet away, nearly unconscious. "John," she whispered. "John?"

*John, can you hear me? Please be all right. John? John?*

Murphy staggered away, still disoriented from grief and anger. He made it back to the road, lit by the flames from the bombed house across the street. The air stank of thick smoke.

He got back into the taxi and turned the key. It was badly damaged and wouldn't start. "Shit," he cried, banging his hands on the steering wheel. "Shit, shit, shit."

A shadow passed silently across the dashboard.

Murphy looked up to the figure of Peter Frain looming over him, pistol in hand. "Do you have a license for that vehicle, sir?" Frain asked pleasantly, pointing the gun at Murphy's head.

Murphy, battered, bloody, and reeking of gasoline, looked up at Frain. "Fuck you."

"I'm *so* glad you said that." Frain pulled the revolver's trigger. Murphy slumped over, mouth open, eyes glazing, blood running down the steering wheel.

"Michael Murphy," Frain said with grim satisfaction. "Shot while resisting arrest."

Arms pumping, David, Chuck, and Edmund caught up with Frain. "Where's Maggie?" Edmund panted.

Frain holstered his gun. "You two," he said to David and Chuck, "go inside and call the fire department and an ambulance. Edmund, let's get started putting out that fire."

Maggie was cradling John's head in her lap in the flickering light of the blaze when she saw Frain and Edmund approach past the clothesline and the vegetable patch. "He's still out there," she said wildly. "He's still there."

Frain shook his head. "Murphy's been taken care of."

They heard sirens wailing in the distance, getting closer.

"It's going to be all right, Maggie," Edmund said, bending down and wrapping his arms around her.

"I know it is," she replied. Then she started to laugh. She laughed and laughed and laughed, until tears ran down her face and her stomach hurt.

Out of the corner of her eye, Maggie could see Frain and Edmund look at each other with concern. David ran out of the house to join them, taking in the sight of Maggie—hair disheveled, dress torn and muddy, face covered in dirt, arm and hands bleeding. She reeked of gasoline. "Merciful Zeus, she's lost it again, hasn't she?" he said in awe. Beside him, Chuck could only stare in shocked silence.

Even John managed to open one eye. "I say . . ." he managed. "You all right, Maggie?"

She managed to choke back laughter and gave a few snorts and hiccups. "I'm fine, John," she said, smoothing back his unruly hair. "Thanks to you."

Then, to Edmund, "I was just thinking," she said, wiping her eyes with the hem of her dress and then dabbing at her nose. "I was just thinking—how on earth are we going to explain all this to Aunt Edith?"

# THIRTY-FOUR

Back at No. 10 the next morning, there wasn't much time to talk to the Prime Minister about changing jobs.

There were memos to type, papers to file, and notation to take. And when Mrs. Churchill, slim and elegant, with intelligent eyes and a strong jaw, came by his office in the mid-afternoon, the P.M. announced to her, "Clemmie, Chartwell this weekend." While it was easier for Mr. Churchill to take his weekends at Chequers, he preferred the family home.

"Winston, you can't," she said, coming around the desk behind him. She put her hands on his shoulders and kissed him on the top of his shiny head. "It's closed—and there will be no one to cook for you."

"I shall cook for myself," Mr. Churchill pronounced. "I can boil an egg. I've seen it done."

She sighed. "All right, Chartwell it is, Mr. Pug. I'll tell the staff."

Maggie pretended to read over her typing as Mrs. Churchill kissed him again, this time on the lips with an audible smack, and left.

Later that evening, they heard it had been decided: The Churchills would spend the coming weekend at Chartwell, and as Mrs. Tinsley's son was home on leave,

Maggie would be the secretary to accompany them. She was elated by the news. She'd been longing to see Chartwell, the Churchills' private estate in Kent.

And this was her last chance.

Maggie was expecting to take dictation as they drove to Kent in the black Bentley, followed in another car by Detective Thompson; Mr. Churchill's faithful butler, Mr. Inces; and several Royal Marines. She had her pen and paper on her lap, at the ready. But Mr. Churchill was silent.

The city landscape segued into misty gray-green plains and orchards, branches heavy with rosy apples. As they covered more and more distance, the pinker and more cherubic Mr. Churchill's face became and the more his blue eyes twinkled. They rode on in silence for a while, as he smoked yet another cigar.

Maggie was nervous—she wasn't used to being alone with him for this long when they weren't working. She tried not to drum her fingers or tap her toes.

Finally, he spoke.

"Miss Hope, I'd like you to know—while I appreciate your actions of recent days, a dead employee is of no use to me, do you understand?"

"Yes, sir."

"It would be highly inconvenient. I need everyone on my staff alive and kicking if we're going to win this war. Do you hear me, Miss Hope? Kicking, I say."

"Kicking. Yes, sir." She tried not to giggle.

The P.M. gave her a stern look. *Women!* He was not good with women, at least not professionally. Of course, women were to be admired, to be wooed—they were creatures of romance and moonlight and mystery. Then they were to be left in the parlors, the bedrooms, the nurseries—doing God knows what—while the menfolk got down to business over brandy and cigars. He'd had severe doubts about giving women the vote and was not impressed by those who'd made their way into Parliament, particularly that infernal Nancy Astor. However, times had changed. They had indeed changed.

"Mr. Frain tells me that you might be better suited to espionage work."

*What exactly had Frain told him?* "Sir?"

"And from what I understand, you have the intelligence and pluck to be a spy—a *spook,* as they say."

He chewed on his large Romeo y Julieta cigar impassively for a few moments and gazed out the car window at the countryside rolling by.

"In general, of course, I detest these so-called career women. Didn't even see why you women wanted the vote! But Clemmie, my daughters, the women of my staff, the women of England—you've all shown considerable mettle. Courage under fire. And we can always use someone in MI-Five who's proven herself."

She nearly fell over from shock. "Y-yes sir," was all she could manage.

"Of course," he continued, "you could still find a nice young man from a good family, settle down, have a few babies. Four, as Clemmie and I had."

He stubbed out his cigar in the car door's ashtray, rolled down the window, and threw out the end. "Let there be women!" he declared out the open window, as though for all England to hear. As he cranked the window back up, he gave a heavy sigh of resignation.

Before she could even think of responding, he went straight into dictation.

Chartwell in October was even more beautiful than Maggie had ever imagined it: practically a picture-book illustration of the English countryside. A rose garden with a sundial in the center was still in bloom. Glimpses of burgundy, scarlet, apricot, pink, and yellow petals could be seen in the distance. The lake at the bottom of the hill sparkled in the golden afternoon sunlight.

On the south side of the house was another flower garden surrounded by a brick wall built, Mr. Inces told her proudly, by Mr. Churchill himself. There was "Mary Cot," a child-sized brick playhouse he erected for his youngest daughter when she was nine. Between the playhouse and the great house was a large orchard of apple trees—Orange Pippin, Worcester Pearmain, and Bramley's Seedling—heavy with ripe fruit. There was a tennis court for Mrs. Churchill and the children. There was a pond with goldfish and black swans and, of course, the painting studio. Cats, dogs, geese, goats, and even foxes roamed freely.

The house itself was quintessentially English inside and out. "We shape our buildings and our buildings shape us," Mr. Churchill had once said, and Maggie could now see why. It was perhaps not to Maggie's taste, but she could see why the P.M. loved it so—the views of the countryside. It had been built in the fifteenth century and was said to have housed King Henry VIII for a time. Inside was a crest with the Churchill family's coat of arms and Spanish motto: *Fiel Pero Desdichado*—Faithful but Unfortunate.

The house's interior reflected two distinct tastes in decorating: Mrs. Churchill's was elegant, while Mr. Churchill's was surprisingly flashy. Since Maggie had seen only their relatively austere quarters in the Annexe, she was amazed to see so many of Mr. Churchill's personal treasures: an ornate Fabergé cigar box; engraved plates of gold and silver; a gold-headed walking stick engraved by King Edward VII, "to my youngest Minister"; and Mr. Churchill's firearms from the Great War.

She and John sat next to each other in the back of the P.M.'s study as he stood and spoke from his high Disraeli-style desk with a slanting top into the large microphone that would broadcast his speech across all England.

"It is quite true that I have seen many painful scenes of havoc, and of fine buildings and acres of cottage homes blasted into rubble heaps of ruin," the P.M. said.

"Notice how he left out Saint Paul's," John whispered to Maggie. "We wouldn't want to scare people."

"The government? Keep information from citizens during wartime?" Maggie whispered back behind an upheld hand. She rolled her eyes. "Perish the thought."

". . . The British nation is stirred and moved as it never has been at any time in its long, eventful, famous history, and it is no hackneyed trope of speech to say that they mean to conquer or to die."

"Even the secretaries," John said with a sly grin, nudging Maggie.

"*Especially* the secretaries," she said.

"What a triumph the life of these battered cities is over the worst that any fire or bomb can do . . ." the P.M. said. "This is indeed the grand heroic period of our history, and the light of glory shines on all."

John squinted at her. "I think I see your 'light of glory.' "

She elbowed him in the ribs. "Shut up."

"Last time I spoke to you I quoted the lines of Longfellow which President Roosevelt had written out for me in his own hand. I have some other lines which are less well known but which seem apt and appropriate to our fortunes tonight, and I believe they will so be judged wherever the English language is spoken or the flag of freedom flies."

They leaned forward to listen.

" 'For while the tired waves, vainly breaking,
        Seem here no painful inch to gain,

Far back, through creeks and inlets making,
    Comes silent, flooding in, the main.

And not by eastern windows only,
    When daylight comes, comes in the light,
In front the sun climbs slow, how slowly!
    But westward, look, the land is bright. ' "

It was a good speech. A great speech.

And Maggie felt that it—and everything—had been worth it.

The broadcast was concluded, and Mrs. Churchill went up to the P.M. and laid a gentle hand on his shoulder. "Time for dinner now, Mr. Pug."

"Blast, I was just getting started," Mr. Churchill said, lip jutting forward in the beginnings of a pout.

"Oh, Winnie, you're impossible," she said, turning around and walking to the thick oak door.

"I know, Clemmie. You're too good to me. What's for dinner?" he said, making his way to the door.

She turned. "Just what you requested," she replied. "Clear soup, oysters, trout, roast beef with pommes Anna, and glazed carrots."

"Pudding?"

"Cook has prepared your favorite—chocolate éclairs."

"Well," he said, considering. "Then I shall be persuaded." He turned back and gestured to Maggie and John. "Carry on."

"I'll have Cook send up two trays," Mrs. Churchill said to them.

"Wait, Clemmie. There's something I want to do first," he pronounced, walking over to one of his bookshelves. He pulled down a leather-bound book and turned to the first page, where he scribbled a few lines with his gold fountain pen.

"Before I forget, Miss Hope, I have something for you. Read it in good health." Too stunned to speak, Maggie accepted the thick, gold-stamped copy of the first volume of Mr. Churchill's *Marlboro: His Life and Times,* about his illustrious ancestor.

Mrs. Churchill gave a small sigh of exasperation. "Winnie, do you always have to give people *your* books?"

"Why else would I write them?" He gave her his most cherubic smile.

"Perhaps Miss Hope would prefer another book. One *not* written by you."

He looked at her over his gold-rimmed glasses and blinked. "I don't see why."

"I'm honored to receive *Marlboro,* Mr. Churchill," Maggie said, "and shall treasure it always."

"There! You see? 'Honored.' 'Shall treasure it always.' The proper response to being given a book. Most proper indeed. You see, Clemmie?" he said, walking over to her and offering his arm.

"Yes, Mr. Pug," she said, tucking her hand under his arm.

He grasped it tightly and patted it. "Thank you, Mrs. Pussycat," he said, and kissed her on the cheek, causing her to giggle.

As they made their way out the door and into the hallway, Maggie opened the book to see his inscription.

*Dear Miss Hope,*
*K.P.O.*
*Yours with great respect and admiration,*
*Winston Churchill*

"So I've heard you're moving over to MI-Five," John said later that evening, when the day's duties were finished. They walked Chartwell's grounds, through the winding paths of the vegetable gardens, past the stables and the sheds. There were some apple boxes in front of the pig pens. The pigs were inside, sleeping on their beds of hay, snoring and snorting lightly.

"Oh, John," Maggie said, teasing, "you do take me to the nicest places."

He took her hand in his; they fit together well. "I'm very happy for you, Maggie. You deserve it."

She couldn't help but feel a warm rush of pride. "Thank you. And thanks, too, for everything you did, you know, with the code. At Bletchley. With Pierce, that bastard. David told me how resolute you were." They sat down on a low weathered wooden bench.

"You'll still be in London, yes?" he asked.

"I'll be in London, yes."

"And when do you start?"

"Well, I'm taking some time off—a month. I just need—you know—to think about everything that happened."

"That makes sense," John said. "You've been through a lot."

She looked into his face; the bruises from the attack were still evident. "Ah, that British understatement."

"What about your father?"

"He's staying in London for a little while. We're taking it slowly. Getting to know each other."

"Ah."

"It's not easy. Still, I'm glad he's alive, and I'm glad he's here. But it's . . ." She searched for the right word. "Complicated."

"It generally is. And how are you doing after, well, you know . . ."

"The death of Claire?"

"Yes."

Maggie sighed. "I've already mourned Paige, at the

funeral with all of you. Claire? Well, I never really knew her."

"I see," John said.

There was a silence, a companionable one. "And as you know, the twins have left for their tour. And Sarah, Chuck, and I are moving in with David, right?"

"What? David?" Obviously, John hadn't heard. "David and all those women . . ."

"Well, he has that huge flat in Kensington. We'll be the three sisters he never knew he always wanted."

"Perfect."

"Much better than going, well, home. After everything that happened, I just couldn't . . ."

"Of course," John said. "No one would expect you to." Then, "What about your house?"

"Ah," Maggie said. "I'm renting it out."

"Good, good, that takes care of that, then." John's brows knit. "And even after everything that's happened, with your new job, your new flat, you'll still want to stay in touch? Because I'd really like that. After everything that's happened."

"*Especially* after everything that's happened. I can't imagine not seeing you."

"Well. Good." He traced the line of her cheek with one finger.

"Yes. Good," she said, smiling, as their lips met.

## THIRTY-FIVE

THE FOLLOWING MONDAY, Mrs. Tinsley and Miss Stewart were both delighted to see Maggie back at No. 10, if only to pack up her things.

"Now, you *will* be careful, won't you?" Miss Stewart asked. "Goodness, we've been so worried about you."

"And you left us with an *extraordinary* amount of work to do, let me say," Mrs. Tinsley said. "Although," she amended, "we're gratified to see you've come back in one piece."

"It was only a weekend at Chartwell," Maggie said as she packed up her few belongings from the desk.

"Don't be impertinent with me, young lady!" Mrs. Tinsley said.

"We're terribly proud of you, Maggie," Miss Stewart said, her blue eyes threatening to overflow.

"Oh, really," Mrs. Tinsley snapped at Miss Stewart. "Must you praise her? It will only go to her head."

"I just meant—"

"Enough is as good as a feast." Then, to Maggie, "But you will come back once in a while, won't you? Just to say hello."

"Of course I will," she answered, meaning it. *I'll miss you, too,* she realized.

David stuck his nose into the office. "Almost ready to go, Magster?"

"One more minute, please," Maggie said, then hugged each woman in turn. Miss Stewart squeezed her back and sniffled. Mrs. Tinsley gave Maggie's shoulder a few awkward pats. "Well, really . . ." Mrs. Tinsley said, taking out her handkerchief and giving a good sniff.

There was one last task Maggie had to do.

She gave the folder marked *TOP SECRET* with the carbon of her report, as well as the journal of everything that had really happened, to Mrs. Tinsley. "For the archives," she said.

Mrs. Tinsley nodded and accepted the folder.

"And I'll take this one to him myself."

Papers in hand, Maggie walked down the hall, for the last time, to Mr. Churchill's office. She knocked at the heavy wooden door.

"Come in!" he boomed.

She walked in and placed the papers on his desk. "Here's the after-action report, sir."

"Ah," he said, chewing on the ever-present cigar and looking at her over the tops of his spectacles. "Right. You're off to work for Frain, then, are you?"

"Yes, sir."

"Well, our loss is their gain, I suppose," he said, rising to his feet to shake her hand. "Need some Hope in their offices, too, what?" He chuckled, then turned back to his papers. "It's all right to take some time off, but don't keep Frain waiting. He's a brilliant man, but not what you'd call patient."

"Yes, sir," she said, standing before him. "Thank you, sir. For everything." She turned and walked to the door.

As she reached it, he spoke again. "Just remember, Miss Hope," he said, stabbing the air with his cigar for emphasis, "kicking! Kicking, I say!"

Her eyes suddenly filled with tears as she turned to respond one last time. "Yes, sir. Kicking, sir."

Maggie got into David's car and closed the door with a resounding thud. They looked at each other and smiled, then he put the car into gear and pulled out into traffic to drive Maggie to his—and now hers and the girls'— new home in Kensington.

"Would you mind driving by Saint Paul's first?" Maggie asked.

Above the city, the great dome of St. Paul's Cathedral soared. The church, in its different incarnations, had been ransacked by Vikings, struck by lightning, defaced during the British Civil War, and nearly destroyed in the Great Fire of London. It had been rebuilt by Christopher Wren only to be bombed by Nazis from the air and nearly brought down by a bomb planted inside. And yet here it still stood.

The warm autumn evening had drawn a crowd beneath the stern gaze of the statue of Queen Anne. She looked down from her pedestal, adorned with her golden crown, scepter, and orb, a fat gray pigeon perched on top of her head.

Below her, the crowd milled, men and women in khaki, dark blue, and gray uniforms, and women in jewel-toned colored dresses, looking like exotic birds amid foliage. A group of laughing RAF pilots on leave posed arm in arm for a photograph, which a young woman in a red-flowered hat looked delighted to take. The lemony sunlight slanted across the square, and an older woman sitting on the steps, wrapped in a long fringed shawl, fed pigeons crumbs from a bag of bread.

A man in an old mackintosh pulled the brim of his hat down as the car passed. Maggie knew that while Murphy was dead, there could be any number of secret agents mixed in among the crowd. She'd almost gotten used to the fact that she still saw Murphy everywhere, including in her nightmares. She gave a barely perceptible shudder.

"Are you all right?" David asked.

It was strange to imagine a world where men like Malcolm Pierce and Michael Murphy still plotted in the darkness. For that matter, a world where she had a father. One where someone like Paige could have led a double life. Where Sarah almost died. And where bombs still rained down from the sky on any given night . . .

"You all right?" David repeated.

Maggie rolled down the window and felt the warm air on her face.

She wasn't happy, exactly; she was still too raw for that. But she was satisfied. Satisfied and relieved, too, with maybe just a bit of joy thrown in for good measure. Yes, that was it. She'd made it through so much already. She knew now that she was strong. She'd survive. And she had friends and family to support her.

"Fine, David." She smiled at him. "Better than fine."

The sun was setting with a brilliant flare of scarlet, gold, and azure. Maggie lifted her face to catch the warmth of the last rays shining from behind the dome, glad to be alive, glad to be just where she was, with the wind on her face.

# HISTORICAL NOTE

*Mr. Churchill's Secretary* is not a history, nor is it meant to be. It's a blend of fact and fiction, of characters and events, both real and imagined.

This book was inspired by a visit to the Cabinet War Rooms in London and its meticulously researched and wonderfully presented exhibits. One of the audio accompaniments to the exhibit was an actress reading the recollections of one of Churchill's young secretaries, taken from the memoirs of Elizabeth Layton Nel. As I listened to her words and walked the corridors of the War Rooms, I felt a shiver go up my spine—and knew I'd found an extraordinary setting for a story.

Mrs. Elizabeth Layton Nel, one of Sir Winston's young wartime secretaries, was kind enough to reply to my letter from her home in South Africa in 2004. I told her how much I admired the work she had done, and also how much I enjoyed her memoir. She was generous enough to give her blessing to my using her "mistakes" ("right" for "ripe," et al.) but did caution me that in reality the secretaries *never* would have had any time for either Maggie's intrigues or romance.

We'd planned to meet in London at the Cabinet War Rooms for the opening of the Churchill Museum in February 2005, but alas, a difficult pregnancy prevented my traveling from New York to London. (The indefatigable Mrs. Nel not only made the journey but was honored at the museum's opening, along with Queen Elizabeth.) A widow since 2000, Mrs. Nel passed in October 2007 and is survived by a son and two daughters.

Her inspiring and important memoir, *Mr. Churchill's Secretary*, was first published in 1958 and, after many years, went out of print. A new edition of her book, *Winston Churchill by His Personal Secretary*, was completed shortly before her death in 2007. And so her story, I'm delighted to report, is readily available to all once again.

Another of Winston Churchill's young wartime secretaries, Marian Holmes, didn't write a memoir, but her quotations in Tim Clayton and Phil Craig's book *Finest Hour* and the BBC TV series of the same name were incredibly helpful. When I write that Mr. Churchill calls Miss Hope "Holmes" by mistake, that's an allusion to Marian Holmes.

In fact, according to her diary, Winston Churchill once referred to Miss Holmes as Miss Hope: "He went straight into dictating and I took it down on the silent typewriter. 'Here you are'—he still didn't look at me. I took the papers, he reached for more work from his dispatch box and I made for the door. Loud voice: 'Dammit, don't go. I've only just started.' He then looked up. 'I am so sorry. I thought it was Miss Layton. What is your name?' 'Miss Holmes.' 'Miss Hope?' 'Miss Holmes.' 'Oh.' "

When I read this exchange, I knew I'd found the last name of my heroine.

I was never able to speak with Miss Holmes, who passed in 2001, but Mrs. Nel assured me that they'd had quite the adventure accompanying Mr. Churchill to Russia together.

In addition, *I Was Winston Churchill's Private Secre-*

*tary* by Phyllis Moir was also useful in obtaining a glimpse into the lives of Churchill's typists.

*The Fringes of Power: The Incredible Inside Story of Winston Churchill During World War II* by head private secretary Jock (John) Colville provided an excellent insider's look at the inner workings of No. 10. John Sterling is in no way supposed to "be" Jock Colville, but I did use the name specifically in honor of Mr. Colville.

The excellent BBC TV series *1940s House,* the accompanying book by Juliet Gardner, and the exhibit at the Imperial War Museum in London were instrumental to understanding the time period. Barbara Kaye's memoir *The Company We Kept* was perfect for everyday details. *1939: The Last Season of Peace* by Angela Lambert, *Bombers & Mash: The Domestic Front 1939–45* by Raynes Minns, and *The Battle of Britain: The Greatest Air Battle of World War II* by Richard Hough and Denis Richards were also invaluable.

Churchill's own *Memoirs of the Second World War* and *The Gathering Storm,* as well as William Manchester's *The Last Lion,* Roy Jenkins's *Churchill: A Biography,* and Martin Gilbert's *In Search of Churchill* were all important to understanding this extraordinary man and his time.

Thanks to the Jerome Robbins Dance Collection at the New York Public Library for the Performing Arts at Lincoln Center, particularly for issues of *Dance Observer* from the thirties and forties. The Vic-Wells Ballet was established by Madame Ninette de Valois in London in 1931; Frederick Ashton was named the company's choreographer in 1935. The company was renamed the Sadler's Wells Ballet in 1940, and in 1956 became the Royal Ballet. *Frederick Ashton and His Ballets* by David Vaughan was a wonderful resource for information on the Vic-Wells Ballet.

In regard to cryptographers and the work done at

Bletchley Park, *Bletchley Park People: Churchill's Geese That Never Cackled* by Marion Hill, *Codebreakers: The Inside Story of Bletchley Park* by Sir F. H. Hinsley and Alan Stripp, and *Alan Turing: The Enigma* by Andrew Hodges were first-rate.

In 2006, it was discovered that Nazi agents in England had, in fact, embedded Morse code in drawings of models wearing the latest fashions in an attempt to outwit Allied censors. According to the recently released British security service files, Nazi agents relayed sensitive military information using the dots and dashes of Morse code incorporated in the drawings. They posted the letters to their handlers, hoping that counterespionage experts would be fooled by the seemingly innocent pictures.

Readers may find the image online: http://www.secure.vimigroup.com/news/?p=162

# ACKNOWLEDGMENTS

Thanks to the directors, trustees, and staff of the Cabinet War Rooms and the Imperial War Museum, especially Robert Crawford, the director general of the Imperial War Museum, and Phillip Reed, the curator of the Churchill Museum and the Cabinet War Rooms.

I'm deeply grateful to Victoria Skurnick (a.k.a. "Agent V"), who never stopped believing (and didn't stop sending out the manuscript). Thank you to Daniel Greenburg, at the Levine Greenberg Literary Agency, for passing my work her way.

I'm forever indebted to Kate Miciak, editor extraordinaire, who took a chance. Thanks also to the fantastic team at Bantam Dell: Margaret Benton, Loyale Coles, and Randall Klein.

This novel never would have seen the light of day if not for the ever insightful, ever patient, and always supportive Idria Barone Knecht—writer, editor, and friend.

I was blessed to have had a wonderful mentor and friend in novelist Judith Merkle Riley.

Many, many people offered support, constructive criticism, and advice as this novel went through its various stages. I'm humbled by the generosity of Lia Abbate, Amy Kass Amsterdam, Jonathan Amsterdam, Nassim Asfeti, Josh Axelrad, Jennifer Barnhart, Paula Bernstein, Scott Cameron, Jessica Cohen, Veronica Hart, Kimmerie Jones, Rick Knecht, Christine Lloyd, Edna MacNeal, Maria Massie, Matthew O'Brian, Ji Hyang Padma, Suzanne Phillips, Jana Riess, Elizabeth Riley, Lisa Rogers, Linda Roghaar, Rebecca Carey Rohan, Caitlin Sims, Christopher Steele, and Robin Walsh.

And I'm awed by the collective intelligence of the M.I.T. alums who were patient with my endless questions: Bob Amini, Monica Byrne, Wes Carroll, Michael Friedhoff, Mary Linton Peters, Stephen Peters, Michael Pieck, Erik Schwartz, Doug Stetson, and Larry Taylor.

Thanks to amazing babysitters Katey Parker, Andi Salamon, and Emily Ulmer for the time and peace of mind to write.

Thank you also to Danielle Bruno, Fidelma Fitzpatrick, Aymee Garcia, Robert Gardner, Melissa Leeper, Jane Beuth Mayer, Christine McCann, Kathryn Plank, Audra Branum Rickman, Rebecca Carey Rohan, Christine Serchia, and Jennifer Serchia for being all-around wonderful people.

Last, but certainly not least, thank you to Noel MacNeal, who always believed and who made writing possible, and to Mattie, who loves to hear Mommy's stories.

If you enjoyed *Mr. Churchill's Secretary,*
you won't want to miss the next ingenious mystery
in the Maggie Hope series.

Read on for an exciting early look at

# PRINCESS ELIZABETH'S SPY

by Susan Elia MacNeal

Published by Bantam Trade Paperbacks

# PROLOGUE

THE MIDDAY SUMMER sun in Lisbon was dazzling and harsh. But while nearly everyone else was inside taking a siesta, the Duke of Windsor, formerly King Edward VIII of England, kept up his British habits, even on the continent.

He and his wife, Wallis Simpson, the woman for whom he'd abdicated the throne, sat outside at the Bar-Café Europa, which catered to tourists and British expats. The town square was nearly empty, except for a young American couple walking arm in arm and a few pigeons strutting and pecking for crumbs in the dust.

Wallis, slender and elegant, wore a scarlet Schiaparelli suit, a bejeweled flamingo brooch, and dark glasses. She sipped a Campari and soda, the ice cubes clinking against one another in her tall glass. Next to her, the Duke, slight and fair-haired, toyed with a tumbler of blood-orange juice and read *The Times* of London. He was only forty-six, but the strain from the abdication, and subsequent banishment from royal life, made him look much older.

A shadow passed over his page. The Duke looked up in annoyance, then smiled broadly when he saw who it was—Walther Shellenberg, Heinrich Himmler's personal aide and a deputy leader of the Reich Main Security Office.

"Shel! Good to see you—sit down," the Duke said.

"Thank you, Your Highness," Shellenberg replied in accented English, sitting down on the delicate wire chair. The Duke and Duchess had befriended Shellenberg on their tours to Germany before the war, visiting with Prince Philip of Hesse and Adolf Hitler.

"Hello, Walther," Wallis said.

Shellenberg removed his Nazi visor hat, with its skull and crossbones, to reveal thick brown hair parted in the center and glistening with a copious amount of Brylcreem. "Good afternoon, Your Highness. May I say you look particularly lovely today?" he said to Wallis, a smile softening his angular features.

"Thank you, Shel," she replied, warming to his use of *Your Highness,* which Hitler had also used when they'd visited him at the Berghof, his chalet in the Bavarian Alps. Technically, neither Hitler nor Shellenberg needed to address her that way, as she'd never been awarded HRH status by the current king, a snub indeed. His wife, Queen Elizabeth, referred to Wallis only as "that woman."

As she offered her hand to Shellenberg to be kissed, the scent of L'heure Bleue mixed with Mitsouko—a heady mix of carnations and oakmoss, Wallis's signature scent—wafted around her in the heat.

"They threw a rock at our window last night, Shel." The Duke frowned. "Shattered the glass. Could have killed us."

"I know, sir. Terrible, just terrible." And he did know—Shellenberg himself had arranged the rock-throwing incident in order to frighten the Windsors, leaving false clues to make it look as though British Intelligence were to blame. If the Windsors were scared enough, blaming British Intelligence, they'd come around to the Nazis' point of view, he was certain of it.

"It's terrible," Wallis said, smoothing her glossy black hair, cut down the middle with a narrow white part. "They hate us. The British just hate us now."

"Now, now, dear," Edward said, reaching over to take her hand. "It's not the British people. It's Churchill and his gangsters. And my brother and that wife of his. Silly old Bertie as King George VI, indeed. It's as if I'd never been King!"

"You can't abdicate and eat it too, dear," Wallis said with a tight smile.

Shellenberg cleared his throat. "I've heard from the Führer."

"Oh, how lovely!" Wallis exclaimed, extracting a cigarette from a gold case and fitting it in a long ivory holder. The Duke pulled out his lighter and lit it for her; she smiled up at him as she drew her first inhale.

"He gave me a number," Shellenberg said, knowing quite well the two were having money problems since the abdication. He took a small folded piece of paper from his pocket, put it on the table, and pushed it toward the Duke. If fear alone couldn't persuade them, perhaps money could.

The Duke of Windsor waited, simply looking at the note for a few heartbeats, then reached for it. Slowly, he picked it up and opened it. He read the number and then handed the slip over to Wallis. She examined it, arching one perfectly plucked and penciled eyebrow, then handed it back.

"Quite a bit of money, Shel," the Duke said, pushing the paper away.

"But it's not just about the money, sir," Shellenberg said, placing the paper in one of the ceramic ashtrays and then lighting it, letting it burn away to ash. "Germany has taken Austria, the Sudetenland, and Poland.

We have taken the Low Countries and France. When Germany invades England—and it's just a matter of time before London falls—your people will need you." He looked to Wallis. "Both of you. You know it's only a matter of time now. We're establishing air supremacy, and as soon as we take out the Royal Air Force, we'll invade. Your younger brother, the present king, has aligned himself with Winston Churchill and his gangsters. He won't be permitted to stay on the throne, of course."

"Of course," Wallis murmured. She had no love for either the King or Queen, who had never acknowledged her and, in her opinion, had taken every opportunity to humiliate her. Why her husband couldn't have simply stayed on the throne when he'd married her, she would never understand—or forgive.

"And his daughter, Elizabeth, raised with the same propaganda her father espouses, can't reign either, so . . . And then we'll need you—*both* of you," Shellenberg stressed, "to urge the British to accept German occupation. With you as King, and the Duchess as Queen, of course."

"It's not about me, Shel," the Duke said. "We need to end the war now before thousands are killed and maimed in order to save the faces of a few corrupt politicians. Believe me, with continued heavy bombing, Britain will soon be desperate for peace. The people will panic and turn against Churchill and Eden—and the current King, too, of course. Which presents the perfect opportunity to bring me back as sovereign." The Duke sighed. "Of course, I can't officially support any of this, you know."

"What other options do you have?" Shellenberg asked.

There was a long silence. The Windsors knew they were running out of opportunities.

"Bermuda," Wallis said finally, rolling her eyes and tapping ashes into a ceramic ashtray crudely painted with a bullfighter holding up a red cape. "Churchill and the present royals want to banish us to that godforsaken little territory. Conveniently out of their way."

"Then don't go," Shellenberg urged. "You have the Führer, and the British people, counting on you to step up. To be their King and Queen."

The Duke and Duchess locked eyes. "What do you say, dear?" he asked her.

The Duchess took a moment for a long exhale, blowing out a thin stream of blue smoke. It had been a long few years for her. First there was her affair with him, when he'd been the Prince of Wales. The unexpected death of his father, King George V, had been both shocking and painful for both of them. Their relationship nearly collapsed when Edward had taken the throne, crushed by the disapproval of the rest of the royal family.

They'd thought, perhaps foolishly, that once the family got to know her better, they'd accept her. But no. The Royal family, in particular the newly crowned George VI and Queen Elizabeth, had made it overwhelmingly clear Edward would never be able to marry her, a two-time American divorcée and a close personal friend of Joachim von Ribbentrop's, Foreign Minister of Germany, and still stay on the throne.

Edward had chosen her and abdicated—but it had nearly killed him. And it broke her heart to see him made to choose. Their love had survived, but only just. Even in the bright sunshine of Portugal, they had their good days and bad.

"We're going to enjoy ourselves at the villa of our good friend, Ricardo do Espírito Santo Silva, for now," she replied, finally. "If—and only if—Germany invades . . ." She shrugged her narrow shoulders.

"—you can count on us to do the right thing," the Duke finished. "For the British people, of course."

The three of them nodded.

"Excellent," said Shellenberg, rising. "That's what we hoped you'd say. *Heil* Hitler!"

# CHAPTER ONE

BLETCHLEY WAS A small, seemingly inconsequential railway town about fifty miles northwest of London. However, since 1938, the town was also the home of what was officially known as the Government Code and Cipher School. But those in the know referred to it as Station X. Or War Station. Or just the initials B.P., for Bletchley Park.

The Bletchley estate, the former manse of Sir Herbert and Lady Fanny Leon, was a red-brick Victorian monstrosity in a faux-Tudor style. Now, under government control, it bustled with men and women in uniform, as well as civilians—mostly men in baggy wrinkled trousers and herringbone tweed jackets with leather elbow patches. The house's formerly lush lawns were flattened and worn from all the foot and bicycle traffic. The gardens had been trampled to make room for hastily assembled huts and office buildings.

Although it was a secret to most who worked there, the real business of Bletchley was breaking Nazi military code. The cryptographers at Bletchley Park had a reconstructed Enigma machine used by the Germans (a gift from the Poles), a code key used in the Norway campaign, and two keys used by the Nazi air force. Though they received a huge volume of decrypts, they still couldn't be used for practical purposes. Under the leadership of Alan Turing, Peter Twinn, and John Jeffreys, they were still waiting and working, hoping for a miracle.

The Nazis thought their codes were unbreakable, and they had good reason to believe so. When a German commander typed in a message, the machine sent electrical impulses through a series of rotating wheels, contacts, and wires to produce the enciphered letters, which lit up on a panel above the keyboard. By typing the resulting code into his own machine, the recipient saw the deciphered message light up letter by letter. The rotors and wires of the machine could be configured in an almost infinite number of ways. The odds against anyone breaking Enigma were a staggering 150 million million million to one.

Benjamin Batey, a graduate of Trinity College at Cambridge with a Ph.D. in logical mathematics, worked in Hut 8 trying to break Nazi naval decrypts. Batey had been working for eight months in the drafty hut. It stank of damp, lime, and coal tar.

He worked in one room of a dozen, divided by flimsy partitions made of plywood. The noise from the other workstations drifted about—low conversations, thudding footsteps, a shrill telephone ring, the steady clicks of the Type-X machines in the decoding room.

The harsh fluorescent overhead light cast long shadows across the concrete floor as Batey and his officemate, both youngish men in rumpled corduroy trousers and heavy wool sweaters, worked at mismatched battered wooden desks piled with sheaves of papers. Thick manila folders with TOP SECRET stamped in heavy red ink across them were heaped haphazardly on the floor, dirty tea mugs lined up on the window's ledge, and steam hissed from the paint-chipped radiator. Blackout curtains hid the view.

Usually a prodigious worker, Batey couldn't wait to leave. He had a date.

"So, is she an imaginary girl? Or a real one?" asked James Abbott, his officemate. Abbott was young, but his face was pale and drawn, and he had dark purple shadows under his eyes. They all looked like that at Bletchley. Sleep was considered an unnecessary extravagance.

Batey was not amused. "I don't kiss and tell, old thing," he said, shrugging into a wool coat and wrapping a striped school scarf around his neck.

"I say," said Abbott, putting his worn capped-toe oxfords up on the desk and leaning back, "at least comb your hair. Or what's left of it."

It was true. Batey might have been only in his late twenties, with a face that still had the plushness of youth, but already his dark hair was receding. It could have been genetics, or the prodigious stress Batey was under as a boffin, as the cryptographers were called at Bletchley. Generally, he was too sleep-deprived and distracted to give his appearance much thought, but it hadn't gone without noticing that in the confines of B.P., the boffins were at the top of the pecking order, as far as the women there were concerned.

It was the first time Batey had been viewed by the fairer sex in such a positive light, and, suddenly, he was in demand. And so, while at first he believed it was absolute insanity that someone like Victoria Keeley, who turned heads at Bletchley with her tall, slim figure, pale skin, and dark hair, would be interested in someone like him, he'd slowly grown to accept and even appreciate it.

There was a knock at the door. Abbott's eyebrows raised.

Batey cracked the door open, but it was too late, Abbott had already caught sight of who it was. "Victoria Keeley, Queen of the Teleprincesses—what brings you to our humble abode?" Abbott said, leaning back even far-ther in his desk chair.

Victoria was tall and slender, with a profile as sharp as Katharine Hepburn's and an aura of offhand glamour that came from being a recent debutante who spoke flawless French and rode and played tennis superbly. "Only a tele*countess*, Mr. Abbott," she replied with her best cocktail party smile. "Despite my family's august lineage, I can't quite aspire to royalty."

"Ah, all you lovely girls are princesses to me," he quipped, grinning at her.

"That's funny, I've heard you say we're all the same in the dark." She batted her eyelashes as Abbott gasped and nearly fell over in his chair. "The walls are thin, Mr. Abbott," she admonished, as he tried to right himself.

She turned to Batey. "Are you ready?" She already had her gray overcoat on and was finishing pinning on her black velvet hat. Batey caught a whiff of the pun-gent, oily scent of the teletypewriters she worked with all day. It clung to her dress and hair, as alluring to him—on her, at least—as Shalimar or Chanel No. 5.

"Yes," he said, putting on his felt hat and pulling on leather gloves.

"So, where are you two going?" Abbott asked. He picked up a sheaf of tea-stained papers and rose to his feet. "Mind taking these out for me?"

"Concert," Batey said, as he accepted the papers. "Bach. Fugues. Bletchley Park String Quartet."

"Well, have fun, you two," Abbott said. "*Someone* has to stay here and mind the shop."

In the narrow hallway, Victoria pulled Benjamin close. "I thought this day would never end," she said, nuzzling his neck.

"Not here." He still needed to dispose of the papers in his hand. There was a room with a shredder, and then all the tiny scraps of paper were put into a large bin marked CONFIDENTIAL WASTE.

She was tall in her heels, and her lips reached his ear easily. "We don't even have to go to the concert," she whispered. "I don't even know how I'd be able to sit through it, knowing . . ."

Her tongue swirled in his ear and Benjamin groaned.

"Let's go," he said in a low, anxious voice.

On their way out they saw Christopher Boothby, who worked in the main office, doing administrative work. The two men were wearing the same navy, red, and yellow striped Trinity College scarf. As they passed, Boothby gave the couple a wink and a smile.

Afterward, in Victoria's tiny bedroom in the drafty cottage she shared with one of the other teleprincesses, Benjamin fell asleep.

As he snored lightly, Victoria slipped out of the warm bed and wrapped herself in her chenille robe. Going to his coat, she rummaged through the pockets, taking the papers he was supposed to have shredded and dropping them into a drawer.

Then she crawled back under the covers and gave him a gentle nudge, then a harder one.

"What?" he mumbled.

"Darling, I'm so dreadfully sorry. But my roommate is such a little priss—and if she catches you here she'll tell the landlady . . . who won't approve at all."

"Sorry?" Benjamin echoed, rubbing his eyes. "Right. Yes, of course," he said, standing up and pulling on his plaid boxers.

"Thanks ever so much," she said, "for understanding. Well, and *that*, too."

"Oh, thank *you*." He stepped into his trousers, his features boyish when he smiled. "You know, I really do want to take you out. A concert, the pictures, a nice dinner—or at least as nice as you can get these days. Please, let me take you somewhere."

"You're a sweet boy, Benjamin Batey," she said with a sigh, getting up and kissing the back of his neck as he finished buttoning his shirt. "A very, very sweet boy."

She helped him with his coat, scarf, and hat, and then sent him on his way. The door clicked closed and she waited as the sound of his footsteps receded.

Then she picked up the white Bakelite receiver and dialed. "Yes," she whispered into the telephone, "I have something you'll want to see. I'm leaving for London now. Should be there in a few hours, give or take. Yes, of *course* I'll use an alias."

Then, "I love you too, darling."

Claridge's hotel in London was a large red-brick building located in fashionable Mayfair, still elegant despite the removal of all of its lavish wrought-iron railings, which had been taken down to be melted for munitions. After her long train trip in the blackout, Victoria was grateful to check in, under an assumed name, and retire to a warm, damask-swathed room, worlds away from the shabby indignities of Bletchley.

After placing the decrypts carefully on the bed, she went into the marble bathroom and drew a bath, noticing that Claridge's had "forgotten" the five-inch watermark for hot water rationing. She turned on the tap and out poured a scalding stream, to which she added a liberal handful of sandalwood-scented Hammam Bouquet bath salts. She sighed as she undressed, then slipped her long and elegant limbs into the bath, reclining against the slanted back of the tub. Benjamin was just such an easy target. He was lovely, really. It wasn't his fault, the poor dear. . . .

The front door clicked open, then closed quietly. With the water still running, Victoria didn't hear it. Then there was a loud thud. "Darling, is that you?" she called, lifting her head.

There was a silence, then the bathroom door creaked open.

"Darling?" Victoria called, sitting up in the tub. "You? No, not *you*!"

The shot went directly between her eyes. She slumped back into the bath, bright red blood streaming down her face and into the water, turning the froth pink and then crimson. As her pale slim body slipped down under the bubbles, her mouth fell open into a perfect *o* of surprise.

PHOTO: © LESLEY SEMMELHACK

SUSAN ELIA MACNEAL is the *New York Times* and *USA Today* bestselling author of the Maggie Hope mystery series, including *Mr. Churchill's Secretary, Princess Elizabeth's Spy, His Majesty's Hope, The Prime Minister's Secret Agent,* and *Mrs. Roosevelt's Confidante.* She is the winner of the Barry Award and was shortlisted for the Edgar, Macavity, Dilys, Bruce Alexander Memorial Historical Mystery, and Sue Feder Memorial Historical Fiction awards. She lives in Park Slope, Brooklyn, with her husband and son.

www.susaneliamacneal.com
Facebook.com/Susan Elia MacNeal, Author
@SusanMacNeal